family path. Both touching and funny in equal measure, *It Could Be Worse* is ultimately a relatable story of growing up and standing up for ourselves. I enjoyed it very much!"

—**Deborah Goodrich Royce,** national bestselling and award-winning author of *Reef Road, Ruby Falls,* and *Finding Mrs. Ford*

"A poignant debut about a woman who finds herself amid life's many challenges, complete with childhood flashbacks that create a heartrending story of love, loss, and the strength to overcome."

—**Emily Liebert,** *USA Today* bestselling author

"In her powerful debut novel, *It Could Be Worse,* Dara Levan examines the many sides of complicated family relationships. Strong characters, childhood flashbacks, buried secrets, and a gut-wrenching decision combine to create a compelling narrative that lingers long after the last page is turned."

—**Patricia Sands,** bestselling author of *The Promise of Provence*

D0367576

Praise for
It Could Be Worse

"Readers will cheer for Allegra Gil, the spirited narrator of *It Could Be Worse*, who faces boundary-busting parents, a not so easy-peasy pregnancy, the madness of motherhood, a health scare, and the everyday angst of work/life balance with wit and grit. If life gives you lemons, read Dara Levan's delightful debut novel."

—**Sally Koslow,** bestselling author of *The Real Mrs. Tobias*

"Visceral and moving. A must read for anyone seeking to understand the impact of parent-to-child narcissistic abuse. Inner child trauma is so powerful, so lasting, so tough to overcome. Levan conveys trauma with complexity, compassion, and empathy."

—**Andra Watkins,** *New York Times* bestselling author

"A powerful and poignant story about letting go. Dara Levan skillfully explores the effects of narcissistic personality disorder on the entire family. This is a book I will remember for a long time."

—**Jean Meltzer,** international bestselling author of
The Matzah Ball

"*It Could Be Worse* is a portrait of unconditional love—siblings, spouses, friends, children, and chosen family. Its waltz-like cadence crescendos with this pitch-perfect truth: *Love is kind. Love doesn't hurt.* If you need to step out of soul-sucking relationships once and for all, these words, and this book, are a mighty guide."

—**Laura Munson,** *New York Times* and *USA Today* bestselling author and founder of Haven Writing Retreats

"With a unique melodic structure, *It Could Be Worse* is an authentic, emotionally resonant novel about how the past deeply affects our present experiences. Dara Levan's extraordinary understanding of human nature and astonishing ability to lay bare the deepest parts of our souls is poured into Allegra, her brave, relatable protagonist, as she seeks to break free of the chains of her childhood and soar on her own terms. The gorgeous prose and raw, unflinching narrative both heal and inspire. A stunning debut."

—**Samantha M. Bailey,** *USA Today* and #1 international
bestselling author of *Woman on the Edge* and
Watch Out for Her

"There's nothing more complex than the dynamics of a parent-child relationship...or the secrets that lurk in our past. Dara digs into the landscape of a heartbreaking family with powerful characters and seamless, lyrical prose. A debut with heart."

—**Rea Frey,** bestselling author of *The Other Year*

"A captivating, empowering read about reclaiming oneself and building the life of your dreams after years of being eager to please but never good enough. Perfect for book clubs."

—**Julie Valerie,** bestselling author of *Holly Banks Full of Angst*

"In her debut novel, Dara Levan beautifully weaves the past and the present in the life of a young mother who struggles to cling to the rose-colored view she has always held of her high-powered father. As the rhythm of the novel moves backward and forward, Allegra confronts some cold, hard truths about this parent she has kept on a pedestal while navigating her own way along the

IT COULD BE WORSE

DARA LEVAN

A REGALO PRESS BOOK
ISBN: 979-8-88845-419-0
ISBN (eBook): 979-8-88845-420-6

New York • Nashville
regalopress.com

Published in the United States of America
1 2 3 4 5 6 7 8 9 10

For Todd and Madeline—I love you unconditionally and forever.

CHAPTER ONE

My life was about to change. But when, I had no idea. Timing is everything. And not just in music.

The bench creaked beneath me as my fingers explored the major and minor keys. Maybe I'd imagined the stuck middle C? It was difficult to discern with the chorus of other instruments in the music shop. Thankfully, my father had agreed to meet me here. A lifelong pianist, he'd be able to detect any imperfections.

A vibration in the pocket of my short swing dress startled me. Withdrawing my phone, I read the text letting me know he'd arrive soon. Nearby, a girl gripped a shiny cello and grabbed the thickest string like she was about to launch an arrow, fingers dancing in front of her eyes as if nothing else existed. The woman, likely her mother, seemed embarrassed and yanked the girl away.

The girl moaned faintly as she trailed behind her mother out of the store. My heart sank for these two strangers, but my father's entrance distracted me. With an air of authority, he held the door open for them and smoothed his thick, silvery hair. He nodded to the store manager while buttoning his Polo shirt and tightening his leather belt.

A new wave of discomfort, more persistent and painful, tugged me back to the present. My phone buzzed again, and I noticed the bars on my cell were low. Hoisting my body from the bench required the momentum of a full aria. The stirring inside me increased while I waddled toward the lanky salesman behind the desk.

"May I make a quick call?" I pointed to the phone. The man smiled and took it off the wall. I was never so thankful for a long cord. I stretched it and wondered about the one that connected me to my baby, and the kicks quickened as if my little boy felt my own intensifying emotions. My clammy hand moved toward the tender musical movements inside me.

On the third ring, she picked up. "Who is this?"

"Mom, it's me, Allegra. Did you call?" I held the receiver closer, and the silver hoop in my ear fell to the floor.

"I can barely hear you," she said impatiently.

I shrugged out of my cardigan, trying to cool down. "We're still at the store. I'm at the front and worried, Mom. I keep having pain in my stomach, and I may be going into labor." I inhaled through my nose, employing the calming technique I taught my patients in therapy.

"Your father's a doctor and a brilliant one, you know. So, ask him—I'm sure you're fine. I need to run. I have a nail appointment."

Before I could respond, my mother hung up.

As my dad came closer, I waved Mozart sheet music in the air like a white flag. His belly collided with mine in an attempted hug. I settled for a shoulder squeeze, relieved he'd come to help me—yet again. I'd called on him numerous times since my pregnancy hormones started surging along with my indecision. Hormone haze. That's what my husband, Benito, named it.

The palm fronds outside brushed the bay window. I glanced at the cloudless, cerulean sky, grateful that we lived in Miami.

Dad positioned himself on the smooth bench. After adjusting it, he motioned for me to join him. I briefly wondered if it could hold our weight as I eyed its wobbly legs. I picked up where I'd left off, the third stanza on the second page. My tummy tightened, and I tried not to wince.

"The sound is off," Dad said, evoking his professional voice. I always knew when he was talking to patients because his pitch would drop, and he'd slow his pace. It's what my brother, Jack, and I had termed his "Dr. Curt" voice. He used it now as he leaned closer to the keys and struck each note, one by one. "I could swear I heard a defective key," he said. Yes, Dr. Curt heard, saw, noticed everything. He was always right. He had to be.

Maneuvering two beings, even a smidgen, felt like hauling a human house. As my breathing slowed, the baby kicked, mimicking the lullaby his soon-to-be grandfather now played. Even at sixty-two years old, Dad remembered our special song. His deft fingers glided up and down the keys. I quietly rubbed my stomach for fear of interrupting him, but the cramping crescendoed.

"D-d-d-dad."

He didn't respond as he pumped the brass damper pedal. I leaned to the left, my jaw clenching along with my insides.

"Allegra, why are you pushing into me?" Dad lifted his hand from the baby grand and placed it on my upper back.

I tried to relax into his palm. "I don't know what's happening," I whispered. "There's a squeezing sensation in my stomach. It's erratic but stronger each time." I cradled the bottom of my belly as the next cramp began.

Dad placed his warm hand over mine and told me to hush. His keen gunmetal-gray eyes moved like a metronome from my scrunched face to his wristwatch. "It seems you are having mini contractions. But it's nothing to worry about. This is how the body prepares for birth. Just like dress rehearsals before your performances at camp."

The pain ceased as my muscles relaxed, temporarily transporting me to those summers in the woods: the fragrant pines so different from my familiar palms and Ficus trees, the lake that wasn't salty, the sound of teenage voices holding harmonies the same way we held our hands.

Dad refocused his attention on the shiny black and white keys. He straightened his bifocals and played a few chords. Johannes Brahms's serene lullaby coaxed me back toward the baby grand. Seeing Dad's diligence and focus, I didn't dare disrupt his solo. Those solid, skilled hands had excised tumors from such young patients. His mastery of musical and medical skills mesmerized me; I remembered watching instructional videos in which he artfully taught students how to use a scalpel.

I loved listening to my father in this rare time, just the two of us. My hands drifted to my belly, waves of life lulling beneath the gentle tune. Then I recognized the familiar melody—"Cradle Song"—the one he used to play when I would sit on his lap as a child.

Only when he finished the final note did he notice me. "This isn't the one, Allegra." Dad cracked his thick knuckles before rising from the bench. "The piano is mediocre." He raised his voice, loud enough for everyone to hear. "I know the store manager; he is an idiot. You shouldn't settle—ever." He pushed the bench back in place, my cue to exit the premises.

"Where'd you park?" I asked, following him to the door.

"Outside."

"Oh, D-d-d-dad." I laughed. "Ben says I'm a smart-ass like you."

"Your husband is clearly brilliant." He chuckled and poked my bicep. "Your stomach isn't the only thing that has grown, sweetheart."

I crossed my arms, ashamed, as heat flushed my cheeks. Maybe I should have put the cardigan on again. Then I saw the store manager and excused myself.

"Sir?" I tapped him, and he turned around. "Thanks for your time. And I'm sorry for my father's abruptness. He means well and just wants the best of everything."

I peeled the remaining purple nail polish off my pinky as I strolled back toward my dad. He didn't bother hiding his disappointment when he looked at me. Leave it to Dr. Curt to detect the most subtle of defects—whether in a piano or in me.

CHAPTER TWO

I shifted slightly, and the screen went blank, prompting a search and rescue mission for the remote control. I reached between the cushions beneath me and nearly pulled a muscle in the process. Nope, not there!

Memories of watching movies and falling in love with Ben bonded the tattered threads of our cozy couch. Who knew that same sofa would become a physical hazard over the last few months? With concerted effort, I rose to a vertical position and headed to the bathroom, needing to pee for the third time in thirty minutes. I grinned while imagining a tiny finger tickling my bladder. Each flutter in my stomach ruffled the dormant feathers of my first years on earth. Vivid daydreams, directed by estrogen and produced by progesterone, broadcasted footage from my childhood. I noticed a pattern of syncopated spasms in my lower belly. These cramps felt different from yesterday.

"Ally! Was that you?" Ben toppled into me and nearly splashed both of us into the toilet.

The ballet classes during summers at camp finally came in handy as I balanced at the edge of the seat and leaned into my sweet husband. "I'm fine, honey. Thank you for checking on me. What's with the panic?"

He clicked the stopwatch. "I wasn't sure if it was you or Cookie. It sounded like a yelp," Ben said.

As if he understood, our two-year-old Bichon scampered into the already small space, his black and white ears bouncing with every leap, his wet nose brushing my knee.

"Sixteen and a half minutes apart, *mi amor*."

I loved it when Ben spoke his native Spanish to me. His hand gently supported my lower back as another contraction started. Immersed in the moment, I was determined to soak it in. Of course, I'd memorized no less than ten "how to be the perfect parent" books, and clearly Benito had done the same. He wanted to jump in the car right away and rush me to the hospital.

"My dad thought I had another few days at least. I doubt Peanut will plop out of me this second. I'm going to shower, okay? It may be my last one for a week." I stood and planted a kiss on Ben's full mouth.

I licked my lips, savoring his scent as I shaved my legs—well, the parts I could reach, anyway.

"Now I'm ready, sweetie." My shirt swished against my leggings.

Ben, his hair tousled, waited in the car with the engine running. He only touched his gel-scrunched curls when he was nervous. "Are the contractions coming quicker? I didn't want to hurry you, so I came to the car to cool it off."

He'd not only packed the bags, which were already in the trunk, but he also had the AC on full blast. I drew a heart with my index finger on his forearm. How did I get so lucky? We balanced each other in all the right ways—me, the creative, right-brained one, while he preferred spreadsheets to sheet music and numbers to words.

We arrived at the hospital and began the endless wait. I had long planned a play-by-play of how pregnancy, labor, and delivery ought to be. I'd envisioned a swift delivery, especially because prenatal Pilates and yoga classes I'd taken supported this outcome. But after eighteen hours of contractions, I was still only two centimeters dilated. This detail hadn't appeared in the notes of my well-researched playbook.

★ ★ ★

Ben's thumbs pressed the buttons on his Blackberry, a repetitive clicking that echoed the pounding in my head as his scuffed shoes tapped like Morse code across the square tiles. "When is this happening?" He paced from the back wall to the door.

"Um, darling, we can't schedule a birth like a meeting at the office." I tried to focus on Sting's voice crooning from the boombox we'd brought with us, which rested on the peeling Formica shelf.

He slurped the last drop of tepid coffee from his Styrofoam cup. I looked at him, longing for one small sip. Ben bit off the end of an ice cube and put it on my parched lips. Sunlight slowly shifted, lingering on the lower half of the sterile wall. Our baby, who we'd named Julian, lessened his kicks as the music sounded, just as he'd done throughout the last trimester, when head-phones hugged my swollen slope and played Beethoven's sonatas. A knock on the door jolted me from my reverie. The familiar sound of heavy footsteps moved toward us.

"Oh, thank goodness you're here!" I exclaimed. My pound-ing heart slowed a bit. Ben's eyes darted from me to my father. My husband's all-the-feels face said everything. Words weren't necessary.

"I'm always here for you, Allegra." Dr. Curt planted his stocky frame in front of Ben's body. My sculpted husband dwarfed his aging father-in-law in stature, but size didn't matter when it came to commanding respect.

My father peered at the blood pressure monitor, the beeping shriller now. He withdrew his hands from the lab coat pockets and untangled three tubes while muttering something about incompetence. He pushed a few buttons, altered the angle of the bed, and crossed his arms over his chest. Nurses popped in and out of my room. As a revered pediatric neurosurgeon in the area, my father could still call in some favors, like securing me a private room. Employees wouldn't dare question his presence on the floor, even though he wasn't on staff at this hospital.

Someone I didn't recognize poked her head in the doorway. She squinted above sapphire spectacles, her observant eyes scanning the space.

"Oh! Dr. Curt—what a wonderful surprise to see you here. One of the nursing students paged me, concerned about a man messing with the machines. Is this your daughter?"

Dad strode toward the petite woman. After scrubbing in at the nearby sink, he shook her hand and beamed. "Yes, my favorite and only daughter. Can you believe I'm going to be a grandfather?" A crescent moon dimpled his cheek as he turned toward me.

"We will take great care of your little girl. Do you sleep in your lab coat? I don't think I've ever seen you without it." My father and the woman chortled in unison.

"You must know him well." Ben laughed too, which was one of my favorite sounds in the world. "He even wears it to dinner."

My father's eyes blazed into Ben's, and my husband stepped backward. Dr. Curt often donned his cape, otherwise known as a "lab coat," to sneak into spaces where he didn't have privileges. Somehow, he demanded reverence from everyone in his presence. This made me feel protected, first as a little girl, and now as I was about to become a mother.

"D-d-d-dad, please don't leave." I laced his hand into mine and pulled him closer.

"I want to stay, but your mom keeps calling. She needs lunch; you know how hangry she gets. After I tend to her, I'll just be a few feet away." He let go of my clammy fingers, patted the crown of my head, and left the room. I felt like I couldn't breathe. How would I do this without him? My chest stung and my pulse doubled.

"Ally, *mi amor*, I am here. I will not go anywhere." Ben stroked my forehead.

"Babe, I know. But I'm so scared. I've never done anything this big, especially medical, without my dad. What if something goes wrong?"

Ben softly kneaded my neck. "You've got this. We've got this." Then the beeping sounds became louder, and blinking blue lights glowered at me from the monitors.

"What's wrong?" I thought I might birth my own heart before my baby.

Before anyone could answer, my father's footsteps again sounded from outside the room. "My dad is an expert, you know," I said. "And I need him here right now!" I leaned toward the left, my watery eyes bulging. Like a freaked-out flamingo, I craned my head upward from the propped polyester pillows. I needed to see the numbers on the blood pressure machine Dad had taught me to read years ago.

I didn't want the on-call doctor. Where was Dr. Gold? He'd reassured me for thirty-eight weeks that despite the rising numbers on the scale, I was still "healthy and beautiful." Of course, I had rolled my eyes and quipped, "Sure, if you call a whale out of water a sight for sore eyes!" Dr. Gold had initially told me our baby would be about eight pounds. But I'd stretched exponentially over the last seven days like those miniature sponge shapes that expanded in water.

"Can somebody stop that irritating sound?" I pleaded.

The doctor on call, a.k.a. Dr. No-Bedside-Manner, stopped the beeping and snapped that if I didn't progress, I may need a C-section. She then grumbled something about checking on another patient, and I was relieved when she left. Ben was about to head to the nurses' station when she returned. I'd heard feedback from friends and in the waiting room that suggested this obstetrician was intolerant—not what I needed at this moment or ever. Dr. No-Bedside-Manner barked orders in clipped phrases through her thin, cracked lips. Contractions came quicker, and so did my desire to finally meet my baby boy.

Determined to keep pushing, I tried to ignore the chatter around me. Extracting my baby?

I'd dreamt of a natural birth, the way God intended, ever since I was a little girl. Then I felt the hospital bed moving as if in slow motion. The monitors flashed like a displaced disco ball. I should have been nursing my son by now, the wrong vibe for this new venue. The operating room felt sterile and serious, a stark contrast to the nurturing ambiance I'd fostered earlier. When had I arrived here?

My shoulders shot up, and my neck tensed. Those breaths I'd practiced in Lamaze class constricted instead of calmed. Alarming, high-pitched sounds triggered a chilly sweat above my upper lip. Frenzied arms reached above mine, checking monitors and stats. A syringe appeared in my foggy peripheral vision. I heard the dreaded word—*cesarean*—then I remembered it being mentioned before, but I hadn't wanted to accept this route. Dr. No-Bedside-Manner's earlier hypothesis had been correct.

I understood that a C-section was the only safe option. I had to trust the next few hours, and I had to trust myself. The doctor who'd deliver my precious Peanut into the world would hold a new life in her hands.

It was official; women who wore the "natural birth" badge of honor had to be sadists. I asked copious questions while the doctor sliced my stomach open. As I gripped the bedrails, my hair clung to my collar bone. The vent above my head blew frigid air. My chest and back were sticky with sweat, and the contrast of hot and cold kept me intermittently grounded.

Information was my balm. I longed to tear down the curtain that separated me from seeing what the hell was happening. My world had always felt unsafe. Now was no different.

Just after midnight, all eleven pounds, seven ounces, and twenty-two inches of my bellowing baby boy entered the world. My body quaked from the drug cocktail pumping through the IV. My back molars clattered like a skeleton's on Halloween, and my father wasn't there to explain why this was happening. Startled by my body's uncontrollable actions, I remembered the alarms. "How's his Apgar score?" My mouth was a megaphone that blared at the nurses as they bathed my newborn.

"Everything is good, Mommy. It was a nine both times."

I got the meaning of that number, thankful my father had taught me some medical lingo, like how to know if your newborn was thriving. Qualitatively. Quantifiably. Completely. Wait. Mommy? Oh, they were talking to *me*. My throbbing head sank into the bunched-up pillow.

A receiving blanket swaddled my son. The nurse placed his warm, rosy body on my chest. As I stared into his navy-blue eyes, all the weeks of worrying about each stage of development dissolved. Julian's head seemed like a strange form for a newborn who was lifted, rather than pushed, from my body. I asked the nurse about the shape I couldn't name. (I'd barely passed geometry.) She reassured me that Julian's malleable head would return to round within a few days.

I released a puff of air, now thankful for the unplanned C-section. "Hi, sweet boy. I am your mommy." Julian gripped my index finger with his chubby little hand. Even after the pushing, pulling, and prodding, my senses remained heightened. "I've waited forever to meet you, felt you growing inside me, and here you are. I wonder if the due date was off, you robust quarterback."

I'd miss the waves of life ebbing and flowing when he'd lived inside me. "I knew you'd be huge! And you're holding your head up already!"

The books I'd read to him must've kindled our connection at eighteen weeks when hearing developed in utero. My proof? Julian quieted almost instantly upon hearing my voice.

Ben rubbed my neck with his thumbs and asked if family members who'd been eagerly awaiting this moment could visit yet. My brother Jack and his partner, David, had been texting Ben incessantly. What I really wanted was to be flanked by Ben and my father. I loved my mother, but her babble made me bonkers. She talked without periods or commas. But it was all or nothing; I didn't want to hurt her feelings or those of my in-laws and the others in the waiting room.

"Not yet, honey. Please let's be a trio for a few more minutes. Look at this *punim*, this yummy face. He has your mouth. And what a head of hair! Just like you and my dad." I rewrapped the blanket and placed the cotton cap on Julian's head. Ben's lips brushed mine before I turned back to our child. I touched each plump finger as liquid love cascaded down my cheeks and dropped onto his.

My eyes misted again, and the fear from before morphed to awe, leaving me utterly breathless. Ben reached toward me. Just when I thought I couldn't love my husband more, he cradled our baby, our miracle, in the crook of his arm. Julian yawned, and his teeny eyelids fluttered.

"Are you ready to teach us how to be a party of three?" I cooed, glancing from Julian to Ben and back again. "You're the luckiest little boy in the world because your daddy is amazing."

CHAPTER THREE
ALLEGRA' 6

"*Baruch atah Adonai, Eloheinu melech ha'olam,*" Grandma began the Shabbat blessing, murmuring as she swayed. Her ivory hands pressed together, shielding somber eyes. The flame flickered, dancing on the back wall of the tiny kitchen.

I balanced the braided challah on one hand and waited for my turn. The scent of honey mixed with dough enveloped us. I recited the prayer and then sang it in English. Music made my grandparents smile, temporarily transmuting their pain from the loved ones they'd left behind.

Grandpa raised the Kiddush cup, swallowed a sip, and shared the sweet wine with me. Jack wasn't here tonight, so luckily I got a double ladle of chicken soup. Friday nights couldn't come soon enough. Grandma and Grandpa always greeted me as if we'd been apart for decades. The weekend sleepovers, Shabbat rituals, and trips to the mall together felt like hugs.

Then the nights came, when fondness replaced the fear I'd felt at home. Though only four-foot-eleven, Grandma gave mightily. She looped her slender fingers through my corkscrew curls.

"My *shayna punim*, let's bless your mother, father, brother, cousins." Grandma included everyone in the bedtime wishes. Her touch, up and down, a rocking chair that lulled me, lingered even days later.

"I love learning Yiddish, Grandma. Will you please teach me how to say 'I love you' in Polish too?"

She scooted toward me, adjusting the thin buttercup quilt. Her lips lightly pressed to my forehead. Then Grandma fluffed the flat pillow before handing it to me.

"One day, one day. It's time for bed now. Grandpa can't wait to take you to Publix tomorrow morning. This time he'll teach you to choose the perfect melon." She rose and reached for the light.

Moments later, when I sneezed, Grandma returned with tissues.

"Why do you cut these in half?" I wiped each nostril with both hands. "I use double the amount."

She cradled my chin in her soft, small hands. "We save so we don't waste. Oy, what if we run out? Sweet dreams, *bubbela*, my sweetie. I love you."

I didn't need a clock. In the morning, the daffodil drapes became a sheer screen for the sun's spectrum of tangerine and yellows. Its fiery radiance roused me from deep, unperturbed sleep. Grandpa's door was always wide open. They didn't lock theirs—then again, my nightmares lived at home and thankfully stayed there. I skipped to my grandpa and crawled into his lap.

"Good morning, Ally. I'm glad you're already dressed. Grandma is almost ready for us." His bass tone was perfectly pitched for a man with quiet strength. He disappeared into the carpeted closet, where a dusty accordion stood next to the glimmering green wrapped bits of forbidden bliss—Andes candies—while telling Grandma he needed to get the instrument so "Ally could practice her music." He winked when he sneaked me a candy the second she turned her back.

They were survivors of a different type, escaping the persecution of Poland. They'd gained freedom yet left and lost loved ones. And they loved me, no matter my size, shape, or achievement, whether I truly wanted to play that ancient accordion or not.

The only male family member on my maternal side, Grandpa loved me with his whole heart. Even a few years later, when he had a stroke that left him without speech and stole his independence, he'd sigh peacefully when I hugged him.

My last memory of Grandpa, a month after Jack's bar mitzvah, was him stripped of his dignity, sitting in a diaper at seventy-nine. Every time I hugged him goodbye, fear filled my being and made it tough to tear myself away. That time, the gong of grief reverberated. I kissed the top of his bald, blemished head. The scar from his shunt stared at me.

I looked at his legs, covered in navy knee-high socks with the gold stitching at the toes. My brown eyes met his fading blueish-gray ones. We shared the same passion for music, and though Grandpa could no longer speak, his gaze was a prelude to the afterlife that was soon to embrace him.

CHAPTER FOUR

O ur little boy slept the whole car ride home in his plaid baby seat. The rhythmic rise and fall of his tiny chest captivated me. I pulled up his socks, fighting the urge to kiss each of his ten tiny toes. Again. The passenger seat felt too far away for our first ride together.

Julian's mouth puckered when we entered the driveway as if he sensed our arrival. Ben unlocked the front door while balancing him on his shoulder. Propelled with new motherhood adrenaline, I entered our home like it was the first time I'd seen it. The carpet seemed greener, as if it'd been fertilized. Our couch looked even cozier, a new snuggly blanket draped across it. A baby-blue congratulations card teetered on the edge of the cushion. Had it only been seventy-two hours since we'd left? We stepped across the familiar threshold and began this next act in our new roles as parents.

Ben beamed, and his eyes glowed with a hue I'd never noticed before. Maybe my hormones had rubbed off on him? I cracked up at the thought of men rocketing a human out of a tiny hole, or in my case, being split apart. The men I knew could barely tolerate a stubbed toe, let alone cramps and contractions.

My chest tingled, and my left breast dripped before Julian made a peep. My body responded before my brain—it had rehearsed for motherhood long before I'd even become pregnant. I sensed Julian was awakening and would be ravenous.

Ben kept repeating, "Isn't he perfect and super easy?"

I listened, cautiously optimistic, and remembered what I'd taught expectant parents during my clinical fellowship about the "hospital honeymoon" phenomenon—which prompted me to return a call from a few days ago. My client had left a few messages, and I preferred to be fully accessible rather than hire an office assistant. She had known I was near my due date, so the delay was forgivable. But the recording captured so much more than her request for a callback. It had saved the tremble in her voice, the staggered inhalations as she repeated her phone number.

I snapped on the baby carrier and adjusted the padded straps, then wiggled Julian into it.

The long-lasting anesthetic still numbed the incision, so I ambled toward my client notebook. She answered on the first ring as I lowered myself delicately into our new denim glider.

"Oh, Ally, I'm glad you called. I was worried. You always get back with me the same day."

I wedged the flat cordless receiver between my ear and neck. Julian drifted in and out of sleep as I rocked him back and forth. "All is well. More importantly, how are you?"

I listened as my client wept, worried about her preschool-aged son. He'd bitten another kid and this time had broken the skin. She couldn't seem to convince her husband that their child may need an evaluation. Julian startled. His tiny trumpet summoned me with a blast.

"You had the baby! This can wait. I cannot believe I forgot."

I offered my finger to Julian as an appetizer, which soothed him for the moment.

"It's okay. I'm here for you. And we can have our phone appointment as scheduled next week." Julian whined and continued sucking on my finger.

"I can't believe you just gave birth and you're talking to me."

"It's my job, and I love it."

"Ally, it's your calling. I am blessed to have you in my life."

"And your son is blessed to have you."

The sound of anxiety transmuting to calm was sometimes audible. The tone of her voice told me she'd be fine until next week. I clicked off the phone, and Julian squirmed with mewls and squeaks. Donning the baby carrier proved easier when he slept—taking it off was tricky. The phone slipped to the ground as I sang to Julian, hoping Joni Mitchell's "Circle Game" would pacify my bambino. I thought this brilliant contraption would be simple. Not so much. By the time I pried it off me, I needed to change my shirt and Julian's drenched onesie.

"What happened to the two of you?" Ben took the carrier suspended from my wrist.

"I needed to call a client." My lower back tensed. Julian's head tracked the sounds of our voices, moving from me to Ben.

"We just got home! I thought you told your clients you'd be off for the next four weeks."

Ice cubes clanked as Ben poured ginger tea into the glass. My friends said you could "pump and dump," but I didn't agree. So tonight's cocktail—and for the next year of nursing—would be a decaf beverage. It paired well with the Thai food that would be on our doorstep soon.

✶ ✶ ✶

Although Ben and I agreed that babies would not sleep in our room, our firm convictions softened like butter left on the counter overnight. A borrowed bassinet doubled as a bed and diaper station. Despite my training in child development, I'd succumbed to the pervasive propaganda and put Julian on his back. The "back to sleep" campaign couldn't be avoided.

Fearmongering messages were everywhere, stamped in bold print even on diaper boxes.

At two a.m., Julian screeched like a section of clarinets and oboes. Ben bolted toward the bassinet, tripping over his flannel pajama pants. I tried to intercept what might've been a collision but couldn't coax myself upright, the slightest movement a mini marathon. Ben caught himself just centimeters away from the cream dust ruffle.

"Holy moly, babe! Nice save."

Ben already had our baby in his arms, swinging him like a human hammock. He brought Julian to my side of the bed. As I attempted my first solo feeding, Ben's breathing returned to normal.

Somehow, even in a sleep-deprived delirium, I sensed that— at a soul level—this tiny human had begun to transform me.

CHAPTER FIVE

With a grimace hopefully hidden from Ben's view, I shakily crawled onto the hot leather seat. Thank goodness he drove a sedan lower to the ground than my recently acquired, gargantuan mom-mobile. Just the thought of driving to our usual place prompted pangs, but I never bailed on my word. Any movement sparked a sensation like my stitches would shred and my stomach might unzip itself. Every speed bump and brake jolted me. My insides rearranged themselves like a disorderly game of musical chairs. The seatbelt dug into my distended belly, which made each start and stop even more uncomfortable.

Ben winced and muttered, "Sorry," every time I gripped the thick console. It had only been fourteen days since we'd become parents, but I had thought I'd feel stronger by now. If he looked at me once more while moving, we'd hit a palm tree.

I hobbled into the bustling restaurant, breast pads shoved into my beige nursing bra. Even though it was eighty-seven degrees, I intentionally wore a dark plum, long-sleeved T-shirt. No chance my jiggly arms would make an appearance. Deeply empathetic and an emotional sponge, I already anticipated a possible let-down at the mere sight or sound of a baby. As Ben held the door, I heard a familiar, friendly hoot.

The boisterous hostess welcomed us from behind the register. "There they are. We've missed you!"

I waved back in return, unable to find words and almost unable to comprehend language. I took a deep breath. "It's great to be here." I wanted to believe it.

Sitting at our typical table and ordering the usual at our favorite bagel joint gave us a sense of normalcy. I asked the waitress for a dozen assorted rugelach to go in case I forgot. This would be a sweet thank you for Aunt Arden. I appreciated that she'd offered to watch Julian so we could have adult time together.

My teeth sank into the toasted pumpernickel bagel, which was generously smeared with cream cheese, each bite a delicious morsel of doughy, delectable bliss. The thinly sliced, just-salty-enough lox brought back memories of brunch on Miami Beach with my beloved grandparents. But after thirty minutes, everything seemed too loud, too bright, too much of everything. The buzzing fluorescent ceiling lights. The air conditioner kicking off and on. The nauseating combination of pastries mixed with pungent tuna fish salad.

I thought about parents I'd counseled for years and how they'd describe the painful experiences with their autistic children. Though I grasped the concept intellectually and compassionately, the sense that even my ears' cilia stood at attention gave me a gut punch of perspective. I felt like shrieking but chewed on the inside of my cheeks instead. Everything hurt. I didn't want to disappoint Ben; this was our first—albeit quick—date alone. I had committed to the idea that our incredible life wouldn't be permanently altered by parenthood. For months I'd heard comments like, "You have no idea how much everything will change," or, "Enjoy your alone time while you still have it." The same was true for unsolicited labor and delivery stories that spawned from family members and strangers.

I tried to tune out the noise. I believed in creating my own rainbows and refused to let anyone else's misery darken our future. I would do mothering and motherhood differently. The little and big things. And it started today. I rubbed Ben's fingers, noticing the fine hair on each knuckle as I attempted to use the centering skills I taught my clients. My entire being felt like it was short circuiting.

"Sweetie, are you alright?" Ben finally put down his bagel.

I glanced at his nearly empty paper plate. Ah. He was good to go.

"I'm fine. How was the whitefish salad? This is awesome to be here, just us. Well, with nineteen other sardines crammed in this place."

Ben folded the napkin into its original rectangle. Then his eyes trailed from my forehead to my chin. I pressed the tips of my fingers together in a triangle as my throat tightened.

"Ally, you look wiped." He reached for the flimsy check. For the umpteenth time, I wondered why bagel stores only accepted cash. And why were the numbers like hieroglyphics? I could rarely decipher them and never knew the total. Thank goodness for my honey, the math whiz, who could understand complex numbers and scrawly writing.

With his arm around my waist, which felt more like an inflated inner tube, Ben guided me toward the parking lot. I had no idea where we'd parked. In fact, I had no clue what day it was either. An invisible film shrouded my senses. I'd swung from overstimulated to muted, and the contrasting sensations caused me to stumble as I clutched the car handle.

Mental clarity and clear intuition usually guided me. I didn't do hazy. But I needed complete silence. So strange for a bubbly extrovert. What I didn't realize was how piercingly persistent Julian's wails would be, setting off a siren in my central nervous system, and when he escalated, my chest thumped and my pulse quickened. As we rode along in the car, even the mere thought of his high-pitched cry rattled me. And we weren't even home yet.

"Hurry up, babe," I urged Ben. "Come on. I need to feed Julian. And I need to get this horrible harness off my body. Like, now."

As we pulled into the garage, I unlocked the seatbelt and unhooked my wide bra strap.

Julian's cry cleared the earlier fog. "I'm coming, sweet boy! I can't run yet. Mommy's doing her best." I waved at Aunt Arden while Ben embraced her. She said Julian had napped the entire time, waking thirty seconds before our garage door opened. I wondered if babies had a heightened sense of smell, especially for their momma's milk.

What a dose of reality. On what planet did I think even five minutes of solitude could happen?

My little insatiable vampire tore and tormented my tender nipples. Though I could be impatient with myself, surely feeding a child shouldn't be painful—hell, moms did this in the wild. Hadn't my mother repeatedly professed how natural and easy breastfeeding was? Why was this so hard for me?

As Julian's feeding time inched closer, I fumbled with the buttons on my shirt—false advertising that nursing clothes made this easier. He writhed and wiggled. He never seemed full, day or night. And speaking of nights, I desperately needed sleep.

Not in the normal postpartum way. My back ached and breasts throbbed. I was certain new nerve endings sprouted by the hour.

My nipples tensed as I trekked to the nursery. The sparse milk I produced gurgled in Julian's silk-skinned stomach.

Finished, he smiled at me as I rocked and read to him in the glider chair. His round eyes like blueberries, tracking each word as I pointed. Then Julian spewed his meal on my shoulder, the floor, and the Winnie the Pooh hardcover collection, which had been a beautiful gift from my college roommates. Luckily, spit-up could be cleaned with baby wipes. But the stench of undigested milk had become my perpetual perfume, lingering long after showers and scrubs, covering any remaining sweetness of the bagel shop. I'd dreamed of being a mother since I was a young girl. Dreamed of the day I'd cradle my own child.

No matter what. No matter how.

CHAPTER SIX
ALLEGRA' 9

Four eyeballs fixated on the television. Dad reclined in the oversized tufted chair. Mom lounged on the settee in her pink silk pajamas. They blasted the morning news shows. Every Sunday, same breakfast, same channels, same everything. They didn't notice when I slipped out the back door.

I bunched my lilac blanket into a ball and shoved it under my arm. The leash clicked and Keri panted, eager to go outside. Glistening pupils met mine, ready to play. Taking her for weekend walks was one of my chores. Jack and I argued over who'd do the baths, but I usually relented. I couldn't stand conflict or seeing my brother unhappy.

After Keri tinkled, we traipsed to the backyard, and I released the leash. She scampered toward my favorite tree, the tall oak with its arching branches and uneven limbs.

"Keri, sit. Daddy will be mad if you jump in the lake!" Tripping over a root, I scrambled toward her and grabbed the collar just in time. She wasn't a puppy anymore. But I guess a three-year-old terrier couldn't be trusted. "Good girl. Sit right there, sweetie, while I fix it." I kept my bare foot on the leash like Daddy had taught me. Then I smoothed the wrinkles on the square blanket and moved it to the left, where the area was flatter.

I arranged her bowl, food, brush, and squeaky ladybug toy. I gently drew Keri toward the blanket. She rolled onto her back, and I brushed her strawberry-blond fur.

"I'll rub your belly in a minute. You're so patient. More than me, that's for sure! Mom and Dad always say nine-year-olds should be able to wait until they're asked to speak." I patted the area where her back leg met her tushy. "Maybe I can teach you ballet—that leg kicks so high." I rolled onto my side, snuggling in the shade with Keri and making up a story about the tree. The Spanish moss swayed, wisps of sage green flowing in the air. The canopy of branches let in just enough sun.

"Where are you, Allegra?" Daddy hollered. "Do you have that damn dog?"

I sat upright and scooped out a cup of brown pebbles. Keri loved lunchtime. She barked and leaped into my lap. The breeze off the lake lessened the humidity.

"D-d-d-daddy. We are over here." I waved while pouring water into the other stainless steel bowl.

Mom trailed behind him. I wondered if Jack was still asleep. "Did you take Keri to the bathroom yet?" she asked, rubbing vanilla lotion onto her hands. The smell, even out here, made my head feel heavy.

"Yes, an hour ago. We've been playing house. I'm pretending Keri is my baby girl," I said, beaming up at my mom. Then I saw her footprints. She had tracked dirt from the nearby bushes onto my favorite blanket, the black muck oozing between the soft lavender fibers.

"Then come inside now. You still need to make your bed, clean the dishes, and finish your other chores." She turned toward the house and walked away. I didn't immediately follow, but we all knew it was just a short matter of time before I would.

CHAPTER SEVEN

I had interrogated the pediatrician, consulted with Dr. Google (again), and spoken to several friends. Julian was only four months old. Moms strolled by me at the park, sipping their cappuccinos while their newborns napped. I was driving to a "Mommy and Me" class, which had been marketed as supportive but seemed more like a brag-fest.

Once I arrived, I dropped my quilted diaper bag, nodded at the other moms in the room, then reapplied sheer lip balm. I hadn't realized how much I'd picked at my mouth on the way there. My chest constricted as I listened to the women prattle. Apparently, these moms had babies who slept all night and napped twice a day.

"The twins are so easy. I feed them, change them, and then they're out cold."

The other women bobbed their heads, their perfectly placed ponytails swishing in sync. One woman with highlighted, beachy-waved hair chimed in. "My mom comes over three days a week because my little one has a tough time during the day. I couldn't work from home without her. At least the colic is getting a bit better."

I changed Julian's diaper and rubbed cream on his chafing bottom. First, my cervix had failed me. Now, I couldn't get Julian to sleep through the night. I told Ben I should've come with a warranty. Gaggles of mommies gasped when Julian hurled all over the primary-colored carpet. How could I predict his splatters of undigested veggies?

"Sorry about that, everyone. He had squash four hours ago," I said, twisting my hair into a tighter bun.

The teacher handed me a few wet wipes. "Thank you," I said, meeting her eyes for a moment. I scrubbed as she strummed a guitar.

I studied my bustling baby boy. Julian seemed thinner and more irritable these days; I'd mention it to the pediatrician at our next visit. I knew behaviors revealed patterns. Just the day before, I had a client in my office dealing with her daughter's eating disorder, and by the end of the session, she'd had a breakthrough about when it had begun. Yet, I couldn't figure out what was wrong with my baby. My own child. Why wouldn't he sleep?

At the end of the silly sing-along, I tucked Julian into the portable car seat, snapped the plastic buckle, and headed toward the elevator.

★ ★ ★

The days were hard, but the nights were worse.

"Babe. I just fell asleep and thought he did too."

Ben turned over but didn't move. I'd nursed Julian for forty-five miserable minutes and waited in the nursery until I heard his blissful, rhythmic breathing.

"B-E-N!"

"Huh? What?"

Exhaustion mixed with agitation irked me. How did he sleep through the deafening concerto night after night? My voice escalated. "I am *begging* you to wake up."

Ben stirred and tried to pull me toward him. Oh, hell no. I was not in the mood. "Why'd you wake me? Are you…?"

Julian's howls escalated.

"Do you hear our son? I just fed him. Please. I know you work in a few hours, but I'm crashing," I cried, curling into a fetal position.

His answer? Syncopated snoring.

I stomped on the warning-wrapped cardboard diaper boxes as I got up. Somehow, this felt empowering. Screw the "back to sleep" campaign. Deciding to trust my gut, I repositioned Julian onto his stomach. Tortuous tirades and nocturnal nursery trips proved our baby couldn't sleep on his back. I'd arrive at Julian's next check-up with an arsenal of research, prepared to provide it if needed. Just in case. One, kids dying in their sleep must be connected to a preexisting condition. How did babies sleep on their stomachs for decades without issues? This defied logic. Two, Julian could scale the plastic-lined mattress like Spider-Man junior from a mere four weeks old. Surely this indicated some sort of distress. Three, babies communicated with body language.

Julian was trying to tell us something.

When I told this to our wide-eyed pediatrician, I whispered it as if at the confessional of a church on a Sunday. Yep. Julian's doc had just been indoctrinated as a priest, even though he was Jewish like me. After hearing about our desperate two a.m. Hail Mary, his jaw dropped farther.

Ben had wedged Julian's writhing body with rolled beach towels. The ratty turtle-patterned towels became a thick buffer between the wooden slats of the crib and Julian. We tiptoed out together, quietly closing the door behind us. At first, I felt guilty, as if we'd just imprisoned our baby. Then relief washed over me. Quiet. Not a peep. Ben spooned me, and we passed out.

But Operation Towel only worked until it didn't. The night after the pediatrician visit, the strong lil' stinker somehow flipped over! When we told the family about Cirque du Julian, they fawned over how "advanced" he was because of this milestone. I knew better. Our newborn insisted we, the two zombies, attend to him. He was clearly overcooked; I joked that Julian's due date must've been off by a month. My momma instinct, which I was just learning to trust, told me this was not normal. Images tinged with worry disrupted me during the night. In the dreams, Julian writhed and wiggled in my arms. He clutched his clavicle and throat. I'd awaken drenched. Ben thought it was all just new mommy jitters. I felt otherwise. In the same circumstance, I would tell my friends, clients, and anyone else worried about their infants to seek guidance from a specialist. I decided to consult my expert on everything: Dr. Curt.

Ben stayed with Julian so I could drop by my parents' house on Saturday. The pineapple palm in their front yard was covered in spikes, ripe and ready to deflate me. Or rather, deflate me even further, if possible. Still, I walked past it, kicked off my flip-flops at their door, and trudged inside. My mother didn't even look up from her agenda.

"Stop worrying, Allegra. Babies are resilient. Anyway, you must be imagining this because spit-up is also normal," Roberta said.

I fiddled with my car keys. "Where's Dad?"

"Oh, the hospital. Some emergency. They always know to call the best."

I nodded absently and headed to my old bedroom's over-full bookshelves. Shoot. I must've donated the textbook from grad school on child development. Tracing the titles left behind, my finger tripped on a homemade leather bookmark. Ruby, my best friend from camp, had once pressed that bookmark into my hands outside our cabin under the shade of more pine trees than I could count. A celebration of a first solo? Something to cheer me up when something had gone wrong at home? I couldn't recall, but what I did remember was that she was now a pediatric therapist. I saw the phone that still sat on the table next to my old twin bed. How many times had I reached for that exact receiver to call her?

She picked up on the first ring. "Ally! I was just thinking about you." Ruby's sparkly soprano voice lifted my spirits.

"You've put a smile on my face since we were eight years old, sweet friend. Just calling to say hi before my little guy is due for a guzzle," I said, hopefully masking my concern.

"Ally. Spill. And I don't mean the milk. What's up?"

I dabbed lavender essential oil on my left wrist, then told her everything.

"Honey, why'd you wait so long to share? You know I'm just a call away. Listen. Listen to those whispers. Isn't that what you'd tell me?" She cleared her throat. "And yes, go see a frickin' specialist." Though she was in Minnesota, I could picture her forehead wrinkling and her flummoxed face. "Love you, mean it," she said, signing off in her usual way. She must've been between sessions because she didn't drop any F-bombs.

I flopped back on my childhood bed. I had been floundering for months. Ruby was right.

I needed help.

CHAPTER EIGHT

r. Singh's slender fingers touched Julian's neck. He continued to palpate the area, and Julian whimpered when the doctor pressed the tender spot just above his belly button.

"I know, little guy. That's where it hurts. Thanks for letting me know." As if he understood, Julian immediately quieted.

Dr. Singh suspected reflux—the same hunch I'd had within the first few weeks of motherhood. I'd questioned my judgment, though. After all, I hadn't gone to medical school like Dr. Curt and the specialist in front of me. I stared at the empathetic man, his hazel eyes holding my gaze. His head nearly grazed the ceiling.

"You're planning on giving my baby that vile liquid?" I swallowed, even the thought making my mouth dry. "You think he pukes now; how will you pump barium into his little body?" The doctor's framed diplomas covered the walls as if seconding his suggestion. "No chance it'll stay down. I know this may sound nuts, but he is discerning and no dummy. And I can already tell he's a sensitive kid."

Julian's eyes blinked at me, following my hands as I pointed to my shirt.

"I need to wear three sweatshirts if I even go near his room, or he starts puckering like a goldfish looking for food! He smells me from far away as if my breast milk is so tantalizing that it wafts into his nursery, luring his little lips." I ran out of air. I'd heard such stellar things about this GI pediatric physician. I frowned while digesting his recommendation of a barium swallow study.

Dr. Singh felt that it was necessary to flood my teeny human's esophagus with the liquid chalk. I placated him with a polite nod. Barium would temporarily turn my baby into a glow stick. A burning sensation seeped into my stomach as I envisioned this extensive exam.

"Do you think it's my breast milk? Can it *spoil?* Does it have an expiration date? I stopped eating curry and garlic. How can I fix this? There must be another solution before resorting to such an invasive test, right?" I said, my head drooping like Eeyore. *Gosh, I could use a Pooh Bear hug right about now. Perhaps a spoonful of warm honey too.*

Dr. Singh gestured for me to sit on the black plastic chair across from him. God bless this gentle giant. I lifted my chin. He didn't interrupt and listened actively. I swayed back and forth to soothe Julian, and for the first time in what felt like forever, I felt seen and heard.

"Let me ask you a question. How much milk do you produce when you pump?"

Momentarily distracted by his voice, I drifted to the rehearsal room at camp. Tenors reserved a seat in my soul.

"Allegra? Are you comfortable discussing this?"

Sweet summer camp memories mixed with the salty present. "Yes, yes, I am. Sorry." I sniffed, wiping my eye with the corner of my lilac jacket. "What was the question?"

He repeated it.

"Well, the most I've ever pumped is about two ounces, and that's a win. I don't understand how my friends fill freezer bags to the top. No joke, I've offered to store some because they're running out of room!" I bobbed my head. "Oh, quick funny story: I started baking one day and could not stop. My mother asked me why. I told her I knew there'd be visitors when the baby arrived. And surely they'd be hungry, so I needed to prepare. I've mastered the art of maximizing refrigerator real estate." I twirled a strand of hair. "Do you think seventeen foil-covered trays are excessive? Hurricane season has started. And what if my neighbors need a nibble?"

Dr. Singh grinned. "That's a first. I think you took nesting to the ninth power. I enjoy hearing your stories, but may I be candid with you?"

I nodded, taking an audible breath that sounded more like a choke.

"You know, it is okay to stop breastfeeding Julian. You've tried for five months. That's quite a long time. It doesn't work out for everyone." Dr. Singh closed the manila folder and leaned forward.

As if he understood, Julian grimaced and nearly wriggled out of my arms.

"I've tried everything. Even bought those miserable nipple guards. Can't get this boy to latch on properly. And Julian flips out the second we're done. He's a human version of the Hungry Caterpillar! I'm wondering if Eric Carle covertly wrote about newborns. And…" I stopped mid-sentence. Turning toward the stroller, I dabbed my cheek with Julian's blanket.

Then wrapped him in it before putting him back in the plaid carrier.

"My father is right. Maybe I am starving him. Oh, Dr. Singh, I have no words, which is a rarity for me. My dad is a pediatric neurosurgeon. He's the smartest person I know and rarely wrong. He's been saying for weeks that Julian isn't getting enough food." I searched in the diaper bag for my car keys. "Do you know my incredible father, Dr. Curt? He trained some of the docs here. Anyway, he and my mother carry on about breastfeeding like it's an impeccably performed symphonic piece." My voice vibrated with worry.

Even Julian didn't make a sound. Unusual, too, because when he wasn't wailing, he was babbling and chewing on his circular teething toy. Today he stayed still.

Dr. Singh spoke softly, emphasizing each word. "It is more than okay. You can stop breastfeeding. The formulas are filled with nourishment and adequate nutrients."

Adequate? I didn't *do* adequate. If it was not excellence, bordering on perfection, I was not interested. No way. Not happening.

"What about the research on mother-child bonding? And I've also read that kids who are breastfed have stronger immune systems. What if I give myself a deadline, like another four to six weeks?" I scooted farther forward on the stiff chair. "I feel like I've failed my firstborn."

No reply. Nothing. I looked up and met Dr. Singh's kind eyes. He rolled his stool closer, narrowing the space between us, and tentatively touched my arm.

"This has been hard. Allegra, I've been practicing for more than twenty-five years. I also have a wonderful wife and four healthy adult children, only one of whom was breastfed. Not only is it okay, but it may be best for your body. You need to heal, and the self-imposed pressure isn't good for you or Julian. If he's anything like you, your little boy will sense your frustration and all the other feelings. Don't you want what's best for the both of you?"

Picking at the label on Julian's empty applesauce jar, I wished I could stuff my shame into it. "I don't care what's best for me. Whatever is best for Julian is what I will do." I sobbed as months—maybe years—of emotions released. "If aborting this mission is what's healthiest for my baby, then..." I started hiccupping erratically.

I clutched my aluminum bottle, drank the cool water, and held my breath. Instead of disappearing, the hiccups tripled in timing and intensity. "I joke that he's my bulimic baby. Totally twisted, right? And now, not only does he hurl as much as he poops, but I've been starving him. No wonder he shrank from plump to emaciated in a matter of months! And it's all my fault." Horrified about the outburst, I stood up, unlocked the stroller with my right foot, and reached for the brass doorknob.

"Ally, wait. Please," Dr. Singh said.

My ponytail swatted my neck like a horse's tail flicking away flies. I peeked at the narrow hallway. My escape route awaited.

"Please consider what we discussed. You are not a failure. I see a loving mother and overachiever who is tough on herself, demanding unrealistic expectations. No matter what you decide, let's schedule the swallow study. Julian may need Pepcid or something stronger. And just as importantly, be gentle with yourself. It's a learning process for both you and the baby." Dr. Singh suddenly seemed more like a doctor exploring my head than one who explored the digestive tract.

Before my tear ducts could betray me again, I managed a meager, "Thank you," and dashed to the check-out desk.

CHAPTER NINE

ALLEGRA' 14

A muddy slide of pine needles merged with the damp dirt. My best friend Ruby's shimmery rain boots shielded her high-arched feet as we headed back to the bunk. My parents refused to buy me a pair, citing the impracticality and cost. How much could they be? Sure, I loved the brands that everyone else wore. But even a knock-off? At least they'd packed a windbreaker for me. The sun beamed like a dimming flashlight, lighting the mucky path peppered with gravel.

"How hot is Henry? He killed it tonight. Pitch-perfect, and not to mention those tights." Ruby hooked her arm in mine. "Bummer I'm not his type. You think I could change his mind?"

Raindrops lingered on the edges of maple leaves. The drizzle had ceased seconds before the last act. My cold toes, soaked in my thin canvas sneakers, tingled. Ruby's idea was a welcome distraction.

"If anyone could convince Henry, it would be you. But I am happy for him that he came out; we've all known since fourth grade. I love that he rocks who he is." I pushed the branch that jutted out in front of us, and then I skipped ahead.

Ruby shrieked as the tree rebounded and its remaining water doused her fishtail braid. "Ally, you *didn't*."

This was the rare time I appreciated being the taller one. I was a few feet ahead of her, but Ruby's sprite frame and years of ballet boosted her speed. She came closer, giggling as she wrung her scarlet hair.

"You got me yesterday," I chortled, turning my head over my right shoulder to look at her. "I told you to stay tuned. Besides, maybe a bit of freezing water will wake you up."

She snapped the back of my bra strap. "Now we're even, Al. Love you, mean it."

We bounded up the splintery steps to our bunk and made it right before lights out. We'd have been in big trouble if this was years ago—good thing we were in the high school division now. Then again, I wouldn't have dared to dabble in tardiness as a middle schooler.

My formerly white shoelaces stuck together like overcooked linguine. Prying the sneakers from the wet socks that covered my feet was a workout. Ruby rested one palm on the porcelain sink. Her other hand scrunched makeup wipes.

"Don't you think it'd be easier if you used regular mascara?" I asked. "That waterproof gunk clings to the lashes. I mean, it's perfect for performances, but just for rehearsal? What a chore to remove, yeah?"

She ignored me and continued rubbing her upper lids.

I used a sliver of Dove soap to lather my cheeks. We brushed our teeth and synchronized our chatter between foamy spits of toothpaste. Our bunkmates were already in bed. Some read. Others listened to their Walkmans. We whispered until our counselor came over to shush us. We never ran out of things to discuss, especially this summer because we'd both gotten our periods during the year. Ruby taught me how to insert a tampon. When I asked my mother about it, she changed the subject.

Shame spread not only in my undies, but it bled into my sense of self. "Diaper-thick pads make a squishy sound, you know? And oversized sweatpants barely camouflage my butt," I said to Ruby.

She replied with heavy breathing, joining the chorus of slumber that blanketed the rest of our bunk. But I didn't care. I was exhausted too, exhausted in the most wonderful way. Even my cheeks were sore. My face wasn't used to so much smiling.

CHAPTER TEN

Julian slept in the car seat, and his serene state provided a much-needed pause. Even I craved more time in the moving cradle. The ride didn't feel long enough. If I went home now, the internet would lure me. I drove in a daze, attempting to digest and determine the next steps.

The scorching sun glinted off the silver car in front of me. I didn't want to bother Ben. He had another full day of back-to-back meetings at the office. At least it was better than the spring, when taxes were due and nobody was ever on time. I'd never get Ben's passion for plugging numbers and pondering equations. I preferred crunchy, dark-chocolate-covered pretzels to crunching numbers.

Time to gather info. Mobilize the forces. Find the silver linings. The four-way stop sign provided just enough time to dial his number. "Hi, D-d-d-dad. Do you have a minute?" I pushed harder on the brake. It was Friday, so he wasn't doing rounds. I knew his schedule to the second. He was probably exercising on the stationary bike.

"What's going on? You sound stressed." As Dr. Curt often commented, I was one of the only people in his life that understood him. I felt the same about my father.

My hands prickled, and I loosened my grip on the steering wheel. "Just left Dr. Singh's office. Remember the pediatric GI doc I told you about?"

"Mmmhmm." I heard him stop pedaling.

"He wants to thoroughly assess Julian. B-b-b-barium study, abdominal CT scan, and b-b- bloodwork. What do you think?" I could predict the next question. But I waited obediently for him to ask it.

"Where did he go to medical school? And where did Dr. What's-His-Name do his residency? You need to compile his background information before he goes anywhere near my grandson."

Pulling over to a gas station, I shifted the car into park and withdrew my plum Moleskine notebook from the glove compartment. "Undergrad Dartmouth. Medical school Johns Hopkins. Residency? I'm not sure." I searched for a pen. No luck. So I poised my lip liner at the top of the paper just in case I needed to take notes.

"Okay. He sounds competent. So, what else did he say?" Dr. Curt interrogated.

If I had called my father while driving, and if this question had snaked into our conversation a second earlier, I might've skidded off the road.

"He thinks I should switch to formula and the b-b-b-bottle," I sputtered, mouth dry.

"Good idea, Allegra. It's enough already. You're clearly starving him. I mean, why else would he scream every time you are done feeding him? That is not normal. At least you haven't used the damn pacifier. Smart choice to listen to me." My father's voice was laced with tough love.

I leaned into the cushy seat and pressed the lumbar button, needing a bit more support. I glimpsed Julian's full lips in the rearview mirror. Cracking the window, I inhaled relief and the tropical Miami breeze. "Thanks, D-d-d-dad. You're always here for me. Don't know what I'd do without you." I turned around and fixed Julian's sock, sighing as I hung up the phone.

Only a mile or two later, I unbuckled the straps that kept Julian safe and melded myself into his warm body, inhaling the sweet scent in the soft space of his head. He slept on my damp chest as we entered the house and continued to doze after I put him into the mesh playpen.

After washing my hands, I plopped on the couch. The air conditioner kicked on, and the hum of white noise soothed me. Relishing the stillness, I tried to synthesize all that had transpired.

The quiet interlude didn't last long enough. Julian's larynx and lungs, high-pitched instruments, soon blared their duet. I lifted my soaked shirt, preparing for what would be one of the last times I'd nurse my baby boy.

CHAPTER ELEVEN

Julian's ballooned belly met mine, full at least for the moment. My cheek merged with his downy crown, which rested on my shoulder. Though he rarely burped, my over-washed palm tapped his back. The books stated burping a baby helped digestion.

"Sweet boy, I didn't know I could love you more every minute." I patted his arched back, a reminder of reflux and imminent regurgitation. "After talking to your grandfather, I think it's time to try formula. I'm so sorry, Julian. I feel like I've failed you and myself."

I positioned him upright in my outstretched hands. Then we resumed. Shifting to the left, he sucked on my flaking nipple. When he settled into a rhythm, I rubbed my itchy nose on my V- neck shirt. It was damp. Had he already regifted the milk?

Then I realized the wet area was a landing pad for a different letdown. My flight of tears.

✳ ✳ ✳

Why did it seem darker? Was I dreaming? And where was my baby? I bolted off the couch.

"Honey, I have Julian." Ben rose from the armchair and drew me toward him. "When I came home, you were both snuggling and asleep. You must be totally wiped out. You haven't moved in an hour."

I wrapped both boys in my achy arms. "Oh, Ben." I resisted the urge to tackle and take him down with me.

Just hearing the heaviness in those two words seemed to be enough. "What happened? You never sleep that deeply. Something's up. *¿Qué pasa?*" Ben pulled away, studying my puffy, mascara-streaked face.

"Formula. Bottle. Baby." I couldn't string a cohesive sentence.

Ben required a more concrete explanation. Of course, it was totally clear to me. He laid his glasses on the end table, staring at a disoriented, disheveled wife.

I made another feeble attempt.

"*Mi amor*, I've been worried about you. And gosh, you have tried and tried. For twenty-one weeks, one hundred fifty-two days."

Leave it to Ben, the human calculator, to figure this out in his head.

"My father agreed with Dr. Singh," I affirmed, probably more for me than Ben. "So tomorrow I'm going to call the pediatrician." Though I knew there was no chance I'd only speak to just one doctor. "To find the formula that best mimics breast milk. I need to wrap my head around this, babe. But I will. You know me. I always find a solution."

The next day, my thoughts woke me before the blazing sunrise. I devoured detailed reviews of nearly every formula available and determined the winner. After I bought some from the store, mixed, bottled, and warmed it, Julian chugged the faux milk like a fraternity pledge being hazed. Even before it came back up, the mustard-yellow powder smelled like expired blue cheese. I had thought spit-up stank before—this gunk reeked from mixing with Julian's overabundant stomach acid. More than once, I swallowed and stifled a gag. But I was grateful he'd started sleeping more peacefully.

The new formula nourished Julian despite the unpleasant aroma. Within the week, he plumped up like a heated marshmallow in the microwave. My lil' bruiser was back. Now I had to heal the bruises in my heart.

After the dreaded barium exam, Dr. Singh confirmed Julian did, in fact, have severe gastric reflux. Duh. No kidding. He prescribed a liquid proton pump inhibitor (PPI)—otherwise known as how to torture a tiny human. Loading the ten-milliliter plastic syringe, I aimed—sometimes missing the target—and squirted the medicinal salve onto my hungry boy's tongue. Julian's rosy mouth puckered. Every time, each morning and evening, sparked a crying concerto. My heart heaved. His hungry wails and writhing body made the required thirty-minute delay before each feeding excruciating. Thankfully my breasts shrank a bit, beginning to return to a desert terrain. One droplet dripped like a memory when I held Julian.

"It's okay, my sweet boy. This hasn't been easy. But we got through it, didn't we? Together."

CHAPTER TWELVE

ALLEGRA' 10

I stood outside the locked heavy door, my tentative fist knocking on it. "D-d-d-daddy. I don't feel good. Something is wrong. I need you."

No answer. I didn't want him to get angry. Shuddering at the shadows on the wall, I'd barely made the trek across the house to their bedroom. Keri followed me and licked my bare heels. "D-d-d-daaaaadddeeee. I think I'm going to—"

The door opened, and Dr. Curt towered over my rumpled nest of curls. "What's wrong, Allegra? I have to rise early." He tightened his terry cloth robe and tamed an unruly piece of white hair. "A VIP patient is flying in from Paris and coming to the hospital because of my expertise." As if listing his resume at two a.m. would coat my stomach like Pepto Bismol.

I shook silently, afraid if I opened my mouth once more, undigested dinner would splatter all over my beloved father.

He felt my forehead with the back of his hand. "Oh, Allegra, you're burning up! At least 101. Come with me." He led me toward the maroon leather sofa in the family room.

"D-d-d-daddy, bag or a bucket, please. I don't want you or Mommy to get upset if I mess up the couch," I murmured, rolling onto my right shoulder.

"I already thought of that. Done." He handed me a stainless-steel mixing bowl we'd last used to make tuna salad. Daddy aggressively shook the fragile glass thermometer. "Here. Lift your tongue and place this as far back as you can."

I listened and did as directed. He wiped crusty saliva from the corner of his upper lip.

"I was correct, of course. 101. Boy, this is bad. Really quite dreadful. You leave on Saturday."

My ticket to freedom. My haven. Where I was free to be me. That was all I needed to hear. Without much warning, curly noodles spewed from my mouth. Everything looked red.

"Is that b-b-b-blood? Am I going to d-d-d-die?" I gasped during intermissions of retching and heaving. I couldn't stop.

He inspected the putrid pile. Thankfully, it had landed in the bowl. So smart, always prepared, he'd lined it with the perfect-sized plastic bag.

"No, you had a pizza bagel for lunch. The noodles are from dinner," he replied, as if I could even remember the day of the week. I swore I heard one of my ribs crack like a tree limb struck by lightning. "Wait right here, Allegra."

I'd thrown up eight times. Even if I wanted to move, I couldn't muster the strength to sit up. He left me. Alone. Keri whimpered, panting near the rolled-up needlepoint rug. I rubbed my hands together, trying to quell the quivers.

"I just remembered I have something to make this stop," he said, back by my side.

Daddy's mirrored medicine cabinet housed the contents of a professional pharmacy. He always told me to be prepared for any situation. Maybe this explained his obsessively stocked stash.

A gleaming, pointy object appeared. I had to be hallucinating from dehydration.

"Is that a needle, D-d-d-daddy?" My wavering voice was a jagged vibrato. Gagging and dry heaving from the stench, I couldn't comprehend how the bowl between my knees nearly overflowed.

"Yes, it is. Would you rather continue vomiting the entire night? Or shall I save you from more misery, Allegra?" he grumbled, gripping the narrow syringe.

I couldn't take much more. I had nothing left.

"Pull down your pants. Hurry up. I need to give this to you immediately," Daddy commanded.

Gingerly, I exposed my bare bottom. Clutching my stomach, I bent over, certain my butt matched the flaming flush on my face. I flinched at the sudden sensation. "That hurt! Why does my backside burn?"

Keri cocked her head, which rested on her paws.

"Oh, it's nothing. I slapped you—it wasn't hard. You should be grateful, Allegra. I utilized this method so you wouldn't feel the insertion of the needle," Daddy said. He tossed the empty syringe into the bucket.

I never threw up again. Not that night. Not ever.

CHAPTER THIRTEEN

Why didn't anyone talk about the fourth trimester? Night sweats, mood swings, achy joints. Zero interest in sex. This was not in the book. Maybe I could have written my own show or fulfilled my childhood dream of becoming an arts reporter. I was glad I'd listened to my parents, though. My therapy profession provided security and stability. But somebody had to alert the others. What a bait and switch! What happened to the flood of maternal hormones that allegedly made this *au naturel*? I'd do it again, but it would've been nice to have a warning label on motherhood.

And the dreaded car seat, which felt like shoving Julian into a straitjacket. My folks repeatedly said, "Somehow you survived without all of these fancy contraptions." Maybe they had a point. By the time I'd buckled him in again, both Julian and I were sticky, sweaty, and spent.

On the way to Dr. Singh's office, I glanced in the rearview mirror. Newborn blue eyes had transformed to a toffee-brown, and I wanted to nibble on Julian's chubby cheeks. And that smile. I'd never get enough of it. Ben teased me that I'd keep the photo paper industry in business. Drool drizzled down Julian's ivory skin. His mouth hung open like a panting poodle, and something about the goofy grin made me laugh.

"Whoa, look at this kiddo!" Dr. Singh exclaimed when we finally walked into his office. The diaper bag under the stroller's pulled-back sunshade and my water thermos in the cup-holder were all in their proper places. "He's thriving! How wonderful to see this, Ally. I haven't even examined him yet, but it's clear you chose wisely."

I beamed and joined Dr. Singh in gazing at Julian. "I cannot believe it's only been four weeks. It's a remarkable difference. He's even sleeping better. And now that he can crawl and roll over, Julian prefers his tummy. How adorable is my little guy?" I pulled the mini-photo album from the front pocket of my purple diaper bag. "I mean, seriously! How cute is that *tuchus*! When is it illegal to stop smushing it? I can't take it!"

We both laughed. Dr. Singh agreed Julian's belly down, butt up position mimicked a yogi child's pose.

"I'm grateful for you in more ways than I can express." My pitch dropped and my voice faltered. "You gave me permission to stop breastfeeding." I twiddled with the edge of my knee- length skirt. Something within me had shifted, my foundation altered. "Writing in my journal is how I process, and I haven't yet identified it. I do know you impacted my life in a seismic way."

I looked down at my clasped hands, pausing after each word. My speech needed to be smooth and articulate. This ran deeper than the "breastfeed or bust" ads and the incessant information about a higher IQ for breastfed bambinos. Well, that was a total load of crapola. Julian had been sick often and didn't even go to daycare. My mother told me about how she and I had bonded in those early months. But Roberta didn't understand, nor had the ability, I now began to sense, of bonding with anyone. The only bonding that ever occurred was during her frequent dental procedures. As if the crowns in her mouth elevated her self-appointed throne.

We left the doctor's office. With Julian propped up, I tucked his squeaky monkey into his pudgy arms. No more breastfeeding, and he was thriving. I was doing it. We were doing it.

Consumed with my thoughts, I didn't see her coming. I swerved the stroller to avoid trampling the toes of my client with the biting preschooler who was no longer biting. We had made sure of that together too.

"Ally! What a surprise to run into you here," she said while helping me gather the scattered diapers and onesies strewn across the parking lot.

"Literally. My goodness, I'm sorry we collided. Good thing my little guy's already buckled in!" I smiled sheepishly, moving Julian's monkey, which had landed on his tray.

"Oh, what a cutie pie. It feels like forever since I had babies. What's his name?" She tickled the bottom of his feet.

"Julian. And he's due for his feeding soon, so I need to get going." I winked at her son, who tugged at his mother's hand. "I hope you have a lovely weekend."

As if he, too, wanted to get on the road, Julian pursed his lips, blew air, and seemed riveted by the music he created. Just as I clicked him in his car seat, a teeny ladybug landed on my wrist. Ladybugs meant good luck. Ladybugs were my favorite. I counted its seven dots aloud to Julian, and I knew we'd be okay.

CHAPTER FOURTEEN

"Ally, I promise it's fine." Ben tucked a strand of frizzy hair behind my ear. "Besides, you checked with six families. Not one bad reference."

We'd tested our nanny cam the prior week, but I didn't trust technology. Tomorrow morning started a colossal day. And no chance I'd leave the house if this machine malfunctioned. I ignored him, headed to the laundry room closet, and hit record. Who needed movies when we could watch Julian babble in his crib? Bringing the monitor with me to the granite kitchen island, I joined Ben and we clinked glasses. My pour of pinot noir was more robust than his. I savored the hint of cherries that lingered on my tongue.

We finished cleaning baby bottles and dishes. Ben crooned and cooed at Julian while I sprawled on the sofa. He knew I needed a night off to be ready for tomorrow, but I had no idea what else he had in mind. When Ben returned to me, he clasped my hand in his, bringing it to his waist, before slowly pulling me to a stand.

"What are we doing?" I asked as he sashayed forward, his cedar-scented aftershave a familiar foreplay.

He cupped my face in his olive hands. "I'll be right back, *mi amor*."

Braless and barely shaven, I stood right there and wondered how he could find me attractive. Forget that my C-section scar hadn't fully healed. My attempts at breastfeeding hadn't helped shed the baby weight. I felt fat, and my nipples were still cracked. Mix that with sleep deprivation—the perfect birth control. Then I noticed the custard-colored stains from Julian's spit-up on my shirt.

Ben returned clad only in silk boxers. My pulse pumped double time. I reached toward the lamp and turned it off as his solid manhood turned me on. Discarding the sleep shirt before he spotted the stains, I released my clip, and my hair spiraled to my bare shoulders.

"You feel that, *mi bella*?"

He pressed my palm against his chest, right where his beautiful heart pounded. We swayed to the sultry sound of salsa music I hadn't realized he'd put on. *Did I feel that?* I didn't know if he meant the drumming beneath our hands or further below. We hadn't made love since the baby. Though Dr. Gold had given us the green light, I just wasn't feeling it. I had visions of breast milk squirting Ben in the eye like a water gun. Then the times he tried to relax me, I worried our moans would wake Julian when we climaxed.

Tonight, I couldn't resist my sensual, sumptuous Benito. Every strum of the guitar reverberated from the speakers to my skin. His tender touches aroused and dampened me in all the right places. I didn't care this time if we woke the baby. My longing for his body, for intimacy, for welcoming all of him inside me mattered most.

I slept better that night than I had in a long time, yet when I woke, my stomach clenched.

Handing my child to a stranger who'd be responsible for keeping him safe terrified me. But I knew my clients needed my presence. The doorbell rang five minutes early. Ben would view this as auspicious.

I'd deliberated about what to wear to my first day back at work and settled on a flowy linen dress. I preferred espadrilles, but my toes hadn't been touched by a nail tech in weeks. I settled for ballerina flats instead. Just the thought of buttoning a pair of pants, or anything, made me feel claustrophobic. I couldn't believe the swelling hadn't ceased.

I opened the door—and my pursed lips—clinging to the last few minutes with Julian. Had I actually agreed to have a stranger watch my baby? "Thanks for arriving early, Louise."

She greeted Julian with a drawl, each syllable separated like strings on a banjo. He reached for her immediately. "Go ahead, Mommy. I've got him," she said. Julian giggled as Louise spun him around. "My four kids and ten grandbabies all adore me."

The back of my trembling hand grazed Julian's cheek as I swallowed the impulse to snatch him back from Louise's arms. "I love you, my sweet boy. Mommy will be home soon," I murmured over my shoulder before I could change my mind.

How'd my mother leave me and Jack, and when we were just three weeks old? Roberta told me she preferred work—we had live-in help, after all. She said she didn't want her brain to rot, and moms who stayed home were useless. Julian would be six months old next week. I hadn't started the day, yet I yearned to hold him. I'd decided just to work a few mornings, and right now, even that tortured me.

Each client surprised me with the kindest gifts. That woman who'd been worried about her son touched my heart. "Thank you so much. I can't believe you found a lavender ladybug!" I said. I turned it like a kaleidoscope, marveling at the pastel prisms it cast on the wall.

She beamed. "Well, the color was easy. Your entire office is shades of purple. And when we ran into each other a few weeks ago, I heard you counting a ladybug's dots with your son. Ladybugs are good luck, right? May this one bring you as much luck and light as you give to so many." I put it on my teak desk next to the framed photo of Julian.

At the end of our session, the drumming in my left breast increased. I'd stopped nursing Julian weeks ago, yet the whole area throbbed, swollen and tender to the touch. I longed to be home in comfy loungewear, preferably one of my organic bamboo cotton shirt dresses. Ben teased me and called them "muumuus." I didn't mind. So many things I could mind about, but I picked my battles. And my muumuus called to me. As did my little boy.

I closed the last of my clients' files and nudged my new lavender ladybug to catch the midday rays from the window. Rainbows of light covered my walls and filled my heart. I'd have to tell Julian. He might not yet understand, but I knew he'd love it.

CHAPTER FIFTEEN

ALLEGRA' 12

My mother, finally satisfied with her cache of expertise, decided to pick through each wavy strand as I sat on the deck in my backyard. Bugs. So many bugs. And not the cute kind. The sharp comb raked my tender scalp.

"Here's another one!" Roberta's crimson fingernails extracted an unhatched egg from my hair. A win because she loved being right, even when she wasn't.

Roberta crowed that "only a great mother would endure this laborious effort for her kid." It must've been true because she worked full time at the school and still made time for me. I'd heard her say the same thing before. About Popsicle stick construction projects I had to build for class. About teaching us to tie our shoes. About staying home when Jack and I were too sick to go to school. This act warranted extra appreciation, evidently because of my place on the cheerleading team. Maybe chopping off my hair would've made this easier, but I refused. My mother continued to complain about the tiny critter extermination.

"No way will I even cut an inch, Mom! It's never been this long. And I need to put it in a ponytail for practice and competitions." My jaw clenched and lower lip protruded.

Even as a young girl, when I felt strongly enough about the cause, I didn't relent. A perfectionistic pleaser, it scared me to fight back. I didn't do it often. But I'd won this minor scuffle. I guess my appearance trumped the extra time required to de-lice my hair. Roberta must've decided the longer locks would look better too. She pressed the comb harder and harder through every section of hair. I imagined that my mother had put aside the tool and just used her nails. But I knew better than that. At least, I was pretty sure.

"You have no idea how much having children will hold you back from the things you love."

I blinked rapidly. "Well, I love you, Mommy."

She answered with more rough movements through my long strands, from my scalp to my split ends. Again. And again.

CHAPTER SIXTEEN

Cramps are nature's dress rehearsal for birth. My monthly rent arrived every twenty-eight days, as regular as the sunrise, both when I was a teen and an adult. The heavy periods were tough to endure in high school, not to mention mortifying. Pads piled into my underwear like a deck of cards, yet I'd still leak; some days I barely made it through a class. But it was an unrealized gift that my body clearly communicated with me, a blessing when Ben and I planned pregnancies.

Planning was my forte. Now married and mindful, I thanked my uterus for fostering a fertile habitat, ready at any moment for seeds to be planted. Hyperaware and deeply intuitive, I could feel my egg descend each month. Like other aspects of my life, I assumed this was common. I'd gotten pregnant with Julian on the first try. (Of course, I kept a hidden ovulation log.) I had purchased several brands to confirm my hunch. I hadn't even been late yet. Before unwrapping the sticks, I sensed something stirring. All five tests had confirmed that a human grew inside me.

My curiosity grabbed the wheel again and drove itself right to the pharmacy. Julian was napping, and Ben was analyzing some spreadsheet or another. I knew they both would be fine for a while. As I paid for the plethora of hopefully positive results, the teenager behind the counter stared at me like, "You're back here again?" I made a mental note, should more be necessary, to find a drugstore in another county. This was getting a bit embarrassing. At this point, I might suggest to Ben that we buy stock in these companies.

Delayed gratification was in a league of its own regarding maternal nudges. I couldn't wait. I managed to give a hopefully charming grin to the connect-the-acne-dotted boy. What I wanted to say, like Ruby's son often did, was, "Please don't judge."

Dashing to the restroom at the back corner of the store, I tore open the foil package. I squatted over the sticky seat, certain that if public bathroom squats were an Olympic sport, I'd have a fair shot at a medal at this point. I squirted all over my ring finger, but enough liquid hope dripped on the stick. After washing my urine-soaked hands, I placed the test perfectly flat. I followed directions to the letter and set the timer on my phone. Hands shaking and heart hammering, I fervently hoped nobody would come into the restroom.

Those seconds felt like a century. The faucet dripped. The fluorescent light buzzed. The smell of bleach infiltrated my nostrils. Then I spotted the faintest sky-blue line. Just to confirm, I raced home and glimpsed that gift on the stick two more times.

Just like with my pregnancy with Julian, I hadn't even missed my period yet. A woman's instinctual indicator surpasses science. I couldn't wait to tell Ben.

★ ★ ★

"Bennn!" I shrieked. My sweatpants puddled at my ankles as I hopped into his home office. I nearly plunged into the corner of his sleek desk. Lucky I didn't, because stacks of spreadsheets covered it.

"I knew it! And I betcha it's a bambina!"

I grabbed Ben's unshaven face. His wire glasses went airborne. We hugged tightly as the density of the past year's struggles dissipated. Yet just as I'd known about this pregnancy only a few days before the positive tests, I had a foreboding feeling. I scheduled an appointment with Dr. Gold, begging him to do an ultrasound. It was too early for a heartbeat, but still. When I got to his office, he ran a specific hormone test, HGH, and the numbers seemed a bit low. He told me not to worry.

Baking the cake for Julian's first birthday began as a distraction. We explored every aisle of the grocery store, noting the different food groups, colors, and shapes. If I couldn't control what I could create inside my womb, then on the outside I'd concoct the most perfect creation.

"This is confectioner's sugar, sweetie. When I blend it with butter, it makes the yummiest frosting." Julian tried to poke a hole in the thin plastic bag.

Determined to make a multi-tiered train cake, I cruised around town and searched for items in two more stores. We found the vanilla extract and flour. Julian charmed the lady at the bakery, who offered him a sparkly sugar cookie. "Oh, he's such a cutie. And so well-behaved," she said as Julian's cherubic face molded into a wide grin.

I didn't have the heart to tell this kind woman that we didn't give him sugar yet. Maybe it'd be better that his taste buds sampled sweetness before the birthday party? If I knew my boy, he'd not only scoop the cake with his bare hands but likely dive into it face first.

Inside me, something was growing. Stronger? Bigger? I wanted a specially made microscope to see my own insides. But

I tried to focus on my little boy holding a cookie nearly the size of his head as he watched the sugar crystals twinkle in the store's lights. Nearly one year old. And maybe just about to become a big brother. I crossed my fingers and encouraged him to take a bite.

CHAPTER
SEVENTEEN

My brother captured the moment when my baby boy smashed his cheek into the lopsided birthday cake. Flecked with organic frosting, Julian's sticky fingers grabbed for his grandparents, who pulled back as if sprinkles were infectious. Ben and I beamed at our one-year-old son.

When Jack hugged me goodbye at the airport the following week, I must've clutched him harder than I realized. "What's up, Ally?" He tilted his head.

The flutters in my stomach hadn't ceased. They were more like broken moth wings than hopeful butterflies.

"I think I'm going to lose this baby," I whispered. "Something doesn't feel right. I can't explain it."

Jack pulled back, peering into my eyes. "That doesn't sound like you, Ally." His own eyes brimmed with moisture. "And you're telling me this now? Right before my business trip? How can I board that fucking flight?"

But I forced him to leave. He only went after another huge hug, letting me go slowly, squeezing my shoulders like he always had. My little brother sometimes seemed too wise for his age.

Just days later, pink-tainted stains confirmed my sinking suspicion.

"You've got two choices, Allegra. I can do a dilation and curettage, or you can do this naturally," Dr. Gold explained when he examined me. He removed his gloves, the snapping sound of latex all too familiar.

"I can't do a D and C," I murmured. "Just the thought makes me queasy. And what if, even if it were a minuscule chance, it could leave scar tissue? What if I couldn't conceive again?"

Dr. Gold said he'd support either decision. I felt confident in my choice. A part of me died in that office, along with whoever had been growing inside of me.

Ben had always anchored me. I knew I'd dial his number the second I got back in my car.

The convenience and efficiency of a surgical procedure wasn't worth the risk. Ben agreed. Motherhood meant everything to me. I couldn't imagine life without my son in it. And I knew, saw it already, Julian would be an older brother. If not now, hopefully sooner rather than later.

The bleeding started within hours. My uterus responded to our conversation. Every merlot-colored clot that plopped into the toilet tore another piece of faith, and I knew the weeks that ensued would be brutal. This was the first time in my adult life I couldn't rally or find the reason why.

I shifted into survivor mode as I'd been trained by my folks to do. Every clot that exited my body became a dagger. A heart-wrenching reminder that what should've been Julian's baby sibling disintegrated into what could've been and what wouldn't be.

CHAPTER EIGHTEEN

ALLEGRA' 8

Swim team and gymnastics, plus full academic days, were scapegoats for the throbbing in my head. One day, I couldn't hold back. I had to complain, so crying and faint, I told my mom about the headaches.

"Oh, it's because you're active, Allegra. You're fine. Just deal with it," she said. Then she returned to filing her long nails.

Those years hurt. My head, heart, and sense of self were stomped on like the springboard in front of the vault I wouldn't dare jump over. Friends who excelled at the bars, beam, and other physically risky routines thrived on adrenaline. A fearful echo accompanied me each time I accelerated. It repeated with each pounding step.

"Why do you always stop?" my gymnastics coach asked again, clearly confused. "You nailed the splits and cartwheels. Balance and flexibility are your fortes. I don't get it."

After four years of bi-weekly practices, I finally confessed.

"I could get hurt, Coach Dee. What if I fall?" I tugged the end of my ponytail. "I just can't do it."

Such a paradox because I was bold in all other areas. I performed on stage, loved to sing and dance, and asserted myself if a friend felt threatened. But standing up for me—that was another story. I dropped gymnastics, but the headaches mysteriously endured.

CHAPTER NINETEEN

I could barely breathe, suffocating in my own sorrow. I typically bounded out of bed, but even the idea of standing up felt like a workout. I lost my appetite both for food and fun. Why couldn't I just be grateful that we had one healthy, thriving child? It was time to get up, get moving, and go forward. I couldn't change the past—I needed to get vertical. One morning, I drew lines on my lids with violet eyeliner. I donned a silk shift dress and sparkly chandelier earrings.

Counseling and consoling a caseload of trauma survivors triggered me. Especially the women who'd survived rape. And the teen who had decided to terminate her accidental pregnancy. I wailed the whole way home, hoping for an emotional drought before cooking dinner for Ben and Julian. Good thing I'd splurged on that waterproof mascara. Scrubbing the purple glitter from my puffy eyes became a ritual. I even threw makeup remover wipes in my bag, a lesson from Ruby all those years ago.

Ben didn't know how to soothe me. He whipped up surprise meals. He showed up with orchids and café con leches. He didn't give up. Yet nothing he said or did could anesthetize my pain. No amount of bedazzled accessories or vibrant clothing could ease the absence I felt with every waking breath.

I wanted to try again the moment my cycle became regular. We decided to switch to a new doctor who worked in a smaller practice. Dr. Bradley was compassionate and versed in state-of-the-art medicine. Unlike my experience with Julian, I would know all the doctors well before my due date. We told him about the emergency C-section and the difficult recovery. My plan was to birth another baby before turning thirty. I informed Dr. Bradley about my ovulation schedule, birthing scenario, and even my favorite brand of home pregnancy tests.

"You're quite a character, Ally!" He chuckled while inserting the metal speculum high into my vajay. "This is going to be entertaining."

For the first time in months, I giggled and then burst into full-on cackling. I almost pished on his gloved fist. "Oy, I'm behaving and just warming up. You sure you can handle my sarcasm?" On my left, laminated posters colorfully mapped the reproductive anatomy. The wall behind Dr. Bradley displayed ads with images of the latest and greatest birth control devices. "And I promise, even though this needs to be a planned C-section— Julian was the size of a manatee—I will no doubt yammer during the entire procedure." I slid back up as instructed while the waxy paper wrinkled beneath me.

Dr. Bradley raised his eyebrows. "Why don't you heal first? I don't just mean physically, but emotionally. You've been through a lot," he said, rumpling the remaining hair on his head. "Your body will know when it's time. And you have no fertility challenges. Based on your bloodwork and exam, the miscarriage had no known cause."

I brushed a piece of hair off my forehead and blew upward. One stubborn strand of bangs, even after being finessed with a flatiron, wouldn't stay put.

"I'm a woman on a mission. I am working on acceptance—this wasn't meant to be, though it hurts in a way I cannot even describe." I grimaced. "You don't have a uterus expelling a life you loved even before he or she was born." A tiny teardrop landed on the vinyl exam table.

Dr. Bradley exhaled in resignation. "Just take care of yourself, Ally. And stay on those prenatal vitamins; they'll boost and replenish you," he advised, lathering his hands.

"Oh yes, of course. And I read in multiple sources they're fabulous for my nails and hair. I may just keep taking them for the rest of my life!" I spread my arms, hoping for a brief hug, before holding myself back. Dr. Curt and Roberta rarely made physical contact, yet I adored touch. I'd have to ask, even plead, to hear the precious words "I love you" from my parents. They usually replied, "Allegra, we just aren't as emotional as you. Words don't mean anything anyway."

I patted my empty abdomen, sending love and support to the eggs waiting inside.

CHAPTER TWENTY

Sunlight shimmered across the turquoise water, beckoning me toward it. The drapes, tied back with a braided rope, framed our placid pool. A lilac orchid petal floated near the steps. I had a sudden urge to jump in fully clothed.

"Honey!" I called to Ben. "I'm changing into my swimsuit. Want to join me with Julian in a few minutes?" Though I abhorred squeezing into the one-piece, I craved the cleansing bath of chlorinated water.

As I stepped into the pool, my calves and thighs relaxed. Once the water reached my waist, I grabbed the foam raft and pulled myself onto it. I rested my head back, palms facing upward, and closed my eyes. The recollection of Dr. Bradley's guidance drifted over me as droplets from the ends of my hair dripped onto my neck. The sun's rays shone through the clouds like an old-fashioned film projector.

"I see Mommy!" Julian's squeal stirred me from my meditation.

"Hi, sweetie. I'm so glad you and Daddy are joining me." I slid off the raft, swam to the side, and he jumped into my arms. I admired Ben's dewy chest, which conjured up images I oughtn't have while holding our child. My husband raised an eyebrow as if reading my mind. The three of us played "I Spy" with flying objects and insects. Julian pointed to a dragonfly, wondering what the "thing" was called. Then Ben spotted a sippy cup, mildly irritated that it was on our patio floor rather than in the kitchen cabinet.

By now, Julian could swim to the end of the pool. He also knew how to float on his back.

My father had instilled the importance of drown-proofing kids. He told me and Jack disturbing, detailed stories of kids he'd seen with brain damage that even he couldn't fix.

Ben and I positioned ourselves a few feet apart, and we timed Julian, asking our energetic minnow to swim back and forth between us. He loved this game. Then I heard a door slam and looked behind me.

"Oh, I'm glad to see you're in the pool. It's time that Julian takes off those stupid swim crutches. It's enough already; you are making him weak," a bass voice boomed.

I shaded my forehead with my hand, squinting because the clouds had dispersed. My mother trailed behind Dr. Curt, yapping on her phone.

"It's fine, D-d-d-dad. He can swim without them. Right, Julian?" Ben was already removing the neon orange floaties. Gripping the edge of the concrete coping, I pulled myself up and out of the water. "Mom, can you please hand me the towel?"

She kept yammering and tossed it to me. I noticed my father staring in my direction. His eyes moved from my neck to my stomach to my thighs.

"I see you're still pleasantly plump. You've got my genes, kid. We just can't eat whatever we want. At least you have my brains," he said, smirking as I wrapped the towel tighter. I felt like a human Tootsie Roll.

He began to unbutton his rayon shirt. "Why don't you take a break? Go inside, make us lunch, and I'll swim with Julian." My father retied the string on his steel-blue swim trunks.

Ben nodded at me from the deep end.

I made the usual. Chicken salad. Cantaloupe. Freshly squeezed OJ. I tapped the tablespoon on the side of the sink, the peace from earlier replaced with humiliation. As if being in front of them in a bathing suit wasn't hard enough, one of my parents always made a critical remark. The fork chimed against the metal bowl as I blended the low-fat mayonnaise.

"Babe, you've been in here for a while. Is lunch ready yet?" Ben poked his head in through the sliding glass doors, his wavy hair dripping water on the kitchen floor.

The chicken now looked more like suntanned cream cheese. I'd lost track of time. "Please come in here and help me carry everything out." I flipped my hair backward. I couldn't stomach another comment from my father.

Though I was glad my parents had joined us today for family time, I wished I could dive back into the water and wash away the shame that shrouded the earlier joy.

CHAPTER TWENTY-ONE

ALLEGRA' 7

I ignored the hazy goggles suctioned over my eyes. The plastic domes, opaque with moisture, obstructed my parents' faces when I came up for air.

Daddy dunked me in the deep end of our pool at home, just like the donuts I wasn't allowed to eat. I remember the boasting: "Allegra and Jack were drown-proof before age one." Every day, after Daddy returned from rescuing another patient, Jack and I had to practice what we'd learned from our swim instructor, who Dad claimed was the best swim teacher in Florida.

She scared the shit out of us. The wiry woman reeked of chlorine and impatience. Those Saturday lessons lingered long after I dried off.

The swim coach never understood why my freestyle and breaststroke forms were impeccable until the detour, when I'd dart away from the drain, believing everything Daddy had said. He'd told me that if I swam near the drain, it would suck me in. My breathing grew shallow as I got closer to the deep end. *Fear the world. It is unsafe. But we'll throw you into an activity that requires fearlessness. And by the way, you'll be the center of attention during competitions.* When I had bombed gymnastics, my parents flung me into the water instead.

The pool was the only place I ever felt physically strong. Water was weightless. And water didn't judge. At swim meets, the rest of the school of fish flanking me were lean and bony. No fat to trim from my teammates. But in the pool, I swam away from the scornful stare of my mom and dad, diving deeper with each stroke.

CHAPTER
TWENTY-TWO

I envisioned growing, birthing, and raising multiple kids. One for every day of the week.

So did Ben. We wanted to fill our home with loving chaos and boundless memories. I even named my babies before conception. Didn't tell a soul, though.

When I casually mentioned expanding our family to my parents, they exchanged a knowing look.

"Wait until Julian gets a bit older and then tell us if you want another one. Your father didn't even want kids. I had to convince him." My mother dabbed powder on her nose.

Though the doubts my parents deposited in other areas of my life drove many of my decisions, I remained unfazed by their endless commentary. The pages of my future photo albums were filled with at least a family of four. So the following month, I secretly decided to track my ovulatory cycle. Again. Before even being one day late, I knew it already.

"Benito! I think I'm pregnant, and it's a girl," I shrieked in December.

Ben, the balance to my bubbly whims, was the annoying (but probably necessary) voice of reason.

"Babe, c'mon. Didn't the doctor say we should wait a bit? And seriously, how could you even know? You haven't missed your period, right?" His eye roll didn't escape my hawk-like gaze.

I heard that old message in my mind, those seeds of distrust that my parents had planted.

Shaking my head, I stepped toward Ben.

"Yeah, I must be imagining that my breasts went from a B to a D already," I retorted, ripping off my cotton T-shirt. "Want to feel them and let me know, dear?"

Ben's eyes widened. I stood right in the middle of our window-framed family room. We hadn't saved enough money to purchase curtains or blinds for this area of the house.

"What the—"

I silenced him, reached for his chin, and drew his full lips toward mine. After I pulled away, leaving him stunned and speechless, I said, "What do you think now? And I couldn't care less if our nosy neighbors see me making out with my hot husband."

Convinced that my body was talking to me, I scattered the sticks across the bathroom counter. Tough to decide which one to use first. I tinkled on a few. And sobbed when the result wasn't what I expected. Was I losing my mind?

My bras felt like compression socks. My tummy molded itself around buttons like silly putty. Hours after I'd taken off my underwear, I'd see indentations above my C-section scar. I discovered, during middle-of-the-night web digging, that after a miscarriage, the body can mimic pregnancy. Deeply disappointed and heading toward devastation, I withdrew from my saddened swamp before being strangled by my own weeds. I couldn't sink. Instead, I poured love into chocolate molds, making animal-shaped lollipops for Julian and his friends. Tying the cellophane bags and curling the ribbon eased my angst.

Two months later, I was nearly certain a little human grew inside me. The stirring sensation, inner knowing, awoke me from a deep sleep. Why should I be up alone? I cleared my throat with unnecessary vigor. Ben kept snoring. I marched to the tiled bathroom and casually—oops!—dropped an unboxed Dove soap in the shower. Sliding open the peeling pocket door, I glanced at my husband. Damn it, he was still out cold.

I didn't have the heart to wake him, though I both envied and admired his ability to literally sleep through anything. In fact, it had baffled me when he'd roll over during Julian's first months and mutter, "Did you nurse him yet?"

"Uh, yeah," I'd reply. "Our baby vampire is never sated. The little stinker sucked relentlessly on these melons four frickin' times already! How did you not hear him wailing?"

But this time, I snuggled back under the sateen sheet and tossed and turned impatiently.

Ben continued to sleep as I awaited the sunrise.

CHAPTER TWENTY-THREE

My leg bobbed up and down like a buoy on a rocky sea. Ben kneaded my back as I waited with him and my overstuffed purse for our turn. It was overflowing. *I* was overflowing. Fingers tap-danced on keyboards and hold buttons blinked. I watched other expectant mothers waddle to the window and sign their names on the clipboard. After confirming the pregnancy a few months ago, I had barely slept. Everything about this pregnancy felt different—further evidence this would be a baby girl. And we were seconds away from finding out.

The rubbing alcohol sensation of acid reflux scorched my esophagus. I'd awaken at night choking on it. Ben slept through this as well. I couldn't sing to Julian within my usual broad range—he adored Elmo and the musical show *Little Einsteins*. I'd switch the high-pitched characters to altos and even tenors, and Julian would shake his body in time to the tunes; sometimes he'd bob his head, giggling and grinning. When I opened my mouth lately, my voice cracked, raspy and breaking.

As Ben and I sat together, silent for once, I drifted into a memory. Always a cast member and never the lead, I could still recall the feeling of the Victorian-era corset gripping my teen body during operetta performances at camp. I relished every second on stage in Michigan. I didn't need or want to perform in a main role. The collective energy and collaborative spirit infused me. At the end of summer, when I packed my trunk to return to Miami, I also fantasized about a funnel in which I could forever capture and contain that unconditional love. I'd relinquish shoes, socks, and every other clothing item and swap it for all that mattered. How I wished there'd be a way to pack love into my luggage.

"Allegra? Are you here?" I heard a faint voice ask. Startled from my camp memories replay, I felt Ben touch my chafing elbow.

I plodded toward the door. "Yes, yes, here I come. Please tell me how much longer I need to hold these gallons of water. I'm about to piddle right here in the hallway. And for goodness' sake, there is *no* way I will put even my pinky toenail on that scale," I prattled.

Removing her tortoiseshell glasses, the nurse smiled and pointed toward room seven, much to my delight because it was my favorite number. Clearly, this was a promising sign.

Another woman told me to take off my top and put on the thin robe. I itched my upper lip, and my finger stuck to a dab of wax. The area was red and blotchy from my amateur aesthetician attempt. This kid, unlike my pregnancy with Julian, fertilized my hair follicles. I felt like a Chia Pet in the oddest places.

Ben clicked the Montblanc black pen in his pocket.

"Babe, please, for the love of God, would you stop? I can barely quiet my own noise. I don't need an accompanist," I bristled. Just at that moment, the door creaked open.

"Dr. B! We thought we wanted to be surprised this time, but on the way here, we decided there's no way we could wait. So..." I heard my own babble bounce off the walls. "Please tell me this is the ultrasound when we'll find out what we are having."

I already knew the answer. I'd asked this question earlier in the week when I talked to the assistant who'd confirmed our appointment.

"This may feel a bit cold, Ally." Dr. B started his spiel. The squishy sound of gel was closer.

"I know, I know! All I care about is finding out the sex of our healthy baby and not peeing all over this table. Can you start?" I pressed my thighs together and dug my nails into them.

Dr. B chuckled and brought the ultrasound machine closer. I rocked to the reassuring tempo of my baby's melodic heartbeat.

"You sure you and Ben want to know? You both told me months ago to remind you that you'd prefer to be surprised this time."

My eyes locked with Ben's, and he winked conspiratorially.

"We can't stand it. We want to know. To be honest, it's me this time. This way we can design and decorate the nursery," Ben exclaimed. "And Ally is so convinced it's a girl. You know how she is with that sixth sense of hers."

The device sashayed all over my slippery stomach, stopping to listen to the hums and heartbeats, then sliding past my own gut gurgles. The intervals seemed longer than usual this time.

"This baby has other plans, you two," Dr. B quipped. "He or she—the legs are closed like a zipper."

I had come prepared. I'd read that sugar could get a baby to boogie. "Ben, please hand me my backpack." I pointed to the corner. "Don't ask, okay? I'm not in the mood." The two men in the room stepped back as I rummaged in the canvas bag. I withdrew a small glass bottle of freshly squeezed orange juice and a handful of Tootsie Rolls, then I stood up, unwrapped the sticky pellets, and popped them into my mouth. I chewed the candy while hopping on one foot.

"Umm, honey? Have you officially lost your mind?" I splayed my hands in the air and pirouetted. "I mean, no offense, but what on earth are you doing?" Ben's cheeks flushed with bemusement as he stared at me.

I ignored him, climbed back on the exam table, and asked Dr. B to try one last time. "Okay, but I have about a dozen parents after you, Ally." The instrument slid over my gelled belly. "I am sorry, but we can only do this for one minute. Oh, oh! She just did a flip and showed us clearly that…"

I gasped and nearly made a glee pee right there on the exam table. "It's a girl! You said 'she'! Oh, we changed our minds. Don't want to know."

Always virtuous and straight-arrowed, Dr. B's mouth dropped open, and he seemed about to apologize for the pronoun slip.

"Just kidding!" I grinned. "We are grateful she listened to her mama. Positive thinking works every time. Apparently, this kiddo likes sugar. I'm already in love with her." I wiped underneath my eyes.

Ben and Dr. Bradley's laughter reverberated like kettle drums. Then Ben's excitement amplified; it never ceased to crack me up. He snorted, then cried, then both at once. After a lifetime of repressed feelings, Ben's layered shell had cracked. I giggled, grabbed his face, and planted an unabashed, ecstatic smooch on his damp cheeks.

CHAPTER TWENTY-FOUR

ALLEGRA' 7

"**D**-d-d-daddy! Please stop. You're hurting him," I pleaded as he shook the glass Tabasco sauce bottle. I heard the crunch of green plastic as he broke the seal. Jack trembled as Daddy towered over him, furtively sinking his four-year-old body into the corner of the couch. If only the puffy down-filled pillows could protect him. Daddy's thick hand shackled my little brother's left ankle and dragged him across the couch. The cushion slid toward the edge with him.

"Don't you even think about it, Son. Man up. If you can't stop this disgusting thumb-sucking habit, then I will do it for you," Daddy snapped.

Jack held out his raw, peeling thumb. I gripped my pilling pajama pants and squeezed my eyes shut. My little brother, obedient and terrified, thudded to the ground. Daddy liked when we listened the first time. With one eye still closed, I padded toward Jack. Our dad left the room to join Mom for dinner. They ate alone in the fancy dining room, the one with the sterling silver chandelier. We had meals earlier and usually with our live-in nanny, Irie.

I reached for my brother's other hand, the dry, unscathed one.

"You are Superman—look at your PJs tonight, Jack. How funny; I have my Wonder Woman ones on." I led him to the back of our house, our safe space, where we could pretend our superpowers would protect us from Daddy.

As we brushed our teeth, Jack asked if I could sleep on the floor of his room that night. "I know Superman wouldn't need you, Ally, but I'm scared. What if Daddy comes in and pours the whole bottle of spicy stuff into my mouth?" Jack's tongue stuck out between his teeth on the letter *s*.

We tucked ourselves under the thin covers, and I made up a story about a superhero family whose special powers became stronger the more they loved each other. Jack jammed his other thumb in his mouth and sucked it silently. Within minutes, his little head rolled heavily onto my shoulder.

I stared at the ceiling, wondering if all daddies dipped their kids' thumbs into spicy sauce.

Why did love have to hurt?

CHAPTER
TWENTY-FIVE

Pushing a Target shopping cart that felt like it had pebbles lodged in the wheels, I searched everywhere for my van. I was certain somebody had stolen my car. My panic skyrocketed while Julian wiggled against me. Wandering up and down every lane in the sweltering garage, I dialed Ben.

"Babe! I've called you three times! Some ding-dong stole my car. And before you say something annoyingly pragmatic, I am frantically holding your firstborn son, who's long overdue for lunch." Julian wound my hair in his forefinger.

Ben spoke steadily and slowly. He started to argue but stopped himself and stayed on the phone with me while I meandered aimlessly.

"This is a super-duper start to my birthday week. I am drenched! It's only May, and this heat is unbearable." Julian squirmed. I reached for the top of my soaked shirt, fanning it back and forth to force a breeze for both of us. A pigeon dipped its beak into a nearby puddle. Then it perched on the side mirror of a car. "There it is! Found it! I knew I should've gotten a custom color; every frickin' person in town has an Odyssey, and they're all white like mine!" I silently thanked the bird as it flew away.

★ ★ ★

Glancing at my pink eyelet shirt, I grinned like the Cheshire Cat, giddy with the clandestine confirmation that a baby girl danced inside me. Then I almost dropped the massive cake when I exited the minivan. We'd come full circle as we'd had Julian's first birthday at this park. Despite the excruciating heartburn, which wouldn't cease no matter what I did or didn't eat, I radiated joy. I couldn't wait for Julian to become a big brother.

I'd baked this three-tiered cake to celebrate life, not just mine, but our growing family too. Ben met us near the swings, thankfully securing a picnic bench shaded by the canopy of oak trees. As I moseyed toward him, Julian let go of my hand and scampered toward his daddy. I noticed a tiny bird's nest in the juncture of two branches.

We'd decided to surprise our little guy with a sweet lunch. After the second slice of cake, I handed him a present. Julian wasted no time as he tore the paper off in one motion.

"What does this say, Mommy?" He pointed to the longest word on the T-shirt, which began with the letter "B."

Touching Ben's knee, I took Julian's hand into mine. "Brother! And the whole sentence is 'Best Big Brother.'"

He jumped up and down like a pogo stick then stopped suddenly and stared at my tummy. "Is there a baby in there? I want to see it. Now." Julian began to lift my blouse.

Ben swooped him into the air, flying him up and down like Superman. "Not yet, buddy. The baby isn't ready to be born. But Mommy and I were so excited we wanted to celebrate with you." Ben flashed that sexy smile at me.

I shaped the last bite of cake into some semblance of an airplane, and Julian squealed as Ben flew it toward his open mouth. We wiped crumbs off the table and our faces then headed back to the mommy-mobile. I still couldn't believe I'd succumbed to this gas-guzzling, gargantuan machine that I swore I was too cool to drive.

CHAPTER TWENTY-SIX

Baby number two's due date was written in a Barney-colored marker on the kitchen calendar. My trip to the hospital was planned. After Julian's ginormous size, Dr. Bradley didn't want to risk a uterine rupture. I learned this after initiating and losing a debate about VBAC (vaginal birth after a cesarean section). Ben loved the scheduled appointment. No waiting. No worries. Hopefully. He could add it to his personal calendar.

A sensation that felt like a Starlight red-and-white candy wedged itself in my throat. It wouldn't go away, no matter how many times I tried to swallow it. Baby girl would be named after my grandmother, the same one who'd given me those mints that populated her box-shaped handbag. Adding to our family had been my dream since the miscarriage. It took me a while to recover from the emotional pain. Sadness. Uncertainty. Yes. That's what it mimicked. Yet it was misaligned with how I lived.

After a few weeks, I figured out why, but the revelation wrecked me like the derailed Thomas the Train set Ben was carefully constructing. I marveled at his meticulous work. Funny how I was more patient with people than with putting puzzles together. My honey was dexterous with his hands. He'd even wrap holiday presents because I couldn't draw a straight line with a ruler. We'd heard that a meaningful "big brother" gift could be a strategic diversion. As Ben clicked the last track together, my limbic system reconnected. Heaving with silent sobs, I was officially a train wreck. Percy, Thomas, and Cranky the Crane gleamed as Ben stepped back, admiring and rightly proud of his work.

Shoot. He'd noticed me.

"*Mi amor*, are you having contractions? What's up? Why are you bent over, and what's that sound?" Ben asked, worry wracking his escalating voice.

Averting my gaze, I shook my head to let him know the baby wasn't leaving the station. At least not until tomorrow morning. We'd been in a groove, a party of three, for the past thirty months. We had a schedule, and I couldn't even imagine life before Julian. My thoughts raced. I murmured an admission.

"How can I, or we, love another baby like we do him?" I said, pulling at my split ends.

The rest of my hair curtained my face as my head dropped lower.

There it was. The elephant in the room (not my stretched, swollen body). I'd admitted the root of my intense, erratic emotions.

"I didn't hear you," Ben replied.

You've got to be kidding me. "Oh, please do not make me repeat myself. I barely got that out. What do you think you heard?" I pleaded, squatting on the electric blue "B" of the jumbo letters that formed an alphabet foam carpet. They served as an engaging way to teach Julian. And now as a docking station for my derriere.

Ben sat down next to me. He steadied my shaky hands with his own. "What I got was you don't think you can love anyone as you do Julian, right?"

No. Those were not my exact words. That is not what I said. But that was the gist.

"I fell madly in love with you on our second date, and not only because you learned salsa *muy rápido*." Ben pressed his palm into mine. "We laughed so hard that I farted, right in the middle of the dance floor. Totally embarrassed, I thought you'd say no when I asked you out again."

He moved my hair away from my face, tilting my chin upward. I squeezed my eyes shut.

"My point is, Ally, your passion and huge heart are two of the things I adore about you. It also makes me crazy at times. We could have one hundred kids, and I'm certain you'd love each one just as much."

I thanked him without words. Tearing off his Nike top, I slid my hands into his slick shorts, for once not caring that he hadn't showered after his workout. Grateful that Julian slept through hurricanes, we brushed against each other, two matches igniting. We didn't make it upstairs. He entered and pummeled me, docking in my station, right there on the letter "F."

★ ★ ★

Our bedroom faced east. Today, it drizzled outside, clouds muting the blazing sunrise.

Solid and sensually insistent, Ben stroked me awake. As I rolled over, a spring stabbed my backside. We needed to replace the worn mattress. The mahogany sleigh-bed would stay; we'd purchased it together. Each chip and scratch mapped the first few chapters of our journey.

I reached behind me and laced my hands around Ben's eagerness. Despite the roaring reflux and bout of bronchitis, I longed to have Ben inside of me one more time. I guided his fingers toward my pulsing need. We only had a few minutes before Aunt

Arden arrived. She'd quickly become like a mother to me and had kindly offered to babysit Julian while we were at the hospital.

Ben's breath quickened. "Are you sure?" he gasped, his voice lowering and thickening with lust.

Though I didn't feel sexy, my libido unleashed itself and gushed with desire. I didn't understand my girlfriends who had no interest in sex while pregnant. The first few times, Ben and I both had an image of poking the baby, but now that idea made me want to laugh, an impulse I quickly suppressed. Men could be sensitive about their manhood, and if I erupted into a fit of giggles, no doubt Ben would misunderstand. Nothing like that to kill a mood.

I loved pleasing Ben with words and through music. But I relished ravishing his toned body too. My fingernails looped through his golden-brown hair and then followed the route of his hairline, my tongue teasing and tormenting him as I traveled southward. He was worried, as always, about the time. He pretended to blink, but I saw him sneak a peek at the digital alarm clock. My stash of Bed, Bath, and Beyond coupons proved useful for blackout drapes, but I realized I still needed to reposition the clock. We didn't have to leave for another two hours. The bland oatmeal shades blended into the textured walls. I preferred vibrant colors; however, my practical self chose these drab ones. This was a rental anyhow; the new house would be ready in a few months. Protest poured from Ben's mouth. The rest of his virile body begged to differ.

Sucking his lower lip between my teeth, I huskily told Ben it would be "access denied" for a while. I planned to successfully (surely the second time would be a breeze?) breastfeed.

And I'd learned the hard way that rest, as much as possible, would heal me faster this time.

That was all he needed to hear. Ben pulled me onto him, eager and erect. As I gripped the curved headboard, we found our familiar rhythm. He carefully slid in and out of me. I palmed Ben's tight buttocks, thrusting his length deep into me. Our erotic duet crescendoing, we climaxed together one last time before we became a quartet.

CHAPTER TWENTY-SEVEN

ALLEGRA' 21

I registered for a second psychology class, "Personality Disorders 101." D-day arrived. In April, I decided it was time to broach the dreaded subject.

Delicate buds dotted the dogwood trees. I loved the space between seasons. After four years in Indiana, I still marveled at nature's symphony of transitions, each encore more magnificent than the one before it. Inhaling the aromatic scent of spring, I picked up my pace, and hopefully courage, from the sturdy branches that surrounded me. The ball bobbing in my throat since this morning had now lodged itself in my larynx. Once back indoors, I lifted the receiver.

"Mom, I need to tell you something. I've decided to apply to grad school, and it would obviously be cheaper to live at home, so I need to find an option in Florida. What do you think?" I doodled in a spiral notebook.

"What? I thought you were interviewing for jobs at some newspaper or magazine—I can't recall which ones," Roberta replied, clearly thrown for a loop and once again disinterested in my destiny.

Why didn't she remember? I had been talking about finding a dream job in Chicago my entire life. I silently stewed. I didn't know to censor myself, trusting my mother like a loyal best friend, so I explained the epiphany, realizing I could still impact others as a therapist.

"And having a family one day, being present with my children, would be impossible if I pursued a career in journalism." My words jammed in my throat.

After a ten-week, life-altering internship in Milwaukee, I knew a career as a reporter, or a successful one anyway, would require me to be married to my job. I craved the stimulation of the newsroom and brilliant journalists from whom I'd learned. But I'd also noticed social dysfunction and fragmented relationships. Connection fueled and fostered my existence.

"I told you journalism is an unstable profession," Roberta said, smug satisfaction steaming like freshly frothed milk foam. "It is fine for a hobby, I suppose. Besides, a woman needs to be able to support herself—you shouldn't count on anyone."

I covered the phone with my cable-knit sweater. I hoped it muffled my groan.

"Not everyone is as lucky as I am. Your father is loyal, and we have a perfect marriage. At least if you get this additional degree, you'll always have a job; I'm glad you figured this out now."

That was my mother's feeble attempt at support. I was proud that for the first time, I'd worked through most of this without my parents' input. I hoped they'd agree to pay for the graduate program, especially since my mom was the headmaster of a private school. I yearned for the day I didn't need to depend on them financially or otherwise.

I swapped the sweater for shorts during a quick stop at my apartment, then headed for the gym. A five-mile run would release the rest of the pressure. I'd grab dinner with my room-mate, Lyn, afterward; she'd share her insights over a salad.

My father called me the next day with a similar sentiment. Not totally surprising, because my parents were in tune like the strings on a harp. For him, it was all about practicality, not about passion or purpose. My personality, drive, and perfectionistic tendencies mirrored his. Unlike me, he was a self-professed loner; it was no wonder he became a neurosurgeon. He sliced and diced the brain without dealing with the emotions emanating from it.

The oval standing mirror seemed stunted, shorter than I remem-bered. Surely I hadn't grown. Though the room was spacious, my clothes were crammed into crannies and corners of the stodgy drawers. I opened the closet, and my breath hitched when I saw that my mother's sequined evening gowns occupied half of it. What I'd hoped would be a reunion, moving back home, felt like an off-kilter step backward.

Thankful for the acceptance to graduate school, I focused on gratitude the first few months. I forced myself to jot three positive notes in my journal each night. But the brassy ambiance irked me. My parents blasted their gargantuan flat-screen televi-sion. Turkey bacon sizzled, and the smell seeped into my room. A stench of seared salmon permeated the house. The phone rang constantly; they didn't have many friends, so it was usually a fam-ily member or a life to be saved.

Without uttering a word, my father shrank my psyche like clothes tossed in the dryer on high heat. He wasn't a big conver-sationalist. His presence—like when I was a child and he hid on the floor next to my bed, thinking it would be funny to sit up as

I was lying down and holler, "Hello!"—petrified me. Instilling terror and reinforcing the creepiness of my bedroom, moments like these fed my fear of an unsafe world. And he knew it.

I bought funky bedding and no longer wore oversized shorts to bed as I had when I was a teen. The posters of Depeche Mode and Duran Duran were discarded during my first semester in college. At first glance, my old bedroom seemed welcoming, but stepping into the space and sleeping here again created a land-mine of memories. Flashbacks to nighttime awakenings, shivering in a cold sweat, still lived in this house and roused me. I'd squeeze my eyes shut, hoping to diminish the shadows that slid up and down the walls. My imagination, especially in the darkest hours, overtook logic. I dreamt vividly and often. If my subconscious was on a payroll, it certainly had accrued infinite overtime hours.

The twin bed barely contained my body. What ought to have been a nurturing nest felt more like a paranormal coffin. But I was alive and awake—shouldn't I be grateful?

CHAPTER
TWENTY-EIGHT

Dr. Bradley welcomed us with a wide smile. He didn't ask the usual "Are you ready?" question. After weeks of constant communication, the obstetrician had my number.

"Time to hop on the table and get a mani/pedi," I joked. Wisecracks commenced before the surgery. When my anxiety escalated, so did my humor. "I think we should place bets on how big she'll be." The men chuckled as I continued cracking myself up. It certainly distracted me from the nurse anesthetist who approached my backside with a needle. Seeing that looming instrument, longer than ten conductors' batons fused together, made my spine ache.

Last time, I was exhausted after fifteen hours of labor, three hours of pushing, and then the grand finale. As they started the IV and cold liquid slithered into my vein, I realized I was way too alert this time. Way too aware.

I begged Ben to keep rubbing my curved back. Then I felt a sting from an injection that was supposed to numb the area. They kept telling me to stay perfectly still. The waiting sucked, and it was interesting how at times what I conjured was worse than reality. Because I kept visualizing Dr. Bradley about to lance through layers of my skin and muscle, I asked Ben, who had the added role of a disc jockey, to put on the Indigo Girls, hoping their soulful songs would do the trick.

"Do you feel this?"

"Nope."

"How about here?"

"No."

One more area. "Ouch!"

"Guessing that's not numb?"

"Genius. Super perceptive, Dr. Bradley," I retorted, the corners of my mouth lifting. This man, in a matter of minutes, would have sharp objects in his hand. I'd better tone it down. He suggested we wait a bit longer. I agreed.

Ben balked. I said, "Really? You're not the one about to be carved like a turkey. You're the assistant chef who basted the human who's going to be removed from the oven."

This time felt easier, knowing what would happen.

And simultaneously scarier, knowing what would happen.

The waiting didn't help one bit. But the alternative would be worse. Even with all the pharmaceutical supports, I rewound the mental movie and pressed play. I vividly remembered how my body became a tug-o-war last time. Suddenly, I heard crisp paper being placed on my stomach. I pinched Ben's forearm, feeling dizzy and disoriented.

"What the...?" He looked at me and fetched the nurse.

"Ally, what's going on?" Her beady eyes peered at the monitor. "Oh, I see. Your blood pressure just plummeted."

Oh no. Was I going to vomit? Peace turned to panic. I'd willingly give birth without an epidural rather than bring up the contents of my gut. "Zofran. I need Zofran. Stat!" My pitch rose two octaves.

"Honey—"

Oh, this woman didn't just "honey" me! I had a name for a flipping reason. "It's already in the IV. You told us at registration—" the nurse droned.

"I made it through the miscarriage, two pregnancies, and four years at college. I do not throw up. Ever!" I squawked. Visions of fleeing the bed against medical advice interrupted my vertigo.

"We need to get going and move you." A wide mouth opened and closed like the automatic doors that parted as we entered the operating room. The lips seemed attached to a flushed face. Did this newbie have his driver's license? I was going to birth this baby any minute. Or retch as the youngster yanked and jostled the stretcher, nicking an already chipped corner in the hallway.

IV still threaded into the vein on my left hand? Check. Ben still conscious? Check. Pump of prophylactic Zofran? Check. A fluorescent UFO beamed at me. An orchestra of instruments reposed on the shiny tray. They, too, seemed to hum with restless anticipation, awaiting the conductor. Was I hooked up to an amplifier instead of intravenous fluids? Blaring beeps, a dangling saline bag, and twisted tubes ramped up my nerves. Even the sound of scrubs swishing as nurses ferreted around the freezing room assaulted me, like that time at the bagel joint after we'd first had Julian. Too bad the epidural didn't dull my senses.

A familiar, soothing voice came closer. "Okay, we are all set. I'm going to start, Ally. I'll talk you through every step. Not to worry," Dr. Bradley reassured me.

"I'm a Jewish mother about to have my insides rearranged like a jigsaw puzzle. Bring it on. I'm totally chill. No biggie. Whatevs." I wasn't sure if I said those words aloud or in my head.

Rustling. Crinkling. Clanging. My belly disappeared behind the paper curtain. I clamped my cheeks, tasting metal more than once. I wished I could see what Dr. Bradley was doing.

"Have you torn my gut open yet? What's going on now?"

Mumblings decelerated to murmurs. The clanks of stainless steel mixed with nothingness needled my nerves.

"Yes. Glad to hear you're comfortably numb," Dr. Bradley said.

How cool was my doc? Or were those the magical meds kicking in? The Zofran had thankfully eased the nausea.

"Did you just quote Pink Floyd? This whole morning has felt the way I'd imagine an acid trip would," I chattered. "Let's place bets. Everyone thought Julian was only going to be seven pounds. I know we scheduled this ten days early, but it seems like my hormones conspire and surge toward the end. I'm guessing she's at least eight pounds. Your turn!"

A narrow head covered in netting, like a gnat trapped in mesh, buzzed next to my own. "We cannot definitively predict the baby's size; you'll meet her soon," the woman said.

"C'mon. It's fun! And what layer are you on? Epidermis? Dermis?" Quiet. Nobody answered me. What was wrong?

"Eliza, give me the scalpel. Carol, I need you here. Now," Dr. Bradley ordered, his volume increasing.

I dug my nails into Ben's arm. Something felt wet under my fingertips. "Honey, calm down. *Dios mío*! I'm bleeding," Ben sputtered.

I inhaled through my nose, cold and crusty from the nasal cannula that gave me extra oxygen. I'd nearly ripped it out a few minutes ago, but the nurse had busted me.

"Did you seriously tell me to calm down? And that you're bleeding? Hello—my gut is gushing, in case you weren't aware!" I fought the urge to keep shrieking. Or tear at his other arm. Symmetry. He liked things even. Ben bit his lip. His brows knitted together as the creases in his forehead deepened.

Dr. Bradley's tranquil tone returned. "We had a bit of a hiccup. Everything will be okay. You know you have a tilted uterus, right?"

"No."

"Nobody told you last time?"

"Shall I say 'no' in nine other languages?"

"Ah. That's why it wasn't on your chart," Dr. Bradley said.

"Clearly. I wrote you a mini novel in the medical history." I coughed. Dr. Bradley found the mute for his mouth.

I wanted—no, *needed*—to know what was happening. My body, my baby, my right. "Am I defective? Can you get her out? Why aren't you talking? I thought this was a planned C-section. Easy breezy." My voice cracked. My throat narrowed. My eyelid twitched.

Parched and now panicked, I needed my father. He always knew what to do, especially in an emergency. He'd spent years rearranging brains. Trauma was his jam.

"Sweetie, we've got this," Ben whispered into my damp ear. "You need to trust Dr. Bradley."

No kidding. What other choice did I have? I might've rolled my eyes. Or stuck out my tongue. I was usually an optimist. Time to pivot and recalibrate. Enough with my whining. I was going to savor every second. This may be the last baby we had.

I closed my eyes, transporting myself to the tranquil lake behind the auditorium at Camp Intermezzo. Visualizing the tall Michigan pine trees, inhaling their spicy scent, I heard the waltz of water lapping onto the strip of sand. A trumpet playing Reveille, the six a.m. wake-up "Sound the Call." Then the sweetest sound riffed, joining my imaginary composition. My eyes fluttered, and the scene shifted.

"*Mazel tov*, Ally and Ben! Here's your beautiful baby girl." Dr. Bradley lifted our plump angel above the curtain.

Ben's misty eyes mirrored my own. My husband, too, seemed to have feared the worst.

Kissing my mangled hair, he said, "Honey, she's here. Oh, she's perfect." He was better at masking, or rather, compartmentalizing, his emotions. Another reason we complemented each other. Another reason we harmonized.

"When can I hold her?" I managed, my pitch rising. I gazed at Ben, sensing sweetness mixed with the salty absence of our grandparents and others who'd passed.

Running water trickled over my daughter. Experienced hands held our newborn, carefully cleansing the amniotic fluid. Then a buxom nurse cradled my swaddled baby. She gently placed her on my chest. My child's skin met mine like lips meeting and breathing life into a flute.

"I've waited a lifetime to meet you. Joy, I'm your mommy." I touched each delicate pink digit. I stared at my daughter in utter amazement. "You have blonde hair! Am I seeing things? And your eyebrows are golden! My angel baby. Ben, do we need a DNA test?" I cackled, grateful that my just-sewn abdomen was still numb.

Joy. So fitting. This name matched her cherubic face, round and rosy. I unfolded the nubby, blush-striped blanket. I turned her, certain I'd find translucent angel wings tucked into her tiny shoulder blades. My hands explored this precious gift. I'd hoped one day to be a mother to a girl, have a chance to love her the way I never was. Turning Joy toward me, I promised, feeling my heartbeat against her own, that I would love her wholly and without any conditions.

★ ★ ★

"Honey, can you be more careful? I think two of my stitches just separated," I said, cringing. Every movement caused a painful tug in my belly. Usually, red lights represented wasted time I'd rather spend connecting with friends and family. Today, I wished they were longer as I exhaled and used mantras off the yoga mat.

Ben maneuvered the wheel as gracefully as one could in a gigantic vehicle. My breath trapped in my trachea while we neared the rental townhouse. The final stop. The familiar wooden door beckoned. Now I just had to open it. And enter a new existence.

★ ★ ★

"Mommy, you're home!" Julian exclaimed, not budging an inch from his beloved new Thomas the Train Table. His eyes were fixed on Percy's ride toward Thomas.

My heart heaved. "Oh, Julian, I missed you," I uttered, edging toward my son.

Julian nestled his waves of light brown hair between my knees. He seemed taller. Or maybe I had shrunk? Thankful for muscle memory and those summers at the ballet barre, I cautiously squatted and held his oval face in my hands.

"Come meet your little sister! She couldn't wait to get home and introduce herself." Julian turned his head in the opposite direction. He shot me a look as if to say, "Nice try, Mommy. I'm not falling for that."

From the cluttered kitchen where my fingers gripped the countertop, I couldn't explain to myself why I felt like an outsider in my own home. Ben hugged Aunt Arden as I tried to absorb it all. He tossed the square cushions aside to make room for Joy's car seat. Dishes teetered on top of one another in the sink. Pillows piled on the floor. Ben took Julian into his arms and spun him in the air.

"Again, Daddy, again!" Julian squealed. My two boys, buoyant and bonding, depressed instead of uplifted me.

I couldn't pick up my baby boy like that. Tears pricked the corners of my eyes, threatening to dampen the delight. Julian needed normalcy, not a hormonal mommy with confusing emotions.

When his two little feet touched the ground, Julian hushed. He lifted his chin and his eyes met mine, a mix of intrigue and irritation. "Baby? Is that baby sister?" Julian pointed to a peacefully slumbering Joy.

"Yes, it sure is. She will be up soon. Remember, Mommy said Joy will need to eat and she'll cry sometimes, okay?"

"*J*. Both of our names start with the letter *J*," Julian said, sounding like Cookie Monster in an episode of *Sesame Street*.

I pulled the scrunchie out of my hair and tossed my head back. I hadn't realized how much tension I'd been holding in my body. My firstborn was still speaking to me. All would be well. "They sure do," I said. "What else starts with the letter *J*?"

I wished for more time as just the three of us, and if I kept the conversation going, hopefully Julian wouldn't plow over Joy with his latest train, a surprise gift from Aunt Arden. No wonder she was his favorite aunt.

The weekend whizzed by. Monday came too quickly. Yet another moment I would miss: Julian's first day of preschool. I hid in the bathroom when Ben left with our son; Dr. B said I couldn't drive yet. My toe caught on the corner of a chipped tile. The repetitive drip of the leaky faucet agitated me, and the beveled mirror looked cockeyed. I couldn't believe I had any tears left. Ben had consoled me earlier, promising to take photos, but it wasn't the same. I yearned to swing Julian between us, his hands locked in ours, and hear him shriek with glee. I longed to hold him for a few extra seconds before Ben brought him over the threshold of his first classroom.

I had promised to show up for my kids. To be present. To not ever miss a milestone. I mopped the rest of my tears off my face and hoped I'd never again miss a first.

CHAPTER
TWENTY-NINE

Breastfeeding dropout. I only made it six weeks this time. The stress of building our new house, being blindsided by babysitters, and the not-so-terrible-but-still-tiring twos weren't exactly a recipe for lactation. A different type of letdown.

This time, Ben pushed harder, insisting I stop for my own well-being. And for his sanity. This time, Roberta and Dr. Curt were superficially supportive, like a bra without underwire. This time, I listened. I didn't fail Joy. Or myself.

I'd journaled Julian's early babyhood, documenting every detail. Now, no matter how hard I tried, I couldn't manage the same dedication in capturing Joy's milestones. Sometimes scribbles sufficed: *Slept six hours straight! Now vocalizing more than cries (three weeks old)... Her cooing sounds like she's trying to harmonize with Julian... Smiling at six weeks. Aimed at her momma... Where's the time gone? I can't believe she's twelve weeks old. My velvet scarf, a remnant of a camp costume I somehow saved, is her fave fabric to explore in her hands.*

Joy sucked on her bottle like it was a blend of chocolate and crack. True to her name, she enchanted all adults, even in the middle of the night.

"Where were you?" Ben rolled over as our not-yet-replaced mattress groaned when I thumped onto the bed. Or maybe it was me.

113

"I changed Joy's diaper."

"It takes twenty-three minutes to wipe her?" Ben flopped onto his back.

"It's like something is missing. Where's the willy, I wonder. She's this compact, neat little package of cuteness. I feel like I need to really clean all her parts; I've read baby girls can be prone to rashes and..."

"Honey, think about that face, those dimples!" Ben kissed my cheek. His touch and the warmth of motherhood massaged my heart.

"Gosh, am I glad Joy doesn't puke. But she toots like a marching band! Do you notice every time she's flat she lets it rip? Then I start giggling, and she tries to imitate me. To be honest, it's hard to put her back in the crib. Can you believe she's already ten months old?"

CHAPTER THIRTY
ALLEGRA' 16

I couldn't believe they had pulled it off, and Ruby had kept a secret. Somehow, she'd snagged my Miami friends' phone numbers during her last visit. From miles away, my best friend coordinated the most awesome surprise.

When twenty teenage girls shouted, "Happy Birthday!" I hid my face in my hands, hoping they couldn't see my embarrassment. I hated being the center of attention. That's why I preferred choir at home and operettas at camp. I could camouflage in the group.

But that night, everyone stared only at me. From the sparkly purple balloons to the twinkling tiara they made me wear, I felt so loved. Yet so lost. A messy mix of connection and solitude. It sucked when reality seeped in. My parents had scheduled their quarterly vacation then, and my nanny, Irie, had stayed at home with me. Ruby couldn't come over afterward because of final exams. Apparently, this date worked for the people she'd invited. I tried to swallow the sadness, but I ate it instead. At least my mom and dad wouldn't be giving me "the look."

I savored two huge slices of chocolate chip cake, each morsel delish decadence. I devoured pizza instead of salad. I honestly couldn't remember when I'd last had a slice. Ruby and I twirled the melted mozzarella cheese as it draped from our lips. We tried to sing some camp songs while chewing, which wasn't a wise idea.

But the happiness I felt surrounded by such loving people dissolved like cotton candy. At home later, when I was all alone, my parents called and told me about the tour they'd taken of Paris. They'd be back in a few days. At least I had Keri, who slept in my bed that night, sensing I needed more than food to fill me up.

CHAPTER
THIRTY-ONE

My motherhood journals had gaps, but never more than a week or two at most. Our babies grew and stretched. Their limbs and ligaments, a mix of Ben's and my own, blossomed as they became their own beings. We clapped and cheered with other parents. Joy and Julian leaped from the stage and into my arms. My body became their playground. I melted into their soft necks, inhaling their innocence, and told them how proud Daddy and I were of their performances.

"Where are Beta and Caca, Mommy?"

I wrung my hands behind my back. I guess Ben noticed my glazed, looks-like-mommy-has-a-concussion expression. He played defense and answered with a swift interception.

"Oh, Caca had a patient. It was an emergency, so he couldn't come," Ben said.

He'd mastered some useful maneuvers. He had also memorized the playbook. Dr. Curt and Roberta had decided there was too much traffic, so they'd turned around, gone back home, and missed the kids' preschool show.

It wasn't the first time.

Loyalty trumped being truthful with my children, and I defended my folks. I'd been doing this my entire life, the script like an implanted teleprompter with an automatic sensor. Even when Ben challenged me, bothered by his in-laws' lack of respect,

I reverted to the role of dutiful daughter. Recently, my mother had me drive forty minutes to pick up a pair of shoes for her. The week before, my father stood me up for lunch, claiming he had an urgent case at the hospital.

Julian and Joy, as kids often do, let it go. I usually did as well. This had only happened a few times. After all, my parents worked long hours. They always told me how exhausted they were at the end of the day.

Yet tonight, my kids' crestfallen eyes peered into mine like beaten-down rescue puppies. Those stares stung, the somber familiarity of my own childhood and my parents not showing up for swim meets or school shows. The kids rarely slept at their grandparents' house—they never offered. Besides, Roberta and Dr. Curt carried on about how wonderful it was that they'd had a live-in nanny when I was a kid. As if it were a favor to spend time with their grandkids.

My father's condescending comments about the women who practically raised me and Jack still echoed in my mind. He couldn't stand the sight of anyone fat. Not at home. Not at the office. Not anywhere. Dr. Curt had labeled one nanny "Rice Patty Fatty" and fired her because of her size. Several dedicated nurses at his office were also dismissed because of their less-than-desirable appearances. "Pleasantly plump" and "morbidly obese" were frequently used phrases I'd heard again and again at five years old. And now.

I winced, recalling my first step onto the public square symbol of humiliation, otherwise known as the Weight Watcher's scale. One time, an older woman with frosted hair glanced down at me. Compassionate eyes let me know I was more than my physicality. Five-by-seven index cards waited in the box, blank until the next written measurement. No matter what the number, I never measured up to my father's expectations. Listening to all the adults collectively commiserate, I learned to avoid ingesting sodium the night before weigh-ins. I also wore the exact same outfit each week. Every ounce counted. Ten years old was a bit young to be dieting. Especially without anyone my age to normalize that experience.

Every Saturday morning, we drove to Weight Watchers. Daddy-daughter special time, when my father would share stories about growing up in the snow. I'd wring my hands like a soaked terry-cloth towel, nervous yet excited for our morning of just us. I awaited the loss, hopeful that a descending number would gain my father's approval. My self-worth was an external umbilical cord connected to my father and linked to the scale. Would it ever be severed?

CHAPTER THIRTY-TWO

"**D**o you know there are eight points in a meatball?" Julian asked me after a rare sleepover at Beta and Caca's house.

I choked on my saliva.

"What's the matter, Mommy? Why do you look upset?" My son ran into my arms. Sensitive and observant, Julian tugged on my hands with his strong seven-year-old grip. My folks chatted with family in another room, fortunately out of earshot since my brother-in-law's home was spacious. The smell of rice, beans, and plantains, a family recipe passed down from Ben's Jewish Cuban grandparents, wafted from the kitchen.

"Nothing, sweetheart. I just remembered that I forgot the Father's Day cards you and Joy made for Caca," I fibbed, which was nearly impossible for me. I had forever been a truth sharer and seeker with a refined filter, but the older the kids got, the harder it became to use it. I gnawed on my lower lip and tried to relax my shoulders. Claiming I needed the bathroom, I closed the door behind me. I required a solid barrier between me and my son. If only I could shove down and seal shut all that surfaced.

It wasn't the first time my past had fused with the present.

But this? What the actual hell? I pressed my hands into the corner of the polished marble.

Reddened cheeks and blazing eyes stared back at me in the pewter powder room mirror. After splashing freezing water on my face, I stood straighter and stormed toward my parents.

"I need to speak with you right now, please." I shot the staccato words through my clenched jaw. It was all I could do not to implode in front of the rest of my husband's family, whom I adored.

I got the hand, the five-fingered flick off. Of course, Roberta was gushing to Aunt Arden about her colleagues and how they loved her latest presentation. My mother was clueless, not noticing that Aunt Arden repeatedly checked her watch, averted her blue eyes, and continued to listen—or pretended to, anyway.

I searched for my father, knowing he'd be alone. He preferred fixing machines to human interaction, the ultimate prescription for a control freak. I surveyed the usual areas. No Dr. Curt sightings. Living room corner: empty. Guest bedroom: barren. I finally found him brooding on the overstuffed chair in the office.

"Hi, D-d-d-dad. I need to speak with you and Mom please." I peeled off the rest of the nail I'd bitten earlier.

"Sure. About what topic would you like to speak? I know you can blab for hours." He smirked at me and raised an eyebrow. My father slid his sleek phone into his pocket. His singular focus and ability to be present was one of the attributes I admired.

"Thanks for turning everything off. I'd rather not repeat what I need to say," I began, faltering a bit. The earlier surge of courage evaporated. I tried to muster the badass, brave version of me from the powder room pep talk. "I tried speaking to Mom, but she was immersed in a conversation." More like a self-absorbed monologue.

"You know your mother. She doesn't stop talking. That's why we'll always have separate office spaces at home, Allegra. It saves our marriage—I highly suggest it." Dr. Curt chuckled as he stood up and left the room to get her. What he said wasn't untrue—well, about my mother, anyway. I made a conscious effort to be an active listener. Not only with Ben but with my children and friends as well. They deserved to be heard.

When my parents returned, looking annoyed and maybe slightly amused, I told them to please sit down.

"I have something to say and would appreciate it if you'd let me finish before talking. Mom, I realize this is mildly painful for you. But I need you to not only hear me but listen." I licked my lips and inhaled slowly.

Roberta's spine straightened. Dr. Curt donned the demeanor reserved for only me and the children he healed. His creased forehead relaxed, and he crossed his legs nonchalantly. His gray eyes scrutinized me. Mom's gaze shifted to his as she plotted her next move. I hadn't even begun, and my mother already seemed exasperated. Talk about a resting bitch face.

"Julian asked me how many points are in a meatball. Actually, he told me. I know that he got that information from one of you. Information that my son does not need to hear or know at his age." My words simmered as I stared at my parents.

"Allegra, lower your voice right now! What will everyone think if they hear you speaking to us this way," my mother hissed between her just-whitened teeth.

"Mother, I am not talking loudly. And please, I asked you to wait until I was finished," I repeated.

"Roberta, give her a minute," Dr. Curt said sternly.

"Are you serious? As if taking me to Weight Watchers didn't nearly destroy me, you are now proselytizing to my children? I am appalled. This is not okay. Do you understand?" I quivered, reliving the aftershocks of my own childhood. I hadn't realized, until this moment, the depth of the dysfunction and deep hurt. *This*. This right here I could not, *would* not ignore.

"I can't believe..." Roberta couldn't keep quiet. A blotch of burgundy lipstick marred her front teeth. "You're overreacting. Give us a break. Do you want to write us a script for when we spend time with our own grandchildren? Daddy is trying to lose weight. Isn't that wonderful? Why aren't you happy for him, finally taking care of himself? You know how much he goes up and down like a yo-yo." She hinged forward and reached into her suede Chanel bag.

Dr. Curt leaned back and observed quietly. He'd snagged a seat slightly higher than ours.

Then he put an arm around me and squeezed my shoulder.

He got it. He got me.

"Darling, I wasn't trying to teach Julian or Joy. You know how I get obsessive and tend to talk aloud. It helps keep me accountable." His words coasted from his mouth as if he were reassuring a hysterical, post-operative patient.

For the first time in my adult life, I didn't let it go. My heart's tempo tripled. I hoped they couldn't see it thumping beneath my sundress. Spasms in my lower belly made it tough to take a deep breath.

"Dad. Mom. I get it. And I'm proud of you for focusing on your health." I held up my hand as Roberta's stained lips parted, preparing for the next round. "Hang on. Let me finish, please."

I gripped the edge of the chair and grounded myself in the distressed wood. "Do whatever you want, D-d-d-dad. I'd never tell you what to do—you know that. But I am imploring you to be aware of what you say to my children. We've discussed this before." I fell backward, shocked at my strength.

My mother sighed loudly. "Can we do anything right, Allegra?" She fiddled with the braided strap on her handbag.

"Enough, Roberta. These are Allegra's kids. We may not agree with how she's raising them or all her ridiculous rules. But they are hers," Dr. Curt said, rescuing me. I shot him a relieved look.

As if on cue, Joy darted into the room, her dimples deepening. "Mommy! Where have you been? Hide-and-go-seek with Beta and Caca?" she squealed, and we all laughed. True to her name, my golden-blonde five-year-old radiated light. Somehow this child beamed a rainbow, regardless of the darkest room. Or the people in it.

When we got back home, Ben headed straight for his office. A few minutes later, he asked me to join him. I wasn't prepared for what would come next.

The days Ben balked at my parents' actions were sparse as we were generally harmonious, except when my father would let himself into our house unannounced because he had the key to the front door. But this time, I guess he went too far, at least for Ben. Even though Dad *had* asked to use our computer when his broke. My typically tolerant husband noticed that Dr. Curt had rearranged the icons on his desktop. Ben thought the computer had developed a sudden glitch or virus. He nearly lost it after discovering Dr. Curt had created his own login credentials. All without our consent.

Rapid pacing and the explosive volume of Ben's voice rattled me. I pulled at my split ends as he intensified. "What the hell, Ally? Who does your father think he is?" Ben boomed, and I swear the windows vibrated. My husband rarely cursed. Nor did he raise his voice. This jarred me, and I shuddered. Ben's tone reminded me of a frighteningly familiar rage. Shaking it off, I defended my he-can-do-no-wrong father.

"Honey, I'm sure he just wanted to help. He's exceptional at programming and organizing computers, you know. I think what he did was thoughtful." I scratched my upper arm. Ben continued to bellow about my father having no boundaries. Then he trudged to our bathroom and into a steamy shower.

I shoved away an ominous feeling and forced my attention back to my own daughter. A true joy.

CHAPTER THIRTY-THREE

ALLEGRA' 15

Daddy said unplugged fun would create avid readers. At least it worked for one kid. Me. I loved getting lost in stories—the characters became my friends. Plus, my brother and I were each other's entertainment.

Until they shipped Jack away.

Jack dodged rules. I followed them. Maybe that's why my bare bottom was spared the belt. Disappointment formed Daddy's face most of the time. Not when he looked at me. I didn't think my little brother noticed the sneers when we were younger. But he swore, screamed, and slammed doors in our parents' faces when we became teens. Jack blasted forbidden rap music. Our shared bedroom wall shook like a sonic boom. My books transported me to a more tranquil space, but one night, I couldn't tune out the raging.

"You are a moron. Turn off this crap and study. How many times do I have to tell you this?" Daddy's voice bellowed over the booming beats of the Beastie Boys.

I shot upright, shaking and sweaty with fear. Then I noticed a powdery dust floating to my pale purple carpet. Maybe remnants of plaster.

"Fuck you. You don't get me. You never have. You never will. I know I'm not the son you'd hoped for. And I'm done pretending for you and Mom."

As I inched closer to the baseboard, I noticed a dent above it. Had Jack punched the wall?

I locked my door, straightened my legs in front of me, and sat at a ninety-degree angle with my back against the wall. The pulsing in my head became a dull drumming sensation. My feet prickled. Then went totally numb. But I didn't dare move.

Jack's door banged. Even though socks covered his feet, I knew those steps, that sound, of Daddy stomping away. Keri leaned into me, pressing her spongy paws into my shaky thighs. We held each other, not making a peep. When it quieted, I cautiously creaked open my door, just a crack, and collided with my brother—he was leaving the bathroom we shared.

"Dad is a royal pain in the ass. I've had it, Ally. Don't tell them, but I'm heading out tonight. Mickey will wait up for me."

I hated secrets. I hated seeing my little brother boiling. I also hated breaking the rules. "You and Daddy scared me tonight. Did he hit you again?" I threw my arms around his neck, burying my head into it. Keri leaned into us, her furry body resting on our calves. Jack shrugged and headed to his closet. I was the only one who knew that he and Mickey were more than friends.

The next morning, my parents told me the news. "We are sending Jack away to school for you. His behavior is disrupting your happiness. And this place will fix him. He likes boys, you know. He thinks we don't know about his defect."

I changed my pillowcases night after night. Shoved them under my lumpy mattress and refolded them when the splotches dried. I felt guilty for not speaking up for Jack. But Daddy and Mom knew best.

CHAPTER THIRTY-FOUR

"**W**hat is that on your neck? I've never seen it before." My mother pushed her Gucci glasses higher on the bridge of her nose.

"I have no idea what you're talking about." I shrugged my shoulders and continued scrubbing oatmeal from the glass bowl.

"Turn around, dear." She poked her pointy fingernail into the front of my neck. "There. It's a lump or something I've never seen. Could just be a ball of fat." My mother took my hand and moved it upward. I coughed and dropped the soapy sponge.

I dismissed the tiny growth on my neck, despite my mother nagging me to get it examined. If a master's degree was offered in worrying, she'd have earned it magna cum laude. I ignored not only my meddling mother but also my own well-being.

Besides, I was busy with Joy, Julian, my clients, and new house calamities. It was like a bait and switch. Apparently "newer" didn't mean "better." We sold the first home because it required a ridiculous number of renovations, like when I'd spotted an area of wallpaper, flopped over like a Doberman's ear, in the upper corner of Julian's nursery. I pulled down a tiny piece of the '80s-inspired geometric covering.

Shocked at the black splotches behind it, I'd ripped the rest of it off. Julian's scaly, flushed cheeks had seemed like an undetermined allergy; maybe the moldy discovery was the culprit? I hadn't made the connection until I'd seen what the wallpaper masked. When the pediatrician confirmed my hunch, we hired contractors, put the house on the market, and moved to a new neighborhood in a matter of weeks.

But even a small pressure gate in our new home had punctured the wall. I joked that the Big Bad Wolf better not visit. This allegedly "well-built" house would blow down with one puff or huff. First the moldy bedroom. Now an infrastructure built of tissue paper. What would be next? I wondered about hurricane season.

Ben, irritated with the crappy construction, immediately patched the holes. I searched for aesthetically pleasing but practical options, concerned about our kids' safety and the puppy's constant curiosity. A steep flight of stairs with little beings? A catastrophe waiting in the wings. However, some solutions created other problems. Diamond-patterned carpet on the steps led to Joy and Julian's bedrooms. The screeching mechanism on the gate woke not only the kids but the puppy as well. It was maddening.

Since my father excelled at rearranging brains, certainly he'd be able to figure out a better option. Dr. Curt preferred texts, which I treasured like burrowing in my sleeping bag at camp on a cool summer night. Though he was on staff at nine hospitals, he somehow made time for me.

He responded right away:

I told you building a two-story house was foolish. But here you are. I will think of a brilliant idea.

And he did.

With some house issues resolved, I focused inward. Though I didn't admit it aloud, necklaces did seem slightly tighter. After an evening bath, I rubbed lavender-scented lotion down my sun-speckled shoulders and arms.

When I reached my neck, the Lumpster (my nickname for the nugget) blocked and halted my hands. Before, I could barely find it. Now, it felt like a speed bump.

Begrudgingly, I introduced the Lumpster to Ben. "Whatcha think about us having a threesome?" I said, rolling over to tickle my confused husband. Not only was he conservative, both in and out of the bedroom, but he despised being tickled. Of course, I knew just where to touch him. Ben scrambled to the edge of the bed and then rolled right off it. The cornflower blue carpet muted his thud.

"Honey, you know I don't like that," he said, smiling despite himself. "What was that about a threesome? Have you officially lost your mind?" Ben stretched on his side, cocking his head.

I fiddled with my platinum wedding band. Then I brought his hand to the middle of my throat, which suddenly felt like a boa constrictor mid-meal.

"Eww! What is that?" Ben recoiled and ran his fingers through rumpled hair. He didn't share my interest in others' insides or psyches, and his face blanched as white as a waiting room wall.

"Meet the Lumpster! She's been living with me for a few months or so. And it appears she's grown a bit." I tried to assuage his concern.

"Not funny, honey," Ben said, clipping each word.

"Love that rhyme! Good one, babe." I put my palm on his chest.

"Seriously, *mi amor*. Why didn't you show me this sooner?" Ben crept closer but kept a deliberate distance, avoiding contact with the Lumpster. "And you named this thing? You're too much."

"You've been busy, babe. Me too. I figured it was a pimple or bug bite. Besides, I told my folks. My father consulted with someone he knows well in Miami; he's the best in the head and neck oncology depart—"

"Doesn't 'oncology' mean cancer?"

I stroked Ben's salt and pepper stubble. "Yes. Doesn't mean I have the big C, though I'm suspecting it. How does something that I wasn't born with grow on its own?"

The Lumpster pulsed, and I touched it lightly with my index finger.

"I already had an ultrasound, and it is not clear. My dad found the best endocrinologist, and he's seeing me tomorrow for a fine needle aspiration biopsy. What would I do without my father?" My stream of words turned into rapids. I lifted the now-cold cup of chamomile tea from the nightstand to my lips.

"I wish you'd told me all of this sooner, Ally. Though I know I tend to get nervous about medical stuff," Ben admitted. He clamped his mouth closed as if he had more to say but wasn't ready.

"I've got this, babe. Let's wait until I get the results. Trust me. If my neck needs to be ripped open and excavated, you'll be the first to know."

I quieted, concerned that Joy and Julian might hear us. "Not a word to our family or the kids. I don't want to worry anyone."

★ ★ ★

"Allegra, do not move."

I uncrossed my ankles and closed my eyes, visualizing the serene lake behind the stage at camp.

"You could bleed to death." Dr. Curt's bass rose to a baritone. I shivered, struggling to stay still in this subzero freezer disguised as a medical office. My entire body felt like it was shrink-wrapped. As the needle approached, I envisioned a hidden seatbelt to hold me down. My father frightened me more than the needle nearing its target.

"It's in. Please don't swallow. You may feel a pushing sensation. Signal to me with your finger if you feel pain, okay?" a gentler tenor voice said soothingly. I suddenly got the phrase "play dead like a possum."

Normally, I would inhale and exhale deeply to calm my central nervous system. When a needle that could double for a church steeple stabbed into the Lumpster, not once but six times, breathing seemed secondary to survival.

"I'm done now," the endocrinologist said. I didn't know his name, but I trusted my father.

I sat up slowly. Woozy and disoriented, I tottered to the elevator. My father's arm around my hunched shoulders supported me. "So, what are the next steps?" I asked. We waited in the valet line. Miami humidity surrounded us in its sauna, and I regretted wearing a long-sleeve shirt. Two pigeons cooed on the edge of a flat roof.

"Hopefully, it's a benign growth. But it is unlikely. Oh, did you read the article I sent you?" Dr. Curt reiterated.

"D-d-d-dad. Do you think it is helpful to, yet again, tell me about the rising cases of cancer?" I wiped my clammy hands on my linen pants.

"Oh, Allegra, get over it. That's who I am. I'll be here for you, as always. And I work in trauma, you know," Dr. Curt chided, pinching my cheek.

"I know. You're right." I touched my tender neck. The Lumpster was inflamed, sore, and rather pissed off. Not unlike me, actually.

We luckily got all green lights and little traffic. I usually craved more time with my father, connecting without Mom's interference. However, today I felt at ease, almost relieved, when he brought me home.

★ ★ ★

Dr. Curt called a few days later. He rarely rang unless it was important. "Great news! I was right! It is—" he boomed from the phone.

"D-d-d-dad! Let me take you off speaker. Joy is a few feet away from me."

In the brief time it took me to get the phone, I saw my furrowed brows in the glass reflection. *Note to self: need to pluck.* This was about to turn into a Ficus tree hedge on my forehead.

Wait. Why was my father calling me and not the endocrinologist? I sat by the pool, dipping my feet and ankles into the tepid water. Whoever invented portable phones was a genius. Especially for parents who've run out of hiding spaces to take private calls.

"Now I can speak. Why are you giving me the results rather than Dr. What's-His-Name?" I realized that I hadn't noted the name on the door or grabbed a business card.

"I saw him at the hospital in the doctor's lounge. He informed me your mass is benign. Figured I'd tell you. He's so busy, as I am. Speaking of which, I only have a few minutes between patients." Dr. Curt's words whirred out of his mouth.

"Whoa. Hang on. Back up a minute. Did you say "b-b-b-enign?" I stammered the word on a long exhale.

"Yes. However, he advised, and I concur, that you ought to see a surgeon. The size of the mass—" that word sounded so menacing "—will impact your breathing and swallowing."

I hiked up my leggings, sinking my calves into the water too. "Makes sense. And honestly, D-d-d-dad? I'm not convinced. Why would something appear and grow that I wasn't born with? Seems sketchy to me. I'm on it." My laptop already open on the deck, I started surfing the web for physician reviews.

I didn't like the vibe of the first two surgeons who I consulted. Sure, they were adequate.

But even the minuscule risk that my larynx could be lanced caused me to be even more persnickety. I'd struggled with my speech as a kid and couldn't think of anything worse than being unable to use my voice. How would I help heal others?

★ ★ ★

I answered on the first ring. "Hey. What's up?"

"Allegra, 'hey' is for horses. How about, 'Hello, favorite father'?" Dr. Curt chortled. "Or 'your royal highness'?"

"Funny. What's up? And please, no sky puns! To what do I owe the honor of two calls in a month?" I bit the inside of my cheek.

"I asked around about the best otolaryngology surgeon for my little girl. I recalled an extraordinary physician, Dr. Bean. You can eat off the floor of his operating room. I'm not suggesting you do so—just reassuring you it is immaculate. He is exceptional," my father proclaimed, as if verbally embossing an envelope with his approval. "I will drive you there. You have a terrible sense of direction, just like your mother." My father cleared his throat and continued. "And this warrants taking a few hours off. It's also convenient that Dr. Bean is located sixteen minutes from my office."

Couldn't he have simply offered to take me without including the criticism? I'd been demeaned and demoted. Maybe I'd imagined it. He told me all the time I was hypersensitive; he was probably right.

"I've got this, Dad. You've already had to cancel an afternoon. Thanks for your guidance and support. I don't know what I'd do without you." I stroked his ever-awaiting ego.

CHAPTER THIRTY-FIVE

wo days later, I was lost. The directions said westbound, right? A saffron Porsche 911 zoomed past me, nearly sideswiping my mom-mobile. Reaching for the phone, I started to dial Dad's number. In a rare moment of confidence, I slammed it shut. I turned off the classical music station, opened the window, and rested my elbow on the side door.

I talked to myself aloud, recalibrating my inner compass to navigate the ride. Who cared that anyone cruising by would think I'd had a psychotic break? No passengers. It was only me. Right when I found the parking garage, the sky unleashed, and raindrops splattered onto the hazy windshield.

"Hi. I'm Ally. I'm grateful you squeezed me into your schedule." I shook Dr. Bean's slender hand.

"Oh, of course! You're Dr. Curt's daughter. It is a pleasure to meet you, Ally. Your father shared the case history with me. We can go right to the exam table. Please lie down." Dr. Bean motioned to the flat bed behind him.

Dad had perfectly described the pristine office and the doctor's demeanor. I felt immediately at ease. "Are you friends with my father?" I pushed into the hard exam table, one arm on each side of me. No answer. Just his hands examining my tense neck.

"Mmm. Did you ask me a question?" Dr. Bean said. "Sorry, I was focused on this rather large mass. All the biopsies came back negative. I see you had three ultrasounds as well. Smart. Unfortunately, these FNAs are not as accurate as a breast biopsy, for instance."

"Honestly, Dr. Bean, I want it *out*. I know it'll eventually be an issue, especially where it is, right?" I counted the sunspots on his high forehead.

"True, Ally. But we only need to take out half of your thyroid. If it grows, we can take out the rest." Dr. Bean removed his hands from my neck and put them in his pockets.

"Something just doesn't feel right in my gut—well, my neck, actually," I twittered. No response. Tough crowd. Oh well. "I want it all out. Why risk having to be sliced and diced twice? Like that spontaneous poem? It's an original!" My pulse slowed with a sense of certainty. I quieted while my mind and spirit had an impromptu board meeting. The vote? Unanimous.

At the front desk, the distracted lady behind the counter wouldn't look up from her magazine. "I need to schedule my surgery," I said. "You know, like the reverse of the *Wizard of Oz*? I'm getting gutted rather than gaining organs."

The young woman, her shiny face like a glazed donut, remained motionless.

"Please tell me you know the Tin Man and Scarecrow? I sure hope Dr. Bean's a real wizard!"

I gave up, signed the credit card receipt, and clicked the ballpoint pen. There would be no gift at the end. Just a loss. Was I nuts to voluntarily remove this itty bitty but essential body part?

★ ★ ★

A few days before the surgery, I wobbled, feeling off balance, and tried to get my bearings. After drizzling more maple syrup on the oatmeal, I left the kids for a moment.

"D-d-d-Dad, I don't know if I can do this," I confessed from the tool closet in the garage, the receiver tight against my ear like a plunger. This was my latest hideaway. Joy and Julian hadn't discovered it. Yet.

"You are making the right decision. Why put yourself through surgery twice?" he reassured me. "Dr. Bean can run a cursory pathology report. If it's malignant, he will likely remove nodes to biopsy as well. You'll be fine; I'll be supervising every step of the process."

A whoosh of pressure released from my lungs like a nail puncturing a tire. I felt lightheaded. "Thank you. You're always there for me," I said. Then my synapses awakened. "Oh! I asked if you were friends, D-d-d-dad. Come to think of it, Dr. Bean didn't answer. But since you trust him, I feel confident with this decision."

After much deliberation, Ben and I decided not to tell the kids the details of the upcoming surgery. Jack kindly offered to sleep over. I reminded him no parties; though Joy and Julian adored their uncle and his partner, I was forever the big sister.

"Ally, come on! I'm not a child, for fuck's sake," he retorted.

"Oh, add that to the list. No F-bombs or any other inappropriate language. Remember your niece and nephew are both under the age of ten," I admonished on the other end of the line.

We were a study in contrasts. I, the elder, consumed with learning and excelling in general, was studious and serious. Roberta and Dr. Curt thought sending Jack away and attempting to neuter his sexual preference would castrate his desires. For Jack, we both learned later, this was a blessing in disguise. I existed under their toxic control into my early twenties. Jack left for high school and never lived with them again. Their parenting, if you could call it that, turned out to be his ticket to freedom.

Though Jack detested our folks, he also had distance from them. He partied. Had his first honest sexual experiences. He could live his truth. Jack was spared. I didn't realize until recent years that my brother's presence diluted the impact our parents had on my childhood.

I missed Jack's antics and secretly wished I had the courage to speak up to my parents like he did. But I'd never leave holes in walls or scream obscenities. He didn't come out until high school. My heart hurt thinking about how painful it must've been before they shipped him away. Double doses and second servings of their parental charades. Liquid criticism, snarky syrup, judgment juice. I swallowed it. Again and again.

My breakfast swam upward as I hung up the phone. I swallowed it, willing it back down. I also swallowed the somber realization that I'd not only lose my thyroid but maybe the ability to procreate and expand our family as well.

CHAPTER THIRTY-SIX

ALLEGRA' 9

I woke up tethered and trapped in the hospital bed. Weird to think I'd been born with tonsils and then they were gone. I wondered why humans were made this way, coming to the planet with unnecessary parts.

The man who contributed to my existence hovered like a helicopter during wartime.

Somebody had to double-check the monitors. Supervise the IV insertion. Daddy showed up in his starched white lab coat. Mother stayed in the waiting room. It didn't matter, because my superhero with the crisp cape comforted me.

I was convinced I'd die if Daddy wasn't there to intervene. He told me emergencies happened all the time, even with the most skilled physicians. Messages like, "That doctor is an idiot," or "What a lousy medical school—you can't trust him," wired the circuits of my psyche. He moved toward the door and grabbed the knob.

"Where are you going?" I fidgeted with the fuzzy blanket that covered my outstretched legs. Black music notes smushed between the creases. Daddy didn't answer. I draped my blanket around my shaking shoulders. It must have been two a.m. I knew better than to ask again. I waited and watched him slide a bifold wallet into his back pocket.

"I'm headed to the adjacent operating room. Once again, I'm fixing this idiotic surgeon's work. A patient came via ambulance with his head bleeding." Daddy looked down at me and scratched his chin. His stethoscope wrapped around his neck like a python.

Without his protective presence, systems (and humans) could crash. But now he left my side to rescue another patient, who probably needed him more than I did. The back of my throat throbbed, and my heart pounded with it. I should be appreciative that Daddy hired a private nurse for me. It was only my tonsils, after all. So why was I worried?

CHAPTER THIRTY-SEVEN

"**W**hat time is it? I'm hungry." I scanned the curtain-enclosed cave for a familiar face.

The top of my hand throbbed from the IV needle. I yearned to itch the area under the sticky bandage. Or rip the entire thing off. I tried shimmying the bottom half of my body upward. My head flopped backward. Ouch.

"Babe, what're you doing? You need to take it easy," Ben murmured.

Was the surgery over? Someone's heavy hand rested on the crown of my head.

"You did great. You're in recovery now. You'll be able to go home in a few hours," Dr. Curt interjected. I thought Ben said something to my father.

Ben's voice again. I tried to turn toward my hubby but could not. "Did anyone hear me? I am starving. Feel dizzy. I'm either hypoglycemic or internally bleeding." I didn't recognize the squeaky sounds leaving my own mouth.

My husband's strong fingers spread over my hand. "Honey, I love you. Most people are nauseous after surgery. You? Girl after my own heart. Well, you already have it." Ben choked on the last word as a lone teardrop landed on the gauze bandage.

"Oh, sweetie! It's cancer, right? I knew it. So glad it's out!" I ran my fingers down his forearm.

"How did you know?" He shook his head and winced.

"Something stirred in me. Nagged. Like a woodpecker who got louder and wouldn't quit," I answered. Probably not the right moment to stand on my spiritual soapbox. Ben sniffed. I hadn't seen him so pale and pasty in years.

"The doctor said everything looked clear. But there was cancer on both sides. *Mi amor, gracias Dio*, thank God, you listened to your intuition about taking the whole thyroid out. What if…"

I waved my free arm at him to come closer. "Everything happens for a reason, my love. I'm sure I'll understand why later." I tried again to turn my head toward him but realized I'd bust open the stitches. "So happy I don't have to go under the knife again. And even more so that I can speak. I can handle having my thyroid in a bottle the rest of my life. But if I couldn't talk, well, that would be a true tragedy!"

★ ★ ★

A melodic pitter-patter of steps came from the other side of the door. Then I heard, "Uncle Jack, Mommy's home!"

Ben stood in front of me as we had planned. They were used to Daddy traveling, but I was their anchor. His body buffered the ecstatic duo. Our kids, our everything.

"We missed you both!" Ben ruffled Julian's hair. Jack held Joy's hand.

I quickly rewrapped the cream cashmere scarf. If the kids saw the stitches, they would be terrified. I looked like a character from the Addams Family.

"Mommy, why are you wearing that long thing around your neck?" Joy's green eyes, curious and discerning, roamed from my head to my chest.

"Remember I told you about the doctors? Well, that little ball you noticed needed to be removed. So now the area needs to heal, honey. It'll take some time." I nuzzled my nose into the nape of Joy's unblemished neck.

The first week didn't hurt. I suppose I'd been conditioned to rise to the occasion. I operated on overdrive, business as usual. By week two, I noticed I couldn't maintain my usual energy levels without an afternoon shot of espresso. Before, I had never consumed caffeine after eleven a.m. My skin and entire being was taut and yearning to be stretched. I missed my yoga practice. I tried to bargain with Dr. Bean during a quick call, but he wouldn't budge. He stated it could cause a surge of blood flow and complicate my healing. I tried to explain that yoga would accelerate my recovery.

But in week three, my energy tanked. Caffeine didn't do a damn thing. Nor did the unpredictable naps.

"Mommy. Wake up. I need help with my project," Joy said, her soprano voice jingling at me from nearby. This wasn't the first time since the surgery that I'd nodded off midday. More scars surfaced beneath the skin. And not just from the thyroidectomy.

Dreading the call, I finally found the strength and succumbed to Ben's urging. "Hey, Mom. I'm exhausted." I sipped the last drop of my coffee.

"Tell me about it; I got home a few minutes ago. Barely any of my friends still work, and certainly not full-time." Roberta clicked her tongue.

"I crash by two p.m. It's been harder than I want to admit. I don't mean to complain," I said, hoping she'd get the hint. I tugged at a loose lock of hair, wrapping it around my finger until it spiraled.

"Well, you did have major surgery. You will be fine. At least you don't need chemo. And you had the good kind of cancer," Roberta informed me.

"True. I am grateful." I covered my open mouth to stifle a yawn mixed with dismay. "Anyway, say hi to Dad. I'll talk to you tomorrow." I'd wanted to ask her for help. I needed someone to watch the kids. But I couldn't do it. Besides, she must be tired from working all day.

I retreated to the bedroom—another silver lining was that it was on the first floor. I still hadn't regained my pre-surgery stamina and couldn't imagine trudging upstairs. I sat down in the closet. Pretending to organize my shoes, I cushioned my face into cozy t-shirts on the walnut shelf and prayed nobody needed me. Or heard me. Or noticed my absence.

I burrowed my nose into my old camp sweatshirt, the faded red one. I could barely turn my neck, so this temporarily soothed me. I stayed right there, smoothing my coarse, brittle hair. A few pieces broke off, sticking to my fingertips like the end of a broom. The thyroid meds weren't tweaked. I'd expressed my concerns to Dr. Bean and tried reaching his nurse. I'd even called my primary care doc. Nobody listened because my lab results looked close to normal. Dry, bloated, and puffy skin. Weren't those all symptoms of hypothyroidism?

And the blues too. That must be why I couldn't suck it up as usual. Everything hurt. And not just the incision.

CHAPTER THIRTY-EIGHT

A dreamy Mother's Day gift this year: three days alone. In an isolated suite. Chugging a cocktail called "radioactive iodine." And educating nutritionists in the middle of the night about what I could and couldn't eat. Didn't they study this stuff in school?

Determined to make the best of it, I decorated the bland walls with photos of Joy, Julian, and Ben. The kids had surprised me with sweet notes and cheery drawings of rainbows and ladybugs. It had been five months since I'd bid farewell to my thyroid. I missed it. Badly. Who knew removing such a tiny organ, no longer first chair in my body's orchestra, would cause such disharmony? To prep for my Mother's Day incarceration, I had to stop taking Synthroid, the thyroid hormone replacement pill. Basically, my inner operating system shut down completely. I checked in feeling invincible like Wonder Woman and wishing I still had my Underoos from the '80s.

Only the nurse's eyes were uncovered. I wondered if this was a real hazmat suit. A rectangular metal box glared at me, its jaws opening wide.

She unlocked the two-part mechanism. "Here you go. Swallow these three pills." Such an assertive voice trumpeting from a petite person. Liquid-filled bullets glinted, daring me to ingest them.

"Um, those? They look like they'll detonate upon entering my body. Are you trying to kill or cure me?" Apparently, the absence of thyroid hormones could also cause an increase in sarcasm. I never noticed that on the perforated side-effects pharmacy printout.

The nurse's face, what I could see of it, crinkled. "Glad you have a sense of humor. You're going to need it. This won't hurt. I cannot stay because of exposure to the—"

"You're basically saying I'll be a human microwave?'

"Well, not exactly that but—"

"Being without human contact is more dangerous for me than a malignant cell that got away." I was on a roll. It was likely best the lovely woman had to leave. This was just my opening act. The aluminum door closed behind the nurse. I tried not to think about how the treatment would also shut the door on my uterus as well.

Gratitude and grief could coexist.

I ogled my puffy face and distorted eyes in the hazy hospital bathroom mirror. I'd been without any thyroid hormones for a few weeks. I tried not to panic, picturing the electric blue capsules disintegrating and absorbing into my bloodstream. I normally didn't eat non-organic food. Heck, I'd never even tried weed or a cigarette. Yet what I'd swallowed would obliterate even one cancer cell that might've meandered and mated in my body.

Composers like Chopin and Mozart didn't ease my angst. I positioned myself into a warrior yoga pose, determined to work with instead of against what needed to be done. My fuzzy ankle socks had sticky treads on the bottom, so I felt safe. As I held the pose and my breathing slowed, my chest throbbed with the realization that bad cells would be gone. But my chromosomes could be altered.

In that moment, the drawings became blurry. I knew this night may be the final movement, the finale of our family's opus. But the beginning of my healing.

"Time to get you in that body scan, Ally." The young man waited as I rose from the wheelchair. "I've heard you've been such an upbeat patient. Would you be willing to come back one day and sprinkle some of your positivity on others? We've never met anyone like you."

I looked up at his unlined face. "I've learned to laugh through life. We have a choice: laugh or cry. I choose the former," I said, smiling at him. "Thanks for the kind words. Happy to come back, but not alone—that was the toughest part." The back of my neck tingled with goosebumps. "I can't wait to hug my kids. I always wanted more, but I worry that the RAI mutated my chromosomes."

I folded my earlobe in half like closing a book. I couldn't believe that I had said those words out loud. A gentle hand touched my shoulder and when I looked up, I saw that the attendant was holding a tissue out to me. I accepted it and blew my nose. "Thanks," I said. "What's your name?"

He seemed surprised that I'd asked. "Jean Pierre, but most people call me Pierre." The way he carefully moved the wheelchair and his compassion eased my pain.

That first night, I'd processed it all alone. Not one to pray, I talked aloud to whatever higher power may have heard me. "I'm grateful for my husband. I'm grateful I have two healthy children—maybe the universe has other plans. When the time comes, throw the door wide open. Or slam it shut," I'd said then.

I wiped my cheeks. With the other hand, I grabbed another rough tissue and thanked him.

Every person matters, every interaction, every connection. As Pierre wheeled me down the hallway for the scan, I made a mental note to send him a card. What a sweet soul.

CHAPTER THIRTY-NINE

ALLEGRA' 17

Jack and I missed Grandpa, even though he'd been gone for years. Grandma still lit the white Shabbat candles every Friday night, but her nurse struck the match and stayed with her until the last drip of wax melted. I wished the flickering flame could spark Grandma's memory. She loved to smooth the foil under the candlesticks, something her hands remembered even if her mind did not.

I was grateful my parents had bought me the used brown station wagon so I could come here. Jack said if it were him, he'd leave the car doors unlocked and hope that someone would steal it. I guess it didn't exude a cool vibe, but I didn't care. Whenever I turned the key, a bit of freedom ignited.

When I visited, I brought my nylon sleeping bag from camp and curled onto the floor.

The exhaustion that followed from a restless sleep was worth it. Grandma would open her eyes a bit wider when I sang the *Shema* prayer. Sometimes I'd also sing the *Mi Shebeirach*, a soulful prayer for healing. After all she had done for us, me and Jack, our entire family, this was the least I could do.

It brought back the memories of when Grandma still remembered me. Back then, Grandma's hands didn't shake, and she'd tuck in the corners of the sunflower quilt. Then she'd cradle my chin while naming each family member and reciting blessings. Drifting from the nearby kitchen, aromas of warm challah, honey-drizzled carrots, and baked chicken had lulled me to sleep. But unlike the apartment where I'd spent those wonderful weekends, this place was a single bedroom. No kitchen, for safety reasons. And instead of chicken soup, it smelled like baby powder mixed with damp diapers.

When Grandma first moved here, she'd introduced herself to the other residents in her typical style. Within a month, she'd taught two of her new Christian friends a handful of Yiddish words. One day I stopped by after a tough day at school, the pressures of my junior year too much to bear, all honors and AP classes, plus theater, voice lessons, and being student government president.

"*Bubbela*! Your grandmother was bragging about you yesterday." A gravelly voice echoed from down the dimly lit, peach-carpeted hallway.

"Hi, Ms. Norma! You are too kind."

She raised her rhinestone-bedazzled cane above her head to greet me. "She was *kvelling*. Telling us about your latest recital and something else about you leaving soon for music camp?" she said. I hugged her, still not sure why she resided here. Sharp, witty, and likely a wild one when she was younger, Norma lived next door to Grandma. I was convinced she helped keep Grandma alive.

One time, when Grandma could still sit up, I surprised her with challah dough. She smiled as I braided it, guiding her hand over mine so she could feel that she mattered. I baked it at home and brought it the following Friday. Swallowing was tough for

Grandma, so I dipped the challah in honey to soften it before breaking off a piece and feeding it to her.

When she could still walk, Grandma's nurse brought her to church on Sundays. She didn't realize it wasn't synagogue. But it didn't matter. Music was a universal language, even when time decayed her brain, years stole her memories, and shrinking lobes muted her speech.

Grandma's fire, extinguished from grief and dementia, still glowed when I visited.

Though she couldn't get up, when I sang the Hebrew songs she'd taught me from my childhood, she'd sway ever so slightly.

CHAPTER FORTY

The radiology tech told me not to move. Not to talk. Not to budge. At least breathing was allowed. I had to quiet my mind and still my movements while lying in the cylindrical machine.

Roberta squawked like a flock of seagulls. She'd arrived midway through the exam. "My dear friend was the CEO of this hospital for years. Now we work together as board members of an important institute."

She enunciated each syllable as if she thought the radiology technicians didn't speak English. Even the machine encompassing my exhausted body couldn't mute my mother, who held my hand as she continued to talk. I tried to focus on the camera that hovered over my neck. Auditory torture. Worse than a station blasting heavy metal rock music, and I couldn't change the channel.

When the scan was finished, my mother wanted to grab a salad before heading home. I wanted to grab a pillow and shove my face into it.

"Mom, I look like a blowfish. And I feel awful. Please. Let's go back to your house," I managed, my throat raw and raspy.

"I have no food in the fridge besides oranges, celery, and deli turkey. I'm hungry, and it'll be good for you too. We are going."

After scarfing down spinach leaves under my mother's scrutiny, we finally drove into my old neighborhood. I dragged myself into my childhood home, where I stayed for another three days.

Water had always soothed me. After splashing my face, I exited the double French sliding doors. Summer hadn't scorched the bumpy Chattahoochee deck, so I padded over it and onto the thick-bladed grass, then settled into my spot. The same one where I'd once journaled about my first kiss. Near the oak tree where I'd stepped on a hidden red ant pile as my parents snapped photos of me and my prom date. Where I'd played house and pretended my old dog Keri was my sweet baby girl.

The lake with the floating dock, once white, had weathered to a mottled cream. I used to swim to the dock and lie on it, finding shapes in the shifting clouds. I'd often meet a friend there, a safe space to chat, out of earshot of my folks. Rusty patio chairs were scattered across the gritty sand. I chose the concrete steps instead, grounding my feet into the sturdy warmth. Sitting by the lake, alone again, awareness engulfed me. I nearly drowned in the flood, allowing myself to feel all that had transpired. Biopsies, cancer diagnosis, bloodwork, scans—all of it pummeled me.

Depleted. Dejected. Downtrodden. I dug my toes into the clay-colored sand. The wind blew pages of the romance novel in my lap. Mother's Day had been Sunday. Today was Tuesday.

I missed my husband. I missed my babies. I couldn't be near them for a week. I'd still be radioactive, and therefore it was detrimental for me to be around the kids. Ironic that what killed the cancer was too toxic for healthy people. I had thought my parents would care for me. Boy, was I wrong. They were both at work, and the cupboard was bare.

Books comforted and consoled me. I loved immersing myself in fictional worlds.

Especially the ones where parents unconditionally loved their children. I'd chosen a raunchy novel, figuring it was mindless and a perfect distraction. But I could not focus. So, I moved to the last chipped step that led to the lake. I wondered why they'd never fixed this blemish.

Strange, given their obsession with safety and litigation. And perfection.

Something lightly moved up my hamstring. As the water lapped to and from the shore, I wished my thoughts would float to the middle of the lake and be strangled by seaweed. I couldn't seem to snap out of this unfamiliar foggy funk. I'd been trained to rally regardless of reality.

Acceptance. That word reverberated as if my younger self coached me. An awareness surfaced as if I had emerged from the fresh water. Suppressing the stubborn urge to shove it aside, I acquiesced and lounged on the grass, face to the sun. A teeny critter tickled the middle of my knuckles just north of my wedding ring. Gosh, my hands looked older. Maybe this was why I never sunbathed?

The tiniest, brightest ladybug I'd ever seen danced up one finger and down the next. She dawdled playfully, spending several minutes exploring my dry hands and brittle nails. Engrossed in her movement, I watched as the ladybug opened and closed her delicate wings before pausing on my pinky. I wished she could take a bow. The ladybug flitted away as gracefully as she had arrived. I gazed at the sunlight and listened to the aquatic concerto. I promised myself this unexpected lucky sighting would be an eternal reminder of letting go.

Over the years, ladybugs continued to appear during times of transition. When Joy first went to sleep-away camp, a ladybug landed on the side mirror of the car and traveled with us for an hour. I also saw a ladybug the day after my miscarriage. Yet another one visited the bush in our backyard when we sold our first house. A dime-sized ladybug landed on the slide at Julian's school his last day there. A sweet sign to trust how life was unfolding. I couldn't wait to get back home.

★ ★ ★

I started the ignition, and in seconds (or so it felt in my low-thyroid fog), pulled into the driveway. Perspiration dampened my gingham scarf; I pulled it off and mopped my neck with it.

"Whoa, kids, don't jump on Mommy. Give her a second." Ben followed Joy and Julian, beaming, his arms wide open.

I leaned into their supple bodies and reached above them to kiss Ben. It felt like I'd been gone for a century. I couldn't wait to drive the kids to school and slowly resume our routine.

On the way home the next day, Julian quietly confided in me.

"I probably shouldn't tell you this, but Caca keeps saying that my new school isn't as good as the other one."

Thankfully he wasn't old enough yet to be in the passenger seat. I felt my eyes bulge as I chewed on the straw of my cup, hoping he wouldn't notice. "What do you mean, sweetie?" The straw split down the middle.

"He told me I won't get into a good college, and how much we are alike. He said, 'Julian, you're brilliant like your grandpa. Don't tell Mom I'm saying this, but I think you're making a huge mistake.'"

I drank from the well of self-control so I wouldn't swerve off the side of the road. "Interesting. Thanks for sharing that," I said between gritted teeth. "It's too early to think about college, sweetie." Who the actual fuck did my father think he was? How could he undermine our family decision to switch schools? How dare he. Heat blazed in my chest. Even when he criticized me, I assumed it was well-intentioned, but the sneaky energy of him going behind my back seeped into me like sludge. Good thing I had a long drive to digest it all before sharing with Ben. He would be furious.

When the kids were out of earshot, I told him what Julian had said. "Do you think I'm overreacting?" I twisted my hair into a plastic clip.

"What? No. Are you sure you heard him correctly?" Ben pinched the bridge of his nose.

"Yes. Unfortunately. I deposed our nine-year-old son. And he's an excellent informant. You know he repeats everything verbatim. Both of our kids' ability for recall is extraordinary," I said.

Ben fiddled with his fine-point pen.

"How dare he meddle with a decision we already made. I am in shock. It's so unlike my father, right?" I pulled at my upper lip.

"Do you want honesty or just to be heard?" Ben held my gaze.

What I wanted was to sail away and seek refuge on an exotic tropical island.

"Give it to me. I want your opinion. Straight up like a shot of vodka. Don't water it down."

Ben turned slowly and rested his hand on my waist. "Let's sit down, *mi amor*." He led me toward the bedroom.

Luckily, the littles hibernated in their caves at dusk. My friends teased me about our strict schedule, but I knew my marriage continued to flourish because we carved intentional time for each other. I turned on the faucet, pouring scented Epsom salts into the oversized tub. Ben probably meant for us to sit on the bed. I'd lounge in the bath.

"Ally. I've tried to say this since we got engaged. I know you revere your father. I see it. I hear it. I get it." Ben's teeth grazed his lower lip. He inhaled sharply. "I don't like how he speaks to you, or any woman, for that matter. He's condescending and controlling."

I luxuriated in the lavender scent. And rested my head on the small blow-up bath pillow.

My hands swirled by my sides, making circles in the warm water.

Ben surveyed his supplement drawer and tossed out some expired vitamins. Then he perched on the countertop. He kept talking while I listened with my eyelids half open. "And it's not only with women," he continued. "When Julian shares anything with him, your father doesn't let him finish speaking. Finds some way to correct him, even when nothing is wrong."

I knew Ben had a point. After soaking for a few more minutes, I lifted the cap off the drain, leaned forward, and stepped out of the tub. Towel-dried hair draped my face like curtains closing on a stage. Relieved he couldn't see my expression, I dipped my head downward and braided a wet strand.

"Now your father is weaseling his way into our kids' minds? And that trip to Chicago. Joy, I think she was four years old, lifted your dad's suitcase for him, knowing he has a bad back from years of operating. Do you remember how he treated her? He screamed, 'Put that down now.'" Ben fisted his palms and punctuated his words.

I flipped my head back, exposing flushed cheeks. I may have nodded.

"It was the only time you ever spoke up to him." I swelled with swirly emotions, about to burst.

"And then he didn't talk to us the rest of the day. Stomped right onto the plane. Put on those obnoxious noise-canceling headphones. Your mother just stood there. How could she stay silent and listen to him demean her granddaughter?"

Leaning on his shoulder, I attempted to process Ben's unusually passionate outburst. My neck, forearm, thigh, entire body sank into his; if he moved even one inch, I would topple. A tree trunk decapitated. I nearly yelled, "Tim-ber." Even though I had started the conversation angry at my father, I was remembering his kindness at other times.

"You're right. That was an awful, mean moment. But maybe he had a bad day, honey. We all make mistakes," I protested. "I mean, c'mon. He saves kids' lives for a living. You really think he'd ever intentionally hurt his own family?"

Ben exhaled a gust of exasperation. It was the first time in the decade we'd been together that he didn't relent. "Crap, Ally. Both of your parents. But it's getting harder for me to ignore." He didn't blink.

I shifted from one foot to the other, digging my big toe into the piled carpet.

"Oh yeah? Then why don't you ever stand up for me or our kids?" I said plaintively, my voice lodged in my throat.

"You know how I am; I don't like confrontation. I've been trying to respect your wishes about accepting them. Besides, your parents are who they are." He shrugged.

"So which is it, Ben? Are you angry about it or accepting it? You know any comments would be received differently coming from you. If you're so livid, then why don't you say something?" I clutched the cotton comforter, taking a deep breath so I wouldn't implode. I realized I was taking out my frustration on the wrong person. "I also know that *nobody* is perfect. My dad really tries. We all have our off days, right?" I said.

"Honey. I love that you are so tolerant, so forgiving. But when is it enough?"

I didn't answer.

I didn't know.

CHAPTER
FORTY-ONE

Drool caked the corners of my mouth like crusty icing on a week-old cupcake. Forcing my creased eyelid ajar, I fumbled for my phone to see the time. "Julian! Joy! Ben! Where are you?" I shouted. The house seemed strangely quiet. Slivers of light slanted on my arm like stripes on a candy cane. "It's okay, sweetie. You can come in." I motioned to my daughter, who stood propped in the doorway. She snuggled under the floral duvet.

"Daddy said you don't feel good." Joy's cherubic face was propped on my arm. "But he said I could wake you."

Scenes from the surreal conversation churned in my out-of-order brain. I grabbed the pillow on Ben's side and promptly smushed it over my face. It baffled me that Ben slept nearly upright on this bulging bolster. At least it served a purpose. My thinner, flatter one wouldn't muffle the groan.

In a split second, I started a pillow fight. I needed to create a game. Fast. A distraction from myself. My head throbbed as if bashed by an onslaught of boulders. No rest for the weary. Or the awakened. With every playful thwack, the night before floated further from my mind. The giggles, tumbles, and squeals muted the pounding. I hoped the bile gurgling in my gut would subside.

★★★

"Please come in." I stepped aside so the lithe young woman could enter. "What brings you here today?"

Ella, her lengthy legs and long torso in sync, moved with the grace of an egret. She seemed self-assured, her body like a dancer's gliding onstage.

"I'm incredibly anxious. I've seen therapists for most of my life," she said timidly. "I heard you specialize in mindfulness."

I put down the pen. My new client needed to feel safe and supported; the notes could wait. "I'm impressed with your clarity and honesty. I am sure the other professionals you saw were excellent. My approach is a bit different, and I appreciate your awareness." I uncrossed my ankles and adjusted the lining of my long dress. I sensed this teenager had been dealt a devastatingly difficult deck.

Eager to explain her story, Ella shared about her past. And she continued talking until the timer on my phone dinged. "We're already done? Wow, I've never had a session fly like this one," Ella exclaimed, suddenly reflecting her chronological age of eighteen.

"Let's schedule you weekly for now. And there will be homework to reinforce what we learn here," I explained slowly. "I teach mindfulness to explore and interweave your past with the present. We may even hold a yoga pose while integrating a new skill." My palms pressed together in a prayer gesture. "It is powerful to move our bodies. It shifts you at a cellular level in ways that are long-lasting. You seem wise beyond your years, Ella. I look forward to guiding you in the next phase of healing."

At every new session, Ella's posture progressively collapsed, each story pulling a piece from her carefully composed exterior. Her mother, as described during the intake, seemed to be a pathological narcissist. Ella's parents had divorced recently. Her father couldn't take the constant criticism, condescension, and codependency.

I loosened the knot in my tie-dyed scarf as she continued.

Ella, the oldest of three siblings, had become her mother's narcissistic fuel. She'd learned to interpret and use her body for expression. This required a fine-tuned vigilance. Ella showered her mother with adoration and was careful not to upstage her. Ella's body was a hanger for billowy, drab clothes that shrouded her sinuous physique. As I suspected, she had danced for several years and battled a long-hidden eating disorder. The only control she had in her life was what she allowed into her mouth. During our sessions, the screenplay of Ella's life and its subversive subplots stunned me. She recounted specific examples when she played the role of the perfect daughter, yet Ella's mother appeared to be jealous of her. I cringed and hoped Ella didn't notice.

"I purposely chopped off my hair because that's one of the things people always told me was so magnificent. But how can I change the color of my eyes? And is it my fault that I have long lashes? Or I was blessed with five feet, nine inches of height? If I flunk my senior year and start skipping school, maybe then my mom will pay attention to me." Ella's head dropped into her laced hands.

My eyes brimmed with emotion. I blew my nose into a scented tissue, which sparked a series of syncopated sneezes. My nasal passages conspired against me. "Excuse me. It's just allergies. This will pass in a moment," I said, stifling a snort. I usually did not lie. Not in the personal arena. Not in my professional life. But I couldn't explain to this fragile girl that much of what she shared mirrored my own childhood. Eerily, uncannily so. Not to mention my personal revelations in recent weeks. It would be inappropriate and unprofessional to speak to her about it.

On the way home, I reminded myself that everything happened in divine timing. It couldn't be a coincidence that in this phase of my career, a younger version of myself had appeared in my office. It was as if my neglected inner child had thrown her arms around me and insisted that I listen. I eventually referred Ella to a colleague. Though enormously empathetic, I effectively maintained boundaries. For some reason, though, I couldn't shake the visceral reactions after my sessions with Ella. The migraines that'd been gone for years made a comeback. Dreams—more like nightmares—spilled into the daylight hours. I needed an objective perspective to prevent me from sinking into a quicksand of confusion. And I knew who to call. I sought guidance from Ruby.

"What is going on? I don't get it."

"Ally, you know what's up. You've shared before that Ben makes comments about your folks. And you call me miffed and offended. I can understand why it is upsetting but also know he's coming from a place of concern. You referred that young woman to a colleague. Maybe you need to think about seeking therapy to explore your own childhood." Ruby lowered her pitch.

"I've been seeing someone since grad school, Rubes. How can we provide the best care if we don't unpack our own baggage? She's terrific. Or so I thought, until today," I grumbled, twirling my ponytail.

"You and I both know situations change. Or we outgrow a therapist. I've had times when I needed a fresh perspective. And it doesn't mean anything is wrong with you," Ruby said, waiting patiently for a response.

She's in full-throttle therapist mode. Betcha she's picking at that oversized pink eraser. I held my breath for a beat.

"Al? You there? Did you hang up on me?"

"No, no. I'm here. I think. I mean, physically, but I feel like I left my body for a millisecond." I toyed with my ring. "Ugh. I think you're onto something. Maybe a decade with the same person is too long. I've certainly evolved since Joy and Julian. Motherhood has morphed my perspective in all areas of my life, you know?"

I could visualize Ruby's mischievous lips rising and her twinkling eyes assessing me from afar. I lit a sage candle, then put her on speaker and closed my eyes. Although my bestie resided in Minnesota, miles away from Miami, we sensed each other's moods like twins could.

"Yes. Totally. Love that we can continue this journey together. We are so lucky that we got placed in the same bunk. Amazing, too, our kids are nearly the same age. Are you in child's pose right now, Ally?"

How did she know that? "Guess."

"Duh. It's what you do when turning something big over in your mind. That brain of yours is like a washing machine. What's the setting today?"

"Take a bow," I hooted as the blood rushed to my head. "Do you have any suggestions? I'm thinking you're right. I'm unnerved by this reaction. And frustrated that even though I discharged this client, I cannot stop replaying certain scenes."

I pursed my lips together, restraining myself from revealing more. I switched the subject and shook my head vigorously like a soaked puppy after a bubble bath.

"When will we see each other? Let's plan a trip soon. It's been too long. Miss you tons," I said.

"Let me know when you schedule that appointment. Love you, mean it," Ruby replied, the same phrase she'd said since we were nine years old.

From the moment we'd met, Ruby and I were inseparable. Different religions. Different geography. Different in nearly all ways. A unique, unconditional sisterly love linked through music. Our girls' vacay trip couldn't come fast enough. I vowed to get there by plane, car, or heck, even a slow-moving boat. Whatever it took.

CHAPTER FORTY-TWO

ALLEGRA' 14

I pressed each square, solid button. Today the ringing felt more like a dirge than the usual chirp on the other end of the line. I drew circles in the dirt with my tattered penny loafer, feeling edgy and something else I couldn't comprehend.

"Collect call from Allegra please," I said to the operator, who sounded like she desperately needed Benadryl. Or sinus surgery to remove polyps. I wrapped my cardinal-red cardigan closer. Then I heard Dr. Curt accept my call.

"D-d-d-daddy. What's wrong?" I said. For the first time in my life, I heard honest, raw emotion in his voice.

"It's Grandpa. He…"

No. No. *No.* "Grandpa? Is he? Oh, Daddy…oh no." I clutched my collar.

When Ruby and I had gone back to our bunk two nights earlier, I'd sunk into a strange sadness. I had even written a poem in my journal that night, trying to make sense of the unexpected emotions. My head and heart had a brief family meeting. Grandpa had sent me a message that now I understood.

"When is the funeral?" I choked on the words, forcing myself to ask the dreaded question. With the heel of my shoe, I smudged the circles and drew a Jewish star.

"Tomorrow, Allegra. Shiva at our house with that schmuck rabbi. Who knows if he'll even show up?"

I gripped the handle. *Oh, you mean the rabbi who performed both my and Jack's mitzvahs?* I'd asked my parents why this synagogue. The answer never changed: it was across the street and convenient. Bringing myself back to the heartbreaking news, I asked how I would get to the airport.

"You're not coming home, Allegra. You will stay in Michigan," Dr. Curt informed me.

I thought camp was ruined. Yet I knew Daddy always did what was best for me. This must be a loving decision. Right? I grieved my beloved grandpa among the pines and within the four rustic wood walls of cabin eighteen.

Rather than my mother or father holding me as I bawled, a college-aged counselor, practically a kid herself, absorbed this finality. She consoled me, hugging me, somehow knowing just what to say. Bunkmates hugged me like a tightly knit safety net. Ruby made me the sweetest card during art class. She had all of the girls sign it. A few of them drew pictures too. One night, my bunkmates surprised me with a funny skit to cheer me up.

Maybe if I'd gone home, I wouldn't have received the same type of nurturing. My father was right. Maybe this was for the best.

CHAPTER FORTY-THREE

My hand reached into the opening of the flimsy cardboard box. I parted the plastic. The crackly percussive sound was a dead giveaway. Busted. By my kid, no less.

"Mommy! You said we had to wait 'til tonight! No fair," Julian whined as I folded the flap into itself.

"You're right, honey. One little bite. I need it for one of the recipes anyway. And I found a buy-one-get-one at the market. Look…" I took my son's hand, leading him toward the back of the perfectly organized pantry.

"Where?"

"Behind the bag of apricots." I hugged him from behind.

"Oooo." Julian's vowel climbed an octave higher.

"Don't tell your sister."

"Okay. *Yum.* Is that…?"

"I love this holiday because I find the yummiest dairy-free treats."

"Who is coming?" He spun to face me.

"Since it's the second night, just Beta and Caca. They should be here by six o'clock." I closed the bifold door. "Speaking of which, I need to finish setting the table. Please tell Joy to come downstairs. I'd love for you both to help."

I looked into my little boy's eager eyes. How was he already ten and a half?

"Can we eat it with the meal? I know it's dipped in chocolate, but please, Mommy?"

"We'll see, *tateleh*, my sweet boy." I tickled his sun-kissed forearm. "This holiday reminds me especially of your great-grandmother. She made the best mandel bread." Julian nodded and grinned.

She'd shown up fully for all of us, like a mother to me. I needed Ben's grandmother's grounded mindset tonight. Cookie howled in her crate. Were they early?

"Hello, Allegra. Your doorbell is broken. Again." Dr. Curt sauntered past me.

I looked over his sloped shoulder and waved to my mother. "Come in, and happy Passover! Glad you could come tonight. The kids are excited to see you." I turned my head to call for them.

Roberta grazed my cheek with a perfunctory peck. Scrutinizing me from my head to my toes, she said, "Is that a new blouse, Allegra? Glad it's not sleeveless. You look great in it. I hope it was on sale."

Why were her compliments steeped in judgment?

"Yes. Thanks, Mom. You're welcome to borrow it anytime." I untucked my shirt.

"That's lovely of you to offer, but it would swim on me. You're much bigger busted and broader," Roberta replied.

I pivoted toward the laundry room. Cookie stretched her front legs and yawned. I unlocked the crate, and she leaped into my arms. "Come here, sweet girl!" She licked the point of my chin, and I giggled. Cookie bounded toward my father's lap, her fluffy ears flopping behind her. He maneuvered his body to block her mid-flight, then ruffled the black and white curls on her coat. Dogs loved Dr. Curt.

"Off. Will you ever train this animal, Allegra? Your kids are relatively obedient. How about the damn dog?" he sputtered.

"D-d-d-dad, she's an angel. She wants to be loved. So well-trained and socialized." I tugged at the edge of my flat-ironed hair and saw a dragonfly hovering over the pool.

"She *is* sweet. Always comes right to me. She clearly has superb taste and is an excellent judge of character." Dr. Curt kneed Cookie's belly.

"Caca! Beta!" Joy exclaimed, throwing her arms around them and colliding into their waists. "We haven't seen you in a long, long time!"

Roberta retreated and cut her off. "It's only been three months, Joy. We still work full-time; many of your friends' grandparents are already retired. They have nothing else to do. My teachers and staff need me; being a headmaster is an important job. And Caca, well, he saves lives of little kids like you. Isn't that incredible?"

"Yes! Can you tell me the story about when Caca—"

"Oh, of course. There are many times he saved someone's life. I don't even know where to begin. Last year, we were on an airplane, and a man collapsed. Your grandpa dropped everything and resuscitated him. He'd be dead right now if—"

"Mom!"

"Allegra."

"Stop. Please."

"What? You're so hypersensitive." Roberta patted her high-lighted hair.

"I need your help in the kitchen," I improvised.

"You said dinner was done and ready. I'm confused."

"True. I thought of another dish. Please come with me," I spat through clenched teeth.

Why didn't she ever get my hints? Did I have to spell it out for her?

Roberta begrudgingly followed me.

"Mom, how many times do I need to ask that you are mindful about what you share with the kids? A few months ago, you dove into every detail of a friend's chemotherapy. And someone the kids had never even met! And the constant recounting of Dad's heroic acts—"

"You are overreacting, as always. I am a grown woman, Allegra. Give me a break." She punctuated each statement and stomped out of the room.

I rolled my eyes at the back of my mother's ketchup-red knit top and made a brief stop in the bathroom to reapply my lip gloss. I scrunched my hair and told the woman in the mirror that nobody would ruin Passover. Tapping my lips together like cymbals, I ambled back to the table.

"Mmm. This is delicious," Dr. Curt hummed. "Is this a new dish? You're becoming quite the chef, just like your mother."

"Thanks, Dad. A friend shared this recipe with me. Thrilled you like it," I said, beaming.

"Interesting your friend gave you accurate instructions," Roberta interjected through pursed lips.

"I don't understand." I sucked on the inside of both cheeks.

"I've told you since you were a little girl: Never trust a woman who gives you a recipe. She'll leave out an ingredient or two." She sighed with exasperation.

"My friends are like sisters to me, Mom. They'd never think of doing such a thing." I drizzled olive oil over the roasted root vegetables.

"Oh, your mother is correct. Nearly every woman is threatened by her existence. You do know she is a fabulous cook and hostess," Dr. Curt said. "We rarely get invited to other people's parties. They cannot compete with her." Their eyes locked in affirmation.

I choked. My hands rose to my neck. A half-bitten hard-boiled egg fired out of my cannon into its unsuspecting target: Roberta's lap.

"What on earth? Do you have stain remover? I must treat this immediately." My mother, verklempt and flustered, shot out of her seat.

Seriously? Who wore ivory silk pants to a home with two kids under the age of eleven? "I'll dry clean it for you. So sorry, Mom," I groaned.

"You most certainly will, Allegra."

Ben's eyes narrowed into slits as he noticed the conversation about to derail. "Is it time for dinner yet?" He raked his hair with his hand.

"Yeah, Mommy! We are starving." My children's angelic duet raised the vibe. These two were bottomless pits.

"It is 'yes,' not 'yeah,'" Dr. Curt corrected.

"Caca is right. You must be hungry, because normally the two of you have impeccable manners," I said and winked at them. "Ben, can you help me? The roasting pan is insanely heavy. I guess a pound of sweet potatoes may be why."

Ben trailed behind me, touching the side of my waist. I rotated my neck east and west, wishing I could ease the knots in it. Now out of view, Ben rubbed my lower back. "You look upset."

"I am."

"What did your mother say now?"

"Don't even get me started."

"Okay. I won't. Good idea."

"Oy. You're so literal."

"I know."

"She's as dense as a plank of wood! Like, literally clueless. Which is why I forgive. Again and again." I sighed.

"Not to change the subject, but that was hysterical. The egg episode." Ben's lips turned upward, and I covered his mouth before we both burst into laughter.

"Serves her right. So sick of the inappropriate sharing with the kids. It's enough already." I pierced the serving fork into the sweet potatoes a few extra times.

Ben pried it from my hands and placed it in the sink. "You realize she won't ever change." He faced me.

"I asked her to go to therapy with me when Julian was born."

"I remember, babe. And she said, 'We don't need that. Our relationship is perfect.'" Ben wrapped me in his chiseled arms. I relaxed into his biceps, feeling safe again.

As we returned to the table, I forced myself to blow my breath out slowly before uttering another word. I swore silently after seeing a stain on the pristine lace cloth. "Would you like chicken or brisket?" As usual, I served my father first.

"Both, please. Everything smells extraordinary. You outdid yourself." He licked his colorless lips.

I paused and let this marinate. The potpourri of sautéed onions fused with bay leaves and thyme enhanced his compliment. "Mom, I know you don't care for red meat. I made your fabulous potato *kugel*. I'm sure it won't be as good as when you make it." I placed the ivory dish in front of her.

"Oh, how thoughtful. Thank you, dear."

"I appreciate you joining us tonight. After Grandma and Grandpa passed, we rarely had second night of the Seder. I won't torture you with the Haggadah reading and prayers. It means so much to have this meal together." I raised the Kiddush cup, wanting to guzzle the sweet wine. Or even the kids' grape juice.

"It's amazing, Allegra, how much you are like your grandmother." My mother placed the navy napkin on her lap. "She would've loved that you continue these traditions. And she was overly emotional, exactly like you."

How had she grown in Grandma's love-lined womb? Focusing my gaze on the fading sunlight, my mind flickered like the white candles we lit. I still wondered why my grandmother had cried on Friday nights. "I'll be right back," I said, returning from my reverie.

Matzah balls plunked into the bubbling broth, each splash sparking another memory. Until my first year at college, I had assumed all grandparents had Eastern European accents. The steam fogged my vision as I stirred the soup, inhaling the aroma of the soothing broth. Shreds of meat fell off the bone and floated to the top, swimming in a bath of carrots and celery. The scent of my childhood, or some of it, was also a saline solution that cleansed my spirit. I thought of my grandmother, who would stroke my head each weekend, and how we'd go to the store for contraband—bubble gum ice cream.

"Allegra? Is the soup done yet?" Ben asked, the tone of his voice strange. I'd dipped into a pot of nostalgia. Their ladle of love knew no limits.

"Sorry for the delay. I always think about Grandma and Grandpa, especially during this holiday. I feel like when they died, so did our traditions." I brought two steamy bowls to the table. The kids continued to doodle on their sketch pads. They adored the rainbow pencils from Uncle Jack. They were so bummed he had to travel today. "And the chicken soup. That smell of Jewish penicillin puts me right back in their old apartment."

"I'll eat it, but skimming the fat is revolting, Allegra. Glad you don't mind making it. It makes me queasy to even think about it." Roberta poked the matzah ball with her spoon. "You also love tea like my mother did. I don't care for it; it makes me think about being ill, which you know I never am."

Time to shift the focus. Madam Obvious returns for another episode of "Beam the Spotlight on Beta." After everyone, except my mother, had a second serving, we cleared the dishes. "Who's ready for dessert? Beta brought her yummy chocolate macaroons. I have fruit as well." I pulled my hair into a high ponytail.

"Mommy, can I share the surprise yet?" Julian whispered, a bit too loudly.

"How about you get it? And keep it behind your back. You can give hints. Let's play a word game." I tickled under his arm and elicited that pre-teen giggle.

"Fun!" Julian squealed.

"Why does he know, and I don't? That's not fair." Joy put her hands on her hips.

"He's older, honey. How about you get the other desserts? Thank you for helping." I folded the rectangular linen napkins. The four adults finally had a few minutes to gab. Ben and I drank wine as if it were water while being subjected to travel stories.

"We'd really like it if you and the kids would come over. Wait until you watch our video from Vienna. It's outstanding. Truly," Dr. Curt boasted.

"I'm sure it is. I think the kids prefer movies or cartoons right now." I signaled for Ben to refill my glass.

"You allow them to watch that rubbish? Their brains will turn to mush. Oh, I am disappointed to hear this," my father said, clearly appalled that his grandchildren watched age-appropriate television. I'd never been allowed to watch any at all.

Superficial chatter peppered the rest of the evening. We focused our conversation on the kids. Dr. Curt withdrew to the corner of the tawny couch and tinkered with his cell phone.

Roberta poured herself a second glass while blabbing to Ben. Joy spun the tricolor gold bangles on my mother's wrist. Julian looked over my father's shoulder to peek at whatever he was reading. The kids finally left to snuggle and read on their bean bags, understanding that attempts to get their grandparents' attention were futile.

I cleared the table and scrubbed the sink. As I stacked the silver-rimmed China plates, I thought about the fusion of fragility and strength. Thankful for our spacious home, I glanced across the family room. Dr. Curt abruptly stood and announced they were exiting.

"Let's stay a little longer." Roberta glanced at her grandchildren. "We should take a few pictures. I need updated ones for my office."

Annoyed and agitated, Dr. Curt responded, "Five minutes and that is it. I need to rise before the sun. I have several rather complicated cases tomorrow, Roberta."

My mother brushed Joy's loose curl off her forehead and fixed Julian's part before taking one photo. Dr. Curt snaked toward the double doors, but first, he stopped by the fridge. I didn't see him coming but I felt him before even turning around.

"Thanks again for enduring a quasi-holiday dinner, Dad." I dried my hands on the plum dishtowel.

"For my dear daughter, of course. Not to mention a free meal—that's a bonus," he joked.

"Hilarious. You're a riot," I retorted.

"I know," he snickered. "Roberta, we need to leave. Now," he bellowed toward the family room.

When Dr. Curt spoke, Roberta generally listened. I vowed, when I was younger, not to marry a man who raised his voice. It rattled me like coins in a canister. My mother obeyed this directive from the general. She joined Dr. Curt, raising her hand to wave to us while they began to walk away.

"Bye, Mom. See you in three months, I guess," I said, clearly joking. Suddenly, my father pivoted and pointed an arthritic finger, his manicured nail centimeters from my pupil.

"You've never appreciated your mother enough. You wasted your education, merely working a day or two. Unlike your mother, who still works full time and also makes me homemade meals every night. You are a terrible daughter. You always have been," he roared, the lion unleashed from his lair.

Roberta, to his right, seemed to gloat, and for once had nothing to say. Joy gasped. Julian shrieked. Ben gaped. I froze.

Our quartet, immobilized with shock, cowered as a unit. My jaw refused to cooperate. I had learned in grad school how to handle unexpected, even explosive encounters. But using those interventions now, employing those techniques, would inflame him further. Sure, my father was a yeller. Kids learn how and what they live. He told me that his own mother kept him in line with a stern voice. I'd expected these erratic outbursts that typically targeted Jack. And I noticed his intolerance of others. Part of the package with one so brilliant.

Nobody could ever match his incisor-sharp intellect.

But this unfounded attack on me as a daughter? And in front of my children? I didn't know what to do.

Joy, taking her cue from Julian, wailed louder and ran to Ben. Thankful for my height, I shot a look of disbelief at my husband and held onto Julian lovingly (and to comfort the both of us).

After continuing his tirade about my ingratitude for my amazing mother and spewing a few final sinister words, Dr. Curt stormed out of the kitchen. Roberta followed him like a dutiful dog. For a moment, I thought they'd left. Then the clicking of heels became louder again.

"I forgot my Pyrex dish. I came back to get it." Roberta snatched it up, headed back toward the garage, and slammed the metal door.

I felt like raw spaghetti squash, my insides scooped and rotting. Gutted. "Ben…." I faltered, my throat swallowing the rest. I heard the kids running in the hallway outside their bedrooms.

"I don't even know what to say." He massaged my neck with his soothing hands. I leaned into them, releasing the breath I didn't know I was holding. "How could your father be so cruel?

What did you ever do except be the perfect daughter? And in front of our kids? In our house? Oh, *mi amor*." Ben tenderly stroked my hair.

I parted my lips. Everything and nothing lingered on my tongue. Sweet and sour. Salty and sweet. Mostly bitter.

Absolutely speechless and stunned, I had a fierce understanding of what a stroke survivor experienced. Stuck in my own body, the words wouldn't leave my mouth. I couldn't cry. I felt nothing. My heart punctured, broke, flatlined. Could it be resuscitated?

CHAPTER
FORTY-FOUR

"Are we there yet?" Joy asked for the umpteenth time. She could barely contain her excitement as we neared. Impatient like Ben, she persisted despite my redirection.

"One more word and I will turn around and go home."

"Oh, Mommy. I can't wait!"

"Me too!" Julian squealed.

Such a love-hate relationship with my minivan. Tough to squeeze the monstrosity into compact spaces. Another reason to return the car and end the lease early. The kids dashed past me to the welcome desk.

I stared at the five-page inquisition awaiting us on a ragged clipboard. Geez. Did they also want our blood type? Today's visit to the animal shelter was supposed to be a diversion. A spontaneous field trip to distract and reboot us.

A man, woman, and two teen volunteers greeted guests while we completed the forms. Julian began peppering the woman with questions. "What types of dogs do you have today? Can we pet them? Do you have any puppies? What's your favorite dog?" I gently squeezed his shoulder and smiled at the patient woman.

"I understand you must be super excited!" She beamed at me. "I taught kindergarten for thirty years; many of my students had puppies." Her voice sounded familiar. Perhaps her welcoming Northeastern accent was reminiscent of cousins I so loved.

Joy jumped up and down squealing. "Yes! Please tell us everything! Do you have a puppy that's hyper-alligator?"

I couldn't suppress my smile. "She means 'hypoallergenic.'" The woman plucked the pencil from behind her ear and jotted a few notes on a Post-it, then said she'd come back to check on us.

Three hours later, I was certain we'd memorized each breed. Mission accomplished—Julian's questions fizzled to silence. Joy's prancing slowed to a languid pace. The kids could barely hold themselves upright.

"Ma'am? Did you find one for your family?" an unfamiliar baritone asked.

"No, thank you." I leaned into the counter, lowering my volume. "Honestly, we had a tough night. We came here on a whim to cheer us up. My husband doesn't even know. And besides, he is allergic." I twisted my platinum wedding band, noticing how the diamonds sparkled under the fluorescent ceiling lights.

"You didn't see the poodle?"

I shook my head as his question reverberated in the two-story building.

"We've explored the kennels more times than I can count. There are definitely no poodles here."

"Yes, there is a mini."

A mini what? A mini breakdown? That was yesterday.

"Are you ingesting some kind of hallucinatory drug?" I teased. One of the kids tugged on my denim skirt.

"One moment. You must not have seen him," the auburn-haired man said, his tongue sticking out like an Irish Setter. Long fingers danced across the keyboard.

"Aren't you closing?"

"We closed at six."

"Oh my gosh, I am so sorry! My goodness, it's nearly six thirty. We will—"

"Please give me a second." He held up a hand.

Before I could respond, the woman approached us. "Meet Noodle the Poodle." Her eyes crinkled in the corners.

"Where is he?"

The woman looked downward. The pup gazed at me. He didn't blink. Noodle's eyes looked like licorice Jelly Beans. And then it happened. I kneeled and offered my palm, letting the pup sniff it before I came closer. Why the heck I wore a skirt still baffles me. It's likely the employees got a glimpse of my polka-dotted momma-wear.

Instead of shirking away, Noodle pressed his small cottony head into my thighs and literally wrapped his front legs around mine.

"Am I seeing things? Did you train him to hug?" I raised my chin.

"No. Poor little guy has been in four shelters. Looks like he's drawn to you."

"Oh, boy. This is trouble. I already have a dog and convincing my husband took years. No chance he'll agree to two." I rubbed Noodle's lean belly.

"Let's go into a room—that will be better. I know we are closed, but after fifteen years volunteering here and teaching before that, trust me, I can see when two souls connect."

I tried to say no but was outvoted. "Mommy! Look!" Julian poked my hip. "He's hugging me. His little head is laying on my lap."

"I need to make a call. Be right back." I chuckled while approaching the front desk.

If that man had a tail, he was wagging it under that counter. What a kind face. He gladly handed me the receiver.

"Hi, honey. I need you to make a quick stop on the way home from the office." The words spilled from my mouth.

"Sure. Where?" Ben lowered the music in his car.

"The Humane Society."

"What?"

"The Humane Society." I eyed the man behind the desk.

"CVS? Are we out of toilet paper again?"

Oy. Ben didn't get it. I cleared my throat then popped a mint in my mouth. Irish Setter man grinned at me.

"The Humane Society."

"Are you joking?" Ben's volume cranked up a notch.

"Um, no. I came here to hang with the kids. And cheer us up. You will *not* believe it."

Ben interrupted me. "Whatever you're about to say cannot possibly be more insane."

"It's literally on the way home. We are waiting here for you."

I heard a huff and then a click. Jerk. He'd hung up on me.

About fifteen minutes later, Ben tentatively entered the tiny room. The kids were splayed on the floor with Noodle nestled between them. Normally, I would be aghast at their behavior—they were both wearing shorts and were sprawled on the filthy floor. Noodle angled his pointy face toward the door jamb. Then he promptly paraded toward Ben and hugged him with thin legs that were surprisingly strong.

"Did you teach him to do this?" My husband's skeptical tone conflicted with his smitten expression.

"Ben, I swear, this is exactly why you needed to come. How can we leave this cutie here?" Noodle nudged Ben's knee, and I finally understood the phrase "puppy dog eyes."

★★★

We scheduled a supervised playdate for Noodle and Cookie the following morning. Our hopeful faces smushed against the wide glass divider. No cheering or cajoling was allowed. The Humane Society had a strict protocol to ensure that the pups jived before rehoming them. The two dogs connected instantly like siblings, but clearly, Noodle couldn't keep that absurd name.

I'd consulted several sites and settled on the name "Itzhak," which meant "laughter" in Hebrew; I even called my rabbi to confirm.

I did not call Dr. Curt.

We decided to abbreviate our new fur baby's name to Izzy. We didn't rescue Izzy; our healing pup rescued us during one of the holiest weeks of the year. As I often say, coincidences are actually life's synchronicities. The kids had mercifully stopped crying. They hadn't forgotten about the kitchen combustion. But our fleecy new pup warmed everyone's mood.

Izzy's upbeat disposition (the vet guessed he was about four) revitalized Cookie. She sniffed Izzy's butt and romped around him. I couldn't recall the last time my elder fur baby frolicked. Ben called her a sloth, yet even he loved that our Bichon, a passive pup whose passion was eating, played with her new brother. Cookie balanced Izzy's delicate, dancer-esque grace.

After the honeymoon, Izzy explored (and claimed) his territory. The second week in our home, he lifted his leg and sprayed every corner of the house like a faulty sprinkler. It's often said to be wary of the quiet ones. We learned that also applied to dogs.

Ben's patience with humans clearly didn't extend to four-legged creatures. "I am going to give you back," he muttered while wiping fresh urine off the floor.

"Daddy, no! That is so mean," Joy protested.

"I thought older dogs were supposed to be trained."

"Honey, he's probably been abused. Bounced around from one shelter to another. You heard his story," I pleaded. "We need to give him a little while to adjust."

"Um, he's been living in our house for six months. Twenty-four weeks. I've had it," Ben grumbled and shoved his hands in the pockets of his pressed khaki pants.

I stifled a snicker. Another obvious reason my brilliant husband chose to work for himself. Similar grumblings occurred when all wasn't perfect with the kids. He was a loving, supportive, and devoted father, but even when the kids were babies, Ben griped when gifted an unexpected load in their diapers. I cracked up. Such a control freak. He also didn't appreciate my breezy banter in this moment.

"This too shall pass. It may pass like a boulder-sized kidney stone. Babe, chill, please. Izzy has been a balm for our kids and all of us." I winked at him and bared one shoulder.

"Really? We better be able to train this little stinker to crap outside instead of on Julian's new bed. Disgusting. And must he pee on the baseboards? We just painted them." Ben puffed up his cheeks.

I hugged him. Nibbling on his fuzzy ear lobe, I took a page from the dog's book and licked his cheek. Though he found that a bit disgusting, Ben's mood brightened, and he quit complaining. For the moment, anyway.

CHAPTER FORTY-FIVE

ALLEGRA' 15

Keri pawed at my hand. I petted her head and rolled over with a grunt. Determined to rouse me, she leaped onto the bed and licked my face like I was a bowl of water.

"It's still dark! Sweet girl, please lie down," I muttered, pulling the covers up to my chin.

She whimpered and whined, the pitch a bit deeper than when she was telling me it was time to go potty. I tried to ignore her, but she escalated to a bark.

"What's the matter?" Now Keri nuzzled her furry face under my armpit. I opened one eye and checked the alarm clock, which rested on the white oak dresser. Rubbing my eyes, I sat up and crossed my legs, certain it couldn't be right. I never slept past my alarm. In fact, I usually awakened before it sounded. Our noses touched, hers cold and wet, mine warm from sleep.

"Thank you for nudging me, Keri! I have to shower and get to school." I pointed to the floor, and she jumped down. "And I have a history test; I don't know what I'd do without you." I took her out, then quickly got ready for school.

A mosquito whizzed near my ear. I got in the car and shut the door before it could fly inside. As I drove the thankfully short road to my high school, I missed Jack in a way I'd not felt until now. We could be driving together. Studying together. Hanging together.

But my parents had sent him away. So instead of having a little—well, now *bigger*—brother with whom I could experience life, I felt like an only child. And all because he liked boys. How unfair and unkind. What our parents didn't know, and Jack had told me recently, was he'd finally had his first kiss. I'd never heard him so happy. He didn't even curse during our call. He'd sworn me to secrecy. I didn't tell a soul. I didn't even write about it in my journal because once I'd caught my mother snooping. But I'd cuddled up with Keri and told her. She loved Jack, me, all of us, no matter what.

CHAPTER FORTY-SIX

Ben implored me to hire a dog trainer. His frustration with Izzy's disregard for our furniture had escalated. I thought it was a waste of money. Besides, if I could help humans modify their behavior, I could certainly work with Izzy. I'd also promised the kids we wouldn't return our fur baby to the Humane Society.

His wiry legs wrapped around my thigh. I secretly loved the hugs. But the training books I'd read emphasized firm consistency, especially at this stage. "Off, Izzy. Good listening, buddy." I gave him a peanut-butter-filled treat. Izzy swallowed it whole. Hooking the leash onto his harness, I headed out the door. My phone rang. I ignored it. He'd become my running buddy and came home calmer. Less pishing in the house. More peaceful and compliant. And this made for a happier hubby.

I squatted and poured water into the cap of the bottle. Izzy's little pink tongue lapped it up. A monarch butterfly flitted to the purple bougainvillea blossoms that framed the garage at a house next door. I decided to head east, hoping we'd catch a breeze because it was closer to the beach. Izzy panted more than usual, and my tank top was already drenched. The sun hadn't even risen. I slowed our pace. It seemed cruel to continue running in this stifling heat. I'd jog alone later.

"Sit, Izzy. Down." I dropped the leash, thinking he was ready to follow a few commands without it. The phone chimed. My mother again. I hit "ignore." The first two times, Izzy listened immediately. I paused to guzzle the rest of the water then turned to toss the bottle in the iron recycling can.

"Izzy! Come back here," I panted as I raced toward him. He'd spotted a baby iguana and bolted. Pointy poodle mouth wide open as if smiling, Izzy stopped for a millisecond and wagged his tail. Then he skedaddled. Did he think we were playing a game? Maybe I shouldn't have trusted him off-leash so soon. My phone buzzed. Now my father had texted. I put the phone on silent. And ran faster.

"Do you need help?"

Spinning around toward the voice, I stumbled into a broken sprinkler head. "Ally?"

"Ella? You live in the neighborhood? I had no idea," I sputtered at my former client.

With her hair in a scraggly bun and no makeup, I almost didn't recognize her. Izzy stopped for a second just as a massive Publix delivery truck trundled by him. Ella joined me as we dove for Izzy's back legs.

"No, I'm visiting a friend. How funny to run into you." Ella scooped Izzy up and handed him to me. A chameleon wriggled through the overgrown blades of grass near my feet.

I held Izzy tighter. "Thank you for your help." I tried to catch my breath. "Did you see that truck? What a close call." My heart pounded.

We headed home. I ignored the ringing. Deleted the pathetically few texts and emails. Worried if I didn't, the temptation to reconnect would override reason. Inane written words and vacuous voicemail messages would not substitute for a sincere apology. As if Stevia really substitutes for sugar. Give me a break.

It had been a month since we'd seen or talked to either of my parents. With Ben's encouragement and friends who'd become family, I dodged feeble attempts, ducking and darting away from potential (and painful) curve balls. Prior to this pause, I had talked to my mother at least three times a day. The conversation topics consisted of Roberta's latest accolades or listening to her unsolicited advice regarding diet, education, parenting…well, pretty much anything. Roberta considered herself an expert, not only in her profession, but also in life.

I'd nearly caved at the start of the summer. Detachment defied my DNA. Interesting, too, that the kids never asked about their grandparents.

CHAPTER FORTY-SEVEN

In August, I decided to deal with the lingering debris. And it needed to happen while Joy and Julian were at school.

"Come in. Let's sit outside on the patio." I didn't touch them, wrapping my shaky arms around myself instead. I was a hugger, even though my parents were not. Like a toddler about to touch an electric socket, I leaned in and jerked backward, realizing the imminent danger.

Ben had taken the afternoon off from work; it meant everything to me. Roberta generally behaved better with him by my side. His sturdy hand pressed into my mid-back. He massaged between my shoulder blades, knowing precisely where my body tensed, and brought me back to what was in front of me.

And who.

Taking a moment, I closed my eyes and visualized a positive outcome. I anticipated they'd try to blow off the conversation. Not this time. I pressed my fingertips together into a triangle, right above my knees. The plush part near my nails pulsed like an opera singer's vibrato.

"Mom. Dad. Please sit there." I pointed to the high-backed chairs. I glimpsed the tranquil lake behind them, feeling the hard surface beneath my bare feet. Nature grounded me. I needed all supports on deck.

Another bonus? If they flipped out, I could plunge into the pool.

Taking out my lined journal, I noticed my father cross his legs. Roberta fluffed her freshly highlighted hair. I began to speak.

"Ben and I want to discuss what happened, right here in our home, four months ago. You will most likely have comments. Please do not say a word until I am done. Do you understand?" I wiped my sticky hands on my cropped leggings.

I couldn't see my mother's eyes. Despite the overcast sky, Roberta wore darkly tinted sunglasses. Dr. Curt's eyes penetrated mine as if he were evaluating a new patient. His body didn't betray him. But that gaze grilled me. I stared back, hoping I appeared more stoic than I felt. Ben squeezed my thigh under the table. I wished his hand would remain right there.

Bummer a shot of espresso couldn't boost me with bravery.

Ruby had suggested that I outline my thoughts and put the list right in front of me, visible on the table, in case I regressed, softened, or unintentionally hit the mute button on my internal remote. I thought that seemed weak. But as I readied myself to confront the two bullies, I realized the reason for Ruby's idea.

"What you said to me, Dad, was vile, hurtful, unimaginable. We are still reeling. We have no idea how you could spew such spiteful, cruel words at me. I do not deserve to be treated that way. It is unacceptable. And as if it couldn't get worse, your hateful grenade exploded all over my kitchen, leaving fragments in your grandchildren." My right leg bounced up.

Roberta opened her mouth, but I shook my head and continued. "And Mom, for goodness' sake. You stood right next to Dad, practically delighting in his disgusting diatribe. What you did, or rather did not do, was unthinkable. Leaving without an apology when you both saw the kids were hysterical. Yet you reappeared to get your casserole dish. Utterly bizarre." I wiped my forehead with the back of my hand.

Dr. Curt's bushy brows hiked up like jagged mountain peaks, his eyes stormy.

"I wish this had been an isolated incident. But you both well know it was not." So far so good. I was still vertical. I positioned my water bottle between my legs, squeezing it as if it were a cello. My thighs quivered, yet the pressure of metal meeting skin braced me.

"What are you talking about? You've never told us we've done anything wrong. There must be a miscommunication." Roberta glanced furtively at Dr. Curt, a picture of curated innocence.

I held up my hand, signaling for Roberta to stop. "No. You are well aware. But in case you have forgotten, let me tell you. Ben and I want to be crystal clear about what we will and will not tolerate in our home. It's getting more and more challenging to defend your actions to the kids." I palmed the water bottle, brought it to my dry mouth, and took a swig.

"How do I answer questions like 'Why did Caca call you a terrible daughter?' and 'How could Beta just stand there?' I'm not referring just to the horrific, hurtful evening in our home. There have been so many other times." I crossed my arms. "I say constantly, 'Those are your grandparents'; 'They mean well'; 'We must accept people for who they are'; 'Everyone has off days.'"

Roberta's fuchsia-stained lips parted. Dr. Curt's upper ears reddened.

"Do you realize what you did on Passover? You, not me, not Ben, not anyone else, showed yourselves. You tore off your perfectly placed masks. In case you haven't noticed, Joy and Julian are perceptive, intelligent, and empathetic." I lowered my shoulders and leaned forward. "They see. They feel. They ask questions."

Ben squeezed my hand under the table.

"We can no longer cover for you. Or to be frank, lie. We try to be truthful and transparent with the kids. This is exhausting. And it feels dishonest." Running out of steam, I slowly inhaled through my itchy nose. "If you'd like to ever see your grandchildren again, here are the rules of engagement: One, do not ever call the kids obese, fat, or any other demeaning synonym. Two, refrain from commenting on any physical attributes for that matter. Period." I let my hair loose. "Three, please be mindful of oversharing. The kids have their entire lives to hear about trauma and tragedy." I forced myself to swallow. "Four, we'd appreciate you tending to your own wounds. Bleeding onto us and our kids is unfair and unhealthy. And when we say no, we mean it."

A cloud partially covered the midday sun. Chill bumps crept up my arms. I glanced down at my skin and pictured a trail of ladybugs. "And please stop undermining and judging our decisions as a family. It is unkind and obnoxious."

I had another six items on my list. But I stopped there. I waited. I watched. Wrestled with what would come next.

Roberta sat as if a wad of gum was stuck to her bony derrière and prevented her from moving. A tear cascaded down Dr. Curt's clean-shaven cheek. It spread like a Rorschach blot across the pocket of his collared shirt.

Hold your ground. You've got this. Ruby was right. I can't believe they could cook up fake emotions.

"I have more to say, but honestly, the bottom line is this: we will not tolerate disrespect, belittling comments, or any unkind behavior. In our home, we love without conditions. Even if you cannot, please understand we are done with the warnings. We've talked about this for years. If you even come close to treating me, or any one of us, the way in which you did again, we will immediately ask you to leave and never return. Is that clear?" I lifted my chin.

Palm fronds rustled in the right corner of our yard. A spiny iguana that looked like a T- rex dove into the lake. My parents didn't say a word. Ben looked at me.

"Dad? Mom? This is the part of the story where you say something. Anything," I said, pressing play on my default defensive mechanism.

Dr. Curt fake coughed. Once. Then he did it again. Loudly. "Allegra, that was one of the most dreadful moments of my life," he said. "I don't know why I said what I did."

Roberta tugged on her shiny gold necklace. She pretended to scratch her jaw.

"Mother? I'm wondering if you heard even one word." My leg started bouncing again.

"Yes, Allegra. I am not deaf, you know. I am glad you expressed how you feel—"

"It is how we all feel," I interrupted. I could predict the next lines.

"It's good to get it out. Now that you did, we can all move forward." She popped a Tic Tac in her mouth.

I wondered if I would have an aneurysm. It probably would be less painful.

"Mother, I sincerely hope you didn't just hear me, but for once, listened as well. This conversation has been brewing for way too long. I say this with the utmost love and respect for both of you. This is it. We've defended your unthinkable actions, your hurtful words. You've revealed yourselves. So now it's up to you," I said, my tone as firm as the concrete tile beneath me. My eyes bored into theirs. I didn't blink. My contact popped out of my left eye and onto the notebook. I kept going.

"We heard you. We will try to do better. We had no idea we'd hurt you all before," Roberta replied unconvincingly. Dr. Curt said nothing. Instead, he stood and wrapped his arms around me. I pushed my own arms into my sides and stood like the flagpole at camp. A butterfly flitted to an orchid on the tapered palm trunk behind him and kissed a yellow bud about to blossom.

Roberta seemed to look at Ben. It was difficult to see, given the unnecessary glasses still glued to her face. Taking the cue from my father, she then bent toward me. If one could call the light touch of arms meeting a hug, well, that happened. She patted my back as if this gesture would make it all go away. My mother couldn't resist having the last word, though. "I'm crying inside. You know I am not as emotional as you," she uttered, her purse already dangling on her wrist.

More like a robot. I had never seen my mother cry. Not even at my graduation, at weddings, or at funerals.

Dr. Curt and Roberta left through the yard and got into their car. I stayed outside, breathing in the crisp and blissfully dry air. When I'd rebuked a nasty comment or expressed anything deemed negative, I had been immediately shut down. This was the first time in my life I'd stood my ground. And stood up for my family in a bold, unwavering way. I headed inside after the sound of Dr. Curt's engine faded into the distance.

"Honey, I am so proud of you." Ben turned the bronze lock on the front door. As he got closer, I saw his eyes fill like the swimming pool behind us. "I have never, ever heard you so strong, calm, and just, wow," he said. "What you did blew me away. Are you sure you're not an attorney?"

I reached up and handed him the nearest paper napkin. "This is ironic. I am consoling you now," I joked. "Tell me what you're feeling, sweetie."

Ben paused and looked past my shoulder. While it was hard for me to wait, I knew he needed to organize his thoughts.

"That's a good question. I guess most of all, super proud of you. I've never seen you talk to them—or anyone—like that. And then a bit scared. Remind me to never piss you off!" He wiped his eyes.

I reached upward, pulled him nearer, and laced my hands around his taut neck. As if at the ballet barre, I *relevéd* onto my toes and pressed my cheek into his.

"I couldn't have done that without you, and I appreciate your support. That was harder than my cancer surgery." My voice halted, the adrenaline evaporating like rain puddles in sunshine. "You know how much it means for someone to show up for me. I also know the timing sucked. For you to come home midday and be here—I'll never forget this."

Ben hugged me longer than usual. And he didn't even check his watch. After he went back to the office, I sat on the kitchen stool for several minutes. Stunned at my courage, I rewound the scene in my mind. I doodled hearts and figure eights on the crumpled napkin.

What a robotic response, or lack thereof, from my mother. It was creepy. Of course, my father teared up a bit. He did love me. A question gnawed at me as I drew circles on the granite with my index finger. Gathering my purse and keys, I headed toward the garage. The question would have to wait; it was time to don the mommy cape and careen through the carpool lane.

CHAPTER FORTY-EIGHT
ALLEGRA' 8

She approached the tire swing, stomping toward us. This would be the third time in two days Sammy, the meanest girl in camp, butted into our playtime. It was so annoying.

"Get off. You've been on there too long." She lunged toward us like a panther.

Ruby lowered her eyes to the ground. We'd just gotten our turn. It wasn't fair. Not just the short time on my favorite activity, but also how mean Sammy acted. She didn't pick on me for some reason but always picked on my best friend, who squirmed on the seat, unsure of what to do next. I dug my dark purple and gray sneakers into the dirt.

"Did you not hear me? It is my turn. It's been my turn for like fifteen minutes. Coach will blow the whistle soon." Sammy clenched her jaw as her face reddened.

On a whim, because I hated seeing Ruby hurt, I joined her on the swing. Then I rose on my tiptoes. My best friend lifted her chin enough so I could see her wide, frightened eyes. I nodded at her and hoped she knew what I was about to do. Taking a deep breath, I used my weight to hold her there until she was ready, then pushed with all my strength, like I did during dance practice, and launched us back up in the air. I held onto the rusty iron links, leaning my torso forward and back to create momentum. Ruby matched my movements, and together we rose.

Sammy hollered again. We ignored her and swung higher. Then we heard the warning whistle. I looked straight ahead, avoiding Sammy's screams. Ruby did the same.

The bell rang and we had to head to the cafeteria. Playground time was over. I hoped Sammy's bullying was too. I was dizzy from spinning and swinging, but this girl wasn't going to hurt my best friend anymore.

CHAPTER FORTY-NINE

I slid the phone from my purse pocket and flipped it open. "Hey there. Got a minute?"

"Hi! Are you alright?"

"I am."

"I have about three minutes," Ruby replied.

"You crack me up. Precise and punctual as always, like me," I said, my tone sprinkled with sarcasm.

I heard puffing, and then she shrilled, "Tell me everything!" I would've bet she was pointing and flexing her calves like we did during ballet warmups.

"First of all, I wanted to thank you. No chance I could've handled myself this way without your support." I eyed the tank level in the guzzler, also called a minivan, which was on empty. Such irony.

"So. Did your dad throw a tantrum? Mommy Dearest race to an emergency pedicure?" Ruby joked.

"Ha. Hilarious. Not far off, actually." I briefly recounted the meeting, then said, "We can catch up later. I'm relieved that it's over. And hopefully they'll change. I didn't realize until today how much I'd been carrying." I massaged the base of my tense neck. "It's like emptying a brick-filled backpack. I think, as I process it all, that I was terrified they'd never speak to me again. My mom called last week, asking us to spend Saturday at their house.

That's a big step, although they refused to cancel their breakfast date with the usual suspects. Whatever. Happy we are moving in the right direction." I exhaled and twirled my hair.

"I'm insanely proud of you. I've had the phone right next to me all morning. Glad you called. Love you, mean it."

"Love ya back," I replied, loosening my grip on the phone.

★ ★ ★

I stretched my head backward, resenting the cloudless sky. Apparently, rain dances did not work.

"Come in, everyone." Roberta had a phony smile plastered on her sunscreen-lathered face. The kids didn't need encouragement as they zipped from the doorstep past their grandparents. "Let's have lunch first," she said.

Ben pursed his lips. I pulled my mother aside. "Please tell me you bought gluten-free bagels or bread."

"Oh, you're still on that ridiculous diet?" my mother scoffed, rolling her eyes.

"It is not a diet. I keep telling you Julian is allergic." I dug my nails into my palm.

"Your father asked an immunologist and confirmed there's no such thing. I also asked some teachers at my school, and they concurred. Though we do have cousins who have celiac, by the way." Roberta reached for her sugar-free Sprite.

"You've never told me that. Seriously?"

"Oh, well, it doesn't matter. I haven't talked to them in years." Roberta snickered, poking me like a mean middle schooler with a pointy pencil. "You seem annoyed."

"Uh. Yeah, this would've been helpful to know. Both Julian and I haven't had gluten in more than five years. We feel great.

The bloating and stuffiness are gone. Don't need bloodwork to confirm what our bodies have shown us. And I brought some snacks." I unzipped my striped beach bag.

Roberta retied her silk sarong then motioned for everyone to move to the backyard. She hated trails of crumbs nearly as much as the breeze deflating her blonde bob. Making a concerted effort, she had agreed to the pool party, though I'm sure much complaining ensued behind closed doors. She wouldn't allow the pups to come, despite the kids begging. It still astounded me that pets had ever lived under this roof. Unbeknownst to me, my mother had invited a few other people, which I discovered when the doorbell rang. My heart sank. I quickly adjusted my attitude like a magnetic clasp on a bracelet. Surely the talk we'd had recently would help a bit. I believed that people could evolve. Especially when motivated by love.

A shrill sound scorched my ears. As if the unexpected invasion weren't upsetting enough, Roberta had invited the most self-absorbed of her group, a significant statement given nearly all her friends "were such narcissists," in her own words. I didn't get it. Why spend time with those about whom you whined the minute they were gone? The irony was that Roberta also ranted about her best friend, the one who perpetually canceled their breakfast dates. At least she was predictable.

I scooted into my old childhood bedroom and sank into earlier years, when I'd cried myself to sleep. When I'd whimpered as they belittled Jack. When I'd returned from camp, dejected. I shuddered as I shut the door. Why did my clothes feel constrictive? I swore for the umpteenth time that in whatever other ways I may mess up my kiddos, a lack of love wouldn't be one of them.

Joy and Julian would feel, hear, and sense how much I loved them unconditionally.

"Babe, where've you been?" Ben said, pushing open the door.

"Sorry. I needed to take a breather. If I didn't disappear, my mouth would've gone on autopilot. And required an emergency landing. What the hell? Can you believe they invited friends?" I chewed on my upper lip.

"Ugh. Nuts. This is their way, I guess, of having an adult playdate," Ben offered.

"And it's the first time we've been here in months. Did you hear what Joy said?" I muttered.

"No."

"She told my mother she hopes Caca won't yell at me again."

"Oh, boy." Ben's eyes widened.

"Yuparoo. Leave it to an eight-year-old to say it like it is. Fortunately, my mother ignored it. I guess that's one advantage to being oblivious. A silver lining of sorts." I rolled my eyes. "Suppose we should join them."

The kids had already devoured the scant meal. Carrots, cheese, and grapes. Roberta had invited her alleged friends, and this was the spread. Good to know the sparse portions weren't personal.

Ben dove into the chlorinated crystal water. He swam toward the steps and tickled my dangling feet. Julian had forgotten to bring his goggles. The kid's eyes were already bloodshot. My portable cottage cheese and sour cream, otherwise known as my thighs, stayed shrouded in jeans. The thought of baring my body in even the most conservative swimsuit made me itch.

Thankfully, Dr. Curt's fully stocked cabinet included Benadryl. Ben knew. But he no longer pushed. It wasn't worth it.

It was nothing short of a miracle that I'd never been bulimic (my emetophobia squashed that possibility) or anorexic (I got hangry if I skipped a meal), despite my folks' constant commentary about "Did you notice how this one gained weight?" or "So-and-so looks sickly, she's too skinny." One couldn't win.

I appreciated the three-foot overhang and loved watching my kids dart like tadpoles in the pool. Weightless in the water, they felt free to frolic, and I, a fish out of water, stood outside the aquarium.

My folks immersed themselves in senseless conversation. The unwelcome guests turned out to be a blessing in disguise. They distracted and diverted any potential misfires. I sneezed again, feeling as stuffy as the stagnant air. Since everyone was occupied, I ducked back into the much-needed air conditioning. Nobody would notice my absence.

CHAPTER FIFTY

Ice cubes clinked in the cylinder glass as I filled it with cold water. The tinted windows lowered the electrical bill. But they also provided a layer of protection and a one-way lens through which I could safely view my family. I meandered to the immaculate living room. The needlepoint pillows on the sofa, stuck in the same spots. A square glass coffee table with hardcover books, never read, placed there for show. It astounded me that the short pile carpet remained pristine. Almost.

Keri had left her mark not just in the corner near the baby grand, but also in my heart. Dr. Curt had strategically shifted the antiquated instrument to cover the stain, yet I pinpointed the location like a pathologist staging a tumor. I remembered everything. Like my father. Hard to believe it had been years since I'd cuddled with my canine protector. Keri had parked her robust body between our bedrooms. The gentle gatekeeper. But I still never felt safe, especially at night.

Since I had noticed an empty paper towel roll in the kitchen, I scoured the laundry room where my parents kept extra supplies. Though the black wire crate was gone, I sensed Keri's spirit and wondered about the afterlife. I'd mentioned this to Jack and his partner, David, and they'd teased me ever since.

My dad had stayed in the animal hospital waiting room. I held Keri in my trembling arms as she peacefully transitioned, stroking her soft belly as she took her last breath. The man who rearranged brains for a living and professed to love animals so much couldn't stomach euthanizing his dog. I couldn't stand to see my father sad. Grandma had died two weeks later.

Then, as so often happens in life, sorrow and joy merged. That's when I had met Ben. A party I nearly skipped became the best night of my life.

I stroked the surface of the baby grand piano, its keys yellowed from being overexposed to the sun. It stood upright, durable, proud of its history, despite its faded exterior. Such a shame my father didn't play anymore. I found myself sitting on the simple walnut bench. Melodies flowed through my hands and onto the keys. Bach's Minuet in G major. Ms. Mida's reminders about sitting up straight and curving each finger transported me to my youth. Then I looked up and saw my kids towel-drying their bodies. I started to stand, but my pinky toe caught on the wobbly leg.

"Ouch. Crap. That hurt," I blurted. My toe throbbed and pulsed in time to my heart. It was mind-blowing how the littlest things invariably hurt the most. I spun back around. The craftsmanship from Vienna had a refined finish. My father wouldn't tolerate imperfections.

I pivoted to inspect the precious piece, worried that I'd marred the glossy veneer.

Crouching lower to get a closer look, I inspected every inch of the fluted legs. Another chord resounded in my mind. In the old house, where I lived the first nine years of my life, a quilted velvet cushion had sat on top of the bench. My first dog, Bach, had tugged on the polyester ties with his teeth, and Dr. Curt snapped at him, kicking him in the mouth. That was the end of the bench cushion. My dad never replaced it.

It was miserable sitting on that hard surface.

Staring at the chipped corner, I spotted a tiny triangle that reminded me of a canine tooth.

I scanned the area around me without moving a muscle. Right. Left. Forward. My unquenched curiosity prevailed.

I opened the lid and held it upright, the way one would cautiously lift a newborn from a crib. My eyes widened. I didn't blink. A collage of sheet music lay strewn within the shallow encasing. I gingerly explored each sheet. The fragility that rested between my fingers unnerved me.

The menagerie of composers represented my father's favorites. One paper, dated 1900, must've been an original or a high-quality copy. What a find. Better than the time I snooped in my mother's bathroom drawer and found what looked like a balloon. (After consulting my middle school friend, I learned it was a diaphragm. Yuck. Gag. Ick. A daughter's nightmare. It confirmed that my parents... I still couldn't bring myself to say the "s" word.)

What started as wonder went from minor to major. How odd for my father to leave these treasures in such a slovenly fashion. Most of the music looked alike, playing hide and seek inside the bench. As I reached the second-to-last sheet, I noticed a contrast in color between it and the others. When I touched it, it felt thicker and textured.

It was blank.

Or so it seemed.

I turned it over. I felt the color leave my face, and lightheaded, I sank to the floor.

I scurried under the base of the piano and grabbed the brass damper pedal. Sunlight beamed through the vast bay windows. Flashes of light landed in just the right places. And my mouth nearly unhinged.

Paragraphs instead of stanzas. Letters instead of music notes. A signature at the bottom. Surely this couldn't be true. There must be a mistake.

I scanned the words. It wasn't hieroglyphics. It appeared to be modern-day English. But it didn't make sense. I rubbed my eyes, hoping that would clear the image in front of me. This further irritated my irises, my contacts crispy saucers from the unflinching stupor. I released my clothespin grip, and the paper floated to my crisscrossed lap.

My father. My daddy. My teacher. My everything. This had to be a mistake. No chance.

Not the honest healer who saved lives.

Dear Dr. Curt,

I thought you ruined my career, my life. But after seeking counsel from my pastor, I now know you could not. And I'm writing to you for me.

Immersed in my secret sleuthing, I didn't hear the French doors slide open. But I did hear muted steps nearing the living room. I quickly folded the letter, praying it wouldn't rip. Why did people use such fancy-schmancy paper anyhow? So impractical, eventually ending up in the garbage. Except this one. I would finish reading it the second I could be alone. I slid the letter into the space between my waist and belly. Thankfully I was still flexible. I rolled over into a child's pose, preparing for a convincing performance, grateful, too, for whoever invented Lycra. These straight-cut indigo jeans had a bit of stretch. My chest thumped and fingertips tingled.

The lake behind the dance studio. Go there, Ally.

My serene sanctuary. Scenes from summer rehearsals that soothed me. I pictured the two-person canoe. A vivid orange life preserver hugging my chest. Ruby's melodic voice tinkling in time with the birds. As my breathing slowed to a rhythmic tempo, a leather shoe clomped nearby and landed like a soldier's boot about a millimeter from my clammy forehead.

"What on earth are you doing, Allegra?"

I poked my head upward, early for Groundhog's Day. His looming frame cast a sideways shadow across the angular light rays. "I'm stretching my b-b-back. It's been a bit achy because it's that time of the—"

"That's enough. Do not say another word. The thought of my little girl…"

"Oh, c'mon. You deal with b-b-boatloads of blood every day. Plus, I have two kids. So clearly, I can procreate, which means—"

Dr. Curt shook his head like a metronome. "Enough, Allegra. What a detestable image you've made me conjure."

I exhaled with concerted effort. I'd dodged a bullet. The years of improv theater training proved useful off the stage as well. Every word, every move, every lesson served a purpose.

Just as he did in the operating room, Dr. Curt conducted his personal life in a methodical manner. Shaken and shocked, I briefly considered that maybe my father was a bit calculating.

He spun on his heels. As I stood on one leg, the other at my knee, in a tree pose, I watched him stalk away. I pressed my palms together and thought about that first paragraph. Who had written this letter? Why was it hidden in the piano bench?

Somehow, I'd comically redirected my father for now. And I had no idea what to do next.

CHAPTER FIFTY-ONE

ALLEGRA' 4

My father played the piano, and I sat on his lap, a captive audience, studying the sounds emanating from the majestic instrument. Like the Big Bad Wolf, he'd huff and puff with frustration. One thick finger tapped the white key. Then another three depressed the black ones. My favorite times were when Daddy practiced scales.

"This is middle C." He curled his strong hand around mine.

"Like this, D-d-d-daddy? Is that right?" I put my first finger on the shiny rectangle.

"Almost, Allegra." Daddy turned his hand upside down, taking my own and molding it into a little hill. "You don't push the keys with flat fingers. See? You curve them," he said, showing me the right way to play.

I walked around the piano and peered inside. Running my fingers over the ridged strings wasn't the same as him teaching me the letter of each key. The magical mechanism that produced melodies captivated me. Each tiny hammer touched a thick and thin wire.

Other days I'd stand to the side, afraid to climb onto his bent legs as he sat on the bench. I could tell Daddy was upset with himself. It scared me sometimes.

"Why can't I get this right the first time?" he'd say, banging the piano shut after practicing the same stanza over and over.

My perpetual curiosity prompted a string of questions. I watched Daddy's graceful hands as they glided across the keys. He seemed to know everything about nearly all areas of life. My father archived volumes of information.

CHAPTER FIFTY-TWO

The second act of "Let's Pretend I Never Found It" opened with a persistent child. "Mommy! Daddy wants to go home," Joy announced from the kitchen.

"I am coming, sweetie." I hoped my elevated pitch didn't betray me. In the car, I toyed with the radio dials, my hands sticky and my hair damp. Music had been a salve for my soul, yet no station or genre slowed my triple-timed heartbeats. I wriggled in the seat, the paper crinkling and reminding me of what I withheld. My limbic system must've synched directly to my gastric one via an invisible cord. When one jerked, the other rioted.

"Babe, can you put the pedal to the metal?"

Ben glanced at me sideways. I winced and pointed to my belly button.

"Ohh. On it."

I needed space. Thank goodness we'd left the powder room near the garage. Ben had initially wanted to omit it from the architectural plans, feeling four toilets were a bit excessive. Turns out our kids produced prolific lavatory performances.

In the safety of the bathroom, my bowels erupted. I continued the courtesy flushes between each movement. I almost dropped the letter right into the water, forgetting it was still concealed in my waistband. I snatched it just in time, mid-flight, a successful interception. That could have been a disaster. *Nice save, chiquita*. Shoving it back where it belonged, out of sight, I scrubbed my hands like a surgeon.

Another similar idiosyncrasy we shared—both of us were clean freaks. Dr. Curt bumped it up to the next level; he disinfected public toilets with soap before planting his ass on them. He told me he preferred his thorough method to sitting on paper towels. I'd mastered the hover and squat, even on turbulent flights. We showered and washed with the voraciousness of those scrubbing evidence from a crime scene. We dried our hands with equal intensity. Ironic because I'd endured teasing from both of my folks for being a "germaphobe." As I frequently taught my clients, children learn what they live.

The kids were bathing. Ben buried himself in a slew of spreadsheets that I still didn't understand how to write or read, not even one line. Dropping my rattan espadrilles near the door, I treaded toward the back of the house. I breathed in through my nose for four beats, held my breath, and exhaled for seven. Then I peeled off the soggy tank top and hung it over the glass shower door.

I should've worn shorts this afternoon. But childhood messages are difficult to delete. Roberta had told me forever that I looked better in pants. Who cared that it was eighty-nine degrees? My legs seemed to have expanded in the denim fabric, which stuck to my freshly shaven calves. I cautiously pulled the fabric away from my skin and shimmied out of the jeans. The letter coasted to the carpet in one piece.

Plowing through my pajama drawer, I searched for a worn-in nightshirt. Though it was only four p.m., it felt like midnight.

I craved the comfort of a snuggly piece. *Ah. Found it.* The one Ruby and I got together a few years ago in Maine. Ruby didn't share the same passion for purple, but she acquiesced. We bought the same shirts.

I crawled to the corner of our carpeted walk-in closet. Reaching for my cell phone, I activated the flashlight. My hands shook as I unfolded the paper one quadrant at a time. I couldn't read it. My befuddled brain and the rest of me felt detached. I'd counseled others about dissociation. But this was the first time I'd ever experienced it. My attention drifted to the rows of color-co-ordinated clothing directly across from me. Shaking my head, I frowned at the camouflage cargo pants with periwinkle hearts on the pockets. Such a sucker for anything in the purplicious family. And hearts to boot! Then my mind drifted like a helium balloon released into the sky, floating to an earlier time. If only I could let go of the string attached.

Fat genes. I thought it was fat *jeans* back then. Speaking of which, I spied the ripped vintage pair I'd been searching for since Julian's birth. How strange and timely they appeared now. My father had clarified what he'd meant many years ago. I even remembered what we'd ordered at the restaurant that day. Grilled chicken over arugula for me. My father devoured a filet so raw it practically mooed.

"Now that you have your own little girl who's expanding by the minute, I need to tell you the funniest story," Dr. Curt said as he sliced his steak, cutting it into equal pieces. "We'll get back to Joy in a moment."

That comment seared into me like a cow branded with a scorching iron.

"When you were about eight years old, adorably naive and concrete, you told a plethora of people that you had fat jeans. In fact, you were so literal, we had you tested to make sure you were not retarded. I mean, certainly that would be close to impossible, given my genetic makeup and the geniuses on my side of the family." He held the fork to his lips. "But we had a psychologist evaluate you, just to be sure. Your brother, even though he's defective in other ways, has a higher IQ than you. Yet you did better in school. Anyway, I digress."

My pulse quickened. I mindlessly chewed on my lower lip until I tasted blood. Sucking on it, I hoped he wouldn't notice.

"Mommy was mortified."

Why the hell did he keep calling her that? I'd called Roberta "Mom" since high school.

"I sat you down—surely you remember this—and explained the difference between 'genes' and 'jeans.' Isn't that an absolute riot?" he said, mostly to himself.

What I wanted to say and what emerged from my mouth conflicted.

"D-d-d-dad, I don't remember that at all. Maybe I blocked it out. It seems unkind, you know?" I crunched on a chunky ice cube. I wanted to yell at him. I wanted to wail. I wanted to wake up from the nightmare. But I didn't want to risk upsetting him. I'd borne the force of his fury too many times.

Somewhere hidden in Dr. Curt's composition there must've been variations on a theme. How could a man who healed others hurt me? And he told me we were so much alike—it didn't make sense.

"Oh, get over it, Allegra. You have always been so over-sensitive. I thought we had the same sick sense of humor," Dr. Curt retorted.

My mouth opened then immediately shut. I wanted to protest but thought better of it.

Another battle not worth fighting. With my father, it was wise to take the path of least resistance. His eyes had looked like blurry half notes, his eyebrows like sideways treble clefs. The image in my mind of my father's face seemed distorted. I eased into a child's pose, my hands outstretched and forehead touching the floor, in the cocoon of my closet.

CHAPTER FIFTY-THREE

I ascended each level of the winding garage. A woman's arm dangled out of the window of her cobalt sedan. Whoever built these structures attached to hospitals and doctors' offices must've loved Legos. I worried I might be late for my follow-up appointment with Dr. Bean.

After finally finding a spot, I discovered that parking was still difficult. I'd hoped downsizing to a smaller vehicle would be better. Ben had surprised me with it, which was beyond sweet. And it served a dual purpose: I felt somewhat trendy again.

The ominous clouds decided to unleash a typical torrential Miami afternoon downpour, and of course, the one available space was on the uncovered level. Drying my bare arms with the bottom of my shirt, I wrapped my soaked hair into a knot resembling a lumpy Kaiser roll.

Once inside, I shivered and chit-chatted with the nurse. They should've renamed Dr. Bean's waiting area "the icicle cube." I was called back to the exam room. But I'd learned at the last visit that like the lines at Disney World, this could be a façade.

My cropped athleisure leggings lived up to the promise of dry-wicking fabric. My favorite four-letter word was *sale*. They were a fab find. But the windbreaker stank like a mildewy bath towel. It, too, had dried. I wished my doubts would evaporate with the water. If my father could conceal something so incomprehensible, what if Dr. Bean wasn't all he seemed?

How could I trust him? To make matters worse, my father was the one who had recommended him.

Like a periscope, I moved my eyes from one wood-framed diploma to the next. Undergraduate degree: Johns Hopkins. Medical doctorate: Duke University. Residency: Columbia Presbyterian in New York City. Dr. Bean's qualifications stared back as if challenging me. I saw the light above the door turn from yellow to green.

"Hello there, Allegra! It's wonderful to see you." Dr. Bean extended his hand. "This weather is dreadful. Let me ask someone to get you a dry cloth. You must be cold." He poked his head into the hallway. Did Dr. Bean seem especially thoughtful and courteous today?

"Tell me how you are doing." He handed me a small towel.

"Well, I cannot believe it's been a year. I'm adjusting to life sans thyroid. Pills apparently can't substitute for the real thing. Wish you could've removed it, fixed it, then replanted it. You know, like a refurbished laptop." I traced the scar on my neck.

"Glad to hear you still have your sense of humor. I didn't cut that out." He chortled.

"It's how I survive. Sarcasm is immortal."

"Tell me how you've been feeling." Dr. Bean scanned my face and waited.

I began belting out some of Katy Perry's "Hot N Cold" lyrics. (Okay, I butchered them.) Writhing my body and wiggling my rear, I danced until he interrupted the spontaneous performance.

"What a voice! I did not know you could sing." Dr. Bean's eyebrows shot upward.

"My range isn't what it used to be. I've always been an alto, but now I'm lucky if I can hit a low C. Ever hear of Camp Intermezzo? I went there for several unforgettable summers. Now I only sing in the shower. And torture my kids on long road trips," I blathered, barely taking a breath between words.

"That's amazing. I played piano and viola as a kid. One of the reasons I chose to be a surgeon stemmed from my fascination with instruments," Dr. Bean shared.

He also played the piano. My vibe went from sharp to flat.

"I wish we could talk about this further," he continued. "However, I have a jam-packed day. Please lie down so I can palpate your neck."

"What's the point of that? Can my thyroid regenerate like a lizard's tail that was lobbed off at its rear?" I replied.

Dr. Bean's cheeks pulled upward as he chuckled. "No. I am checking the area for any swelling. All is well. The radioactive iodine did its job. Do you have any questions?"

What tumbled out of my mouth stunned me as much as it seemed to shock Dr. Bean. "Yes," I said. "Would you consider it unethical to have a child with a resident if you were the attending physician?"

"Pardon me? Wh-wh-why are you asking?"

I'd never heard him stutter before. Maybe music was his balm too.

"Just curious. You know I am an avid reader. And I also had a client recently who shared a story that got me thinking." I shrugged my shoulders.

"I cannot imagine anyone doing that. It would be unthinkable and extremely unethical." Dr. Bean cleared his throat and coughed. He reknotted his silk, pinprick blue-and-yellow tie.

I trusted him. My heart heard truth and authenticity. And his eyes emanated complete sincerity. I needed to trust myself. Dr. Bean's response drew me deeper into a dungeon of dread. The letter and its contents lingered, a residue so putrid it infiltrated my senses. Though it was hidden in my closet, I could smell the stink of duplicity. I'd placed it in the deep pocket of a blazer. If the letter had been with me right then, no doubt it would've disintegrated in my clammy palms.

I hadn't slept well since unearthing Dr. Curt's shocking secret. I grappled with what to do. Who to tell. What to make of it all. The song from *HMS Pinafore*, an operetta that I'd performed at camp in the 1980s, echoed in my head. Incredible how Gilbert and Sullivan embedded timeless themes like deception within witty lyrics: "Things are seldom what they seem, skim milk masquerades as cream." If I admitted to Dr. Bean what simmered in my brain, it would feel like betraying my father. Dr. Bean knew him as a brilliant surgeon and colleague.

On the drive home, I thought about withholding in general. From little things like taking the kids to the park to the bigger ones, Ben had heard it all. Communication powered my world. Not sharing, for me, felt analogous to lying.

CHAPTER FIFTY-FOUR

ALLEGRA' 17

My lips parted and my tongue touched the roof of my mouth, but no sound came out.

Viscerally wrong on indescribable levels. I'd only lied once to my parents.

I pursued passions from camp, hoping to continue them during the year. Skipping school was not one of those activities, but during senior year, after I'd already been accepted to university, my friends prodded me to do something "normal." (I'd declined marijuana, alcohol, and cigarettes, even when everyone was doing it.) I caved to the pressure, figuring that a quick breakfast would be tastier than first period political science.

When my parents returned from work that night and finished their dinner, I motioned to my mother. "Mom, I need to talk to you about something important." I hopped from one foot to the other.

"Can it wait? I'm watching the news," Roberta said with an air of annoyance.

"No. It can't. Besides, I keep telling you that what you watched at six p.m. will be the same as at eleven. It's called sensationalism. We discussed this in journalism class today. You're the best audience." I laughed.

"Surely this isn't an emergency, Allegra." She stayed put and cranked up the volume.

"Depends how you classify that, Mom." I twirled two strands of hair around my finger.

"I'll talk to you at the next commercial."

I retreated to my bedroom. Always waiting for my mother. Always when it was convenient for her. I tapped my short fingernails on the glass top of my desk.

The door was closed. Roberta opened it without knocking. I inched toward the bed and gestured for her to join me.

"I have to say something. I am scared to tell you. It's a big deal." I could barely look at her. I folded my upper lip into a crease.

"What? You? You never do anything, unlike Jack. Well, that would get a call from the principal or a teacher, though." Roberta smirked. That was not a kind thing to say about my younger brother. But certainly true. Sometimes I wondered if he had the right idea. It was exhausting being the good girl.

"I…I, um…so, something happened today." I wrung my hands.

"Allegra, get to the point already. I don't have all day." Her right leg jigged up and down.

"It's nighttime. I would've called you earlier, but I didn't want to interrupt you at work. When I try sharing something after mealtime, you're watching the news or talking on the phone," I pleaded. "This has been hard for me to hold in."

"So. Tell me. Are you pregnant?"

"What? That would require me to have sex. And you know I'd come to you about that for sure." My eyes bulged with disbelief.

"Well, what are you carrying on about? Did you get a B on a test? Spit it out." Roberta checked her diamond wristwatch.

"I skipped school today," I said feebly. I uncrossed my legs and brought them toward my chest.

"Why are you telling me?" she asked.

Warily lifting my head, which had been buried between my knees, I glimpsed at what seemed like a grin on my mother's heavily moisturized face. "That's a good question." I scratched my nose; it had started to twitch.

"What teenager skips school and then tells her mother?"

"One who runs smack into her mother's best friend!" In a rare connective moment, we cackled as I told her the rest. "I guess because I've never done this before, going to the nearest bagel store wasn't the wisest choice," I confessed sheepishly. I returned to peeling my split ends like string cheese. This comforting habit drew my eyes downward and sideways. I could not look at my mother.

"I'm glad I heard it from you, Allegra. And it is kind of funny, don't you think?"

I looked up, attempting to suppress my surprise at my mother's reaction. "Yes, truly hysterical. I'm relieved you now know." I leaned toward my mother, craving the comfort of a maternal embrace. Instead, Roberta stood up and briefly touched my hand.

"Goodnight, dear. Good talk. Sleep well," she said, sauntering out of the room and closing the door behind her.

Pulling the comforter over my head, I exhaled with such relief the wood ceiling fan seemed to spin faster.

CHAPTER FIFTY-FIVE

I forced my eyes to focus on the wrinkled paper. It took every ounce of willpower to resist the urge to clean my closet. Besides exercise and journaling, gathering unworn clothing to donate brought me joy. I was both a hunter and gatherer. I reread the shocking letter in my closet. Dramatic irony at its finest. A true comedy of errors. Well, based on the contents of the note, perhaps a tragedy.

I clasped my hands and reached them behind my back, then stretched them over my head.

I slowly turned my head right to left and back while inhaling deeply and exhaling gradually. I flicked on the nightlight, hands quivering as the letters on the paper became clearer.

Dear Dr. Curt,

I thought you ruined my career, my life. But after seeking counsel from my pastor, I now know you could not. And I'm writing to you for me.

As I promised years ago, I haven't told Jon about us. But I thought you'd like to see a photo, which I've included, of your son. He's an angel, a kind human being who loves to learn, especially science. Jon is also musical. He's already taught himself how to play the piano. Can you believe he is now ten? He's brought such joy, light, and love to my life. I never married. I wonder if that's why he's so independent. Or maybe it's the genes. You would know best.

You hurt me—I never thought I'd recover. It was hard enough to heal from the heartbreak while I was still your resident. Then to deal with the pregnancy and how you immediately abandoned our relationship. And your—our—unborn child? Despite all of that, I'm proud to share that I am now the attending for the pediatric neuro department at Boston Children's Hospital. You taught me resilience in and out of the hospital.

But now I think about my blessings, and I've found gratitude in the grief. It seemed like the perfect time to send you a note as Jon begins a new decade of life. I hope you're using your talent to teach instead of take.

Wishing you well, Dot

Who was this woman? Did my dad really have a kid before I was born? And why did my father save this letter? The words and message unnerved me. Nobody was perfect and mistakes happened. But what if the letter was a fake? Given the high esteem in which Dr. Curt was regarded, both locally and internationally, he could be the target of a jealous colleague. I remembered from my own internship how grossly competitive people could be. Something didn't register. My neurons fired like floodlights exposing a nighttime burglary.

"Ally? *Mi amor*, where are you? Everyone is starving," Ben shouted from the family room.

I had no idea it was already dinner time. I gnawed on my lower lip and sighed. Today's meal would be an Uber delivery. "Sorry, I got on one of my closet cleaning kicks." I walked into the kitchen, stretching. The kids bought it. Ben did not. The eleven lines between his brows deepened. *Not now, babe,* I tried to communicate telepathically. I couldn't go there. Why worry my husband when surely this couldn't be true?

Thinking must burn calories. We devoured grilled chicken, green beans, and broccoli. I was still ravenous, so I poured a cold glass of almond milk and dunked a homemade snickerdoodle cookie into it. One of the benefits of being married to someone hyper-focused on his work was that he forgot about my odd behavior. When we went to bed, Ben cradled me from behind. We eventually fell asleep.

Bizarre dreams and fragmented images repeatedly awakened me. I wished there was a way to speed up the sunrise. With it, a new day would dawn. One that would explain or make sense of the madness. I couldn't take it anymore. 5:15 a.m. Ugh. My knees creaked as I straightened my legs and stumbled out of bed. Tiptoeing out of the room, I threw on dirty running shorts and a loose-fitting tank. I scribbled a quick note to Ben with a heart. Time to pound the pavement. I had a full caseload today.

As sweat streamed off my body, endorphins flowed and provided a much-needed lift. After the first mile, fuchsia and tangerine rays spread across the sky. Five miles later, I turned around and headed home, switching off the music and listening to the blue jays chirping instead. I'd decided to put the letter into an imaginary drawer for safekeeping. It'd be unfair to my clients if

I let it interfere with me being present for them. Unfair to my family too.

A steamy fifteen minutes of singing and exfoliating did the trick—that, and blasting Abba's "Dancing Queen." Acoustics were perfect in the shower.

CHAPTER FIFTY-SIX

"Joy! Julian! Pick up the pace," I piped, drinking my second cup of steaming coffee. "We're going to be late."

I loved driving the kids to school. Buckled in safely. Minimal distractions. Sacred space. They didn't have phones yet, much to their dismay. Our most meaningful conversations occurred on the road. Joy once asked about God, and that if he was everywhere, why couldn't we see him? She then wondered if God was a boy or a girl. Julian had asked about blow jobs and dildoes. No chance he'd have the nerve to do that while looking me in the eye.

I'd rarely had any bonding time with my own mother. Irie, our live-in nanny, did the schlepping. Our morning routine consisted of Cheerios and fat-free milk. When Irie didn't drive us, at least in the first neighborhood where I lived, we would sometimes carpool. That stopped when we moved to the house on the lake. In fact, we lost touch with all the families. I had such fond memories of sneaking Doritos and Skittles at the Hildsteins'. The Lanskis' house had forbidden snacks too. The banned food cocooned me.

Daddy would feel the television when he got home. If it was warm, he'd berate Jack especially, knowing his dutiful daughter would never break the rules. Come to think of it, the few times we spent in the car together were on our trips to Disney World.

When Jack and I got rambunctious (in other words, laughed and carried on as siblings do), Daddy threatened to smack us. Jokes and jibes, unless generated by him, were forbidden.

Driving Joy and Julian cut into my schedule. It could become burdensome. But I loved it.

If Ben ever asked Roberta if she'd help, the answer was always no. Even on the weekends, my mother would bike near the beach, just minutes from our house. Yet she didn't have (or rather, make) time to stop by and see her grandchildren. The mere suggestion of changing a standing appointment (haircuts and manicures) prompted a vexing response. As I dove deeper into mothering Joy and Julian, I gathered snippets like newspaper clippings of the important moments my parents had missed.

My phone buzzed, startling me. "Hey! Awesome timing, Jack. I'm waiting for the kids to finish their karate class." I straightened in my seat. We didn't speak regularly. Life got in the way, which made me sad. "Where are you? Vegas? Virginia? Zimbabwe?" I said, stifling a laugh.

"Funny, Al. I'm home." His pitch dropped. "What do I hear in your voice?"

"What do you mean?" Damn it. I was certain I sounded like my usual chipper self.

"I dunno. You sound weird."

A line of birds perched on the taut traffic light wire, their balance and grace inspiring. "Must be the connection. The other parents are watching their darlings. I'm sitting in the car to avoid the mommy mafia." I jostled the keys.

"No, no. It's not that. You don't sound right," Jack pushed back.

I tried to change the conversation by asking about David. But once Jack's radar went off, he wouldn't quit. Empathy was yet another reason why I adored my younger brother.

"C'mon. I know you. And I feel it. Something isn't right," Jack persisted. I heard him click a pen.

"Love and hate that you know me so well," I groaned. I gripped the jagged part of my house key.

"So? What's up? I'm not getting off the phone until you at least give me a clue."

"Fair enough. Before I say another word, I want you to know I've held this in for a while. I haven't even told Ben," I began.

"What? Do you have cancer again? Ally. Are you dying? I am freaking out. Tell me. Now. Go," he shrieked.

"We were at Mom and Dad's last month." I turned my wedding band for the fourth time. "First visit since Passover and the separation from them, remember?"

"Mm-hm."

A waterfall of dismay and dejection rushed from my mouth as I began to tell him the story.

"*What?*" He sounded as stunned as I felt.

"Yup."

"What else did the letter say?"

"The kids are almost here. You're on speaker," I interjected, fumbling for the phone.

"You cannot leave me hang—"

"Say hi to your favorite uncle." I pushed the button to close the door after the kids climbed in.

"Hi, Uncle Jack," the kids sang in unison.

"How are you two? Did you both win Olympic medals yet? What have I missed?" Jack teased.

They erupted into a glorious chorus of giggles. "Where's Uncle David? We want to say hi to him also," Joy said.

"He's at an appointment right now. But maybe we can stop by Friday afternoon and see you all," Jack said.

Julian and Joy chanted, "Yes! Yes! Yes!"

I finally had the phone back on my ear. "You're off speaker now. I obviously can't finish what I was saying. Can you meet me somewhere this week?" I puffed my cheeks with air.

"I'm free tomorrow after five o'clock."

"Perfect. I had a cancellation. Heads up: this will require something stronger than water." I checked the rearview mirror and sighed.

"Oh, boy. Shit. I'll meet you at Myko's. We can grab some sushi. And it's two-for-one sake night."

I chuckled. "Now I really feel like the older sister. Of course you'd know. I'd have no clue about twofers unless they were sales on handbags or shoes. I can't wait. Love you."

CHAPTER
FIFTY-SEVEN

ALLEGRA' 10

Daddy didn't believe in God. But he did believe in surprises.
Valentine's Day scenes fluttered like moths in my
mind. Flitting, doubling their wingspans, and boosting a
bittersweet memory. Daddy once gifted me a pair of dangly heart
earrings. Another year's treasure was a sparkly amethyst ring. But
this year, when I crawled into bed the night before, I saw a burgundy heart-shaped box. Untying the glittery bow, I salivated
at the mouthwatering sight. Milk chocolate truffles cradled in
paper accordions beckoned me.

What a treat, and such a kind gesture! Daddy knew how to
make a girl feel so loved, so special.

The next morning, I thought it'd be deliciously rebellious to
sneak a bite before breakfast.

After all, the closest thing to dessert I was allowed were low-
fat graham crackers. When Jack managed to finagle the occasional
bag of Chips Ahoy cookies by sneaking them into shopping carts
at the grocery store, I ate them when nobody was looking.

Little by little, I pried open the top of the box and licked
my lips in anticipation of chocolate melting in my mouth. But
the package was barren, like trees in winter. Wrappers, carelessly
crumpled and empty, blanketed the base of the box. I wondered
if it had all been a dream.

Still dazed, I wandered into the family room. Predictably, Daddy sat on his plush chair, or "throne," as he called it. One hairy leg was thrown over the chair's arm. I looked away. For some disturbing reason, this man, whose precision bordered on obsessive, never noticed that his splayed position gave all who passed by a clear view of his crotch. Other times, he'd roam from room to room, wearing thin gray boxers. At least he wore a loosely tied velour robe.

"Daddy? I am confused. Am I going crazy?" I yawned, approaching him from the back. I didn't want to chance an embarrassing encounter with his private parts again.

"To what are you referring, my favorite valentine?"

"I looked inside the pretty box—you know, the one you left on my nightstand last night?—and it's empty."

Daddy chuckled, shooting me a sheepish grin mixed with self-deprecation. "Oh. That. You know I cannot control myself with sweets. I ate them all," he confessed.

Mommy jumped to his defense. "I hope you appreciate your father, Allegra. He started getting you gifts because you were insanely jealous of the attention I received. I mean, I *am* his wife. So sweet and thoughtful, your dad." Mommy's words dripped like a recently tapped maple tree. Her syrupy statement solidified the importance of gratitude.

I pinched the skin between my thumb and forefinger. Daddy taught me this helped with headaches. Maybe it would make the sadness go away too. After the initial shock, I regrouped and realized that my father was always honest. Just like he'd taught me and Jack to be.

"That's okay. I understand. You tell me that I have fat genes, so I guess eating chocolate wouldn't be good for me anyway," I said, instantly forgiving him.

"That is true, my darling daughter. You've got the Curt curse. It's another thing we have in common. You're one of the few people in the world who understands me." He squeezed my shoulder.

CHAPTER
FIFTY-EIGHT

his dive had been here since we were in middle school, though we hadn't developed a taste for raw fish until much later. I loved supporting family-owned restaurants. The food was fresh and the staff was welcoming. Ben and I had celebrated my one-year non-cancerversary here with a sumptuous sushi boat.

The willowy hostess opened the door as I approached. "Hello," a sparkly voice greeted me. "So happy to see you, Ally!"

I remembered when the hostess's daughter had slept in a stroller near the black lacquered bar. She was a calm infant; I couldn't recall her wailing or even making a peep. Ben joked about importing what must be a special Japanese formula and why it wasn't offered on the menu as a to-go item for new parents.

"How many people tonight?"

"Two—me and Jack," I said. "I'd appreciate you seating us somewhere quiet and private." I needed to gather my thoughts and ground myself. I twisted my hair into a bun and then released it. Appetizers danced on the menu. I couldn't steady my hands. Speaking the words aloud. Showing Jack the letter. All of it would make it seem real.

I could recognize my brother's confident gait anywhere. He strode with the pride of a peacock. I was thrilled that he chose to live his truth despite our parents' rejections and rancor.

In our younger years, he'd drag his legs and hunch his shoulders. Not now.

"Oh, it's great to see you!" I rose and averted my eyes downward, the tears threatening to trickle. "Love those shoes. Ab fab. Let me guess: Prada, right?"

Jack hooted and spun me around. We hadn't hung out, the two of us, in a few months. "You know it! And on sale too."

"My favorite four-letter word. So glad you told me about that outlet mall. Honestly, I used to think your fashion choices were extravagant. I couldn't care less about name brands, but my flat feet thank you. I now own four pairs of Prada sneakers," I reported.

I wondered if I could continue the mindless banter. All night if I had it my way. I didn't typically avoid tough topics. But this letter was in a league of its own.

"Why don't you order for us? Surprise me. I need to tinkle. Be right back," I said over my shoulder.

I chose the handicapped stall. I needed space to stretch and give myself a stern speech. "Girl, you've got this. You're the older one." I raised my chin, hoping I was alone in the bathroom. "Get a grip. It's the right thing to do. Besides, maybe he'll see something I don't. And he'll show me why this can't be true." Splashing cold water on my face, I thanked the genius who invented waterproof eyeliner and mascara.

I returned to the table with calm conviction. My brother knew me well. A sake mojito with ginger awaited me. I guzzled it, hoping he wouldn't notice.

Jack stroked his impeccably trimmed goatee.

Uh oh, I thought. *Here it comes.*

"Al. What the heck? You're acting like me. Either you are thoroughly dehydrated or insanely nervous. Spill." Jack tapped his manicured fingernails on the laminated menu.

"Knock the glass over? No way. And miss a drop of this anti-oxidant-infused liquid?"

"Hilarious. Now I know something is up. Talk to me." Jack's determined hazel eyes deepened to a rich toffee.

I folded the burgundy napkin into a triangle then unzipped the canvas messenger bag. I normally carried smaller purses. Withdrawing the file folder, I cleared the area in front of me.

"Jack."

"Ally."

"I don't know where to begin. I had a whole speech planned. I'm sure you're shocked. Ben thinks I should run for Congress. He told me I'd be brilliant at a filibuster," I quipped.

"He's right. That's a fuckin' riot. And so are you. I leave town at five a.m. for Philly. As much as I don't want to rush our dinner, whatever you need to say, please spit it out." He planted his hands on the table and pitched forward.

"This is going to shock the hell out of you. I don't—"

Jack reached for the folder.

"Wait! Are your hands clean? Are they dry?" I asked.

He withdrew the letter with the precision of a kid playing the game Operation. If my folder had a buzzer, it would've stayed silent. A dot of lime-green wasabi flecked the end of my chop-stick. I brought it to my mouth, and as the blistering taste hit my tongue, I reached for the icy water. I sucked edamame beans out of their salty pods.

"What the…" Jack started.

"I know," I managed.

"This is insane."

"Tell me about it." I gulped the rest of the water.

"Where'd you find this letter?" Jack unbuttoned the French cuffs on his starched shirt.

I told him about the bench; he never took piano lessons. Our parents steered him toward soccer and football. He hated it. A boy going to poetry readings or, heaven forbid, the ballet class Jack yearned to take—what would people think? The fear of rejection surpassed Jack's aversion to aggressive sports. Until he hit puberty, my brother did as he was told. He adapted his mask accordingly.

I continued, sharing that I'd fooled our father, thank God. Then I remembered and told Jack that I was never allowed to get sheet music from the bench. My scales and songs were in books, organized on the shelves next to the piano. Dr. Curt couldn't stand clutter.

"I'm fairly certain he does not know I have the letter." I exhaled, swaying a bit, and clasped my hands under the table. I thought I'd pass out. Face-plant right into the mound of sticky rice.

"Yeah, I haven't heard him even mention the piano in a few years. You're probably right," Jack affirmed.

Okay. Breathing, please resume to normal. "I can't wrap my head around this. It's totally gutted me." I put an ice cube on my wrist.

"What does Ben think about it?"

"Um. About that…"

"Shut up. You didn't tell him? Are you fucking kidding me? The two of you share, like, literally everything. Never understood it. David would puke if I told him about my bodily functions." Jack shook his head.

"I'm afraid he'll be upset, see Dad in an even worse way. What if Ben doesn't let my kids see their grandfather anymore? What if this rocks our marriage?" I reached across the table and squeezed Jack's hand to steady mine. "This has been harder for me than, well, I don't even know what to say. I've been preoccupied with the kids and work. I didn't realize how heavy..."

Jack seemed to teleport. Suddenly he sat to my left. With his arm around me, I finally felt safe to unzip the emotional girdle in which I'd contained it all.

"Let it out. I'm here, Al. My gosh, I feel awful you waited so long to tell me." Jack rubbed my upper back as I shook silently. "And you're the one who taught me about being honest, that nothing good comes from repression." He handed me a tissue. Only my brother would have an impeccably folded Kleenex in his pocket.

"You're right. You've been so busy I didn't want to add to your plate." I blew my nose.

"Speaking of which, let's eat a few more pieces. This rainbow roll is divine," Jack said. I hadn't eaten since lunch. My blood sugar dipped like a pelican swooping into the sea.

Being hangry wouldn't provide clarity. It wouldn't help this situation. I ordered a lychee-tini. Good girl gone bonkers.

Jack read the letter again. I casually snuck a peek at the accordion on his forehead, which shortened and lengthened. I made a mental note not to mention it. Jack's vanity drove him to Botox, fillers, and goodness knows what else delivered via needles. No need to remind him to schedule a derm-spa day, as he called it. I adored my brother and loved the spectrum of animated expressions when his face thawed. Especially tonight, as I gauged him from across the table.

"Who the heck is Dot? Do you ever remember hearing Mom or Dad talk about someone with that name?" He looked up from the paper.

"No. I've been wracking my brain, and you know my recall is super sharp." I sighed. "I hoped to piece together additional information. I'm at a loss."

Loss. What a word choice. A short yet linguistically loaded one that sparked new meaning in this moment. I sat and stared back at him, wringing my hands on my lap.

"When you mentioned that name, I had the funniest flashback. We both loved the *Wizard of Oz*. I think you were five, and I was eight. You asked Mom why we couldn't meet Dorothy," I said, shuddering at the parallels between the great and powerful Oz and my father. Maybe he wasn't as omniscient and omnipotent as he seemed. Discovering this letter lifted the curtain. I feared what else we'd uncover when we drew back the rest of it.

"Well, you're like a private investigator, Al. Now that you have that nugget, can you find out who the fuck Dot is? And if we seriously have a brother we never knew about?" Jack chewed the rest of the salmon sashimi, then veiled the letter with the fastidiousness of a skilled surgeon. In this one way, his methodical movements reminded me of our father. It was one of the reasons he succeeded as Vice President of Marketing for the publishing company where he worked. A former editor, Jack had shifted to the corporate world after falling in love. Two pay cuts prompted him to leave the magazine industry. Jack knew he couldn't be happily married to both David and his job.

"You don't seriously believe what is on that paper?" I jabbed my finger at the folder. I stared at my brother expectantly. He did not reply. But he held my gaze.

Sometimes silence is an answer.

CHAPTER
FIFTY-NINE

Night after night, I scoured the internet like a raccoon searching for a meal. I couldn't find a morsel of information about this woman Dot. Tried searching all Dorothys in the Pennsylvania area too. Nada.

The phone rang at ten thirty, a peculiar hour for someone to call me. I grabbed it and sprinted to the bathroom. "Everything okay?" I gasped.

"Why?"

"It's kind of late, Jack," I whispered, turning my head to confirm that Ben still slept.

"Oh, sorry! I forgot you have little people and awaken early. We just finished dinner." He chortled.

"Well, now that I nearly had a heart attack, what's up? No chance you're calling to tell me about a new Netflix series," I said, retying the drawstring on my shorts.

"I couldn't stop thinking about our conversation. Tried to push it out of my mind. I kept seeing the letter," Jack said.

"And?" I pulled at the loose thread on a soft purple towel. His voice rose. I knew my brother was about to detonate.

"I found a lead. There's a neurosurgeon who works at Boston Children's Hospital. Her first name is Dorothy."

I lost my grasp on the receiver. Thankfully, the thick bathmat muted the emergency landing. "Say that again." The sensation of a stone in my throat came back. An anxiety encore lodged in my trachea. I barely breathed.

He repeated what I thought I'd heard.

"Oh my gosh, Jack. I—I—I can't wrap my head around it," I sputtered.

"I'm so sorry to call at night. But I leave for a meeting in the morning. It didn't feel right to hold onto this information. And I may be tough to reach the rest of the week."

I heard the tension in Jack's voice and pictured his neck tensing in the same place our father used to grab.

"It's okay. It's more than okay. You've somehow, ever since we were little, been able to see right through their nonsense." I pulled the towel down and turned on the faucet. "Remember when I first told you I thought Mom and Dad may be a bit self-centered? I think it was while I was finishing grad school."

"Yes. I remember every word of that conversation. I was shocked that you'd just noticed that in your mid-twenties. I was the failure in their eyes. You were like a perfectly trained puppy. Unreal. I don't think you ever mouthed off to them," Jack said.

"You did that for both of us!" I laughed, relaxing my shoulders and placing the wet towel on my forehead.

"That's for damn sure. They treated me like an alien. Remember when you and a few of your friends thought it'd be fun to put a full face of makeup on me?" Bittersweet sarcasm coated his words.

"I do. Dad flipped out. I cowered in my room like Keri after Dad yelled and hit her with a newspaper. I hid under my sheets until mid-morning. They were probably thrilled I'd skipped a meal," I said.

"Go back to Ben. Speaking of my brother-in-law, when the hell are you going to tell him about the letter? You're an open book—you've kept this from him for weeks. This is totally unlike you," Jack chided.

I avoided the question as my shoulders shot back up to my ears. How could I rock our happy home? What if it changed everything in our lives? And underneath it all, I felt shame. Still, nothing was confirmed yet.

"I'll tell Ben after I talk to Mom; I'm going to be direct and ask her. I appreciate your call—I think," I said halfheartedly. "Seriously, what would I do without you?"

★ ★ ★

Ben was snoring, so I headed back to my closet and tentatively reread the letter. When had my closet morphed into an evacuation zone? Taking the cobalt clutch from the top shelf, I unzipped it and withdrew the envelope. I opened the flap and took out the photo, then studied the wallet-sized image of Jon. Holy shit. The color of his eyes. Those long lashes. Jack. An uncanny resemblance.

Every path led to a cul-de-sac.

Early the next morning, I decided to call my mother before my family awoke. It seemed to be a safer route than going directly to the source. My mother confirmed that she knew a woman years ago, Dot, whose full name was Dorothy. She wondered why I asked.

"When Jack and I met for dinner, I teased him about his longing to meet the real Dorothy." A squirrel scampered up the coconut palm tree.

"That is hysterical! He was so frustrated with me and your father. He begged us for a pair of those ruby slippers. You know Jack. When he makes up his mind, it's nearly impossible to convince him otherwise," Roberta replied. "Just like me. I love that about Jack."

"If Dorothy wasn't from Oz, who was she? I think you and dad may have mentioned her name once. But I don't remember meeting her." I sat at the shallow end of the pool and dipped my toes into the water.

"Dot is a person from our past. She doesn't matter anymore." Roberta's tone was matter- of-fact, as if she was talking about her latest mole removal.

"That's such a shame! I cannot imagine letting go of Ruby or any of my friends. They are like family," I blurted, stopping myself before I said something I'd regret. A heron spread its wings and flew from the podocarpus hedge.

"Who needs anyone but a husband? You get attached to people. I still marvel that you chose to be a therapist, given your challenges with being so emotionally engaged," Roberta said. "You shouldn't trust anyone besides Ben."

Well, she had thrown the door wide open. Would my mother finally understand why connection meant everything to me?

"That is my strength. Thanks for acknowledging it, Mom." I pressed my fingertips on my chest and massaged the area near my heart. "Empathy and compassion, in my opinion, helps me see others' perspectives from all angles. It's interesting that you perceive that as a weakness." I splashed the water, kicking my feet up and down.

"Here you go again with the psychobabble. I don't have time or desire for my daughter to criticize me."

Before I could respond, the dial tone on the other end of the line did it for me.

CHAPTER SIXTY

ALLEGRA' 11

The sun baked my fair skin while I waited on the edge of the cart. Sometimes I paced.

Other days I watched the ribbed balls roll back and forth as I feigned interest to please my mother. Sweltering, sweaty, and so bored.

Adults stopped for frequent water breaks, which seemed more like an excuse to reapply lipstick. The women would engage in a game of grown-up gossip. That wasn't the first time I felt invisible.

"Can I play with you, Mommy?"

"No, you don't understand the rules. Sit there and wait. We'll all go to lunch after this round," Roberta said to the putting green ahead of her. I hung my head as another drop of sweat splatted onto the pavement. They never let me step on the golf course.

Same routine every single Saturday. My mother wore a bright orange, collared shirt and a pristine skort. No sunscreen, which would explain her current prune-shriveled face and crinkled neck. I related to that ball as it disappeared into a hole after getting thwacked with clubs.

I comprised a captive audience of one unless Jack was dragged along with me. He understood even back then how to wriggle himself out of their grasp. My brother invented reasons why he couldn't be the caddy. A meek, sensitive child, Jack escaped the wardens by sailing and canoeing. Smart and savvy then and now. This was before his hormones surged. With the whoosh of testosterone, his emotions raged as well.

My beloved books kept me company; I wished I could teleport into fictional worlds.

Especially the stories in which mothers spent time with their daughters. Tucked them in at night. Savored ice cream and other childhood delights.

Routine could've been Roberta's middle name. Same course. Same outfit. Same strokes. My mother seemed to crave and fill her voids with consistency. Lunch after hours of bouncing in the boring golf cart finished me off. A smorgasbord of shame.

"You had one already. That's enough." Roberta tapped my hand, which was half wrapped around the flour-dusted roll. Same restaurant, same sticky, vinyl booth, same server. The public humiliation of being restricted from a second serving still stung. It wasn't just the waiters and waitresses. It was the skinny, brunette best friend too. The four-eyed parental surveillance suppressed my appetite.

During weekly dinners, I had more freedom. Our nanny, Irie, cooked comforting Jamaican rice. Unbeknownst to her employers, she watched soap operas and wrestling matches at night, hooting and hollering at the TV, which Jack and I found hysterical. I heaped another pile of calming carbs onto my plate. No chance I would be allowed to do this at Sunday brunch, the only meal that our family ate together.

CHAPTER
SIXTY-ONE

I couldn't wait to pick Ruby up at the airport. My brother had bought me a radar detector—time to test it. He never got speeding tickets. Hope I had his luck today.

With a purple Sharpie, I checked off the descending days on the kitchen calendar. When I learned about the change, or rather addition, to our plans, I'd felt dejected. Then a bit guilty for the former feelings. Our visit was supposed to be a party of two. But how can you say no to your best friend bringing her mom, who had recently finished her fourteenth round of chemo? Besides, I adored Ruby's mom, Anna.

While sitting in bumper-to-bumper traffic, I thought about my own mother. Roberta would send my father or a taxi to retrieve me on college breaks. Yet I was my mother's no-matter-what-the-hour chauffeur. Jack, adept from a lifetime of self-protective lying, ejected excuses from his mouth like the tickets from a parking meter. My father went along for the ride, and I now wondered why he didn't speak up for me in matters regarding my mother. He'd often make me question myself, my judgment, maybe my entire existence. And he'd recently proclaimed that I was in competition with my mother. Bizarre.

As I pulled into the bustling Miami International Airport, I crunched on the remaining ice cube in my soy latte. I found a parking space and sprinted toward the American Airlines terminal. I touched the azabache, a jet-black gemstone that Ben had given me on our honeymoon. It swung on the silver chain as I bounded toward the baggage claim area. Flight arrival announcements blared from the speakers in both English and Spanish. I walked on the pastel undulating waves painted on the asphalt and made a note to snap photos of the new art installations, vibrant images of Florida's ecosystem.

Ruby dashed toward me with perfect posture. We nearly knocked each other over. I squeezed my soul sister like she was a juicy orange. "Oh, girl, it is so good to hug you," I shrieked, feeling Ruby's heartbeat thump against mine.

I pivoted and threw my arms around Ruby's mom, her hair now prickly sprouts. The remaining reddish hues must've died with the malignant cells. Anna bent toward me with the grace of a heron, lean and agile.

"I have a fabulous weekend planned for us," I said. "I told Ben he's on round-the-clock kid duty, and he can't call or text unless a child or animal is literally on fire. I cleared my schedule. I want to make the most of every second you're here!"

It wasn't long before we were driving over the Venetian Causeway. We cruised toward the hotel with the sunroof open, taking in the balmy breeze. The women gazed at the placid water on each side of us; they said they couldn't wait to lounge at the beach and swim in the ocean. I noticed a few tinsel pieces in Ruby's hair as the sunlight shimmered on it.

After self-parking, I could barely contain myself and almost spoiled the surprise. I babbled about my kids and Ben to keep the banter engaging. The darn elevator stopped on every floor, and our room was on the seventeenth.

"Oh, Ally! You've outdone yourself, dear." Anna's face glimmered like the iridescent paper that covered the basket to which she pointed.

Jack had a high school friend who'd hooked us up. Ruby and Anna, enthralled by the unexpected room upgrade, headed straight to the balcony. I wanted them to tear open the cellophane around the gift basket.

"I could move here. Permanently. Not just Miami—this view, this weather! This is wonderful," Ruby chirped. "Such a feast for the eyes!"

I smiled to myself as the women chattered and soaked it in. Seagulls soared in the expansive, clear sky. I promised we'd collect shells later as we listened to the concert of waves spraying the shore. But I couldn't stand one more second of the suspense.

"Please, you two. The ocean won't evaporate. I promise it will be here for your entire vacation. I have one more thing to show you," I cajoled, motioning toward the end table.

The women finally untied the ribbon and ripped open the translucent wrapping. Some of the basket's contents rolled onto the floor.

"What? No fucking way, Ally!" Ruby's jaw slackened.

"Sweetheart, your language," Anna admonished, and put a hand on her bony hip. "My goodness, you are a mother now. Please tell me my grandchildren don't use these abominable words." Her long vowels lingered, punctuating her plea.

Ruby grinned at her mom, then flicked her fiery curls over her shoulder. "If they did, rest assured they would impeccably articulate each syllable," she retorted. It was amazing how Anna spoke to Ruby. Instead of sounding judgmental, her words communicated love.

"You thought of every detail. You got tickets to the exhibit I've been wanting to see at the Bass Museum. And Tchaikovsky's *Swan Lake* tomorrow night? This is dreamy! I think you missed your calling as a travel agent or party planner," Ruby squealed. Those years of singing clearly kept her lungs and diaphragmatic breath support going strong.

I squeezed my best friend's forearm. I'd give her a lung or any other major organ.

Anything—though the liver would be tough because I'd recently discovered red wine. I needed to keep it. A far cry from my dry four years in college, where my only act of rebellion or risk had been the second ear piercing.

The next day was a blast. Anna purchased a vibrant abstract piece by a local Colombian artist. I introduced her and Ruby to Cuban cuisine; we went to Ben's favorite restaurant. They devoured the pico de gallo and fried yuca. Later, we collapsed in a collective carb coma onto the plush hotel beds.

"Let's take an Uber tonight. There's a popular piano bar nearby—we can head there after the show," I suggested. I'd join them as spectators of the lavish scents and opulent colors of my Miami.

As we approached the Arsht Center, the women agreed we'd chosen wisely. The valet line snaked around the building. I heard staccato chattering, mostly in Spanish, too fast for me to interpret. Ruby and I settled in our seats. Anna joined us a few minutes later with chocolate-covered almonds and champagne. Decadent delight and bubbly bliss.

"Why are the lights still on?" Ruby asked. It was 8:02 p.m. Anna loosely knotted her pashmina.

"Ah. It is early. We are on Miami time, *mi amiga*," I said, smiling. I loved listening to the orchestra warm up. I hummed the *A*, inviting myself to harmonize with the string section. The bowing and plucking took me back to concerts at camp.

"Reminds you of that smokin' hot bass player, right?" Ruby tipped her head toward me. "And how we sobbed at the end of our shows, especially on closing night."

"Totally. I can smell the pine trees. And that musty odor of sweat mixed with polyester. Can you believe the costumes we wore? Our kids would be horrified." I grinned.

Ruby's eyes sparkled, and she drifted elsewhere. I knew that sultry gaze. "What if our kids found out about my boyfriends?" Ruby had her first kiss and other explorations in the woods.

"I always became just friends with the few guys I kissed. So unfair. You, on the other hand, my wild *wahine* friend. It's a miracle you never got caught," I said.

"Remind me to tell you about the practice huts when we were in high school division and—"

As if on cue, the lights dimmed. Elbows up and out, the conductor lifted his birch baton.

CHAPTER SIXTY-TWO

How old were we? Like, seriously? Far from the office, it was unlikely I'd run into a patient. Screw it. I scurried to the stage like a lab mouse given a shot of adrenaline.

"Hey, do you know any songs from the eighties?" I slicked back my frizzy hair with my hand. "It's my favorite decade."

The man peered at me with curiosity. He straightened all of his four-foot, ten-inch frame and tightened the rubber band that held his wispy hair. "Do you know this one?" He hammered a few bars, and I nodded.

I clutched the microphone like a life preserver. Still sober yet feeling bold, I belted the first few lines of Madonna's "Borderline." Did I hear a hint of vibrato? Holy crap, I thought it'd disappeared decades ago. I stuck out my chest and flipped my hair. The confidence of a child who hadn't been hurt by the world infused me with courage. I shimmied my shoulders and shook my butt. Madonna had better not make an appearance; she used to own a home nearby.

Ruby hooted and hollered while gyrating her slender hips. So many other options—Billy Joel, Elton John, Queen…the list went on. Ironic that the piano man chose this song. Sweat soaked my violet blouse, and I ignored the mortifyingly moist area under my armpits. The stench of middle-aged sweat mixed with bourbon and bustling silicone boobs permeated the room. This was one of the more tame, conservative joints. Speaking of which, I got a massive whiff of weed and nearly gagged. Ben would be mortified if he saw me carrying on like a lunatic. Oh, well.

Damn, this felt liberating. Thankfully, I was sleeping at the hotel tonight. I handed the microphone back to the pianist with a sheepish grin.

Ruby rushed to the stage, extending a hand to help me jump down.

"I didn't think you'd have the balls to get up there, especially in your hometown. Holy shit, Ally! You did it." She threw her arms around me. "I am so proud of you."

"Did that just happen? Let's leave before I see someone I know. Dark spaces are not my thing, but I'm glad there are tiny spotlights tonight." Awareness of what I'd done made me dizzy. My shoes stuck to the tacky floor as we pushed through the sweaty bodies jammed together.

"Not so fast, my friend. Let's do a shot. Pick your poison. Tequila. Vodka. Goldschläger?" Ruby batted her eyelashes at the bartender.

"Are you nuts? No way. Remember my twenty-first birthday?"

Ruby motioned to a waitress. "Who could forget it? It was epic! Good thing we didn't have cell phones back then. If that night had been documented, it would've gone viral."

I propped my elbow on her shoulder and smiled. Oy, my crazy bestie.

"What the hell. I'll never understand why I regress when you visit. Are you joining us?" I asked Anna.

She shook her head. "Oh, it's much more fun watching the two of you. What a fabulous encore to an exceptional evening," she said, her face glowing with amusement.

★★★

The next morning, I fumbled futilely for my overnight bag. Head pulsing and eyes squinting, I finally found the Tylenol.

"Strong. *Fuerte*. Coffee. Now."

Ruby and Anna rested in the nautical striped chairs in my bedroom and were already dressed, looking as if they'd walked off the pages of a Ralph Lauren catalog.

"Morning, sunshine! What're we doing today?" A sly grin spread across Ruby's face.

"This is why I drink wine, and just on the weekends. Please tell me you didn't record any of our shenanigans on your phone," I moaned.

"She wanted to, but I snatched it out of her hands," Anna said.

"Thank God. I would be horrified. Glad we kept the proof in the liquor and not in photos. At least one of you is rational." I rolled over to my side.

Ruby drew back the aqua curtains. "Get your bootie out of bed! I can't believe you slept this late. It's gorgeous outside."

I pressed my face into the down pillow. "No chance it's later than seven a.m. Ever since the kids, I can't sleep in," I grumbled.

"Dear, it is eleven o'clock. We didn't have the heart to wake you. You needed the rest." Anna's inflection was a maternal tonic.

I sprang off the bed, went airborne, and landed in Ruby's lap.

"What? I feel terrible! You've been waiting around for me, and on the last full day we have together? I wish you would've woken me sooner." My pitch dropped. "Fortunately, I didn't plan anything specific for today's itinerary."

"Why don't you two spend the afternoon alone? I've already crashed this party, and you've been beyond gracious. I made a few appointments at the spa. It looks magnificent." Anna handed me a water bottle.

What a wise woman; she knew I'd protest. Did she still see me as the little girl, the perpetual pleaser, and now, hopefully, the perfect hostess? I wanted to say no. It seemed rude to leave Anna by herself. But the more I thought about it, I needed alone time with my bestie. We'd reconvene at dinner.

Scorching water pulsed from the shower head and stimulated my skin. I turned the faucet and doused myself in a frigid, two-minute finale, then I returned to the land of the living.

Oversized towels swathed me. This, coupled with round-the-clock housekeeping, made the thought of returning to my real life less than appealing.

My hair would be a tangled, curly mess today. Whatever. No time for a blow dry. I didn't want to miss another minute of precious time. Water, whether sitting by it or bathing in it, brought clarity. Ruby needed to know. We wished Anna a peaceful day and headed to the elevator.

★ ★ ★

Ruby waved to the sculpted, sunscreen-lacquered lifeguard. Wouldn't it be lovely if he'd loan me a bit of his testosterone? It'd be, like, insta-firm abs and arms. And I bet the toned bastard ate endless empanadas. No fair.

"What a hottie! Totally eye candy. He's positively edible."

I elbowed my friend, aghast at her brazen outburst. Ruby was the spicy seeds in a jalapeno pepper. I was the milder exterior.

"C'mon. You know he's yummy. We are married, not dead. It's like going to the MoMA or another museum—look but don't touch," she said.

Rolling my eyes, I informed Ruby that her illicit thoughts were practically illegal. The kid couldn't have been older than sixteen. My stomach lurched. Uh-oh. He was bringing two others who clearly modeled for Calvin Klein ads. As the trio approached, I flicked Ruby's double-pierced ear lobe.

"Ouch! What the—"

"Hi! Thanks for snagging us a quiet spot in the shade. We're moms and relishing the rare time away from our kids," I said, trying to intervene before Ruby said something appalling.

"No way! You both don't look a day over twenty-one," the middle boy said, a glossy grin plastered to his face.

"Thanks, sweetheart. You're a doll. Not to mention those abs," Ruby crooned. A flush spread from my neck to my forehead like a wildfire in the Everglades.

The taller dude said, "Need anything else? It's all-inclusive today. We're running a special."

"Nope! All good. Appreciate you asking," I answered.

A barely clothed, burnt-to-a-crisp girl waded in the nearby pool. Ruby gawked, distracted by the nearly naked young lady.

"If someone wore that at home, they'd be arrested! Is that even considered a bathing suit? It barely covers her north and south longitudinal lines. This doesn't look like a nude beach." Ruby snickered.

And if the skimpy material didn't draw attention, the color sure did. Neon pink with tiny green flamingos that flaunted their wings.

"*Bienvenido a Miami, mi amiga!*"

"What the actual fuck does that mean?" Ruby retorted.

"Welcome to Miami! Our bathing suits are conservative compared to South Beach fashion. We might as well be wearing girdles with waterproof skirts attached." I twirled the tiny paper umbrella, tossed it in the air, and squinted while tracking its carefree descent into my lap. Ruby drank the frothy piña colada, but I did not. The smell of pineapple provoked memories of the nauseating colonoscopy prep that my parents made me have during a college break. I gritted my teeth. Only Dr. Curt would deem it necessary, hypothesizing that I may have an intestinal tumor. I hadn't noticed back then how my father reacted dramatically and disproportionately to minor concerns. Turns out it was irritable bowel syndrome caused by living with an anti-Semitic roommate.

"Where'd you go, my friend?" Ruby tapped my shoulder.

"Huh? I'm right next to you. What'd they put in that cocktail?" I joked.

"I'm serious. You can't fool me," Ruby said, peering above her Chanel sunglasses.

I clinked the abstract-shaped ice cubes, hoping to delay my reply. Across the pool, a family of four played a board game. The siblings were about thirteen and fifteen. Other kids zoomed around the perimeter. I worried one of them would wipe out. Nothing escaped Ruby. We'd been busy and having a blast all weekend. Was it that obvious? I'd been totally present. Or so I thought. I stayed silent, mesmerized by the motion of the water swirling in the stout cup.

"You can tell me anything. Soul sisters forever," Ruby said quietly.

She must've rocked at psychotherapy. Her voice was like an oral sedative. A bit of the ice melted and merged with the cranberry juice.

"You are right. Honestly, it's been painful holding this in. I wanted you and your mom to have the relaxing vacay you both deserve." I looked into the liquid, wishing it would wash away the truth. And wishing I'd brought a visor instead of my hand to shield me from the sun.

"Ally, it's me. If you're hurting, I am too. What gives? Talk to me." It was eighty-six degrees, yet chill bumps appeared on my chest.

"Let me ask you something before I begin. We've never lived in the same city, let alone state. Yet you know me and my family as if we were raised under the same roof," I began. She steadied my shaking hand in her own. "Do you think my parents could hide something surreal, utterly appalling... I could invent a designed-by-me thesaurus to describe what I'm about to tell you."

"Yes. I do." She pushed her sunglasses up onto her head.

"Really? Wow. I'd tell you either way, but hearing that gave me the go-ahead." My voice quivered as I recounted the details of the piano bench, the letter, and its contents. Protective wrapping off. Tight seal broken. I leaned back and closed my eyes. Tropical scents of suntan lotion with saline from the sea surrounded us.

A hand touched my forehead, barely perceptible and gentle like a nurturing mother.

"Ally."

No. No. No. You cannot ruin, like literally, the last day with her. She flew all this way. I pushed my cuticles back with a toothpick. A tiny tear swam down my eye like a lost tadpole looking for its family.

"How do you feel speaking that aloud?" Ruby paused.

"Scared. Nervous. Ashamed. My entire universe, my existence may be crumbling." I tried to take a breath.

"Hearing what you shared, I can only imagine. I have such compassion, my friend." She held my hand and my gaze.

"Why aren't you stunned? You seem calm, as if you had this information already." I squinted, studying Ruby's unruffled expression.

"Are you ready to hear why I'm not as surprised as you may have anticipated? Please be honest. What you told me is already a lot to digest," she said. "There's so much to unpack. Talk about baggage."

I tucked a strand of crunchy, salt-sprinkled hair behind my ear. "How can a person ever be ready for life-altering information? I don't know how to answer that question. But yes, I need your insights—I'm listening."

Ruby pulled a hair tie off her wrist and twisted her curls into a messy bun. "I vividly remember a summer when we were about eleven years old. Your parents arrived early and surprised us at ballet. We headed to the water fountain, and instead of a hug, your father critiqued the *rond de jambe*. Then he carried on about the etymology of the term. And your mom stood there like a tree."

I immediately defended him, explaining that Dr. Curt wanted me to excel.

"Maybe you need more examples. Let me think." She chewed on minty gum. A failed attempt at blowing bubbles stuck to the corner of her downturned mouth.

"How about when you called me after that first weigh-in? Your dad called you a horse and dragged you to Weight Watchers. I can still hear the door slamming as he screamed that your brother was damaged goods. I'd return from visiting you and wonder how you survived in that environment." Ruby leaned forward, sensing my pain.

I smoothed the wrinkles in the turquoise terry cloth towel. "So, he was tough on me. A perfectionist. But it shaped my work ethic. Besides, our folks came from an older generation. We parent differently. How does that explain him lying about—well, he didn't lie. He would never lie. I guess, keeping such a..." I clenched my jaw.

"Cover-up" took on a new meaning. I turned to my straw beach bag and rummaged inside it. There it was. I withdrew the flowy fabric and threw it over my head. It draped across my face, shielding me from both the sun's ultraviolet rays and what I'd shared. But breathing became a challenge.

A peace offering in a cup slid under my shroud. I grabbed it and sniffed before sipping. "Vodka is the answer? Oh, Ruby, I don't need a rerun of last night. Please tell me you don't encourage your patients to use unhealthy coping mechanisms," I chided.

"No, silly. I would never. I'm off the clock, and girl, you are a hot mess." Ruby reached up and tugged at the corner of my caftan like a persistent toddler.

"This sucks. It hurts. It is all kinds of crazy. And I know your father is everything to you. We've always been brutally honest with each other. Ally, you need to see someone. Like, yesterday." Ruby raised her volume to be audible above the hip-hop music blasting from the speakers around the pool.

"I do! She's fabulous. Insightful, intelligent, direct." Another pause. She was not done yet.

"Time for a fresh perspective, and I have an idea. What about a male psychologist? Maybe someone who can do hypnosis. A new approach could likely catapult the processing. I know I'm preaching to the choir." Ruby tilted her head and propped it in her hand.

"Why the hypno? I need to make sense of this and figure out the next steps," I wondered aloud. "It's not like you to reference gender."

"This is deep-rooted stuff. Much of it may be too painful for you to identify and access at a conscious level," Ruby continued. "Also, it could be interesting to decipher man-speak. Any therapist can help, as you know. But, c'mon. Keeping it real. There's a biological difference between how we think, and men, well, they're another breed."

But leave my own therapist, Lilly, and try someone new? This wasn't rocket science. I needed an objective opinion, that's all.

"It's clear and concrete, don't you think? A letter. Maybe I have another brother. I probably need a few sessions to sort through what, if any of it, is true." I forgot to mention the photograph, still hidden in the back of my closet.

Ruby threw her arms around me. Instead of a reply, she held me until the sobbing subsided.

CHAPTER SIXTY-THREE

ALLEGRA' 15

Rain tap-danced on the sloped roof. Maple leaves clung to bending branches and comprised nature's wind section. But the cheers from my bunkmates sounded above the torrential downpour.

I clasped Ruby's left hand and turned my head. The corner of her lip peaked, and she gave me the double squeeze. We hinged forward slowly, her bow more graceful than mine. It didn't matter, though. Our fifth summer here, Ruby had nudged and nagged until I agreed to audition for this production. I'd kept a copy of the sheet our choir instructor tacked to the bulletin board, still shocked to see my name listed in the program.

As we strolled off the stage, I licked a drop of sweat that beaded on my cheek, and I tasted the matte foundation that had melted under the spotlights. Ruby had insisted I use waterproof mascara. Maybe I should've listened to her about the makeup too.

"Way to go, Ally!"

"Your harmony was incredible!"

The rest of the ensemble moseyed toward us. A few of our bunkmates snuck backstage.

Then they cheered, jumping up and down.

One boy, who'd had an entire solo, enveloped me in his arms. Even his sweat smelled divine. Thank goodness the backstage lighting was lower because my cheeks scorched. I'd had such a crush on him for the past three summers. And especially now. He'd never hugged me before, and though I'd noticed how much taller he'd gotten, I'd never felt his strong muscles.

This was a summer of so many firsts.

CHAPTER SIXTY-FOUR

Anna was already in the lobby when we returned. Flabbergasted that she'd packed Ruby's luggage, I eyed the organized stack outside the hotel lobby.

Nothing escaped Ruby. "You think I'm compulsive? If my mom had it her way, we'd be at the airport six hours before the flight. And that's only for domestic trips," Ruby quipped, waving at the taxi driver as he came closer. He rolled down his window.

"*Hola! Mi amiga necesita ir al aeropuerto, pero ella necesita usar el baño. ¿Puedo dejar el carro aquí por cinco minutos?*" I motioned to the curb.

"*No problema, señora.*" The young valet handed me a ticket. "*Muchas gracias.*"

We dashed back inside. Ruby gaped at me.

"When did you learn Spanish? Wow, that was impressive. Not that I understood a word of it—well, except 'bathroom.'"

I cackled as we pushed the molded wooden door open. I wished my bathroom door at home was this heavy. Maybe the kids wouldn't barge in unannounced.

"I told the man you had the hots for him and needed to splash water on your face before you gave your elderly mother a heart attack," I deadpanned.

Ruby uncrossed her legs like a dancer about to take flight. "You can't do that to me. Pushing three kids out of my tiny vajay—I'm about to pee in my pants. Literally!" She unbuttoned her teal Bermuda shorts and dashed into the stall. "I don't even have time to put down toilet paper—ahh."

The woman had no shame. Judging from the duration of the stream, Ruby barely made it in time for her bursting bladder. My phone dinged. I knew it was Ben from the sound reserved for him.

Hey. I hope you had a great time together. You're probably dropping them off soon. When will you be home? We've all (especially me) missed you.

I dried my hands. Well, sort of. The air blowers, while environmentally friendly, never worked. I responded to Ben's text:

Thanks for this time away. When you first told me to stay here, I wasn't sure if that was necessary. Gosh, I needed this more than I realized. Can't wait to see you tonight. Love you and will show you later how much I missed you.

Ruby and Anna insisted on taking a taxi. After much cajoling, I finally agreed and hugged them goodbye. My heartbeat *lub-dubbed* with gratitude; love and friendship filled my veins. Strands of sorrow streamed into me, merging with it all. I rolled my neck and relaxed my shoulders.

Normally I'd be eager to get home to my family. I-95 had burgeoned into a massive maze. I dreaded the drive and headed this far south only when necessary. And the constant construction—I never understood why road repairs couldn't be done during the night. Zero traffic for the first fifteen minutes. Then boom. Standstill.

Turning down the radio dial, I forced myself to sit in silence. Ruby had reached a part of me I couldn't access. Now that a bit of the scab had been peeled back, I needed to rip the rest of it off and tend to what lay beneath. I'd seen Lilly for years, but our recent sessions were more conversational than therapeutic. Besides, what was there to complain about anyway? A loving, incredible husband. Two healthy, thriving kids. A fulfilling career.

Yet the letter latched into me like a fishhook. If I didn't remove it, I would bleed out—that much I knew to be true. Maybe a male psychologist would be interesting. Ruby knew me well, and she was highly intuitive.

I accelerated from ten miles an hour to a whopping forty. Progress was progress. When I depressed the gas pedal, tears fueled by grief misted my vision. I pulled over on the local road and parked behind a gas station. A sixteen-wheeler rounded the corner, and then I was alone. Not unusual that I missed Ruby already, but the intensity differed from times in the past. I ignored the alerts on my phone and turned off the engine. No chance I'd arrive home in such disarray. The kids would worry that Mommy was hurt.

Mommy. A loaded word. My own mom. All weekend, I'd admired Anna and Ruby's closely-knit bond, as harmonious as a gospel church choir. Affectionate, connected, and everything I hoped to have with Joy. I had asked my mother if we could take trips together. Her response varied on an "I'm too busy with work" theme. When I offered to be flexible and cancel appointments, Roberta claimed that her calendar was too full. I suggested local spa days, practically anything, to cultivate the deeper connection I craved.

I'd known for years that my mother wasn't like others. But it was what it was. Roberta's teachers and colleagues loved her—she had told me that forever. I should've been grateful I even had her in my life. I thought about this as I turned the wheel and made a right toward home. My positive self-talk pitter-pattered, dripping erratically like rain from a gutter. I lifted the garage opener cover and pushed each number. Ruby was right—I needed to find a new therapist.

Immediately.

★ ★ ★

"Mommy!" Joy ran into my outstretched arms. "I missed you so much! Daddy said we could only call at bedtime. That was hard."

"Oh, I missed you too. I appreciate you giving me the time with Ruby." I fiddled with the stubborn zipper on my tote. Joy leaped over it like a frog from a lily pad.

"What's in there?" She yanked at the handle.

"You don't miss a thing, sweet girl! Please get your brother first." I chuckled, hugging her tighter.

"Juuuuuu-lee-IINNN! Come downstairs. Mommy is home," Joy screeched, her soprano tone echoing off the walls.

Ben encircled me from behind, burrowing his nose into my sunburnt ear. "We may need hearing aids if they keep this up. How many times must we tell them not to yell across the house?" he murmured. "Can't wait until they go to sleep. And I hope you're rested, because I have plans for us."

I turned to face him and ran my pinky up his inner thigh. "Bedtime can't come soon enough. I've been undressing you in my mind all weekend." The bulge in his blue basketball shorts swelled.

Julian's strong arms squeezed my waist as he pulled me downward. I turned and crouched to meet my son's round eyes, so like my own.

"Daddy said you helped with Joy and the dogs. You're such a wonderful big brother." I beamed at my little boy and ruffled his thick hair. I loved my munchkins. Fiercely.

Unconditionally. No matter what. I hoped they felt that always. I handed two hastily wrapped presents to each of them. "Let's read these books tonight—we will take turns," I said. The kids nodded enthusiastically.

Ben winked at me. I wiggled my rear, a sassy preview of the gift I'd give him later.

★ ★ ★

Much to the kids' delight, we devoured breakfast for dinner (pancakes and eggs). Ben cleaned up, and I tucked them in. Maybe Ruby's risqué impulses had rubbed off on me. I couldn't wait to rub his...

"Again! Let's start over. I love Ramona Quimby—I want to hear her story again," Joy pleaded, dragging my hand toward the bed.

"I'm tired, sweetie. I promise we can read more tomorrow."

Joy yawned, and Julian's head bobbed. Thank goodness, because I didn't know if I could contain myself much longer. What was happening to me? I kissed their foreheads, and agreed, even though it was a school night, that they could sleep together in Julian's room. I continued our tradition of spelling letters with my finger.

Just when I thought they were out, Julian's head popped off the pillow. "I love you so much, Mommy. Thank you again," he said with his eyes half open.

"Love you more." My phone buzzed as I quietly closed the door. *Mi amor, mi Benito.*

Meet me between the sheets.

My typically conservative hubby had made me damp. With five words. I peeked into the bedroom. Cedar mixed with vanilla lured me closer. I couldn't remember the last time he'd lit a candle. My absence was clearly an aphrodisiac.

Faint at first, the pulsing between my legs intensified to a throb. And he hadn't even touched me yet. I bared one shoulder, searing my eyes into his while I stepped out of my satin pajama pants. I crawled toward Ben and stroked the side of his rock-hard forearms. He moaned, ready to enter me. Massaging his palm, my other hand glided over his eagerness.

"I can't last much…"

My mouth muffled his sounds, and I teased him with my tongue, pushing it in fast and pulling out slowly. He cupped my swollen breast and tortured my taut nipples until I nearly purred with need. Digging my nails into the plush-covered headboard, I straddled Ben as if it were our first night making love. The headboard hit the wall in tempo to our erotic salsa. He reached up, pulling me higher, and exploded into me.

"Babe. Whoa. That was…" He couldn't catch his breath.

I doodled on his chest, drawing hearts between patches of his wavy hair. "Do I need to call a paramedic?"

Ben's belly ballooned as he laughed. "Only you would say something hilarious and twisted at the same time. You don't miss a beat. And unreal—you're not even out of breath!"

I tickled him. I couldn't resist.

"Someone's gonna get hurt, and it's not gonna be me," he warned, moving backward and bracing his bare feet on the mattress.

"Aw, fine. I'll stop. You're adorable, all silly and disheveled. And that post-orgasm glow—I could do this all night!" I soaked him in, admiring my winded, gorgeous husband and the twisted sheets, mangled from our lovemaking.

He cocked his head, stroking my temple, and again said he couldn't get over my boundless libido. Something else seemed different because I usually worried about the kids hearing us. Tonight? Not so much.

"What?"

"Nothing. I'm admiring my horny honey." His index finger traced the silhouette of my breast. I shivered with arousal. "That's nothing new, except that after the births and thyroid surgery—I can't explain it. You let go in a way I haven't felt in years," he said.

I nestled the top of my head into his thigh and refused to ruin the mood with the melancholy wave that suddenly threatened to engulf me.

CHAPTER SIXTY-FIVE

After dropping the kids off at school, I headed straight to Dr. Jed Lewis, a therapist specializing in hypnotherapy, trauma, and family therapy. His website, soothing and simple, didn't scream "I'm the best in town." Unlike the others I'd explored, it felt humble and inviting. As if my phone was bugged, Ruby texted me while I waited for my name to be called.

> *So?*
>
> *So what?*
>
> *Did you get in with that doc?*

I crossed my legs and texted back:

> *Yes.*
>
> *Are you actually going to the appointment?*

I rolled my eyes and wrote,

> *Yes.*
>
> *What's with the one-word answers?*
>
> *I'm in the waiting room.*
>
> *Proud of you. I know it's tough for you to ask for help.*
>
> *Who said I was doing that?*

Ah, there's the Ally I know. Smartass central has returned.

Need to go. They just called me. I may hurl.

You've got this. Remember what you've told me for years:
Be honest. Be real. Be you.

I tentatively tapped the waiting room bell. A soft-spoken woman slid the frosted glass window open and reassured me when I started blathering.

"You're not alone. Dr. Lewis sees a few others in your field. It's normal to feel nervous. But if you don't care for yourself..."

"I appreciate the reminder. Oxygen mask on me first before others. I know. I tend to forget," I admitted.

She handed me back the insurance card. "Oh goodness, I didn't even know your name. And here I was, gushing all over the place." She motioned for me to come in.

I tripped over the threshold leading to the office and felt a sturdy hand on my elbow. I wasn't even wearing heels today. Lovely grand entrance. Ugh.

"Are you okay?" a comforting voice said, easing my embarrassment. My eyes met the twinkling ones of the office manager, who, by the way, looked like she'd been at Woodstock. Exactly as I'd pictured her when we'd spoken on the phone earlier in the week.

"I am. Thank you. Lovely to meet you in person," I said. Her zen energy put me at ease.

The woman kept her hand where it was and guided me toward the first room. With silver hair to her hips, she exuded tranquility and inner wisdom.

"You know there are no accidents. It typically takes two months to get a new patient appointment," hippie momma said. She adjusted the clasp on the amethyst crystal pendant that rested on her neck.

"Interesting you say that, because I specialize in mindfulness. And I live with intention too," I over-explained, and then bit my lower lip.

"My name is Dottie, short for Dorothy. I tired of the Oz jokes by my teenage years," she said, grinning. "Welcome to our office."

Don't faceplant. A few more feet. I'm almost there. That's not a common name. I fought to maintain my composure. I believed in signs. Big time. This woman's name and the synchronous significance behind it blew me forward.

A slender man, about six foot three, glided toward us. "Hello. I'm Dr. Lewis. Please come in," he said.

Dottie seemed to vanish. Was she part fairy? I thought I'd heard a slight Gaelic lilt. "Feel free to sit anywhere. Even on the floor is fine," Dr. Lewis said.

I scanned the scant, understated room. Not too "therapy-ish," although I noted a half-full tissue box and a worn-in chenille couch. I opted for the high-backed armchair. It looked supportive, which seemed appropriate.

"What brings you here today, Allegra?" Tingles crept down my spine.

"I love my name. But I prefer Ally, especially if we are going to meet every week. That said, perhaps we only need one or two sessions?" I glanced at the digital clock behind his desk.

"Ally. I am glad you are here. I read on the intake you are a therapist as well, yes?" Dr. Lewis left his hands on his knees while uncrossing his legs.

I nodded, suddenly uneasy and a bit woozy. And grateful for the sturdy arms of the chair, which I promptly gripped. This couldn't be blood sugar. I'd eaten on the way here. I forced a feeble smile.

"Ah. The ultimate question. I am not sure where to begin. But I do know this is uncomfortable, bordering on scary for me."

He twiddled a pen between his thumb and forefinger. "All feelings are valid and accepted, Ally. I want to assure you this is a safe space."

Safe. That word again. Maybe that was where I should start.

"So, speaking of safe, I'm glad you used that word. I sought therapy with Lilly soon after my kids were born. Conflict with my self-absorbed mother seemed to magnify—she refused to join me in sessions. It took me a year to talk about the deeper issues because it's my nature to focus on the positive. Being here and letting someone else in is terrifying." I touched the prongs on my pear-shaped solitaire. "Ironic, given my profession, I know."

He nodded, encouraging me to continue.

"Why am I here? I suppose for two major reasons. It's clear my mother is self-focused, but I didn't actualize the magnitude of it until I became a mom myself." I cleared my throat.

"Go on."

"What I cannot tolerate is how my parents treat my kids. It's as if I became a mother and their masks crumbled. And I can't unsee that which is now clear. Make sense?"

Dr. Lewis leaned forward, his hands casually resting on his lap.

"Yes. You're not alone, Ally. Our psyches, as you know, are powerful. They can push realities aside to protect us or to reveal truths." Dr. Lewis prolonged the word "truths."

Had Ruby or Jack given this man a heads-up? Or was he psychic?

"I'm thankful you understand. The deeper stuff, though, is how demeaning, toxic—so many adjectives I could use—they are to my kids. And they notice all the nuances. My children ask pointed questions. And I cannot continue to defend my parents' despicable behavior." I massaged my pulsating temples.

"So why do you?" Dr. Lewis touched the tips of his fingers together like a tent.

"My head and heart are in constant conflict. It's crucial that I model respectable behavior for my children. Though recently, Lilly threw out the term 'dysfunctional loyalty.'"

Dr. Lewis glanced at me, his eyes brimming with compassion and recognition. "May I ask why you decided to come here rather than continue with Lilly? She seems quite competent," he said.

I was starting to wonder why as well. I didn't know if I could trust this man. The only older male figure in my life, the one with whom I'd shared without hesitation had betrayed…

"Are you comfortable talking about it?"

My eyes shifted from his face to the exit door. Sigh.

Surrender.

"I think for now, I'd like to focus on strategies regarding how to handle my parents in relation to the kids. My husband, who's levelheaded and patient, is fed up. Understandably. He doesn't get why I put up with the nonsense." I pressed my palms together and propped my chin on them.

Should I tell him about the letter and photo I found in the piano bench?

"I'm also here to try a new method, and I'm open to anything. And since nothing's changing, well, I need to change my reactions and approach."

Dr. Lewis jotted notes as I stared at the side part of his gelled hair. Now I got why my patients asked what I was writing in their charts. This man was crafting a novella. Lilly rarely used a pen or paper, at least in front of me anyway.

I touched the fading scar on my neck. "Can you give me a few tips today, please? Nothing I've tried is working. We're having brunch with my folks on Sunday." I hoped to leave with an armory of defense.

Dr. Lewis agreed and briefly brought up boundaries. After asking the kids' ages, he suggested Ben and I answer their questions truthfully. For instance, when Julian asked, "Why does Caca yell at you?" offer no more "he's stressed from work" or "that's just him" excuses. Rather, the empathetic man in front of me said to be honest. To tell the kids it was not nice, and that we did not speak that way to those we loved.

The bigger question that poked at me like a cactus was whether I had the nerve to do as Dr. Lewis advised. What if the kids said something to my parents?

CHAPTER SIXTY-SIX

ALLEGRA' 19

My heart thumped as I jostled the tiny key in the hole. Who knew I'd crave the sound of ripped cardboard? My college roommate's mom sent her monthly packages from overseas. Sometimes an envelope with encouraging stickers. Yesterday, the box that arrived was bursting to share its contents, so heavy she needed my help to lug it upstairs.

The metal door creaked open. I stuck half my head inside the empty space. I even went to the front desk to ask if a package could've been misplaced. Nope. The house mom on duty triple checked. Yet I returned day after day.

Freshman year was such a tender time. I yearned for my mom or dad to reach out more than the weekly five-minute calls. I'd gained weight; jelly beans and juice went from my mouth to my ass. As winter break approached, I woke up sweaty and scared, dreading the day I'd go home, but I longed to soak in the sunshine and lounge by the pool. The darker days of winter weighed on me.

When it was time to return home, I loaded my luggage onto the bus and plopped onto the narrow seat, feeling my flab spill out of my jeans. I boarded the plane and gripped my belly tighter during the bumpy descent into Miami International Airport. I wished Ruby could be at the gate to greet me.

"Hi, Mom. Thank you for picking me up." I tried to bring her closer.

She pushed back and straightened her glasses. "Oh my, Allegra, there's much more of you than when you left in August." My mother's eyes studied every ounce of me like a dance critic reviewing a performance.

"I've missed you!" I picked off the remaining nail I'd been biting in flight and turned to look for my father. "Where is d-d-d-dad?" I lugged the overstuffed suitcase off the conveyor belt.

"He is in the car. Hurry up. You know your father doesn't like to wait." My mother strode a few feet ahead of me.

Muggy air mixed with cigarette smoke surrounded me as we walked through the sliding doors. Blaring horns blended with Spanish banter and rustling palm fronds. "Welcome back, Allegra." Dad turned his head and waved from the front seat.

"Hi, D-d-d-dad. How've you been? How is work?" The seat-belt clicked. I loosened the tight strap. Breathing was challenging enough.

"I rescued another few kiddos. A typical day at the office." He high fived me and snorted.

Roberta chimed in as we pulled away from the curb. "Did Daddy tell you about his latest award?"

I tried to tune out and turn off. Coming home for the first time in months dragged me toward the shadows. I dreaded the days that followed and suddenly couldn't wait to be back at college.

CHAPTER SIXTY-SEVEN

"Why do we always have to go to the same place?" Joy whined from the backseat.

Ben clasped my hand. He ran his slender finger over the grooves of the radiant solitaire. My eyes lingered on it. *I am strong. Strong like this diamond. Nothing will dull my sparkle. I've got this.* "That's where your grandparents like to eat. Not all battles are worth fighting. If it makes them happy, it's fine with us."

My damp palm betrayed me. Ben glanced at me sideways. Answering the kids with that type of reply felt weird and wrong. I felt guilty.

The pair of parrots, otherwise known as my parents, perched on their usual stumps. Same chairs. Same table. Egg white omelet, no butter, scooped multigrain bagel, light cream cheese on the side. Of course, they'd also ordered for me, Ben, and the kids.

I used to think this was a thoughtful gesture. I assumed anticipating others' needs represented affection and love. Is that what it was? Or was it a way to control us? No, no. I was being ridiculous. Air kisses all around. I beamed as Joy threw her arms around Dr. Curt's neck. This one, my spirited girl, insisted on giving and receiving love, even by those who didn't know how.

Dr. Lewis had offered tips about Boundary Setting 101. Restaurants had a time limit. He postulated that people like my parents would behave better in public settings. I decided to be an observer today. No reactions. No facial grimaces. No *audible* sighs.

My mother beckoned the busy waitress with a frenetic wave. She seemed slighted when the young woman turned the other way. Nobody ignored Roberta.

"Excuse me! You, yes, you, Amanda. Come here please."

The poor gal looked frazzled as she smoothed her stained apron. She left the customers with whom she was conversing. "Yes? Did I get something wrong?" She flipped the pad to a fresh page.

"Not exactly. We are regulars here, you know. I guess you're filling in for Deb today. I like my coffee hot. This is lukewarm. Bring me a new one," Roberta scoffed.

"I apologize. I'll be right back." Amanda scurried away like a bewildered chipmunk. She dropped the tray on her way to the kitchen. Ben kicked my foot. I raised an eyebrow.

"Joy, that's enough. Why do you heap sugar onto your grits? It's fattening, and your teeth will rot," Dr. Curt snarled.

Here we go.

"Dad, it's fine with us. Tell me about your weekend. Did you like the movie last night?" I straightened the bow in Joy's hair. Victory. I calmly stood up for my girl. *Check.* Redirected my father. *Check.*

"It was utterly absurd. How such nonsense becomes a blockbuster is beyond my comprehension." He stirred cream into his coffee. "I went to appease your mother."

Roberta turned her torso toward him, then fluffed her already poufy hair. "Isn't your father such a wonderful husband? The things he does for me, for us, for everyone."

You should only know. The benefit to their preordering schtick was a quicker meal. Less time meant less room for belittling. A silver lining. Ben chewed on the last bite of his sesame bagel. I handed Julian a napkin to wipe the remaining cream cheese off the tip of his nose. A flimsy paper flitted to the table.

"Can anyone read this? What's the total?" Ben said, after he waited a polite amount of time to see if his in-laws, just this once, would pick up the check.

Nope. They preferred to tell stories about their own parents' generosity while waiting to be treated. Ben walked to the cash register, and I jumped up to join him.

"They are so cheap, babe. When we go out with my parents, they won't let me pay unless I do it in advance," he groaned.

I rested my head on the space between his shoulder blades. "I appreciate you. Every ounce of you." How could I tell Ben about what my father had done? He'd hate him even more. Ben draped his arm around me, and we headed back to the table. I wished I could activate an invisible funnel cloud to carry me away.

"Amanda, Deb gives us extra rolls and Danish to take home. And no, she does not charge us." My mother's voice rose above the hum of other customers.

Another mental note: discuss the entitlement crap with Dr. Lewis. Obnoxious. Yuck. Gross.

My father, not as thrifty as Roberta, loved to dine out. Distracted as usual, he ignored the kids while tapping on his cell phone. But this time, Julian noticed.

"Caca, why do you use your phone during a meal? Daddy said we aren't allowed to use anything that turns on when we are eating. He and Mommy say it is rude," he stated with such sweet innocence.

I nearly projectiled the last bite of my omelet.

"I am an adult, Julian. I may do as I please. Your parents are teaching you well. Children shouldn't have any technology as far as I'm concerned. So, it ought not to be an issue." He glared across the table at me.

Pushing my fingertips into my lap, I stared back at my father.

"Well, in our home, it's a rule so we can show respect for everyone."

A new waitress came to clear the plates. I bet Amanda had handed in her resignation.

★ ★ ★

With a few minutes left before the bell, the kids would be in the car soon. Jack and I hadn't connected in a while. I tried him on a whim. I'm a planner. My brother? Not so much.

"Hey, Sista," Jack hooted, his baritone warmth spreading the smile on my face. "Please don't tell me you're calling because Mom finally told Dad she's a lipstick lesbian?"

I howled. "How do you come up with these lines? I still think you should consider stand-up comedy. I'll be your agent. No charge." A rare moment, I was the caboose of the long carpool lane. The extra time was a gift.

"So…"

"Yes?"

"You're still grappling with it, huh? I mean, yeah, it sucks. It's insane. But I still think it is unquestionably true." Jack already knew why I'd called.

I paused, tying the ends of my hair into knots and watching them unravel. A metaphor for my life. I understood why Ruby said it was easier to deal with other people's drama than her own.

"I decided to see a new therapist. A man who is an expert in both CBT and hypnotherapy."

Jack knew both all too well. Much to our folks' dismay, those years at the conversion school had further affirmed his homosexuality. "Ally, you know I speak to you straight. I mean, candidly, with sparkles of sarcasm," Jack added.

I gripped the phone tighter.

"I am fucking ecstatic you've chosen a different direction. Lilly seems to be a love, but maybe you've stagnated. And more important, as you've taught me, growth is uncomfortable. I'm wondering what else may come up in those sessions." Jack's voice lowered with an undercurrent of foreboding. My brother could swear and utilize multi-syllabic words in the same conversation—both with equal proficiency.

"Thanks, and what do you mean?" I asked warily.

"Nothing. A hunch, I suppose."

"My kids are next in line. You're literally off the hook. Love you mucho." I hung up and sighed. Joy's usually perky, effervescent demeanor seemed dulled. Julian didn't notice. He nearly banged his head on the corner of the door, totally engrossed in a book.

"Honey, you okay?" I asked. No answer. "Joy? You're awfully quiet. Does something hurt, sweetheart?" I tugged on my lower lip. I heard a slight whimper and instinctually glanced in the rearview mirror.

"Want to talk privately when we get home?"

"Yes, please, Mommy," Joy whispered.

We made it a few steps into the garage. Without warning, Joy spewed chunks of undigested peanut butter and jelly. Before the reprise, I grabbed Joy, held her backward, and galloped toward the toilet. *Don't gag. I can't let her feel my fear. You've got this. Breathe, Momma.* I planted my rear on the cool tile while Joy planted hers on the commode.

"I'm fine now, Mommy. I hope you're not mad at me," Joy said, wide-eyed with fear.

"Oh, sweet girl, no. Why would you think that?"

"I couldn't make it here in time. I made a mess." She wiped the tears from her eyes. I leaned toward her, slowly smoothing her tangled locks. "When I threw up once at Beta's house, Caca and Beta yelled at me."

"What?" I tried to hide my shock.

"Don't tell them. Please. Especially Caca. I am scared he'll get really upset." I brought Joy closer to my chest. "And I feel better now. I think Beta is right. You know how she says, 'little mean girls turn into bigger meanies'? My tummy hurt because Tammy wouldn't sit with me at lunch. I was all alone." Her typically chipper voice sounded somber and dejected.

What the actual? Terrific, Mom. Such a healthy message to send your grandchild. Guess I should be relieved she didn't use the "b" word like she did when I was a kid; this modified version was slightly more palatable. Time to decontaminate my innocent kiddo. I squirted the last bit of foamy soap from the dispenser.

"Sweetie, everyone has off days. Tammy's been your best friend since kindergarten. I know you will work it out." We scrubbed our hands together.

How I wished washing away the hidden hurt would be this easy. For both of us.

I wrote in my journal until my hand went numb. Iridescent butterflies adorned the cover. The unlined, natural fiber paper encouraged me to let go. Sometimes I made lists. Other times I doodled. Buried relics released as I scribbled, excavating my mind onto the pages. I needed deep rest to process the connections that pinged back and forth like a pinball machine. And I had a feeling my next session with Dr. Lewis would be epic.

CHAPTER
SIXTY-EIGHT

"Come in, Ally. How are you doing?" Dr. Lewis stepped aside and smiled. Such a short question that today required a requiem of a response.

"Well, I'm a lot of things. I can't believe it has only been a month since we've been working together. I'm proud that I stood up to my parents a few times. Also dodged a few curve balls. I'm not sure that's the right analogy because sports metaphors evade me," I said. "Anyway, I'd like to read you something." Dr. Lewis's lips released a soothing sound as his jaw slackened, signaling for me to continue. My throat narrowed as my body rewound, replayed, and responded. I didn't pause until I finished reading the entire journal entry.

"I'm realizing such painful parallels to my own childhood. It's not that I never noticed before, but I suppose rose-colored glasses are permanently affixed to my face. Before meeting with you, I figured this was part of my overall outlook." I told Dr. Lewis about asking Roberta to go to therapy with me years ago. My mother's reply was the same each time: "We don't need to go—everything's perfect. You overanalyze everything, Allegra."

"I'm remembering that even when I had cancer, a miscarriage, gosh, so much, Dr. Lewis, my mother repeatedly said, 'It could be worse.' My dad showed up for me, at least for medical procedures. The ranting and raging I forgave—maybe he didn't know any better."

I froze, wondering if I had shared too much, and deliberated about when to show the letter and photo to Dr. Lewis. I ran the tip of my tongue over my teeth. They felt like Chiclets, numb and not attached to my gums.

"She's right in some regards, you know. Both my parents lost family and friends at young ages. Instead, I've chosen to focus on the rainbows rather than the storms preceding them." I closed the journal and placed my hands on top of it.

"Ally, tell me what you are feeling in this moment. Not five minutes ago. Not yesterday. Right now," Dr. Lewis prompted, leaning back in his seat.

I unclasped the mother-of-pearl clip in my thick hair. Tendrils escaped, cascading around my face.

"I am petrified, to be honest," I answered, coughing on my own saliva. "Forgive this analogy, but it's like I just stripped in front of you. And there's much more. Stuff that I haven't even told my husband." I didn't realize I'd been fiddling with the clip until a piece cracked and landed right on Dr. Lewis's desk.

"You can trust me. Speaking of trust, I'm sensing there's something that needs to be explored there." Dr. Lewis laced his hands behind his neck. "How do you feel about spending the last portion of our session doing a bit of hypnosis?"

I inhaled for four and exhaled for seven.

"I had a cancellation, so if we run over, it's not a problem at all. Many of my patients are more at ease when in this relaxed state," he said.

I'd promised myself to try new approaches. Wasn't that what brought me here in the first place? "Yes. Please give me a moment to center myself." My fingers and toes tingled as I wiggled them. The rest of my body felt sluggish, and I shivered because the room was freezing. Then I let go, trusting Dr. Lewis and listening to the calming cadence of his voice.

After an indeterminate amount of time, I heard him say, "Start to bring yourself back to the room, to the present. When you feel ready, open your eyes. I dimmed the lights, so take your time. No rush." His methodical, measured words waltzed in a predictable pattern.

"That was incredible. I remember most of what you said. Did I fall asleep?" I slowly propped myself up on my elbows.

"You drifted in and out of dimensions. And you seemed thoroughly relaxed. Thank you for trusting me," Dr. Lewis said.

"So? Did you get all the answers? Let me guess—you will discharge me today," I joked, stifling a yawn.

Dr. Lewis let out a hearty chuckle, his laugh lines deepening. "Keep that sense of humor, Ally. It's best if we go over what I heard and observed next week. For now, remember to continue reinforcing those boundaries. Saying no to someone else means saying yes to yourself."

CHAPTER SIXTY-NINE

ALLEGRA' 23

I hoped the rabbi wouldn't light a match near my hair—it might ignite. "Mom, please, it's fine. We've been curling, primping, and spraying for nearly two hours." I looked at Marcus, wishing he'd get the hint. He shrugged his shoulders and smoothed my blunt-cut bangs with his hand.

"Every strand must be perfect, Allegra. Trust me. You'll regret it one day when you look at pictures if it's not." My mother continued admiring herself in the mirror. She told the make-up artist to retouch her recently plucked eyebrows.

"*Marcus. Por favor, necesito un minuto sin mi madre,*" I said quietly.

Consumed with caking a third coat of concealer on her face, Roberta didn't hear me. Not that she'd understand it, anyway. I exhaled when she left the room. I'd hold my Benito soon. I didn't care about fashioning the latest bridal look or layering more shimmery shadow on my eyelids. We hadn't seen each other in forty-eight hours. And I couldn't wait one more second to begin our lives together.

Roberta handed Marcus the box of bobby pins he'd requested. With my pearl and crystal comb placed comfortably, he attached the organza veil. In seconds I'd transformed into a bride.

As we'd planned, my soon-to-be husband waited for me in the room next door. I tapped his shoulder, and the photographer snapped shots as Ben saw me in my wedding dress for the first time. Even without those pictures, I'd never forget his expression, a mix of dewy desire and misty eyes. And above all, love.

We signed the *ketubah*, signifying the official marriage of two souls, even before the ceremony. We'd designed an original, which included Shabbat candles, two doves, and our vows written in Hebrew on a lavender and blue watercolor background. Ben's lips lingered on mine, and the rabbi smiled at us. He'd known me my whole life. Ben and I parted, and our bridal party took their positions.

We'd chosen an instrumental version of the theme song from *St. Elmo's Fire* for the entrance of our bridesmaids and groomsmen. Ruby and my college roommate cried; they understood the song's meaning at the deepest level. The women wore iridescent indigo dresses and held ivory bouquets; the men wore matching ties. My dress, satin with capped sleeves and a beaded bodice, was accompanied by an untraditional lilac, rose, and deep purple orchid bouquet I'd designed. These teeny details and others broke the constraints of my childhood.

I approached the *chuppah*, the canopy with four posts under which we'd unite as husband and wife. Ben's eyes glistened, and his cheeks flushed. My father and mother, holding each of my arms, walked me toward my love. Roberta sat down in the front row. My maid of honor straightened the bottom of my dress as my father and I ascended the steps, bringing me to *mi amor*.

Dr. Curt lifted my veil, kissed my cheek, and patted Ben's back. A vision of us sitting together on the piano bench when I was a child flashed in my mind. He'd done the same the times I'd nailed a note. Then my father uttered to Ben, "She's yours now. You can't give her back."

CHAPTER SEVENTY

Maybe my mother was right. Maybe I did suffer from occasional analysis paralysis. I decided I needed a bit of self-care, a rarity for me. Any free time I had was usually reserved for my marriage, kids, and catching up with friends. The facial I'd booked for Saturday couldn't come soon enough. Homework, sports, doctor appointments, and music lessons—I schlepped Joy and Julian from one city to another, answering client calls in between. Brief showers and necessary hygiene like brushing my teeth were the extent of my weekday self-care.

An austere, no-nonsense Austrian woman named Maria taught Joy piano and theory. Her personality was so similar to my voice teacher at camp. To be on time meant you were late. To be adequate meant unprepared. And this teacher's expectations surpassed those of any I had experienced in South Florida. Other than my father's.

Maria was increasingly dissatisfied with Joy practicing on our home keyboard. My excuse: it sufficed because Joy was young and had no intention of becoming a concert pianist. Apparently, this reason proved to have an expiration date. Maria hemmed and hawed. Finally, she insisted if we didn't purchase a proper piano, she'd remove Joy from her roster.

This chiding from Maria prompted a guest appearance by Ms. Mida in my mind. My father desired the best. Anything less, in his esteemed opinion, did not warrant his attention, time, or money. Unfortunately, Maria—much like Ms. Mida—had reached her breaking point. And for other reasons, I did as well.

I hoped the rare moment of solitude would assuage me. Practical, too, because though I loved squeezing my own pores, it was best left to the dexterous hands of a professional. This blissful hour would be calming and refreshing—if I could refrain from chitchatting with the aesthetician. That would be tough. Somehow strangers became friends in most areas of my life. It occurred to me that boundaries shouldn't only apply to my parents.

So, an opportunity to practice. Bummer my insurance wouldn't cover facials or retail therapy. Changing from my work-out clothes to the luxurious robe instantly relaxed my body. Sliced cucumbers and fresh lemons floated atop the ice cubes in the glass pitcher. Hibiscus and chamomile tea bags rested in an oblong teak dish. Mini glass jars of local orange-blossom honey adorned the frosted glass table. Clear containers displayed a mix of dates, shaved coconut, and granola. I lounged on a seafoam green chair right by the rock wall and listened to the comforting sound of trickling water. Low tide and placid, the Atlantic Ocean was a backdrop for this serene space. I could skip the facial and stay right there.

Just as I'd settled myself, I heard my name, and a tall woman guided me down a hallway. Eucalyptus and lavender mist permeated the massage room. The oatmeal mask smelled so delicious I wanted to lick it right off my chin. I drifted in and out of consciousness. The heated mat molded to the back of my body. As the facialist's nimble hands roamed over my cheekbones, my thoughts meandered too. My complexion became clearer along with my mind.

Joy and my father both loved art and music. I'd hoped this would connect them in some way. Instead, he criticized her posture and technique. But that wasn't the worst of it. He also chastised me.

"A keyboard for my granddaughter? I taught you better, Allegra. This is preposterous. It's clearly not a money issue. A piano would look perfect in the empty corner of your living room," Dr. Curt had said on more than one occasion.

Ben became frustrated with the unsolicited commentary. He couldn't stand that his father-in-law, who took but never gave, would spend our money. One day, he had a brilliant idea. Leave it to my honey to devise a logical, thoughtful solution.

"You know, instead of your father telling us what to do, why doesn't he give us his baby grand? It sits in their house collecting dust," Ben said.

True. Plus, one would think gifting the precise instrument upon which two generations had played would become a meaningful heirloom. After months of Ben's encouragement, I finally broached the topic. I followed my father's lead, waiting until he inevitably brought it up. Again. Which he did after sharing about a piece he'd once mastered. I shuddered, thinking of him sitting on the bench.

"D-d-d-dad, we love your idea about a piano. Wouldn't it be so special if the kids learned on yours? Julian is starting lessons next year," I said.

"Allegra." He widened his stance. "That is an immeasurably valuable instrument. You'll have it when we die. Besides, it's not like you and Ben cannot afford to buy one," Dr. Curt countered. I swiftly changed the subject.

Later at home, after downing a glass of cold hibiscus tea, I knocked on my husband's office door and gave him the update. He slammed his laptop shut.

"What the hell! Are you serious? You'd think he'd be thrilled to give it to us while they are still alive. And there he goes again with the fiscal assumptions. I know how much that piano means to you; why don't you offer to buy it?" Ben suggested.

I scratched my scalp. A wet sensation seeped under my fingernails. "I can't do that. Tell me you are joking," I replied, wiping the blood from my fingertips. My head tilted as I waited for Ben's reaction. "Oh my gosh. You are totally serious."

"Yes. I sure am."

I hugged him, trying to tame my tongue. "Honey. I need to tell you…" I couldn't do it.

So instead of saying what must be said, I buried my head into his chest. Ben still didn't know about the piano and its bench buddy—and what it concealed. But how to tell him? When? What would he say? And what if he wouldn't let the kids see their grandfather again?

Telling the love of my life, my best friend, my everything, would make it real.

CHAPTER
SEVENTY-ONE

Though I rarely did family counseling, this mother-daughter referral from one of my esteemed colleagues seemed divinely guided. My first professional mentor taught me certain principles, an integration of modern mindfulness and traditional therapy, one of which was finding other ways of connecting rather than physical touch.

Today was the exception.

I'd worked separately and now together with them. An only child, Mia had lost her beloved father suddenly. Her mother, Raquel, sprang into action, procuring a full-time job at a clothing store, though she hadn't worked in years. As was often the case, emotions—especially grief—that had been repressed reared their heads like a jack-in-the-box. On the brink of sinking into a marsh of melancholy, Raquel dragged herself out of bed one day to come to my office. Over the course of our sessions, the pale, emaciated ghost of a woman had strengthened into a resilient soul.

Raquel, with seven-year-old Mia behind her, looked frightened and frail. I fought to maintain my composure. The change was drastic.

"Come in, you two!" I hoped my peppy tone would uplift her.

"Can we speak first?" Raquel raised an eyebrow. "Honey, can you please sit in the waiting room for a few minutes? I'd love it if you'd make me one of your beautiful drawings." She hugged Mia, her downtrodden eyes meeting mine. I motioned to the rainbow-hued beanbag and shut the door. Before I said a word, Raquel bent over, clutched her stomach, and sobbed.

My next move surprised me. I sat on the cushy rug right next to her, sunlight streaming from the transom window, and hugged Raquel until her tears ceased.

"I can't do this anymore. I have nothing left." Her chest heaved. "No matter what I do, she lays into me. If I organize the clothes as told, it's not good enough. She criticizes me in front of my employees. How can I expect them to respect me if I'm constantly undermined by her rants and unannounced visits? I know she owns the shop. I get it. But this doesn't seem right." Raquel dried her eyes with the back of her hand.

The ornery boss had started to sound more like a sociopath than simply a tough cookie. Raquel kept talking. Apparently, this dreadful woman had been spreading lies about her to the other managers. She also blamed Raquel for decreases in sales, even though the team consisted of twenty managers. Even worse, the owner invented tasks, taunted Raquel for not completing them, and made her feel like she was crazy. One of Raquel's strengths was her organizational skills. In fact, as she grieved the loss of her husband, Raquel overcompensated by developing rigid schedules and productive, yet fun, activities. She and Mia barely had a second of downtime.

Many of our recent sessions were focused on art therapy and meditation to alleviate Mia's recurrent nightmares. This was so like Raquel to divert the focus from herself. Momma bear. Taking it for the team. Why hadn't I seen the signs sooner?

"Raquel, you deserve better. And I need to remind you about self-care and that *you* matter." I handed her another tissue. "Goodness, I had no idea it had gotten this bad. The last you shared, your boss was moody and demanding, but what you're describing is gaslighting. She sounds like a full-blown narcissist."

Breaking one of my own self-imposed rules, I proceeded to tell Raquel about the woman for whom I'd worked. As a fledgling therapist, I hadn't known any differently. I fervently wanted to work for and learn from this guru. I was her favorite clinician until I asked about unethical billing; she'd submitted double time to insurance companies for single sessions.

I crisscrossed my legs and pressed into my knees. "From that day forward, my boss acted as if I didn't exist. Refused to speak to me. Didn't make eye contact. I had to pull over and use the same coffee shop restroom on the way to the office because the tension made me physically ill."

While sipping tepid mint tea, I realized it'd been ages since I'd thought about that experience. Even speaking about it made my stomach spasm. Amazing how the body remembered.

Raquel shifted in the beanbag and unwrapped a butterscotch. "But I need the money. And Mia does not know; she's in school all day and aftercare. I get myself together, put on my big girl panties, and all is well in the evening," Raquel said feebly, shrugging her small shoulders. A faint tap interrupted my reply.

"Can I please come in, Mommy? I finished my picture." Mia's long braids bounced on her backside as she trotted into the room like a pony. She proudly presented the nine-by-twelve piece of pale pink construction paper.

I handed Raquel the box of tissues and steadied myself.

"Let's give Mom a minute. Why don't you come sit on the couch with me? I'd love for you to tell me about your artwork." I hoped Mia would oblige.

"But I'm not an artist, Ms. Ally. You see that person?" She pointed to a cloud. "That's Daddy watching over us. Me and Mommy live in the rainbow, and Daddy colors it so it protects us from the sky. Why is Mommy crying?"

I held out my upturned hand. Mia placed the paper delicately on it. Then she straightened the satin bows in her hair.

"You are an artist. We all have creativity within us if our hearts are open to receiving inspiration. Before we talk, why don't you sign and date this beautiful drawing?" I offered her a ballpoint pen.

Her almond-shaped, emerald eyes widened to ovals. She dropped to her knees and straightened her little slumped back. Mia wrote her name in the lower corner of the paper. With a sunny smile, she handed it back to me. Raquel edged over to us, wiping the remaining mascara from under her eyes.

I facilitated a nurturing, honest conversation between mother and daughter. I explained how art can sometimes be interpreted by the viewer differently than what the artist intended, and that is the beauty of it all. Then I quietly observed the girls, one a bud, one a blossom, and soaked it in.

I told Raquel we would schedule a follow-up, an adult-only phone session. I knew grief often clouded judgment—this toxic work environment was depleting Raquel's reserves. And Mia needed her mother.

After they were gone, I grabbed my car keys and left the office. Before I knew it, I'd pulled into a spot in front of the music store. They'd rearranged the sections. But the baby grands were assembled in the exact same space. A white Baldwin beckoned, and I sat on the plush, modern bench.

"May I answer any questions, ma'am?"

I whipped my head around. That voice sounded vaguely familiar.

"Do you remember me? I came here with my father years ago. The baby—I was pregnant the last time I was here—is now almost eleven years old," I said, flabbergasted that the same man stood before me.

"I remember your father. Quite discerning and knowledgeable. Did you ever purchase a piano?"

This could not be a coincidence. Maybe I'd take lessons again. "No. Which one do you recommend? And kindly show me the appropriate benches for all ages and sizes."

My joints ached that night, which was strange because I hadn't exercised yet this week. I told Ben that perhaps I was fighting a bug. He surprised me by putting the kids to bed. While he did that, I wrote in my journal, and my pulse quickened. A page tore as I pressed harder, writing zealously. Something about Raquel's situation had struck a chord. An archetype, beyond narcissism, nagged at me.

A disorder about which I hadn't read since grad school popped into my mind. Sociopath. That word reverberated over and over. When I felt this type of nudge, I followed it like the Tin Man skipping on the Yellow Brick Road to the Emerald City.

Ben worked his magic. The kids didn't tag team him with their typical delay tactics, so he came back earlier than I expected and leaned over my shoulder.

"Sociopaths? I thought you were in here resting, babe." He ran his hands through his hair. "This doesn't seem like a bedtime story. Why don't you give that hamster wheel of yours the night off?" He grabbed the book, closed it, and locked the door. Then he dropped his navy joggers on his way to the bathroom. Water whooshed like white noise from the faucet. "Come in here," he shouted.

Bossy. But I loved it. Wowza. How could I say no to that? I giggled at the sight of Ben, buck naked, head back, legs outstretched in our bathtub.

"Join me." He ran his tongue across his gorgeous straight teeth. He wasn't usually spontaneous. Then again, ever since my staycation with Ruby, he'd stunned me more than once. I stripped and did as I was told. The warm water and safety of his arms soothed me. With his firm thumbs, he rubbed the base of my neck and shoulders.

"Honey, I can't tell you how much this means to me, you showing up. I know you're on a big deadline. I think something must've triggered me." I exhaled into him. "I need to tell you—" This secret, the letter, couldn't stay inside me much longer. But how could I ruin our evening? I shut my mouth and started over. "Being with you is a salve for my soul. I'd love to—"

"I know, I know. Raincheck?"

"Hell, yes," I said, lying back into his sturdy chest.

I continued to ignore their calls and texts. Dr. Lewis suggested subtle distancing, but it was tough. Not with Dr. Curt because he rarely reached out unless there was an emergency. Or a pseudo one inflamed with drama and doom. Roberta detested anyone ignoring her. Plausible excuses were getting increasingly difficult to invent.

One strategy I'd implemented, which seemed to work because my mother was so self-absorbed, was that I would call only when there was a built-in boundary. On my way to the office or right before picking up the kids. The best time? When Roberta herself was at work. She and Dr. Curt defined themselves by their own praise and perception of success. So even if she picked up the phone, the call inevitably ended quickly because someone or something took precedence over her own daughter.

But I found myself increasingly agitated with being treated like week-old leftovers.

Tossed aside. Tolerated at best. And the secret, a simmer at first, became a rapid boil. I didn't know how much longer I could keep it from Ben. Or from my own mother, for that matter. Did my mother know her honorable husband had knocked up his resident? There was only one way to find out.

CHAPTER
SEVENTY-TWO

ALLEGRA' 9

My father demanded the best. Of himself, his children, his entire existence. Anyone or anything he determined was flawed didn't deserve his time or money. He'd hand-picked my piano teacher, a graduate of Juilliard and reportedly preeminent in Florida.

Ms. Mida knew her worth and wasn't shy about sharing it.

"Well, Roberta, if Allegra must end early—again—I cannot continue to hold her place. You know I have a rather lengthy waiting list," she said, an exasperated exhale blowing Bach's minuet right off the music stand.

I stiffened as if I'd developed dowels that affixed my rear to the antique bench. I both admired and feared Ms. Mida. But it made my father happy to hear me practicing on his precious, prized piano. It was one of the few times I felt heard, both literally and viscerally. How could my mother take this from me?

"My husband will be rather displeased. This is absurd; you know the only reason we are pausing lessons is that she's going to Camp Intermezzo in Michigan for the summer," Roberta countered.

Ms. Mida respected my sanctuary in the woods. I was counting the days until I'd see Ruby and other friends. She'd recommended it to her finest students. But my piano teacher wouldn't relent.

"Fine. Then this will be Allegra's last lesson." Roberta pulled out her checkbook, scribbled onto it, and shoved it under Ms. Mida's flaring nostrils. Then she zipped her leather tote and threw it onto her shoulder. My father didn't say a word when we got home; there was no standing ovation. We left that day and never returned. I wondered how life might've been different if I'd continued with Ms. Mida.

CHAPTER SEVENTY-THREE

Mom. Please give me a few dates you're available. Lunch works best. I'd love to meet just us. Hope you're having a great day. P.S. My treat.

I hit "send" before losing my nerve. If I catered to Roberta, meaning on her terms and offering a free meal, she'd be more likely to say yes. My phone dinged almost immediately. Not surprising, as Roberta was one of the most compulsive people I ever knew. Fascinating how we become like our parents or choose the opposite.

What a lovely idea, Allegra. Why don't we meet at the cafe in Bal Harbour on Friday?

Of course, she picked an extravagant place. It'd be the cheapest deli in town if roles were reversed. But this was safer for me. I could make an emergency exit if necessary. Yes. An outdoor, elegant establishment. Such fond memories of my younger years there. My father used to take me for key lime pie on daddy-daughter dates. One of the few times I'd eat dessert in front of him. But I couldn't do it. Too tender, too painful.

Friday works for me as well. I'd prefer to go somewhere else, though, and I need to pick up the kids after. Let's meet at Smith and Wollensky instead.

Ding. This time I held a handful of files and couldn't respond. *Ding. Ding. Ding.* She persisted. Resending the message three times. Like Pavlov's pup responding to the bell, I caved and glanced at my phone.

> *I still do not understand why you don't have live-in help. Such a waste of time and energy taking your kids to and from school. That's what your father always told me; he is correct. See you Friday at 12:30. Mom*

★ ★ ★

My hair nearly broke as I twisted it into another knot. I'd normally call Ben, thinking aloud and anticipating the conversation. Cranking up the AC didn't dry the perspiration on my upper lip. Crazy now that I thought about it. Meeting with my mother, alone, for a meal. It required the same preparation as rehearsing for a camp choir performance. Or prepping for a colonoscopy. Either scenario necessitated planning and a strong mindset.

I blasted eighties rock music and turned up the volume, determined to rally the courage needed for this conversation. Some of my faves, like Def Leppard, Bon Jovi, and Prince kept me company.

I'd intentionally reserved a corner table. Air kiss, air kiss. After a robotic greeting, my mother sat across from me. I preferred a booth but also knew Roberta would kvetch about the "unbearable size of the seats." Predictable as ever, she ordered a Greek salad with grilled chicken, no olives or onions, and dressing on the side. I told the waitress to please double the order, again aiming to avoid potential pitfalls. Everything was easier that way.

I listened as my mother gossiped about her friend's new husband. Roberta insisted this man wasn't good enough because he, unlike Dr. Curt, didn't have a medical degree. He was a mere radiology technician, after all. I continued to feign interest as she gabbed about her work and other superficial subjects.

After twenty-two minutes, I excused myself to use the restroom. Was I invisible? Had I become an apparition? I could have sworn that was me staring back in this mirror. And my mother was totally clueless. Time to head back and do this.

The scrumptious smell of lobster, filet mignon, and cappuccinos wafted from tables. With purposeful steps, I ambled to the corner. My mother gave me the "wait a minute and don't interrupt me" finger. More fucking hypocrisy. She and my father judged the kids for even owning a phone. Yet she rudely used it in the middle of an upscale restaurant?

I fought the urge to flick her off with a different digit.

I waited. And waited. I contemplated ordering myself a heavy pour of Sauvignon Blanc.

Maybe straight tequila with ice. She wouldn't even notice. The food finally arrived, and my mother ended her call. Priorities.

"Mom, I need to speak with you about something serious. I'm okay. Everyone is fine." I didn't blink. "And it is important that you listen. This will be a discussion; I promise we'll talk it through. But I need to share a bit before you respond, and I'd appreciate your full attention." Like that was even possible for her without a frontal lobotomy.

Roberta put down the fork, and I touched her hand. I recounted the day, months ago, when I'd discovered the letter from Dot. I articulated every word and paused purposefully so

Roberta could process this shattering news. This must've been beyond horrifying for my mother to hear.

Roberta listened or appeared to do so. She tried to interrupt, but I did not allow it. I kept speaking.

"It means the world to me that you've remained calm, Mom. I realize this news must be shocking. I have questions but don't want to overwhelm you," I said, studying my mother's mascara-framed eyes. She was uncharacteristically collected. Weird. Like in the eye of the storm. I clamped my mouth shut.

"I know."

I blinked. I itched the inside of my ear. Cocked my head like a curious Goldendoodle. "You know what?"

Roberta kept going. "I know about the child. I did not know about this letter. Such a shame, too, that Dot couldn't get over it. It's not like your father did this on purpose, you know." She reached into her handbag, extracted a bottle of lotion, and squirted a drop onto her palms, rubbing them together.

"Raising this kid would have ruined our future and the life we created," she said, emotionless, as if talking about a blurb she'd read in the paper. Then she picked up the fork and stabbed a piece of romaine lettuce.

"I don't know what to say." I hid my trembling hands under the marble table.

"Well, there isn't anything to discuss. We will never speak of this again. And your father...oh, how it would destroy him if he found out that you know. He loves his little girl. What's in the past should stay there." She sliced the chicken and popped a piece into her mouth.

Was now a good time to tell her Jack had read the letter too? Before I could respond, Roberta kept talking between bites of crunchy cucumbers.

"If anyone heard about this little mistake, your father's career and stellar reputation would be ruined. Not a word about this to anyone, Allegra. Ever. Are we clear?"

Crystal clear. I'd never be able to unsee or unhear what was revealed. It was as if I'd been transported to an alternate universe, but this was real. I downed a third glass of water. Nothing could dilute the deranged interaction I had experienced.

"Mom, thank you for your honesty. It's a lot to digest. I am at a loss for words, which you know is a rare occurrence. One thing is for sure: I appreciate you confirming that Jack and I have a half-brother. To be frank, I thought it couldn't be true," I confessed. "And who is Dot, anyway?"

Roberta also confirmed what Jack had deduced. Dot, a first-year resident, had been supervised by my father, the attending physician in the department. As I integrated the information, I visualized the twisted strands of a double helix. Unaware until this moment, now a mother and wife in my late thirties, how deeply codependent Roberta and Dr. Curt were. Crazy I never realized it until today.

A child had been born. And he wasn't wanted. The deception. The lies. The lack of remorse. My father had shredded what I thought was our eternal bond. Who was this monster?

Roberta asked me for singles at the valet, assuming I'd pay for the parking. While we waited, she asked to see Joy and Julian, citing that her usual Sunday lunch club had canceled, so she had an opening in her calendar.

My mother rarely offered to take the kids, but for some reason she did today. On a whim, I agreed. Ben and I needed alone time. Now more than ever.

CHAPTER
SEVENTY-FOUR

Ben held my hand as we strolled on the boardwalk and watched the world wake up.

Sizzling orange and fuchsia rays reached across the Atlantic Ocean, the water a serene, moving mirror that lapped toward the shore. Frothy waves made rippling marks on the sand.

I wanted to tell him. I needed to tell him. It was killing me—both the waiting and the shame. But I'd wait until processing it all with Dr. Lewis on Monday.

My phone buzzed, bolting me back to the present. Ugh. Of course. Something had come up and my mother wanted to bring the kids home early. I grimaced. "Honey, we need to get going."

"Why? I thought we were also grabbing a bite. The kids are gone until one." Ben pulled the baseball cap over his wind-blown hair.

I rolled my eyes and wished it were possible to take the surf home with me.

"Well, that was the plan. Supposedly my dad has an emergency at the hospital. And you know my mom finds watching two kids exhausting," I said, my chin puckering.

Maybe it was a blessing. Saved by a text. For the moment, anyway. Timing can be a vaccine. As it turned out, the kids' earlier-than-expected arrival prevented them from further poisoning.

"Mommy, why does Beta always watch the news or talk on the phone when we're over? She ignores us," Joy asked when we got back home.

I swirled the suds of dish soap in the stainless-steel sink. A few bubbles floated above me. Then I dried my hands on the plum and sage plaid towel. Julian nodded, agreeing with his perceptive younger sister. "And we don't get to go over there a lot. We clean up without Caca or Beta even asking. It scares me when Caca screams."

Why did he look nervous? My alarm bells were blaring.

"I don't feel safe there, Mommy. It's why I don't like to sleep over. When I have nightmares, they get upset if I ask for a hug. Besides, their door is always locked," Joy added.

Between the lunch with my mother last week and rapid-fire revelations, it was almost too much to take. I spun the amethyst beads on my left wrist. Feeling a bit lightheaded, I stepped toward the sofa for support. Then I invited the kids to join me on the couch. I wanted to be fully present for them, now and forever. They needed to feel heard. And never invalidated. Their feelings mattered. They mattered. Another promise I'd made to myself the second I knew I was pregnant. And given how I'd begun to awaken, to notice and understand the depth of my own childhood, this felt more important than ever, almost urgent. I asked them to repeat what they had said. Maybe they were exaggerating?

Instead, the kids slowly shared more. Caca had locked them out of the house. Beta told them stories about me and Uncle Jack, most of which were embellished or inaccurate. Where was

Ben? He needed to hear this right outta the mouths of our babes. I heard a click. A key in the door. Timing truly was everything.

"Daddy!"

Ben scooped Joy into his sturdy arms, twirling her, as she loved to watch her pleated school uniform skirt swoosh like a parachute.

"Babe, come sit with us. The kids were sharing a few things," I implored my distracted husband, hoping his sometimes-slumbering internal sensor would activate. *I know you want to open the mail and check your burgeoning inbox. I need you present for me, for all of us,* I tried to tell him telepathically. By some miracle, Ben had left his phone and leather briefcase in the trunk.

"Where were we, Julian and Joy? Tell Daddy what you started to say," I said.

The seal broke, and the kids poured the contents of their vacuum-packed container of incidents all over us. At ten and almost thirteen years old, Joy and Julian had blossomed into insightful, empathetic preteens. ("Tweens," as Joy had recently corrected me.) They interrupted each other, finishing thoughts and filling in details.

My husband had noticed the way Dr. Curt and Roberta treated them—and me. But hearing our kids recount times when they were alone with their grandparents seemed to throttle him. I thought about the night when Julian went to his first sleepover party. It wasn't too long ago. Had I known then what I knew now, no chance Joy would've been there.

Ben had asked my mother if Joy could spend the afternoon and evening, and he offered to drop her off. Roberta had agreed to bring her home. Only one kid—who, by the way, was polite and easygoing. Neither grandparent worked the following day. Joy texted us, within a few hours of being at their house, that the promised "just the three of them" dinner date she'd been so excited about was canceled. Why? Caca had a late lunch and therefore was not hungry.

But that wasn't the worst of it.

The texts had blown up both of our phones. All my hubby wanted was a romantic evening with me. We'd nearly polished off a bottle of our favorite Cabernet.

When Joy wrote, "*Beta said she's too tired to drive me home. She keeps asking me to sleep here. I want to come home. She is making me feel bad,*" Ben was baffled. We had a one-glass rule. We'd each had two that night. Not drunk. But mildly buzzed. Then confusion fermented to fury and frustration. "One night, just us. A date at home. Quiet time to chill. This is unreal." Ben peeked at the empty wine bottle and slid off his velvet slippers.

How selfish and disgusting. Our emotions surged like high tide. In the past, I would've asked Ben to handle this because I feared upsetting my folks. Boosted by atypical anger, I snatched the phone and called my mother. But I couldn't do it. One ring and I immediately hung up. Instead, what I'd normally consider cowardly, I texted both of my parents. Self-preservation also meant knowing when and how to deal with situations as they arose. After an exasperating dialogue, Roberta didn't budge. Dr. Curt ignored the entire group text.

No comment. No words. Nothing. Nada.

The Uber driver had waited in the sloped gravel driveway. I chatted with him in Spanish after seeing his flummoxed expression in the mirror. He talked about his two grown daughters—he'd dreamed of having them live here instead of in Guatemala. With compassion vibrating in his baritone voice, the driver couldn't comprehend the cruelty of "abuela and abuelo." I couldn't, either.

Unconditional love transcended language. It was universal. The kindhearted man could've been speaking in Latin or French. It didn't matter. I felt seen and heard. It both touched and disarmed me.

I didn't want to waste more of the gentle man's time or gas, so I suggested he turn off the ignition. My mother told us they'd bring Joy to the car. But we'd been waiting for thirty minutes. A dead palm frond snapped and dropped from a nearby tree. My head jerked. I spotted Joy.

My angel girl nibbled on her nails and trailed behind her Caca. Ben got out of the car to thank his father-in-law. Then my father jabbed a finger at me, signaling for me to roll down the window.

"Your daughter broke Mom's phone. Now we need to go to Verizon tomorrow to buy a new one," Dr. Curt hissed.

I slid out of the backseat. "D-d-d-dad, you've got to be kidding me. Where is Mom? This entire night is insane. Do you realize we couldn't even d-d-d-drive to get our little girl? And now you berate me for her reportedly ruining Mom's phone? Perhaps both of you ought to consider spending time with your granddaughter rather than shoving an electronic babysitter in her face. All she wants is your love. That is it. She was excited to spend a few hours with you," I sputtered, finding the brakes in my mouth and screeching to a halt.

My abdomen quivered like a dog about to be beaten. This must've been how poor Keri felt, fearing the wrath of her combustive owner, Dr. Curt. My voice cracked. My torso inflamed, my body boiling despite the fall breeze.

The dark sky disguised the etchings of his face. But I saw enough. My father's gray eyes froze to a sinister steel. Thin, shriveled lips clamped shut. Legs apart and staked in the ground, a pit bull primed to pounce. But the worst part?

Utter, total silence.

I turned and clutched the door handle, about to retreat to the car.

"Your mother told me you're searching for a piano. We've reconsidered your offer. If you want it, it's yours. For twenty thousand dollars. I'll sand and revarnish the bench this weekend. That damn Keri with her endless chewing."

Joy sandwiched between us in the sedan. Ben looked over the top of her head. And mouthed to me, "I am so sorry."

Those words, that phrase, had meaning unlike any before. I thought cancer hurt. Sorry. A sorry situation. A sorry life. A word I had never heard either of my parents say. And probably never would.

CHAPTER
SEVENTY-FIVE

ALLEGRA' 12

Smoke from the sizzling steak swirled around his silvery hair. The gleaming knife sliced through the middle as liquid rushed onto the plate. Smug satisfaction spread across my father's cleanly shaven face. He craved meat as much as precision.

Ruby's mother had sent Omaha steaks the day before she arrived to visit me. How'd she know it was the perfect "Thank You for Hosting My Daughter" gift? The delivery man poked the doorbell, prompting Daddy to drop his crystal tumbler. The stench of scotch saturated the kitchen. Keri chased her stubby tail, anxiously waiting for a human to respond. Mom, furious about the ocher shards, pointed to the paper towels.

"Allegra, clean up this mess immediately. After you wipe the floor, use the Dustbuster." She pumped the salad spinner, continuing to extract water from the chopped romaine lettuce.

Our pup waited patiently, eager for a bite to drop into her drooling mouth. With one hand, I petted Keri's curly fur. With the other, I reached above her body and opened the whitewashed wood cabinet door. Mom had requested a new glass; her semi-matte lipstick had lined the rim of Daddy's, and he would be irritated.

My father smeared unsalted butter across the steamy slab. His narrow tongue repeatedly ran across his lower teeth. He ignored Mom's nagging about fat content as she nibbled on carrots. Irie had the day off. Otherwise, my father wouldn't be cooking. I both loved and hated Sundays: loved because we ate together as a family if my parents stayed home, hated because I left the table hungry. But I'd learned to deal with the pangs; it sure beat the discomfort of mealtime jibes.

"Allegra, you ate enough; you are going to gain more weight. It is truly astounding that you are still hungry." Typical lines from my parents' playbook—Ruby couldn't believe how they treated me. She insisted Midwest cows tasted better. One year for Hanukkah, Ruby had sent me a stuffed cow with rainbow udders. A few other silly gifts arrived for my birthday. On our late-night phone calls, I begged her to stop with the jokes or I'd become a vegetarian. Her twisted humor secured her a spot in our home; my parents already loved Ruby. And not only because she was thin and talented. I felt lucky to have such a loving best friend.

I cringed, hearing the crumpling sound of newspaper rolled up again.

"Bad dog!" Daddy hollered, smacking Keri's damp nose. I'd told Ruby about this, and when she said it was cruel, I defended him. He always told us dogs, like children, required discipline to behave properly. When we were younger, Jack would crouch on the ground, cowering behind Keri, and I'd sing or attempt some other distraction. Now, when Daddy smacked Keri, Jack told him to lay off and stop being a lunatic. I molded my lips into a smile, shooting Jack a "zip your mouth" glance.

But the fighting escalated. And so did my nightmares. Keri started sleeping at the end of my bed. At twelve years old, I'd grown to my full height of five feet, nine inches. Even though my twin bed was narrow, I shrank and smushed myself toward the wall so Keri could be my fortress.

CHAPTER
SEVENTY-SIX

My head drooped like an overripe coconut. I could barely lift or turn it. Flashes electrified my dream time, illuminating what I would prefer to keep in the dark.

Thankful it was Sunday, I poured my sadness into homemade blueberry pancakes. Joy's jubilance, sweet like the Vermont maple syrup, began to uplift me. I doodled with the batter, creating hearts, rainbows, and the kids' initials.

Then I treated myself to alone time in the park. Trees grounded me. Though these were palms, black olives, and oaks, they still reminded me of summers at camp. Ben bristled a bit when I told him that I'd leave my phone in the car. "Babe, I really need to disconnect on all levels. I won't be long. Promise." I gave him a peck on the cheek.

My shoelaces untied and tangled. So irritating. I nearly tripped on my way out the door. Not much had bothered me until recently. Branches crunched beneath my sneakers. Each step, each breath, each move forward defogged my brain. As I picked up the pace, I thought about the cruel and downright disturbing evening. My daddy, the rooted trunk of our family, had revealed himself again.

Entirely, indisputably, and devastatingly.

Inhaling the tropical air, I adjusted my sports bra. Normally I wouldn't notice the material clinging to my chest, but every cell seemed inflamed. And although I was outside, I felt contracted with emotional claustrophobia. Women chatted with their mothers, pushing strollers and rocking sleeping newborns. Ahead of me, a lithe grandfather lifted a toddler out of a bucket swing.

I gently massaged my temples. I couldn't erase the images and interactions that'd incited a dull throbbing. I walked and walked. Jogged. Sprinted as if being chased by a bobcat. Pushed myself to the brink of exhaustion. Then I spotted a mature tabebuia, blossoming unusually late, its yellow blooms like delicate earrings adorning the long limbs. I sat under it. A few petals rested on its gangly roots. A palette of such stark contrast.

Tough and tender. Delicate and durable. Fleeting and forever.

Sitting cross-legged and losing track of time, I stretched my neck backward and allowed my eyes to slightly close. The sun sifted through the leaves, alternating light and shadows on my face. The aromatic perfume of spring shifting to summer drifted toward me. A rainbow of hibiscus blooms spread their petals toward the sunlight. Purple and white orchids budded between their green waxy leaves.

I loosened my ponytail, and a wisp escaped. Tears dropped with it as my heart thumped like a rabbit's foot. After using strategies I'd taught to my clients, I hopped back into my headspace. My breathing slowed, and if I had a pulse oximeter, I knew it'd be close to normal. So why the physiologic responses? Fear? Excitement? Anxiety?

It was fascinating how we taught what we needed to learn.

★★★

The next day, I stood at the familiar oak door and had a tough time coaxing myself to open it. A closed door protected. Unlocking it could…

As if he already knew, Dr. Lewis sent Dottie to escort me into the office. "How are you?" She touched the upper side of my forearm.

Somehow, I sensed in that moment an unveiling of my soul.

"Just a bit surprised, I suppose. You're typically in the back. I appreciate your kindness," I said. She held my gaze for a second longer than usual.

"I understand." She rubbed my arm.

I hadn't even made it to the threshold and already felt supported. I squeezed Dottie's hand and took a deep, cleansing breath, then stepped into Dr. Lewis's office.

"Good afternoon. Would you like to share about the past few weeks? Or shall we dive into the hypnotherapy feedback and observations? It's your session, your choice." Dr. Lewis reclined in his chair. I noted the on-trend sneakers, surprised he owned any.

Pulling at my lower lip, I paused to think about his question for a bit, then answered with a quick recap of my recent revelations regarding my parents. I shared that maintaining boundaries was getting a bit easier with my mother. But my father, despite the ugliness I'd witnessed, proved to be much tougher.

"Incredible insights, Ally. How are you feeling about what you called this 'awakening'?"

I released a puff of air. "It hurts. It sears. I find, even in our sessions, when I talk about these incidents, including telling you about the letter, it's as if I'm having an out-of-body experience. I've tried to tell Ben. I simply can't. I'm so afraid to unravel our family, our marriage." I couldn't catch a full breath. "Like my mouth is moving, and I'm sharing someone else's story. These are facts. These things happened. Yet I still cannot believe these are the two humans—if they even classify as such—who birthed me." I paused, twisting my wedding band. "Telling Ben will make it real. I feel so ashamed of my father." I traced the line of the scar on my neck. The lump there was gone, replaced with a thick one in my throat.

"Dissociation is an unsettling feeling. I am affirming what you already know. But it doesn't make it easier," Dr. Lewis said. His expression seemed clouded. He rubbed his right eye and put on his glasses. "Change and expanding our consciousness isn't comfortable. This is the perfect time to transition and talk about our hypnotherapy work. I honor your progress, Ally."

He explained that while I was in the hypnotic state, he'd asked me a few questions, most of which I remembered. "You let go. You trusted me and the process. Before I go further, I want to thank you for being receptive." Dr. Lewis paused.

Wow, what a humble, kind man. He was thanking me. I nodded, encouraging him to move forward. My anticipatory anxiety began to dissipate, and curiosity took its place.

Dr. Lewis reached for a separate notebook dedicated to hypnotherapy notes.

"Within minutes, so much became clear. Shame, invalidation, and triangulation were the most prevalent themes. Your mother seemed to be judgmental, and in her eyes, you were never enough. I realize that's a lot to digest." Dr. Lewis looked up from his speckled journal.

"Please go on. This confirms much of what I've noticed in recent months about how she treats me and also my kids." I leaned forward.

"Your perceptions, experiences, and connections to your father seemed more complex and layered. You'd answer a question, but then quickly and consistently defend him. You also mentioned a letter from a woman he impregnated. Speaking of children, when we touched on his treatment of your kids, your responses were unwavering. What do you think?"

I took off my strappy wedge sandals, grateful I'd worn stretchy pants instead of a dress today. Then I sat on the floor and pushed my back into the edge of the firm couch.

"I'm absolutely flabbergasted that I went there. Everything you described makes sense. Can you please tell me more about my father?" I pressed my hands onto my knees.

Dr. Lewis uncrossed his legs. He turned the lined page, and his movements seemed to be in slow motion.

"From what I gathered, he can do no wrong. Another significant finding is, and please stop me if you have questions or it is too much to process, that your parents may be codependent. It's difficult, at least with the information I currently have, to discuss them individually. That said, your father appears to be the domineering one of the two. Does this seem to align with what you've noticed?"

Yes. Yes. Hell to the yes. "They rarely argue. Even with all my training, I didn't notice dysfunction in their relationship. It's all I knew, and it seemed to work for them. Yet as you're speaking, I'm sensing there is more." I picked at my split ends.

Dr. Lewis nodded. He asked if I had read any of the books or articles that he recommended last time. "We have a few minutes left. Are you familiar with narcissistic abuse?"

CHAPTER SEVENTY-SEVEN

I couldn't decide which hurt more: the pain of awakening or withholding it all from my Benito. A silent inferno. I needed to extinguish the blaze within me. My foot tapped in triple time as I waited for him to answer the line.

"Honey," I said.

"That would be me," Ben joked.

"I, um, we need to speak."

"Isn't that what we are doing?"

"Hysterical. I am serious," I retorted.

"Tell me we are not having a third child."

"No. Unless my tubes miraculously untied themselves."

"Serious as in, let's meet somewhere? Or serious like you want to pontificate about the latest research on meditation?"

I didn't answer. My silence sufficed.

Ben rapped on the metal door. "Come in," I called, straightening the file folders on my desk.

"I'm officially worried." He strode toward me in his pinstripe suit.

"I asked you to come here because the babysitter said she could stay later. And I figured we won't be interrupted; everyone else has left for the day." I wrapped my arms around Ben's waist. My husband ate like Pacman gobbling those pellets and didn't gain an ounce. Still tight and trim, Ben only exercised when walking the dog. Well, unless you considered chewing an exercise. And if it were, I'd be a waif! Holding him temporarily tempered my inner turbulence as my cheek met his.

Ben preferred the couch. But he agreed to the beanbags. He wriggled on one until he got comfortable. I sank into the rainbow-hued bag. I looked at him tentatively and twirled a strand of hair.

"Remember when we went to my parents' house a few months ago? The first time we all saw each other since that crazy Passover kitchen combustion?" I rolled my head from side to side. *I can do this. I must do this. I am doing this.*

"Of course. Why?"

My ribs expanded as I inhaled deeply. "My mother's stunt—inviting her friends to join us—was totally innocuous compared to what I'm about to tell you."

Ben's entire body tensed. I wished I could press a button for help. For both of us. "Remember I didn't go in the pool that day? I tinkered on the piano while you all swam."

My eyes looked past his at the sunset photograph framed in pale lavender. I paused. Ben's mouth opened, but I lifted a finger to it. "You know how I believe everything unfolds in the time and way in which it should? This information left me shocked and stupefied. And totally ashamed. In fact, it's taken me weeks to grasp the idea that it could be, um, that it *is* true."

The words tumbled out of my mouth like rocks falling from a mountainside, and the burden of all I carried lessened. I told Ben about the letter and showed him the photo of Jon. I extended my legs, pointing and flexing my feet. Ben began to interject, which normally I'd allow, but this time I feared if I did, I'd retreat and stay in that safe, shadowed space. I hadn't realized until that moment how much I'd kept from my husband.

A lone teardrop trickled down his cheek and landed in the cleft of his angular chin. "Ally. This is horrible, *mi amor*." He caught another one before it splatted on his cufflinks.

"Why are you crying? I still can't...I think I'm numb, like after the miscarriage." I dropped my head between my outstretched legs.

Ben skooched his beanbag over until it met mine. I brought my legs under me, and he put his head on my lap. His eyes glinted up at me as I massaged his temples.

"We obviously need to talk about this," Ben said. "But to answer your first question, I'm sad because you waited so long to tell me. And for you to deal with this by yourself. I don't know how you have been functioning."

Who knew summers performing among the Michigan pines would become dress rehearsals for my own survival? I'd adopted roles, even wore invisible costumes, to protect my family. I adored my husband. He'd stood up for me when I couldn't advocate for myself. More often with Roberta in his gentle, charming way. But with Dr. Curt, not so much. There were times in our marriage my parents' antics caused unnecessary friction and angst between us.

Maybe this is why I couldn't bring myself to share until now. Maybe I was afraid that Ben would see me in a different light. Or that this secret could unravel our family unit. Or make it real. Before I could release the bubbling brook in my head, Ben beat me to it.

"Who else did you tell about this horrific letter? Besides your mother, who apparently already knew," he asked.

Another reason I loved this man—my ethical, honest, loyal hubby. Yet this right here? Uncharted, foreign territory. If I told Ben that Ruby knew first, he'd be hurt. But hopefully he'd understand about Jack.

"Jack. He knows. Honey, I had to tell someone. I grappled for days, literally didn't keep much down," I admitted, kissing him lightly on the forehead. I reminded Ben about my brother's childhood. I had to be the perfect child to compensate and quell the heat in our home. Jack told our folks to fuck off daily. He got it. He saw it. He knew it. I never did.

"I still feel like I'm talking about a horror film or dystopian novel." I shuddered at the mere thought. "And you know I don't even watch or read anything dark."

Ben flipped off of the bean bag and onto his stomach. He stroked the stubble on his chin. "I'm glad you're seeing this Dr. Lewis. It's fascinating that what you heard after the hypnosis session equates with this letter. Ally, it makes sense. A sum of parts," he added, propped up on his elbows.

"What do you mean?"

Instead of replying, Ben pulled me toward him. I relaxed my head on his shoulder. Rays from the setting sun streamed into the room through the transom window. If not for the kids, we would've slept right there, entwined in solidarity. The ladybug paperweight projected muted prisms on the wall, the light lingering longer as summer approached. Florida forecasters had the perfect profession. Rain. Sunshine. Humidity. Or a combo of all three. Half of the time they were wrong but got paid anyway. I hoped this wouldn't be an active hurricane season.

My knees buckled as I rose. Ben supported my back, bracing me like a two-by-four, and piloted me toward the car. Though I'd typically delay our return and head to dinner, I could barely keep my eyelids open.

"I'm sorry, babe. So wanted to have a date night. This wasn't exactly romantic." I yawned between each syllable.

His eyebrows peaked and forehead lines deepened. Good thing Ben didn't play poker. He'd lose every game. But he did muster caring words, even if his face conflicted with what came out of his mouth. "I understand. It's fine. Let's pick up from Whole Foods," he said.

★ ★ ★

Our new sitter, Sandra, texted us that the kids were tucked in bed and asleep. It had been years before I could trust another human with our children. One nanny, when Julian was twenty months old, had fainted in the rental apartment. I remembered arriving home from work, greeted by my wide-eyed toddler at the door. It took several minutes to rouse the woman. I thought she was dead.

Then there was the time, barely able to stand straight after my second C-section, I was flipping a feta and spinach omelet for myself in the pan. The baby nurse asked me to make her breakfast. Instead of saying no, I obliged and whipped up eggs for her as well.

Jackie was the final straw. By then, we had bought multiple cameras for the main areas of the house. I originally resisted, teasing my girlfriends that it was excessive and obsessive.

Although quite tempting, I didn't watch each episode of the Nanny Cam Nightmares. But in one clip, Jackie was filing her nasty toenails on my dining room table. The wood was covered with dust from her pink emery board. How could this be? Sweet, responsible, and respectable Jackie? I couldn't help myself. Rewinding the tape, I scanned a few other snippets from the month. I hit pause on the remote.

Joy lay naked on the terry cloth-covered pad. Alone. On an elevated changing table. At four months old. She could've rolled over and...

I couldn't go there, even now as I floated in and out of consciousness in the car. I'd been forced to fire others in the past. But Jackie jarred me in a way that began to make sense. I pondered the patterns. Minor requests, but important, like not using a pacifier, were disregarded. I was intent on teaching my babies to self soothe. My parents always said, "We trained you at an early age. You and Jack slept through the night the first week. Babies should cry themselves to sleep and never sleep in your bed. And pacifiers will ruin their teeth." I'd heard these messages my entire life. Jackie had repeatedly ignored me. Back then, I didn't have the courage to confront her. And nobody's all good or all evil, right? I was glad we could even afford to have help.

More scenes replayed themselves in my head as Ben drove. Was Jackie narcissistic? Then my mind made another detour as I drifted in and out of sleep on the ride home. Bosses. Friends. Professors. People patched together, a quilt sewn with thin and thick threads of control. A tightly stitched beguiling blanket of deception. Each square unique. Yet eerily, uncannily similar.

What would happen if I unraveled it?

CHAPTER
SEVENTY-EIGHT
ALLEGRA' 14

 'd returned from camp obsessed with the brand Esprit. I wanted a sweater or even a T-shirt—anything—with that coveted tag on it. My parents refused to buy me Edwin jeans because "name brands were costly and impractical." Welcome to the fashion-forward eighties! They could afford to purchase the entire store. It wasn't about the money. Always about the principle. And often about instilling a sense of superiority. I never felt worthy.

Assimilating into school meant everything to me. Daddy treated me to an Esprit sweater during our annual day date. Jewel-toned threads woven through fine wool—I couldn't wait to show it to my mother.

"Mom! Look what D-d-d-dad got me!" I barely made it inside before tearing off the tissue paper. I held the sweater in front of my budding chest like an Olympic medal.

"How much did that cost, Allegra?" She tilted her head.

"Eighty-eight dollars on sale. Every one of my friends at camp wore this brand; Ruby let me borrow her Esprit sweatshirt, and I loved it. I heard it's freezing at school. I'll wear this tomorrow!" I stretched it from sleeve to sleeve so she could see the entire sweater.

Roberta flashed her coffee-stained fangs at my father. "Drive back to the store right now and return that ridiculous thing. It is an unflattering cut, and it's obscenely priced. You two know better." She rolled her eyes and released a puff of air.

I shoved it back in the bag and darted out of the room. I hoped to hold back the tears. No chance. I couldn't make it. Those words. That look. All of it. Fat, ashamed, and shattered again like stained glass.

CHAPTER
SEVENTY-NINE

"**L**et's go to the beach! Spending the day with the three of you would be the best birthday gift." I loaded the last plate into the dishwasher.

Ben didn't love the sand. Or eating anything messy with his hands, like a gooey, freshly baked chocolate brownie. And relaxing, otherwise known as sitting still while awake, wasn't his jam. I joked Ben had two buttons: off and on. Awake or asleep. Sitting or standing. Now that the kids were older, I promised him that we could leave them to stroll along the shoreline.

We didn't make it there in time for sunrise. On our way out the door, our rescue pup Izzy decided to gift us with a ginormous mound. Right in the middle of the kitchen. As I cleaned up the mess, I decided that delays or other unanticipated kinks would not affect my day. No matter what.

Though it was a bit humid, the breeze and our bright Tommy Bahama beach umbrella provided shade. I laughed while watching Ben and Joy chase the cloth napkin that had somehow escaped from the cooler. Julian looked at the water. Much like his father, he detested seaweed and unknown creatures touching him. He also preferred predictability. Joy zipped past her pensive brother and dove right in.

"Why'd you get me wet? Ouch! There's salt in my eyes," Julian protested, blinking rapidly and wiping his eyes with his hiked shoulder.

"You're fine, sweetie," I said.

Joy ducked her head into the water, then dipped in and out, trying to engage him like a playful dolphin. I drew a rainbow in the sand with my finger, contemplating nature versus nurture. These two loves of my life were similar in some ways yet starkly different in others. Just like me and Jack. But my kids had already bonded deeply. That's the nurture part, I suppose. What an honor and privilege to be their mother.

I stood up and walked toward the kids, the waves lapping the seashore, the rhythm echoing my own ebb and flow. As I neared Joy and Julian, I spotted a heart-shaped shell and scooped it up. Minuscule moments, like the specks of sand beneath our feet, a sandcastle that held my heart. Like the one I now tucked into the pocket of my swim skirt.

★★★

"What an amazing afternoon, babe." I rested my head on Ben's bare upper back. "Thanks for agreeing to it. I know chilling by the ocean isn't your cup of tea."

I looked in the mirror and then began rinsing the black one-piece bathing suit in our bathroom sink. Suddenly, I felt as if I'd swallowed curry—my stomach gurgled, and acid rose in my chest. Crazy how my body responded to this vision of myself, to this fabric. The power of intention is mind-bending. I kept the pharmaceutical industry in business. The proton pump inhibitors—ironically the tiny magical pill was my favorite color—suppressed the heartburn.

Ben yawned like a languid, satiated lion. Why didn't he make the connection that the positive ions from the salty air morphed him from Buzzy Ben to Buddha Ben? Maybe if I mentioned it one more time, then…

"It's all over your face," he joked. "Please don't start with the mini yogi sermon, Professor Ally."

"I have no idea what you mean, sweetheart." I snickered with feigned innocence.

Snuggling closer to him, I traced the path of hair from his chest to right above the elastic of his shorts. He squirmed and wiggled, still ticklish, like in the earlier days when we were dating. I coaxed him toward the bathmat that I'd recently washed. Though he protested, the bulge in his boxers lit up.

Ben insisted on celebrating not just holidays, but all birthdays and milestones. I was more comfortable giving than receiving, and I baked creative cakes for family and friends. But when it was my day, I craved connection, not confections. So this last gift? I eagerly unwrapped and devoured it.

The kids continued to celebrate me with a surprise brunch. Their hand-made cards made my morning. Then I spoke to Ruby, Jack, and other dear ones. I breathed in gratitude as the sun melted into the sky, streaking it with hues of pinks and purples on a palette of pale blue.

Prosecco coursed through my veins, uncorking deeper emotions that flowed freely. "Honey, why do you suddenly look serious? You concerned about a patient or that upcoming presentation?" Ben asked.

Should I rain on this party? That seemed unfair. Yet I wouldn't withhold more info from him. That was torture.

"I love and hate that you know me so well. Are you sure? If I start, please know this won't be a quickie. And I'm referring to conversation—I saw that twinkle," I warned.

Ben nodded and placed the remote in its holder on the wall.

"Them. The two vessels that brought me to the planet," I said.

"Huh?"

"Roberta and Sheldon." I'd realized recently that using their names distanced me a bit, making it easier to speak about them.

"Ohhh. Oh. What about them?"

I paused to gather my thoughts, hoping I'd be coherent. After downing a liter of water, the effervescent buzz dissipated.

"When I told you about the letter, I sensed you had strong opinions, thoughts, feelings, all of it. You nor I had the energy to delve deeper that night. While I appreciate the space, it's been weeks, and you haven't even asked to read it. Why?" I tried not to sound hurt or frustrated.

The bubbly bottle wasn't the only thing uncorked.

Ben groaned. "You want to talk about this now? I was about to fall asleep. And we had such an incredible weekend."

I turned to face him. "Yes, now. I was totally transparent and asked first if you were up for this. It's eroding my insides."

My husband averted his gaze and stared at the ceiling. "I don't know where to start. We can get to that horrific letter in a minute. Let's talk about you. About us. About our family unit," he said.

Where was he going with this?

"Your migraines are back. They haven't been this bad in years, since you were a teenager. I'm worried about your health, *mi amor*." Ben twisted his plain gold wedding band.

"Oh, you're sweet. I am fine," I lied.

"No. No, you are not. You've been snippy with me. Snapping at the kids. I've never seen you act like this, Ally. And you're usually the patient one in this house. It's like we are all walking on eggshells so you don't crack open."

I listened, my eyes widening and neck tensing. Was this a mistake? Maybe some things were better left unsaid.

Ben continued talking, a stream of observations flowing from his mouth. His professional, analytical mode agitated me and allayed my fears all at once. Holy crap, he'd noticed the stuttering too.

"I'm not saying these things to upset you. And, like you, I guess maybe I've been holding this in for a long time," Ben admitted. He glanced at me cautiously.

I, too, twisted my wedding ring. He was my world, and he gave me what I'd never had from my folks—unconditional love.

"I'm not upset, honey. I'm grateful you love me enough to say all that you did. I honestly wasn't aware of this dynamic; I promise to work on it. I don't feel it's fair to blame my folks. As each layer is revealed, it aches in places I didn't even know existed. I'm doing the best I can, or so I thought." My voice cracked at the end. I had to talk this out with the one person who could intuit what I could not.

★★★

Ruby answered on the first ring. A minor miracle. I dragged a fallen palm frond off the grass. "Hey, my friend." Just hearing Ruby's voice calmed me.

"Hey to you. You know, hey is for horses. You trying to tell me something?" I teased.

Chortling on the other end of the line. "How do you still remember that? I guess we heard it enough at flagpole," Ruby said. "You're still nauseatingly perky in the morning, Ally. Some things don't change. Blew my mind, even when we were twelve, that you didn't need to do vocal warmups."

I was the luckiest woman in the world. A husband who adored me. A friend who was a soul sister. Two amazing kids. Aunts who were more like mothers.

So why did I feel woozy? I sat down on the grass. "Why do you think I always offered you the top bunk? You sleep like you're in a coma." I cracked up and Ruby joined me. "Remember that counselor, I think it was Sue, dared me to dip your hand in freezing water? You didn't budge. The following year, I had the brilliant idea to shove the bedsprings. You literally levitated."

We reminisced about other fond memories. I wheezed as she carried on. Ruby incited a spark that led to fireworks of laughter. After we both caught our breaths, her tone changed. "I have to tell you something. Please don't freak out."

"What an opening!"

"My mom's cancer is back."

"Oh, Ruby. I am so—"

"I can't talk about it. I won't. We are getting second and third opinions—I need to be focused. Though I appreciate your empathy, it'll undo me." Ruby's pitch dropped from a soprano to an alto. She swiftly switched topics and prodded me to share about family, work, and life.

How could I top that one? My family drama was a droplet compared to that deluge.

Besides, I could talk this through with Dr. Lewis. I was not telling her.

As if she'd tapped my subconscious, Ruby peppered me with questions. I tried to dodge them. Unsuccessfully.

"Fine. You are right. Lots going on, my friend. After what you shared about your sweet mama, there's no need to discuss me today," I attempted.

Ruby wasn't buying it. The woman should've been a hostage negotiator. In my garden, the budding orchids leaned into each other, sharing their secrets. I lowered my voice as I told my best friend more of mine. Not a cloud marred the sky. I wanted to pull the Miami blue over me like a weighted blanket. I divulged the unsettling conversation with Ben.

"Wait a sec. Stop right there, sister. Trouble in paradise?" Ruby gasped.

I continued, forgetting that I hadn't shared the events that preceded our tough talk. I scooped fresh soil and pressed my hands into it. I'd heard this new plant attracted ladybugs. Ruby, both a wise ass and wise woman, encouraged me to consider cutting out my parents. Permanently.

"How could I do that? There must be another way to coexist with them. I'll amp up the boundaries. These are my kids' grandparents, Ruby. What would I be modeling? It feels hypocritical because I live and breathe my family—you know that—and that includes Ben's too." I shifted to my knees, dirt mucked under my nails, and pulled weed after weed.

Ruby, a fiercely loyal friend, knew she'd gone too far with me. But for days after we hung up the phone, the seed she planted began to grow roots.

CHAPTER EIGHTY

ell hath no fury like a Florida Home Depot before a hurricane. Like a grown-up Chuck E. Cheese party, people zoomed up and down aisles, chaotic and crazy.

The tropical storm had picked up speed, threatening to make landfall as a Category Four, even though two days before, the forecasters said it would veer back out to the Atlantic. I hadn't experienced Hurricane Andrew, the most devastating storm that tore through Miami in 1992. My parents had been with me as I moved into the freshman dorm in the Midwest.

Even decades later, Ben and others remembered each hair-splitting second of that night. Though infrastructure, codes, and other protective measures had been upgraded since the 1990s, some Floridians panicked when smaller storms approached. For many in my community, intense hurricanes incited fear and flashbacks.

Since the kids were toddlers, I'd updated my hurricane "in case we need to evacuate" stash. I created a color-coded, neatly labeled binder with copies of important documents. Filled and froze Ziplock bags with water for bathing or drinking. And gathered an admittedly ridiculous abundance of Charmin. I had loved hurricanes when Jack and I were younger, at least the ones in the first house. One year, we slept on mattresses in the hallway. It was one of the few times I felt deeply connected to my parents—not just the physical proximity, but emotionally as well.

Our home lost power if somebody sneezed. So, in addition to the pre-season nesting (or perhaps hoarding), I'd compiled a list of hotels that had generators. I booked rooms for my parents when a menacing storm threatened to make landfall. This one, surprising in intensity even for natives like me and Ben, threw everyone off course.

The cone of concern wobbled and wavered along with our decision whether to ride out the storm or to join the caravan of cars heading north on I-95. Most of my friends chose to leave. Some headed for Disney, which we'd done before to entertain the kids. Others fled to second homes or to hotels out of the state. After much debate, we decided to stay put. We didn't want to leave in case my parents needed our help in the aftermath.

"What the..." Ben studied the screen. He adjusted his wire-rimmed glasses.

I continued bringing in the patio furniture. Julian and Joy knew the drill by now. Second- generation Floridians, an unusual flock, our kids would likely sleep through the entire ordeal. I channeled my pre-hurricane buzz into cleaning. I had smelled and sensed the atmospheric shift the night before as if I were hooked to an oxygen tank, infusing me with energy. Truth be told, I welcomed it when the world around me halted. Forced intermissions and time with the four of us—no electronics, no work, no school.

"Babe. Come here, please," Ben said. He sounded like a viola string about to snap.

I wondered if I had forgotten to fill the cars' tanks. On a normal day, this would have irritated him. My husband didn't understand how driving on empty didn't bother me one bit.

Little stuff rocked him, especially when the bigger things, like a massive hurricane, were out of his control. Before I could conjure other scenarios, he handed me the cell phone.

Hi Ben. We are informing you that we are currently at the Miami International Airport. (You know we prefer Fort Lauderdale; it's a disaster here.) Our itinerary is as follows: We fly to Washington, D.C. (It was the cheapest we could find so last-minute.) Then staying with friends—you know, the rich ones who have that fabulous apartment in Boston—until the storm is over.

I read and reread the text. Many thoughtful friends, including Ruby and Lyn, had begged us to ride out the storm with them. I had insisted that we stay home, worried my parents might need help cleaning up the yard or otherwise.

And they'd left? I'd made reservations for them at the Marriott. How dare they! And they didn't have the decency to call or at least text their only daughter? I could not believe this.

I rarely got angry. Hurt? Yes. Disappointed. Yes. Sad? Occasionally. But anger—no, more like fury—felt foreign to me. I shook. I simmered. I stormed away, seething with a mix of rage and resentment. And so much more. I didn't say a single word. My right back molar nearly broke as I clenched my teeth.

With a half pirouette, I fled up the stairs. Showered. I would wash this away. I turned up the heat and then lowered it after noticing I was about to self-inflict a second-degree burn.

Scrubbed my body. Massaged my scalp. Finished with a frigid rinse.

Wrapping my head in a plush towel, I stared at the flushed face in the mirror. A woman I barely recognized, puffy and pissed off, stared back at me. I needed to get a grip. The last thing Ben, the kids, and the pups needed was more stress. I quickly changed into clean clothes.

Grounded myself with a tree pose and a few downward dogs. Then I joined everyone outside. Ben barbecued the chicken, pounding it flat. Our usual pre-hurricane prep—cook all frozen meats in case we lost power.

I chopped veggies a bit more aggressively than usual. The kids, immersed in a show on the television, didn't notice that their momma was about to implode. After dinner, we turned the air conditioner to sixty-eight. Joy and Julian were delighted— they rarely slept in our room. I gazed at these little humans. Joy, my affectionate kid—when she hugged me, it felt like a human tranquilizer. And Julian, with his ability to focus, to tune out the world around him. How I wished I could.

Sleeping bags. Check. Dog food and toys. Check. Flashlights. Check. Surprise snacks. Check.

We were over-prepared, as usual. So why did I feel this fore-boding sense of doom?

CHAPTER EIGHTY-ONE

ALLEGRA' 16

I had to go back. I must. I would. But my parents didn't applaud my proposition. "Seven summers is enough—time to get a job," they snarled in unison.

Rapid-fire breaths burned in my heaving chest. I needed my artsy tribe: teens and teachers who understood and accepted me. Fat or thin. Sharp or flat.

And no way would I be trapped in the narrow hallways of darkness and judgment here at home. I refueled on connection in the log cabins and onstage. It sustained me during the school year like solar panels heating a pool.

Though the sun shone nearly year-round in Miami, it didn't beam its light into my house. Soggy maple leaves and flattened pinecones covering the ground after summer storms in Northern Michigan grounded me. Once, we'd hunkered in the basement, a cast of cabinmates, staying safe from a potential twister. The tornado missed our 1,200-acre, sprawling, tree-lined campus. The piercing piccolos of alarms alerted us to run for shelter.

Yet I never suffered the gripping fear I did in my own home.

Sounds from string and brass instruments floated from the wood practice huts.

Performers played on sundry stages. Campers convened after rehearsals, licking drips of soft-serve ice cream between laughter.

A magical composition of youth and inspiration. Each summer, we gathered from not only the U.S., but sixty other countries to collaborate, connect, and create.

I'd carefully considered the options. Then I broached the subject with Roberta and Dr. Curt. This was about money. This was yet another "lesson." The message was clear: I didn't matter.

My legs quaked. Lunch rose in my throat. But I made it to the family room where they watched a documentary. Again. I tapped my father on his upper back, and he turned around.

"I'm going to pay for camp, Dad." I gripped the polished Petoskey stone in my pocket. The one I'd made my first summer in Michigan. "I need to go back. I'm not ready to say goodbye." I barely got the words out, shakily held up my hand, and spoke louder.

"Before you say no, hear me out. I *am* going. I will babysit during all my free time and raise the money."

My father sneered at me. My mother raised the volume on the remote control.

"Allegra, while I'm proud of your determination, you can't possibly do that. There's no way you'll be able to make enough money to pay for all eight weeks," Roberta said. She glanced at Dr. Curt, seeking backup. She rarely disciplined us on her own. That would require effort.

"So, you don't believe me? Give me a few months. Let's see how it goes. I am going to make this happen." I ran from the room, but at least I hadn't stuttered. Just the thought of being caged without other inmates shook me to the core.

Rattled but hopeful, I secured a few regular gigs. One family had no rules, no boundaries.

Ten-year-old twins tossed tomatoes at me. I ducked and threw out the filthy fruit. When tamer kids went to sleep, I studied or called a friend. Another house had a pantry stuffed with Oreos, Skittles, and other forbidden goodies.

Week by week, the bills I'd stashed in the corner of my closet thickened. When I counted one thousand dollars, I scheduled a meeting with my parents. I feared approaching them again until I had solid proof. They could easily afford the summer tuition—other campers needed scholarships to attend. It was the principle. They saw life—not just mine, but everyone else's—as the way it "should be." Any ideas or actions that contradicted their rigid, self-righteous ideals were instantaneously rejected like a violent bout of food poisoning.

It was only the three of us. I missed Jack beyond words; he would've convinced them for me in seconds. But by early April, I was ready for the (hopefully) final act.

Over plain grilled chicken and charred cauliflower, I waited until my parents were satiated. Only a brief intermission between dinner and the evening news.

"I have something to show you both." I stayed seated, not trusting my legs.

With Jack gone, I'd stomached a double serving of pleasing the two people for whom I was never enough. I needed to escape to my magical nook in the woods. And it was tough to argue with a wad of self-made cash. They allowed me to return to camp for one last encore.

CHAPTER EIGHTY-TWO

The hurricane birthed funnel clouds. We huddled in the bathroom a few times when the radio siren sounded. The kids, frightened that *The Wizard of Oz* could become a reality TV show, pressed against our bodies. The storm had decelerated. But our collective heart rates raced as if we were running a family marathon. Fortunately, the alerts ceased by about 9:30 p.m. The kids collapsed with Izzy and Cookie burrowed between them.

Though we never lost power, my upper lip beaded with moisture. My knees creaked as I bent to open the bathroom drawer. Ben washed up, brushed his teeth, and we whispered between spits in the sink. Within minutes of lying down, Ben snored. Our kids were blessed with his lights-out gene. Lucky them.

As my eyes grew heavy, the landline phone rang. I tiptoed toward the back of my closet, not wanting to awaken the zombies. Had someone died? Who the hell calls at nearly midnight in the middle of a massive hurricane?

Oh my God. My father.

"Hello. You and Mom okay?" I paced back and forth.

"Yes. Your mother is asleep. I called to tell you about the wonderful time we are having. We've seen two shows, which were remarkably good given it's a traveling cast rather than Broadway. And our friends have treated us to lavish dinners," Dr.

Curt reported. Even though he boasted about his medical school buddy, my father also complained that the home was "filthy and cluttered," which was one of Dr. Curt's pet peeves. One of many.

The winds wailed, and a coconut, now a projectile, slammed into the window. I was literally holding down the fort.

"You want me to do what?" I could barely hear him above the howling winds. Was he kidding? Was this a sick joke?

"Do I stutter too? I said check on our house tomorrow. What if there is shattered glass or something worse? I know, I know, you've been pestering us for years to get impact windows," Dr. Curt snapped.

I murmured an affirmative sound. Then I heard Ben rustle. Glad he'd convinced me to update our windows. I started to shake as I saw two branches snap between bolts of lightning. Maybe shutters were better after all.

Too much to see, to take in all at once. Worried I'd woken Ben, I padded over to his side of the bed. His rhythmic breathing had resumed.

"Allegra? Are you there?" my father asked.

I was but would rather not have been at the moment.

"Yes. I had to check on my family," I said. "You do realize the time, right?"

Instead of asking about us, he sliced into me, his words excavating my entire limbic system.

"Don't speak to me like I'm an idiot. Of course I know what time it is," he bellowed. "You will go to our house tomorrow. Your mother and I don't want to come home and deal with a mess."

Like the Jaws of Life but reversed, he roared and raged. I'd heard this hollering directed at Jack before. But rarely at me.

Only that one time during Passover in front of the kids. And never with the ferocity of a T-Rex.

My fingertips felt frostbitten. My lower lip trembled. Even biting it couldn't still the quivering. I held the phone away from my ear. His volume barely dampened. I didn't notice Ben standing over me.

"Babe. Who is that? It's nearly one a.m."

I mouthed "my father" and promptly put him on speaker. The kids breathed heavily, a sleeping duet.

"How *dare* you reject us! Who the hell do you think you are, Allegra?"

Ben's mouth nearly dislocated. I lay on the cold tile floor, hoping to center myself. My stomach churned and warned it may empty its contents.

"D-d-d-dad. I d-d-d-don't understand." I started hiccupping uncontrollably. Speaking that small sentence took every ounce of effort.

"Are you an utter moron? I *am* speaking in English, a subject in which you excelled! You did not invite your mother and me to stay with you," he spewed.

"Huh? Mom told me, and I confirmed with others in the family, that you b-b-both chose to stay at the Marriott. Which, as always, I b-b-booked for you." My breathing became jagged. If Spielberg could have cued special effects at that moment, I swear steam would've melted the phone.

Ben mumbled, "How long have you been on with him?" He shook his head, horrified, and told me he couldn't take anymore. It was making him nauseated. He urged me to hang up.

I couldn't do it. I froze. Physically. Emotionally. Recoiled and retreated. My inner child popped in to join the show. Dr. Curt continued blasting and berating me. And I listened. The good girl grasping for a shred of my daddy. The strong, smart, and supportive version. The one I thought I knew. Then something inside me snapped.

"D-d-d-dad. I know. I know about the letter. I read it. I saw the photo. You got a woman pregnant, your resident, before you married Mom. I have a second b-b-b-brother." I didn't wait for a response. I stood, ripped the cord out of the phone, and then collapsed onto the carpet.

Debris crashed into the side sliding door. The royal palms stood stoically, guarding the flowers I'd recently planted. None of it mattered. Material possessions and shrubbery could be easily fixed. I'd weathered the eye of the storm.

But could anything or anyone ever fix the decimated piece of my soul?

CHAPTER
EIGHTY-THREE

Wafting smells of turkey bacon mixed with tinges of maple syrup drifted into our home.

The nausea from the night became a ravenous urge to fill my stomach. And the empty spaces.

If Ben hadn't witnessed the deranged diatribe, I would swear that call had never happened. I wrapped my terry cloth robe around my shivering body. Instead of my usual coffee, I reached for two ginger tea bags. An image of my Polish grandma, who'd drunk Lipton black tea, prompted a brief memory. Those sleepovers, that precious time spent with the two people who nurtured me, who loved me unconditionally, even at my plumpest, felt like a lifeline right now. The littlest things, seemingly insignificant at the time, became the most impactful and memorable.

Then I heard Roberta's words in my head. Incredible that she could interrupt me even when I was not with her. In my mind, I heard her say, "I don't like tea. It reminds me of being sick. That is the only time I drink it."

Interesting how memories affect us all in unexpected ways.

Oh, the heartwarming honey. Sweet sunshine that dripped off a teaspoon and swirled with the steeped liquid. I kept stirring until it melted into the hot water. Outside, a mama duck and her darlings waddling behind her distracted me. I wondered how they knew to innately trust the adult who led them.

Ben's arm encircled my waist. "You must be absolutely exhausted," he murmured in my ear.

"Understatement. I think numb?"

"I know this is probably the worst time, sweetie. But no time will ever be right for what I am about to say," Ben began.

I could not take much more. I placed the ceramic mug on the credenza and signaled toward the back door. Our kids were like wiretaps. Thank goodness Ben got the hint today.

"Let's sit down," he said, guiding me toward the stone table. He proceeded to tell me that he was done. Finished. That he couldn't and wouldn't risk losing the woman he adored. His cheery, positive wife. The mother of his children.

"*Mi amor*, it's time to take them out of our lives. What happened last night is unforgivable. I've looked the other way. I've defended them because you've asked that I do so for our kids and the rest of the family. We've talked to them, written to them. They won't change. Your parents' manipulative toxicity is wedging itself into our home."

Had he called Ruby? What the hell? I didn't think I was breathing.

"I can't. They are my parents. And you know how they lie. My aunts, uncles, cousins." I wrung the edge of my robe. "I adore them. Even the ones who don't live here. What if I lose everyone? That's not a risk I'm willing to take. And I've never shared what goes on here with other people, how they treat the kids, me, you. Cutting them out feels plain wrong. Disloyal. Not sure of the right word—I can barely think right now." I pinched the bridge of my nose.

Ben, my love, my acoustic guitar, amplified the decibels and went full-on electric. He refused to accept my response. Shaking his head, Ben's volume intensified, and with it his resolve. A Papa Bear caring for his cubs and their momma with an unwavering stance I had never witnessed.

"When's your next appointment with Dr. Lewis? I'd like to come. Maybe he will have another idea. Because, honey, I love you, I love us, and I'm not letting them hurt our family again," Ben said.

★ ★ ★

He never took a day off. Ever. Yet Ben insisted on driving me to the therapist's office. I tried to dissuade him, insisting I was more than capable of handling myself.

"You are one of the smartest, strongest people I know. This isn't implying weakness. I want to be here. Please. Let me," Ben said, stroking my hair as he pulled into the spot.

I had forgotten to call, which I realized when Dr. Lewis greeted us with a befuddled expression. The men, both taller than six feet, looked over my head. I stood in the valley of those virile mountains.

"I hope it's alright that Ben's here today," I said sheepishly. "I meant to ask."

After shaking Ben's outstretched hand, Dr. Lewis motioned to the two seats across from him. "It's wonderful to meet you." Dr. Lewis leaned back in his chair. "Ally, would you like to begin?"

I started and stopped like a clunky jalopy with a dying battery. I couldn't coherently recount all that had transpired. Ben jumped in the driver's seat and seized the wheel, sensing that I couldn't steer this conversation. As Ben talked, I zoomed in and out of mental lanes, and the room spun. I saw the crash. I felt the impact. Gripping the sides of the chair, I became a passenger, a spectator.

If only the human body had a built-in airbag.

Dr. Lewis listened intently, interjecting twice to clarify what he heard. Then he asked my permission to speak frankly in front of Ben.

"Yes, of course. I appreciate you asking," I mustered.

He explained the depths and nuances of narcissism. Dr. Lewis also touched upon sociopaths and said that about four percent of the population exhibited these behaviors. They were the most dangerous. Not the Jeffrey Dahmers of the world—the ones who lived next door, worked alongside us, were relatives and friends. They appeared and acted deceivingly, convincingly normal.

Unbeknownst to me until this moment, Dr. Lewis's dissertation had been on the spectrum between benign and pathologic narcissists and why, when their cases were moderate to severe, they were difficult if not impossible to treat. He explained that the hallmark of this disorder was total detachment, lack of awareness and empathy, and no connection to self. After the question he'd left me with from our last session, I'd ransacked the research, perusing all journals and other reliable sources on narcissism. Though I'd studied NPD in graduate school, it wasn't my area of expertise. I also ran it by Ruby, and she consulted with a colleague who specialized in narcissistic personality disorder.

What Dr. Lewis said didn't surprise me. Still, as he continued, my synapses fired, synthesizing the cognitive and emotional components of all he shared. As I watched Ben nod, his clear comprehension of such a complex disorder made it painfully real.

Dr. Lewis must have noticed me withdraw, his patient shutting down and on overload. "Let me pause there. It's a lot to process, for both of you," he said.

I blotted my damp eyes with the tissues he handed me.

Ben rubbed my back in a slow, circular motion. "This has been so much, especially on Ally. It's not new. It's gotten much worse." Ben's voice got raspy and then cracked. "And the hardest part is the kids. They notice. They ask. Ally's gotten a bit better about telling it like it is." He shoved his hands in his pockets.

"But she sometimes still defends her folks, and they've gone too far. I am not losing the family we've built. The tension in our house is escalating. And I am not risking my wife's health. She's my everything—" Ben's breath hitched in his throat.

Dr. Lewis leaned forward and tapped his forefingers together. After months of working with him, I knew he was on the precipice of an epic statement.

"Have either of you considered cutting them out? Ally has done well with setting increasingly firm boundaries. She told me about the major sit-down chat you had with them five years ago. It seems, and I imagine it may be heartbreaking to hear, that nothing has changed. This is abuse, even though you can't see the wounds or the scars. And the only way to break the cycle is to end it by completely disconnecting." Dr. Lewis swiveled slightly in his chair.

"I've wanted to say this for a long time," he continued. "But, as you well know, Ally, it's ultimately your decision regarding the path you take and the choices you make. Then again, isn't it intriguing how we are guided? And if we're paying attention, how some decisions are made for us?" He removed his glasses and put them on the desk.

I told him about my fears and the reasons why removing them from our lives seemed impossible. I'd taught my kids that family comes first, always and forever. I didn't know how this would trickle into my extended family, either. My parents each had a PhD in martyrdom and masks.

He nodded and elaborated further. Somatic symptoms, like anxiety and migraines, were common for survivors of narcissistic abuse. Dr. Lewis reiterated that emotional trauma housed in the human body would manifest in myriad ways.

I knew this. I taught this, but was blind when...

"As you suggested, I've been taking that trauma healing yoga class," I shared, touching the faint line near my collarbone. "I had an epiphany the other day that my thyroid cancer could be a manifestation of not being allowed to speak my truth. Maybe the chakra blockages, my higher self, my voice was censored and squelched until that area became sick."

Dr. Lewis put his clipboard on the desk and told us to reach out if we needed him. We thanked him for his compassion and candid insights. I knew in that moment that a battle scar remained on the outside, but the healing needed to come from within.

CHAPTER EIGHTY-FOUR

Ben and I debated a phone call versus a letter. Dr. Lewis suggested that we compose a written document, as did Ruby. My ensemble of friends, who hadn't known about the worst until recently, did as well.

It felt liberating. I broke free and flew from the cage. But to name it—abuse—made it excruciatingly real. Even more real than when I'd told Ben about the secret letter.

It was tougher to contradict facts in black and white. Sure, we had been warned that no matter the method, Dr. Curt and Roberta would spin and weave a distorted web. Nothing upsets narcissists as much as being seen for who they are. Admission and ownership of all they'd done and not done, I now understood, was impossible. Instead of anger or disappointment, an ache of longing for what would never be pulsated within me.

Dear Mom and Dad,

We love you. We always have. We always will. And it breaks our hearts to send you this message, but it's become clear that there's no other way. Your toxic behavior, manipulation, and abusive actions are unconscionable. Love is kind. Love doesn't hurt.

We've tried repeatedly to express this and continued to hope you would change. We've asked you to go to therapy—you've refused. Talks, texts, tears. Though we accept who you are, we cannot and will not accept how you treat us, and especially, our children. They see, they ask, they know. And we will no longer invalidate what they recognize to be true—we cannot because you have revealed yourselves to your grandchildren.

Please do not contact any of us for the foreseeable future. For the health and well-being of our family unit, we must discontinue all communication. We hope you seek professional help, as we have, and wish you well.

All our love,
Allegra, Ben, Julian, and Joy

My finger hovered over the "send" button for a few extra beats. Hitting it was one of the saddest, scariest seconds of my entire life.

We never heard from them. No call. No email. No text. No apology. No seeking (or even faking interest) in owning the years of twisted, toxic behavior. And even more tragic and heart-wrenching beyond comprehension was that neither Roberta nor Dr. Curt showed up—not physically, not verbally, not at all.

They lived only a few towns away from us.

The daddy I thought I knew, the man who'd been my hero, vanished, gone from my life but leaving scars in my heart. The silver linings showed themselves in how my children treated others. How we lived and loved without condition. And how even in an abyss, it was possible to find the rainbow.

During a much-needed, mindless afternoon of retail therapy, the store manager remarked that something seemed different about me. Had I dyed my hair? Got a new style? Had some "work" done, a nip and tuck?

Somewhere between squeezing into jeans a size too small (and perhaps cutting off my circulation), I shared a snippet of my story. Maybe the tie-dyed tube top I tried on catapulted my confidence. Or had I taken the final leap of faith, liberated at last?

A saleswoman standing nearby, who I'd never met, overheard our conversation. She looked at me, her eyes pooling with pain and compassion. "What parent—who, anyone—would ever let you go?"

EPILOGUE

Waves washed over my toes as my feet sank into the sand. I loved this secluded spot we'd found, where the only music sounded from the speakers next to the chairs we'd brought. Standing at the edge of the ocean, I adjusted my striped, magenta bikini and breathed in the salty air. Amazing how much Julian and Joy had matured in just five years. Where had the time gone?

Ruby splashed the kids, diving between the frothy waves, forever young, my bestie. She was intent on staying that way with the help of world-renowned plastic surgeons and was recovering at our home because, of course, the best docs are in Florida. I loved how she loved my kids, my entire family, as her own. And I was forever grateful she had been in my corner since our earlier days at camp.

And my Ben, *mi amor*, my everything. As if he felt my thoughts, he winked and waved from his paddleboard, and his biceps winked as well. I wouldn't be here without his support, strength, and solidarity. How'd I get so lucky? We'd grown as individuals and as a family since sending that email. I didn't regret it for a second. While I missed the idea of my parents in our lives, I realized they had never actually been there.

As I submerged myself into the ocean, the seaweed brushed my ankles. I rose from the water and tipped my head toward the sun. My hair reached my waist; I loved that I'd finally let it grow longer. It curled at the ends, crunchy from the salty sea, and tickled my back as I headed toward the shore. Then I spotted a starfish on the sand. I'd never seen one out there before. A sign of intuition and rebirth.

I touched the spot where the Azabache stone once hung, knowing I'd no longer need its protection. A heart made from rose quartz, a symbol of unconditional love, dangled from the silver necklace in its place.

-THE END-

ACKNOWLEDGMENTS

I thought writing a novel would be a tough task. For me, whittling down these pages is grueling. How can I fit infinite gratitude into a small space? And "thanks" is a tiny word that cannot possibly express my boundless appreciation. Writing and publishing this book has transformed me at a soul level.

I've learned that creating and crafting requires solitude, which I now crave rather than avoid. (My family laughs at my recent revelation that I just may be an introvert!) It takes a team of discerning, supportive doulas to birth a book baby.

Thank you to Anthony Ziccardi, Gretchen Young, Madeline Sturgeon, and the entire Regalo Press team for giving *It Could Be Worse* a home with a heart.

To my beloved Interlochen Arts Camp, a musical sanctuary amongst the pines, I wouldn't be the woman I am without those formative summers.

To the late Dave Adams, my publisher at the *Indiana Daily Student* newspaper. You gave me a mustard seed just before graduation, and as a young reporter, I didn't quite get it. Decades later, I now understand the seed represents growth, faith, and luck.

Thank you to Marta Helliesen, PhD, for answering my questions about narcissism and therapy methodology. Kris Spisak, developmental editor extraordinaire, I'll never forget what you wrote on my early draft; it's tucked in my heart and propels me forward. Huge thanks to Cindy Cunningham, PhD—you helped fine-tune my sentences when I was high-strung.

To the Instagrammers, bookstagrammers, podcasters, bloggers, reviewers, librarians, booksellers, and those in all areas of publishing—you all rock. I appreciate your literary passion and support.

I'm infinitely grateful to the author community and the many people who shared their insights with generosity and authenticity. I wish I could list you all! Huge hugs of gratitude to those who've fortified me on this journey—Samantha Bailey, Julie Valerie, Jean Meltzer, Patricia Sands, Victoria Francis, Meredith Schorr, Josie Brown, Eileen Moskowitz-Palma, Sonja Yoerg, Julie Maloney, Natalie Silverstein, Brad Meltzer, and Rea Frey. To book champions, fellow podcasters, and friends Dan Blank, Julie Michiko Chan, Zibby Owens, and Lainey Cameron—thank you for amplifying authors' voices.

Thank you to my extraordinary publicist, Emi Battaglia. Your guidance, expertise, and professionalism are unparalleled.

To my family near and far, past and present, who've lifted me up and taught me lessons along the way. I love you always. To my fur babies, thank you for the snuggles.

To my framily—Robyn Gottlieb, you nudged me to write and wouldn't quit. So, I didn't either. You've believed in me since college, been there since the beginning, and are like a sister to me. Rachel Frank, the yang to my yin, you asked questions that needed answers, cheered for me every step of the way, and are a steadfast friend. Terry Frank, thank you for noting a rock band poster wouldn't appear in a piano store and for not sneaking a peek at the early copy Rachel read. Endless gratitude to my soul sister Tricia M. Warford—I'm thankful we met in grad school, for our conversations, connection, and forever friendship.

Nikki and Brian Kopelowitz, Samra Vogel, Susanne Hurowitz, Marcia Barry-Smith, Forrest Nelson, Ilona Mandel, Ronit Neuman, Dana Kaufman, Harvey Parker, Taina Rodriguez, Diana Levy, Allison Cagnetta, Marjorie H. Brooke, and so many others. I'm blessed with an abundant village of family, friends, and colleagues in my South Florida community—grateful for each of you. If I missed anyone here, please forgive me. I promise you'll be in the next book. My kids, my loves, my inspiration. Todd and Madeline—this story is for you. It's an honor and privilege to be your mom. And though my husband shares traits with Ben—kindness, loyalty, and steadfast love—I'm lucky he is real, he is mine, and we are forever one. Jarett, there are no words sufficient to thank you for giving me the space and support to transform words into a healing story. You are my rock, my best friend, my bashert.

As an author, you don't always know who you're impacting. Just knowing this novel is in your hands, hopefully inspiring and empowering you, is why I write. And to those who've awakened, accepting what is and may never be, you deserve to love and be loved.

ABOUT THE AUTHOR

Dara Levan is the creator and host of *Every Soul Has a Story*, a podcast in which she interviews inspiring people from around the globe. Her calling to impact others began at the age of twelve in her hometown of North Miami Beach, Florida, when she interviewed the residents of the nursing home where her grandmother lived and

Alison Frank Photography

wrote their stories. As an undergrad at Indiana University, Dara earned a BA in English and pursued a career in journalism but decided to pivot and returned to South Florida to earn her MS in Communication Sciences and Disorders. Dara stopped practicing speech therapy to return to full-time writing. Actively involved in her community, she is currently a board member of the Community Foundation of Broward and board member of Joe DiMaggio Children's Hospital Foundation/Memorial Hospital Foundation and the Community Foundation of Broward. Dara served as a board member of the Goodman Jewish Family Services (JFS) of Broward County and Junior Achievement of South Florida. She is also a founding member of the Circle of Friends for the Alvin Sherman Library Research, Information, and Technology Center at Nova Southeastern University. Dara is a member of the Women's Fiction Writers Association, Women's National Book Association, and the Authors Guild.